PR
Steven L. Kent

THE CLONE SEDITION

"Compares well with the Star Fist series by David Sherman and Dan Cragg, the Lost Fleet series by Jack Campbell, and several series by Ian Douglas . . . *The Clone Sedition* takes the action back to its roots with humans fighting clones."

—*SFRevu*

"Kent is a shameless orchestrator of adolescent wish fulfillment . . . Virtually every chapter of every one of these books features at least some tense action sequences, often elaborately well-done." —*Open Letters Monthly*

THE CLONE REDEMPTION

"An exciting intergalactic adventure." —*Sporadic Reviews*

"Intense . . . An awesome sci-fi story." —*Night Owl Reviews*

"Fans of Ian Douglas, Jack Campbell, David Sherman, and Graham Sharp Paul should find plenty here to enjoy." —*SFRevu*

THE CLONE EMPIRE

"Kent writes a fast-paced and interesting novel. His dialogue is realistic and his universe is well thought out and developed."

—*SFRevu*

THE CLONE ELITE

"If you enjoy military science fiction, then this is the book for you . . . Fast-paced and hard-hitting. Punches, bullets, and nuclear bombs are not held back. The characters face hard choices and don't regret them after they are made." —*SFRevu*

continued . . .

THE CLONE ALLIANCE

"Offers up stunning battle sequences, intriguing moral quandaries, and plenty of unexpected revelations . . . [A] fast-paced military SF book with plenty of well-scripted action and adventure [and] a sympathetic narrator." —*SF Site*

ROGUE CLONE

"Exciting space battles [and] haunting, quiet moments after war has taken its toll . . . Military SF fans looking for stories that combine mystery, action, espionage, politics, and some thoughtful doses of humanism in exploring their not entirely human characters would do well to add Steven L. Kent to their reading lists." —SF Reviews.net

THE CLONE REPUBLIC

"A solid debut. Harris is an honest, engaging protagonist and thoughtful narrator, and Kent's clean, transparent prose fits well with both the main character and the story's themes . . . Kent is a skillful storyteller, and the book entertains throughout."
—*Sci Fi Weekly*

"The first sentence gets you immediately . . . From there, the action begins fast and furious, with dark musings, lavish battle scenes, and complex characterizations . . . *The Clone Republic* feature[s] taut writing and a truly imaginative plot full of introspection and philosophizing." —*The Village Voice*

"A character-driven epic that understands that the best war stories are really antiwar stories . . . A smartly conceived adventure." —SF Reviews.net

Ace Books by Steven L. Kent

THE CLONE REPUBLIC
ROGUE CLONE
THE CLONE ALLIANCE
THE CLONE ELITE
THE CLONE BETRAYAL
THE CLONE EMPIRE
THE CLONE REDEMPTION
THE CLONE SEDITION
THE CLONE ASSASSIN

THE CLONE ASSASSIN

STEVEN L. KENT

ACE BOOKS, NEW YORK

THE BERKLEY PUBLISHING GROUP
Published by the Penguin Group
Penguin Group (USA) LLC
375 Hudson Street, New York, New York 10014, USA

USA • Canada • UK • Ireland • Australia • New Zealand • India • South Africa • China

penguin.com

A Penguin Random House Company

THE CLONE ASSASSIN

An Ace Book / published by arrangement with the author

Ace Books are published by The Berkley Publishing Group.
ACE and the "A" design are trademarks of Penguin Group (USA) LLC.

For information, address: The Berkley Publishing Group,
a division of Penguin Group (USA),
375 Hudson Street, New York, New York 10014.

ISBN: 978-0-425-26449-2

PUBLISHING HISTORY
Ace mass-market edition / November 2013

PRINTED IN THE UNITED STATES OF AMERICA

10 9 8 7 6 5 4 3 2 1

Cover art by Christian McGrath.
Cover design by Judith Lagerman.

This book is dedicated to Fred Watson, a very good friend who doesn't read fiction . . . including my books. I'm not going to tell him about this dedication. Instead, I'll wait to see how long it takes for him to find it on his own.

Good luck, Fred; the clock is ticking.

ACKNOWLEDGMENTS

There are, as always, so many people I need to thank for their help and encouragement. First and foremost, I need to thank the lovely and talented, and let me add *patient*, Anne at Ace. She gave me three extensions on this book . . . Did I mention she is patient?

I also want to thank my agent, Richard Curtis, who really is a wizard. I want to thank my primary readers, Trevor Boll and my father.

Also, I want to thank my long-suffering wife, who really has put up with too much for too long. I really wouldn't be anywhere without her.

Under the smoke, dust all over his mouth, laughing with white teeth,
Under the terrible burden of destiny laughing as a young man laughs,
Laughing even as an ignorant fighter laughs who has never lost a battle . . .

"Chicago," Carl Sandburg

NINE EVENTS THAT SHAPED HISTORY

2010 TO 2018
DECLINE OF THE U.S. ECONOMY

Following the examples of Chevrolet, Oracle, IBM, and ConAgra Foods, Microsoft moves its headquarters from the United States to Shanghai. Referring to their company as a "global corporation," Microsoft executives claim they are still committed to U.S. prosperity, but with its burgeoning economy, China has become the company's most important market.

Even with Toyota and Hyundai increasing their manufacturing activities in the United States—spurred on by the favorable cheap labor conditions—the U.S. economy becomes dependent on the shipping of raw materials and farm goods.

Bottoming out as the world's thirteenth largest economy behind China, United Korea, India, Cuba, the European Economic Community, Brazil, Mexico, Canada, Japan, South Africa, Israel, and Unincorporated France, the United States government focuses on maintaining its position as the world's last military superpower.

JANUARY 3, 2026
INTRODUCTION OF BROADCAST PHYSICS

Armadillo Aerospace announces the discovery of broadcast physics, a new technology capable of translating matter into data waves that can be transmitted to any location instantaneously. This opens the way for pangalactic exploration without time dilation or the dangers of light-speed travel.

The United States creates the first-ever fleet of self-broadcasting ships, a scientific fleet designed to locate suitable planets for future colonization. When initial scouting reports suggest that the rest of the galaxy is uninhabited, politicians fire up public sentiment with talk about a new "manifest destiny" and spreading humanity across space.

The discovery of broadcast physics leads to the creation of the Broadcast Network—a galactic superhighway consisting of satellites that send and receive ships across the galaxy. The Broadcast Network ushers in the age of galactic expansion.

JULY 4, 2110
RUSSIA AND KOREA SIGN A PACT WITH THE UNITED STATES

With the growth of its space-based economy, the United States reclaims its spot as the wealthiest nation on Earth. Russia and Korea become the first nations to sign the IGTA (Intergalactic Trade Accord), a treaty opening the way for other nations to become self-governing American territories and enjoy full partnership in the space-based economy.

In an effort to create a competing alliance, France unveils its Cousteau Oceanic Exploration program and announces plans to create undersea colonies. Only Tahiti signs on.

After the other nations of the European Economic Union, Japan, and all of Africa become members of the IGTA, France discontinues its undersea colonization and joins the IGTA. Several nations, most notably China and Afghanistan, refuse to sign, leading to a minor world war in which the final holdouts are coerced into signing the treaty.

More than 80 percent of the world's population is eventually sent to establish colonies throughout the galaxy.

JULY 4, 2250
TRANSMOGRIFICATION OF THE UNITED STATES

With most of its citizens living off Earth, the IGTA is renamed "The Unified Authority" and restructured to serve as a government rather than an economic union.

The government of the Unified Authority merges principles from the U.S. Constitution with concepts from Plato's *Republic*. In accordance with Plato's ideals, society is broken into three strata—citizenry, defense, and governance.

With forty self-sustaining colonies across the galaxy,

Earth becomes the political center of a new republic. The eastern seaboard of the former United States becomes an ever-growing capital city populated by the political class—families appointed to run the government in perpetuity.

Earth also becomes the home to the military class. After some experimentation, the Unified Authority adopts an all-clone conscription model to fulfill its growing need for soldiers. Clone farms euphemistically known as "orphanages" are established around Earth. These orphanages produce more than a million cloned recruits per year.

The military does not commission clone officers. The officer corps is drafted from the ruling class. When the children of politicians are drummed out of school or deemed unsuitable for politics, they are sent to officer-candidate school in Australia.

2452 TO 2512
UPRISING IN THE GALACTIC EYE

On October 29, 2452, a date later known as the new "Black Tuesday," a fleet of scientific exploration ships vanishes in the "galactic eye" region of the Norma Arm.

Fearing an alien attack, the U.A. Senate calls for the creation of the Galactic Central Fleet, a self-broadcasting armada. Work on the Galactic Central Fleet is completed in 2455. The newly christened fleet travels to the Inner Curve, where it vanishes as well.

Having authorized the development of a top secret line of cloned soldiers called "Liberators," the Linear Committee—the executive branch of the U.A. government—approves sending an invasion force into the Galactic Eye to attack all hostile threats. The Liberators discover a human colony led by Morgan Atkins, a powerful senator who disappeared with the Galactic Central Fleet. The Liberators overthrow the colony, but Atkins and many of his followers escape in G.C. Fleet ships.

Over the next fifty years, a religious cult known as the Morgan Atkins Fanatics—"Mogats"—spreads across the 180 colonized planets, preaching independence from the Unified Authority government.

Spurred on by the growing Morgan Atkins movement, four of the six galactic arms declare independence from

Unified Authority governance in 2510. Two years later, the combined forces of the Confederate Arms Treaty Organization and the Morgan Atkins Fanatics defeat the Earth Fleet and destroy the Broadcast Network, effectively cutting the Earth government off from its loyal colonies and Navy.

Having crippled the Unified Authority, the Mogats turn on their Confederate Arms allies. The Confederates escape with fifty self-broadcasting ships and join forces with the Unified Authority, leaving the Mogats with a fleet of over four hundred self-broadcasting ships, the most powerful attack force in the galaxy.

In 2512, the Unified Authority and the Confederate Arms end the war by attacking the Mogat home world, leaving no survivors.

2514 TO 2515
AVATARI INVASION

In 2514, an alien force enters the outer region of the Scutum-Crux Arm, conquering U.A. colonies. As they attack planets, the aliens wrap an energy barrier around the atmosphere. Called an "ion curtain," the barrier cuts off escape and communications.

In a matter of two years, the aliens spread throughout the galaxy, occupying only planets deemed habitable by U.A. scientists. The Unified Authority loses 178 of its 180 populated planets before making a final stand on New Copenhagen.

During this battle, U.A. scientists unravel the secrets of the aliens' tachyon-based technology, enabling U.A. Marines to win the war. In the aftermath of the invasion, the Unified Authority sends the four self-broadcasting ships of the Japanese Fleet along with twelve thousand Navy SEAL clones to locate and destroy the Avatari home world.

2517
RISE OF THE ENLISTED MAN'S EMPIRE

The Unified Authority Congress holds hearings investigating the military's performance during the Avatari invasion. When two generals blame their losses on lack of discipline among their cloned enlisted men, synthetic conscription is abolished and all remaining clones are transferred to frontier fleets—fleets stranded in deep space since the destruction of the Broadcast Network. The Navy plans to use these fleets in live-ordnance military exercises designed to test its new, more powerful Nike-class ships, but the clones thwart this plan by declaring independence.

After creating their own broadcast network, the clones establish the Enlisted Man's Empire, a nation consisting of twenty-three planets and thirteen naval fleets. As hostilities continue between the Enlisted Man's Empire and the Unified Authority, the Avatari return, attacking planets using a devastating weapon that raises atmospheric temperatures to nine thousand degrees for eighty-three seconds.

The Avatari attack three planets in December 2517—New Copenhagen, a Unified Authority colony; Olympus Kri, an Enlisted Man's colony; and Terraneau, a neutral nation. Working together, the Enlisted Man's Navy and the Earth Fleet successfully evacuate Olympus Kri prior to the attack. Following the attack on Olympus Kri, the Avatari accelerate their attacks, incinerating a new populated planet every three days as they work their way toward Earth.

Despite the mutual threat, the Unified Authority renews its assault on the Enlisted Man's Empire.

2517
DESTRUCTION OF THE AVATARI HOME WORLD

The Japanese Fleet locates the Avatari home world in Bode's Galaxy. While the inhabitants of the planet have become extinct, its automated mining and military systems continue their destructive expansion.

After depositing all nonessential personnel on New Copenhagen to establish a new colony, the *Sakura*, the last ship in the fleet, launches a successful suicide attack on the Avatari planet.

2517
ENLISTED MAN'S EMPIRE RETURNS TO EARTH

Unaware of the Japanese attack on the Avatari home world, the Enlisted Man's Empire divides its military into two groups. One group establishes a colony on the burned-out remains of Terraneau, while the other defeats the Unified Authority, establishing a clone-controlled government.

The clones' hold on Earth proves tentative as remnants of the Unified Authority military attack EME bases on Earth and Mars. After an entire division of EME Marines defects, the clones learn that former members of the Unified Authority intelligence community have discovered how to change the neural programming in clones.

PART I

THE PROVOCATEUR

CHAPTER ONE

Location: Washington, D.C.
Date: July 16, 2519

The provocateur entered the Pentagon at 10:28. He was a natural-born, something that automatically made him a person of interest. He stood in the queue surrounded by clones, calmly waiting his turn to walk between the posts—the security system that would search his identity right down to his DNA.

His brown hair fell just past his shoulders, not the kind of style you normally see in the Pentagon, home of the flattop. His dark beard ran the corners of his jawline. His eyes were green, his skin pale, almost colorless.

He wore a gleaming white shirt buttoned up to the neck, a bloodred tie, and a charcoal-colored suit. The clones around him wore Navy white, Army drab, and Air Force blue.

The provocateur followed the queue past a security station, closer and closer to the posts. Armed guards with M27s stood in full armor behind a wall of bulletproof/grenade-proof glass. Unconcerned about the guards, the provocateur checked his wristwatch, looked around the lobby, tried to decipher the tabs that a nearby soldier wore on his chest.

The posts was a detection device disguised to look like a set of ten-foot Ionic columns. The column on the left, "the sprayer," emitted a burst of air and vapor that dislodged flecks of skin, dandruff, and loose hair. The column on the right, "the receiver," drew in and analyzed the debris. Identity, blood type, genetic information, medical history . . . the posts created a profile based on genetic material, which it transmitted for analysis.

Anyone planning to fool the posts would need to trick the

Census Data Agency, the government information storehouse that tracked citizens from the cradle to the grave, an impossible task.

Criminals and terrorists had tried covering themselves with skin peels, loose hair, dandruff, and eyebrows from other people. They'd tried scrubbing themselves with defoliating sponges, laser shaving all their hair, and wearing wigs on their arms and eyebrows, but the posts still identified them. If flecks of skin showed too much decay or if there were signs the hair came from multiple donors, the posts' computers asked questions.

With the government on high alert, every person entering the Pentagon was searched for metal, X-rayed, and spectroanalyzed for radioactive and chemical residue.

When his turn arose, the provocateur calmly stepped between the posts while its sensors checked his heartbeat, pulse, and brain activity for signs of tension. A set of detectors searched him for traces of chemical agents while an X-ray device identified his telephone, wallet, and belt buckle.

The guard at the far end of the posts asked, "You Leonard Herman?"

"I go by 'Lenny,'" said the provocateur.

"Lenny Herman?" asked the guard.

"That's me."

The provocateur stood over six feet. He had big shoulders that had gone soft with age.

"What's your business here?" asked the guard.

"Floors and sinks mostly," said the provocateur. "My company sells janitorial supplies."

"Janitorial supplies?"

"Yes, sir. We're bidding on the Pentagon contract." The provocateur had a high voice, not effeminate but innocuous. He spoke softly, slowly.

"Who are you meeting?" asked the guard.

The provocateur pulled his phone from his jacket and tapped the screen. "Major Day."

"We got a bunch of Day's working here," said the guard. Never taking his eyes off the provocateur, he accessed the building directory using his visor.

"Major Walter Day."

"Got a branch?"

"Enlisted Man's Army."

Using the equipment in his visor, he contacted Day's office. The conversation didn't show on the security brief, but the communications system recorded it. When Pentagon Security investigated the attack, an officer uncovered the recording.

Once he'd reached Day's office, the guard said, "Major, I'm calling from the main entrance security post. Do you have an appointment with . . ."

"Is Lenny Herman here? Damn, I let the time get away from me. Tell him I'll be right down."

"Yes, sir."

The guard grunted and let the provocateur through.

CHAPTER TWO

Major Day, a standard-issue five-foot-ten-inch clone with brown hair and brown eyes, met the provocateur in the lobby. The Pentagon had been on high alert since the discovery that the enemy had learned how to reprogram clones. Security not only screened for wolves in sheep's clothing, it screened for sheep that sided with the wolves.

"Mr. Herman, thanks for coming on short notice," said Major Day. He shook hands with the provocateur.

"Call me Lenny," said the provocateur, he of the innocuous persona. He shook Day's hand, looking slightly befuddled. Nothing strange there, natural-borns generally became disoriented when they entered the Pentagon. All of the officers were clones; they all stood five-foot-ten; they all had brown hair cut in a military regulation flattop. To natural-born eyes, the lobby of the Pentagon looked like a hall of mirrors.

"I'm glad for this chance, Major . . ."

"Call me Walter."

He clapped the provocateur on the back, and they headed

for an elevator. As they rode to the third floor, Day asked, "Have you looked at the floor plan?"

The provocateur nodded. He said, "Big place. You have a lot of floors to polish."

"It's a big contract," said Day. "Pull this off, Lenny, and you'll be a wealthy man."

The provocateur nodded, and said, "I bet you guys go through a lot of wax and cleanser," as the elevator opened to the third floor.

Day smiled, and said, "Seven hundred drinking fountains, five thousand toilets, seven million square feet of floor space."

"Aren't pentagons supposed to be five-sided figures?" asked the provocateur.

"The original building was pentagonal. The U.A. Department of Defense went with a cube during the rebuild. It's a more economical use of space."

As they started down the hall, the provocateur's voice took on a less friendly tone. "Did you get the cases I sent ahead?" he asked.

"Sure. I shepherded them through security personally," said Day.

"Any problems?" asked the provocateur.

"Smooth as silk."

Major Day didn't notice the way his guest played with the ring on the middle finger of his right hand as they chatted. Day led the way, walking slightly ahead, not bothering to look back as he spoke. In another minute, his trusting nature would cost him his life.

"Your package is in the third-floor facilities locker. That's where we're headed."

They walked down the hall. Most of the people they passed were clones, males, soldiers, sailors, and Marines. Day, an Army man, led the provocateur along the Army face of the building. Army, Navy, Air Force, Marines—each branch had a side.

They reached a service hall, an empty, dead-ended corridor. Day said, "I know it doesn't look like much, but you'd be surprised what goes into keeping this place clean. This is only a locker; our main warehouse is on a subfloor."

The provocateur said nothing.

Day pressed his hand against a security plate, and the door slid open. The lights inside the locker powered on when the door opened. So did the security system. The Pentagon was on the verge of a security lockdown. The entire Enlisted Man's Empire was on the verge of a security lockdown. What happened next pushed it over the edge.

Major Walter Day stepped into the storage area. He asked, "Do you have a family, Lenny?"

Rows of shelves lined the floor. There was a clock on the wall. The time was 10:52. Having been afraid he might have missed his deadline, the provocateur saw the time and felt a sense of relief. Hoping he sounded relaxed, he said, "Three kids. The oldest is my girl."

Day said, "You're a lucky man. Me, I got the Army, but I don't have a wife or children. You civilians get things too good."

10:53.

Bright lights shone from the ceilings. The glare caused the provocateur to blink. He asked, "Where's the package I sent."

Day turned, pointed to the package, and staggered forward. He didn't call for help. He barely grunted as he dropped to a knee and turned to face his killer, his arms already paralyzed.

The provocateur had hit Day in the back of the neck, stabbing the poisoned spike in his ring into the spot where the dying major's spine and skull met. The spike delivered a powerful shock as well as a dose of neurotoxins, paralyzing Day first so that he could not call for help as he died.

The provocateur grabbed the dying officer by his tunic and struck him several times in the face, the spike of his ring puncturing both of Day's cheeks, his left nostril, and his left eye. Unaware that Day had been dead for several seconds, the provocateur continued hitting him, then dragged his body into a blind between a sink and some shelves. He moved his crates in front of the body to block it from view.

The attack left no blood on the ground. It was quick and clean and silent, leaving no mess and attracting no attention. Security cameras in the ceiling recorded it, but no one was watching.

The provocateur opened the largest crate. He pulled out three layers of cleaning supplies from the top. Beneath the supplies was a burn-a-bomb, a collection of benevolent chemicals that wouldn't set off bomb sensors until they were exposed to heat and mixed into a decidedly malevolent compound.

Laced around the chemicals was a heating coil that would work as a catalyst, melting the packaging that separated the chemicals, heating them, and converting them into an explosive solution. The burn-a-bomb didn't pack sufficient power to bring down the Pentagon. The layers of concrete and cement in the floor and ceiling would channel the explosion, spreading the percussion horizontally rather than vertically. In another five minutes, every person on the third floor of the Pentagon would die.

Deeper in the crate, the provocateur found two other weapons—a miniature burn-a-bomb designed to work like a grenade and a porcelain-alloy pistol with ceramic bullets. He pulled the tab from the side of the grenade, allowing an electrical charge to heat the copper coil. The chemicals reacted quickly; in a minute, a whiff of acrid smoke would rise from the globe, signaling that the mechanism was armed.

The pistol, a five-inch tube, had been sent as a precaution. It was a three-shot security blanket that the provocateur couldn't reload once he'd spent his ammunition. He held it between his cuff and his palm, just under the wrist. He placed the grenade into his jacket pocket.

After checking one last time to make sure that the bomb had started cooking, the provocateur closed the crate and sealed it. Hoping to camouflage his handiwork, he arranged his cleaning supplies on the lid. His left hand thrust into his coat pocket, thumb held over the grenade's pin, the provocateur gave the janitorial locker one last scan and left.

He crossed the empty service hall and entered the main corridor. A pair of soldiers walked past him, then stopped. With the building on alert, civilians were not allowed to travel alone. One of the soldiers called out, "Excuse me. Excuse me, are you with someone?" As he turned to respond, the provocateur whipped the porcelain pistol from his cuff.

The soldiers weren't attached to Security, the only department with personnel who carried weapons inside the Pentagon. They hadn't prepared for a confrontation and didn't recognize the tube as a gun.

It was at that moment that the chemicals inside the grenade melded and emitted a trace of acrid smoke. Security sensors in the ventilation system detected the dimethylformamide and pentaerythritol tetranitrate that the smoke gave off, and alarms began to blare.

One of the soldiers said something about escorts, and then the provocateur shot them both. Blood and brains and scalp splattered the walls. The bodies lay in spreading puddles, their white tunics stained deep red.

The provocateur didn't waste time inspecting the damage. He trotted toward the elevators as alarms echoed through the halls. Soldiers emerged from their offices. The doors of two elevators slid open and MPs poured out. The doors remained open, locking the elevators in place, the first step in securing the floor.

As the halls became more crowded, soldiers with MP bands screened people as they entered the stairs. They detained civilians, employees and visitors alike, escorting all nonmilitary personnel to the security office.

Seeing MPs moving toward the two soldiers he'd shot, the provocateur slipped the cylindrical pistol back into his cuff. He turned a corner and blended in with the crowd, then pushed into a different corridor, wading against the tide of clones coming from another direction.

There was no blood on him, nothing to suggest he was dangerous. He stationed himself against the wall in a corner where two halls met, and herds of workers shuffled past him. From here, he could see the door of the laboratory in which key scientists performed the Enlisted Man's Empire's most urgent experiments. The door was inconspicuous, and the hall looked no different than any other hall.

He stood there for ten seconds, watching the door for movement.

An MP grabbed him by the shoulder and shouted, "We're evacuating the floor. Move it."

The provocateur jumped at the contact. He pulled out the little pistol and shot the man, then entered the nearest stairwell. As everyone else ran down toward the street, the provocateur forced his way up against the tide.

This was not a panicking crowd. Most of the clones had

mistaken the evacuation for yet another drill. Combat-tested soldiers and sailors seldom panicked at the sound of alarms. Had they panicked, they would have trampled the provocateur.

By this time, though, Pentagon Security had eyes watching every monitor. The unescorted natural-born pushing his way up the stairs did not escape their notice.

CHAPTER THREE

Major Alan Cardston heard the alarms and ran from his office to the surveillance room.

He saw the emergency screen that identified traces of dimethylformamide and pentaerythritol tetranitrate had been detected on the third floor . . . the makings of a bomb had been smuggled into the building, and not only smuggled into the building but placed near a high-security area.

Cardston knew the chemicals and what they were used for. The officer in charge of Pentagon Security, he had arranged his organization so that the bomb disposal teams, the evacuation teams, and the MPs didn't waste time waiting for obvious orders. The first team to arrive on the scene was the six-man bomb disposal squad. The lieutenant in charge reported the two dead soldiers, but the team did not stop to investigate the scene as they hustled to the facilities locker.

Cardston studied the security monitor. The floors of the Pentagon showed as two-dimensional mazes with white dots identifying his security men. Red pixels would mark the locations of possible intruders. Only one red dot showed on the screen; the person it represented had entered one of the stairwells.

Cardston tapped the dot, switching to the cameras covering the stairs. He saw a natural-born male, tall and pudgy with long hair, dressed in a suit and tie. Using the data gathered at the posts, the computer identified the intruder as Leonard Herman, the owner of a janitorial supplies company.

Cardston looked at the names of the MPs chasing after Herman. The man leading the team was Sergeant Major Gregory Goldsmith.

"Goldsmith, this is Major Alan Cardston. Do you read me?"

"Yes, sir."

On the security monitor, the red pixel moved slowly up a crowded stairwell. Had Leonard gone with the flow instead, he might have been able to escape the building with the flock.

"I've got your target on my screen. He's entered Stairwell Number 121. Do you read me, Sergeant Major? That's Stairwell Number One-Two-One on the north side of the building."

"Yes, sir."

"Take a right at the next hall, and you'll see it on your right."

"I see the door, sir."

"He's moving slowly, Sergeant Major. He's passed the fifth floor and is working his way to the sixth."

"Yes, sir." A pause, then, "We're on the stairs. There are a lot of people in here, sir. Do you have any men on the fifth?"

"Negative, Goldsmith. You and your men are our closest team."

Cardston heard Goldsmith and his men shouting, then the sergeant major said, "Sir, this crowd is going to slow us down."

"Your target has the same problem, Goldsmith," Cardston said. "Proceed with caution; he may be armed, and I want him brought in breathing. Do you read me?"

"Yes, sir."

Cardston stood beside a console in the Pentagon Security nerve center, a dark vault lined with computer screens, phones, and microphones. Dozens of officers worked inside this lair.

Cardston checked the monitors showing the various exits around the building. He saw screen after screen of people leaving the Pentagon as calmly as moviegoers emptying a holitorium.

"How is the evacuation going?" he asked the captain to his right.

"Smooth. Most of them think it's a drill."

"The disposal team has the bomb," said the lieutenant to his left.

Cardston stepped behind the man and watched the operation over his shoulder. He said, "Is it going to give them any trouble?"

He stared into the screen. Three men in armor stood around a crate in a janitorial closet. They had not bothered to place protective walls around the crate. The operations manual called for a flimsy protective firewall, speck knows why. If the bomb went off, it wouldn't matter if it was nuclear or packed with horseshit, that wall would not protect the men trying to disarm it.

"It's a textbook burner, sir," said the lieutenant.

For Cardston, that explained quite a bit. Terrorists and provocateurs made sacrifices when they used a burn-a-bomb. They were easy to smuggle, but they were also easy to defuse. The only advantage burn-a-bombs offered was ease of concealment. Their innards were simple, straightforward, easily disarmed—separate the chemicals before they oxidized, and the bomb became as benign as a child's chemistry set.

"Alert me when the bomb is disarmed," said Cardston.

"It's disarmed," said the captain.

"That was fast," said Cardston.

"Almost not fast enough," said the captain. "Twenty seconds more, and it would have gone critical."

"Major, sir, we're closing in on him," said Goldsmith. "We got a flash on him."

On the display, the five white dots representing the MPs had gained ground on the red dot representing the provocateur. Once he passed the seventh floor, Herman had run out of options. The stairs led to the roof, but the roof access door was locked, and Goldsmith's security team waited one flight below with M27s raised and ready.

The stalemate lasted nearly a minute.

Goldsmith asked, "Major, did he make it out to the roof?"

Cardston looked at the floor schematic. Something had happened. The provocateur couldn't have opened the door to the roof without a bomb or a bazooka or possibly a laser torch, but the red pixel no longer showed in the stairwell.

The pixel had disappeared.

"Bring up a map!" Cardston yelled to the officers around him. When the map showed on the monitor, he needed only a moment to spot the escape route, then he pulled the microphone close and said, "Sergeant Major, one-two-one connects to a service floor. He's entered a machine-and-maintenance area just below the roof."

"Can you see him?" asked the sergeant major.

"Negative, Sergeant Major. We don't have eyes on that floor." Once they had the bastard, Cardston would personally oversee the installation of cameras and sensors. *What a speck-up,* he thought.

"Yes, sir," said the sergeant major.

The flight of stairs leading to the seventh floor was clear. The flight leading beyond it was clear as well. Bright light shone down from the ceiling, illuminating the entire concrete enclosure. The open door to the service floor stood out like a dark cave on a chalk mountain. Goldsmith led his team as carefully as if they had entered an enemy base.

The alarms went silent, but their ringing still echoed in Sergeant Major Gregory Goldsmith's ears. Speaking much louder than needed, he said, "We're going in."

They moved slowly, stepped softly, traveled as silently as possible. Step . . . step . . . step. The door to the service floor hung open.

One step from the door, they paused.

Goldsmith signaled for his men to wait while he checked the doorway. He pressed the muzzle of his M27 against the doorjamb. He checked his men to make sure they had taken their positions, then he counted to three in his head and sprang through the door. MPs on either side of the jamb lunged in behind him, forming a cross fire, covering the entrance from every angle on the off chance that the provocateur had smuggled help onto the service floor.

The floor seemed to stretch the entire length and breadth of the Pentagon. Heavy machinery stood like twenty-foot-tall buttes on the floor, reaching up into the open ceiling. Wires, cables, and vents snaked this way and that above the unadorned light fixtures.

In the center of this, fifty feet from the door, the provocateur stood facing the men. The moment the MPs entered, he smiled, opened his right hand, allowed the grenade to roll across his fingers.

The explosion all but ionized the provocateur's body. It killed the three MPs who had entered the service floor. The two standing outside the door were deafened for life.

Once his team had checked the service floor for chemical and radiation, Cardston surveyed the damage. As men in combat armor swept for traps and photographed damage, the major looked down at the bodies of the MPs he had sent on a fatal assault.

The blast from the grenade had smashed two of them into a wall hard enough to leave bloody imprints. The remains of Sergeant Major Gregory Goldsmith, who had been standing directly in front of the door, lay in the stairwell.

The only parts of the provocateur that remained recognizably human were his feet. His chest, shoulders, and head were gone, plastered all over the walls in every direction.

Cardston stared down at the feet, ignoring the grinding of machinery around him. The Pentagon air-conditioning system was stored in this area, fifteen enormous turbines made of aluminum and sheet metal. Ten of those turbines spun silently. The force of the grenade had split two of the turbines wide open, their chambers and tubes exposed like a metal model of human viscera. Three more limped along, spinning in twisted cabinets.

Cardston saw oil running down vents, dripping into the industrial air conditioner. It wasn't oil, though. It was blood. *You painted the room, you bastard,* he thought as he saw bone and hair and shreds of clothing.

CHAPTER FOUR

Location: EME Correctional Institution,
Sheridan, Oregon

At precisely 08:00, the gunship dropped out of the sky looking more like an oversized insect than a bird of prey. She descended out of the clouds and hovered in place about 150 feet above the forest, her stubby steel-and-carbide body beneath dual rotors gleaming in the sun.

The Sheridan Correctional Facility didn't have radar; the first officers to notice the gunship were the guards in the southwest tower—a nest made of steel and bulletproof glass with window walls and a wraparound balcony. One of the guards spotted the gunship, and asked the other, "Where the speck did that come from?"

The gunship remained a few hundred yards away, looming like a dragonfly looking for prey. At this distance, the guards could barely hear her rotors. The glass walls of the nest blocked the sound.

The first guard flipped a switch on the communications console, and said, "We got a helicopter flying out here. You know anything about that?"

"A helicopter? What the hell is a helicopter doing there?" asked the dispatcher.

"Flying," said the guard. He meant it as a joke.

"What kind of chopper?" asked the dispatcher. "Can you identify it?"

Sheridan Correctional was a federal penitentiary, run by the Enlisted Man's Empire. A few of the guards were clones, retired military. The dispatcher was a local civilian.

The first guard, a natural-born who had never served in the

military, said, "How the speck would I know that? If you want aircraft information, call a specking air traffic controller."

The second guard in the nest was a clone, a retired airman. He leaned over the console, and said, "It's a gunship, maybe a TR-40."

"A gunship?" asked the first guard. "Are you sure?"

"No, sir, I'm not entirely sure it's a TR-40, could be a forty-two." He picked up his binoculars, equipment made for searching prison yards, not skies. "Two racks for rockets . . . Yes, sir, it's either a forty or a forty-two."

"What's it doing here?" the dispatcher asked.

Below the tower, guards started lining up along the prison wall for a better look. There were no military bases near Sheridan, the gunship was an unusual sight. Off in the distance, the gunship dropped slowly until she was almost even with the tower, then she remained in place, as still as a toy on a shelf. She hung in the air about fifteen feet above the tips of the pine trees.

"Are you sure that's a gunship?" asked the dispatcher. "I just checked with the tracking station at Newport. They say there's no air traffic in the area."

"Speck that," said the first guard. "That sure as shit ain't no seagull."

The dispatcher said, "Let me check with . . . hey, Astoria isn't answering." A moment later he added, "I can't reach Coos Bay."

A civilian, he didn't know that gunships carried equipment that could block satellite transmissions; the retired airman did. He ran the military math in his head and asked, "Have you tried using civilian communications?" Military consoles used a satellite link. Civilian lines used underground laser cables.

The dispatcher said, "Hey, there it is; we have it on our security cameras now."

"I told you it wasn't a seagull," said the natural-born guard.

The clone guard didn't join in their conversation. *If that bird is one of ours,* he asked himself, *why didn't we know it was coming?* But gunships were not known for their stealth capabilities. There was no way the Unified Authority could have flown one in without being spotted.

"What's it doing out here?" asked the dispatcher.

Still staring out at the bird, the clone guard said, "Once you broke in, what would you do with a gunship?" A silent moment passed before he answered his own question, "You couldn't land it, not in here. You'd only need it for . . . cover." Speaking to the dispatcher, he said, "We're in deep. They have infantry out there."

The dispatcher shouted, "I tried the landlines; I can't reach anyone!"

"They cut the lines," said the clone guard.

"Who cut the lines? Who the hell are they? What are they doing here?" asked the natural-born guard.

"Here they come," said the clone guard.

Five military transports approached in the air, drifting in behind the gunship, then touching down along the highway that led to the gates of the penitentiary.

Isolated and alone, the penitentiary at Sheridan was protected by gates and walls and a handful of guards. The warden addressed his men over the intercom. He said, "Sheridan FCI is now under lock . . ." Before he finished the sentence, the prison went dark.

"They cut the lights," said the natural-born guard. "What do we do now?"

Raised in a military orphanage, having survived airman training and a life at war, the clone guard had duty programmed into his brain. He said, "We lock down."

"Lock down? With that thing out there? Lock down? Bullshit! I didn't sign up to fight gunships. I didn't sign up for this!" His mind decided, the natural-born guard fled. He sped down the stairs of the tower and disappeared into the tunnel that led into the wall.

The second guard, the clone, hustled to the rail and prepared to shoot. He saw enemy Marines dressed in combat armor marching up the street. They marched in a column. They did not carry guns. Seeing this, he knew that the battle was forfeit.

Unified Authority Marines, he thought, knowing that U.A. Marines wore shielded combat armor. Bullets and batons were useless against men in shielded armor . . . "glowboys" as the EME Marines called them.

The gunship fired her chain gun into the fences that surrounded the prison perimeter. Sparks danced on the electrified wire as bullets tore the posts to pieces. The gunship opened fire on the inside fence.

Across the wall, guards fired at the gunship and the troops on the ground. *Useless,* thought the clone guard, as he chambered and fired another bullet.

The gunship raised a few feet higher and fired a rocket. A thin arc of white smoke hung in the air, like a thread made of cloud, connecting the gunship to the outer wall of the cell block. Flames and smoke and clouds of concrete dust flushed into the air as the façade crumbled in an avalanche. The crack of the rocket still echoed in the air, drowning the dull thud of the demolition.

The gunship pivoted nearly imperceptibly, then fired chain guns at the guards manning the towers. Bulletproof, but not chain-gun-proof, the guards' nests shattered, splattering nuggets of glass around the guards' dead bodies.

The guards clustered around the entrance to the cell blocks on the second floor of the building. With the electricity out, the halls had become dark as a moonlit night, lit mostly by squares of light slanting in from small windows above the cells. A line of emergency beacons shone red along the wall.

A few yards deeper into the darkness, prisoners stood in their prison cells, screaming at the guards. They couldn't hear the battle outside. Concrete walls and shatterproof glass drowned out the sound of rifles.

Then the rocket struck the front of the building, and a thunderous blast shook the facility down to its foundation, followed by a soft rumble as the wall collapsed in a concrete avalanche. Smoke and dust filled the hallway, sunlight slowly creeping in through the miasma.

That first rocket didn't harm the guards, but it sent them scurrying into the building's depths. Outside, beyond the tattered ruins of the electrified fence, men in combat armor marched across the grounds unopposed. The gunship hovered protectively above them, no more than fifty feet from the ground.

Some of the guards approached the ledge where the wall

had been. They saw troops crossing the scraps of the outer gate and the gunship hovering above their heads. Death had come.

One of the prisoners taunted the guards. He yelled, "You better run, rabbits."

"Shut up, Andropov," said the warden. "Shut the speck up."

"Warden, you must really love your job," said Andropov. Once a powerful politician, he knew how to slash at enemies with his words.

The warden raised his riot gun and pointed it at Andropov. "I told you to shut the speck up."

Andropov lifted up his hands, palms out, and backed away, as silent as an altar boy.

"He's right," said one of the guards.

The warden looked down the line. He saw only forty men. The others had run away or died defending the building. Most of the men who remained were clones, retired military men who didn't have it in them to run.

Forty men, he thought. He'd started the day with over one hundred.

Sheridan held few prisoners, all of them labeled war criminals. Tobias Andropov had been a member of the Linear Committee, the executive branch of the Unified Authority. Most of the others had been senators or generals. Had this been a military facility, the guards might have had orders to kill the prisoners, but Sheridan FCI was civilian. No such orders had been given, and the clones who made up the bulk of the remaining guards were created without initiative. They would need orders before they could kill the prisoners; that was in their programming. The warden could have given the order, but he was a civilian; he cared more about his own survival than the survival of the prisoners.

The first of the invaders entered the hall. He looked like a ghost, a glowing silhouette of a man that materialized out of the sunlight. Two more followed. Many more came after them, their armor glowing a dull orange-gold as they entered the shadowy building.

Though he knew it was too late to surrender, the new warden handed his shotgun to the nearest guard and walked out to meet the invaders. He held his hands out so they could see that he came without weapons. Squinting into the sunlight, he took slow steps. He inhaled and held his final breath.

The first of the invading Marines stood about fifty feet off. He did not carry a gun.

Don't shoot me, the warden willed. *There's no need to shoot.*

He came within thirty feet of the invaders before the man on point raised his arm and fired three fléchettes—hair-width fragments of depleted uranium that penetrated both the front and back of the warden's skull.

One of the remaining guards, a clone, raised his riot gun and fired. The buckshot spread, forming a two-foot-wide pattern. Shot that went wide of the invader cut ellipses in the wall on either side of him. The shot that should have hit his shielded armor flashed like sparks and evaporated.

The gunfight lasted five minutes. In the depths of the hall, their shotguns echoing like thunder and flashing like lightning, the guards, shot, pumped, shot, pumped, retreated farther and farther into the hall, gave up ground, unintentionally freeing prisoners as they backed away from the attack.

A clone guard hid behind a corner, gripping the butt of his shotgun as tightly as he could. Fear surged through his brain. As an invader passed his hiding place, the guard rose to his feet, and fired a shot at point-blank range.

The U.A. Marine turned, grabbed at the guard, and the power running through his shields both burned and electrocuted the man. His face and shoulders charred as the clone died of heart failure.

One of the guards threw his riot gun to the side, turned, and ran. The invaders shot him in the back. Blood drained from his body through dozens of pinprick holes. Another guard raised his hands high above his head and tried to surrender. He was a natural-born, something he hoped might save him. The invaders shot him.

Once the guards were dead, the invaders turned on the prisoners. They freed Andropov and most of the politicians, then killed the incarcerated former Unified Authority military officers in their cells like penned animals.

When investigators came to search the scene, they found no survivors.

CHAPTER FIVE

Location: The EMN *Churchill*, orbiting Earth

At the time of his death, Admiral Don Cutter had not heard about the attacks on Sheridan Correctional or the Pentagon. It was 16:00 by the Space Travel Clock, which was synchronized to Greenwich Mean Time, five hours ahead of Washington, D.C., and eight hours ahead of Sheridan, Oregon.

As the provocateur armed his bomb, and the gunship approached the penitentiary, Don Cutter, the highest-ranking officer in the Enlisted Man's Navy and de facto leader of the Enlisted Man's Empire, sat alone in his office.

Cutter maintained a deck for himself and his staff on the *Churchill*, the flagship of the Enlisted Man's Fleet. He was not the captain of the ship or the commander of the fleet. As the head of the Enlisted Man's Navy, he no longer participated in the tasks that he loved. He had risen from commander to "commander in chief," which, in his mind, meant the same thing as being put out to pasture. He had become the kind of officer he had most despised throughout his career. Instead of leading space leviathans into battles, he now settled political squabbles.

He had trouble concentrating on his work. The report on his desk was about the integration of "Martians" into Latin America.

Martians was a derisive term that referred to evacuees from the planet Olympus Kri. Officially, they were *New Olympian refugees.* When the Avatari aliens began the second wave of their invasion, the Unified Authority and the Enlisted Man's Empire had agreed upon a truce as they evacuated seventeen million New Olympians to a mothballed commuter spaceport on Mars, a facility designed to serve as a revolving door for six million travelers. The truce had ended in an ambush, leaving the New Olympians stranded in squalor even as the Enlisted Man's Empire defeated the Unifieds and established a new government. Nearly two years after relocating the New Olympians on Mars, the Enlisted Man's Empire transported the refugees to Earth.

According to the report, the New Olympians weren't any happier in Mexico and Guatemala than they had been on Mars.

It's Harris's headache now, Cutter thought with some satisfaction. He had sent Wayson Harris, the highest-ranking general in the EME Marines, to survey the situation.

But Harris's headache had managed to work its way up the chain of command. Cutter felt it as well. He leaned back and massaged his forehead. "Damn Martians," he muttered.

When the trouble began, the war hadn't been between the Unified Authority and the Enlisted Man's Empire. The clones had been the foot soldiers in the Unified Authority's military at the time, and the enemy had been an ill-fated band of religious revolutionaries. Then the Avatari attacked, an alien force that would ultimately destroy 179 of the Unified Authority's 180 planets. Rather than take the blame for their failures, the natural-born officers who ran the military blamed their losses on the cloned conscription.

After that, the Unifieds had jettisoned the clones by relegating them to deep-space patrols. That was how Cutter had risen to power. As they abandoned the fleet, he had received a field promotion that raised him from chief petty officer to captain.

Having stranded the clones on ships spread throughout the galaxy, the Unifieds thought they had solved the situation. They hadn't. Wayson Harris had figured out a way to transport the ships back to Earth, and the war began just as the aliens launched a second, more destructive, invasion.

Cutter poured himself a cup of coffee.

A light winked on his communications console. The light winked red, alerting him that the message was urgent.

He sipped his coffee, hit the switch, and asked, "What is it?"

"Admiral, I just received a message from Pentagon Security.

They're evacuating the building," said Thomas Hauser, captain of the *Churchill.*

"Is it a drill?" Cutter asked. In his head, he added, *I hope you aren't pestering me because of a specking fire drill, Captain.*

"No, sir."

The admiral sipped his coffee. "Very well. Let me know when you know more."

"Aye, aye, sir."

Hauser signed off.

The door to the office slid open. Cutter looked up and saw something that struck him as strange. The man in the doorway, an ensign, had brown hair and brown eyes and stood the right height for a clone, but his face didn't match everybody else's. He would blend in only as long as no one looked closely.

Without speaking a word, the ensign pulled an S9 stealth pistol from inside his jacket. He aimed it at Cutter and fired. The first fléchette barely nicked the admiral, cutting a quarter-inch crease across his right cheek, slicing part of it from the rest of his face. Before Cutter registered what had happened, the ensign fired a second shot that hit him in the forehead, killing him instantly.

Cutter did not fall from his chair. His corpse slumped against the backrest, and his arms dropped over the sides.

CHAPTER SIX

Location: Mazatlán, New Olympian Territories

I had come to conduct a summit, but when it was over, I would stay for the waves. The days were hot. The evenings were dry and comfortable. Steep, brush-covered mountains reached out like arms around this town, and stretched into the ocean.

I woke at 07:00 and jogged four miles to the end of the

beach, then I turned and sprinted on the return trip. Now that I had finished my run, I stripped off my shirt and shoes and strode into the water. I didn't have a mask or fins, so the swim would probably be brief. I planned to swim a few hundred yards out and float for a while. It wouldn't matter to me if the currents swept me out to sea. Warm water, colorful fish, an acceptable place to die.

Anyplace else, this water might have felt warm, but this ancient shoreline stretched along a desert. As I stepped out, the water rolled up my feet and calves, and the bracing cold made me pause for just a moment before I pushed farther in.

The useless fears began gnawing at me by the time the water reached my thighs. I looked back at the shore and thought about slinking back to the hotel, then I dived in and swam.

My hosts kept careful watch on me. A car filled with policemen had trailed me as I ran; now a pair of boats patrolled the shore as I swam—twenty-five-foot motor cruisers with the words SHORE PATROL hand-painted in foot-tall letters along their sides.

Seeing the boats, I stopped to tread water and consider my options, then I stroked out for a chat. As I approached, I yelled, "Gentlemen, I know how to swim."

"Yes, sir, General Harris. We can see that," one of the sailors called down to me.

They were all natural-born, almost certainly refugees from Olympus Kri, "Martians." They wore white uniforms of some sort.

I lowered my feet and started treading water again, my body rising and dropping as foot-tall swells rolled by. "I'm only a hundred yards offshore," I said. "If I get a cramp, I could swim back one-handed."

The men on the boat didn't answer.

I gave them a few seconds, then added, "Go back to the dock."

"We can't do that, General."

"Why not?" I asked.

One of the sailors shrugged, and said, "Orders."

Another said, "You know, there are sharks in these waters."

"Sharks?" I asked, now feeling less confident. There had

been a time when the thought of sharks didn't bother me. That time ended about a year ago. Now I needed to muster my confidence to swim in water more than a few feet deep.

"Sure, there are sharks. This is the ocean. They live in the ocean," said one of the sailors. He had a slight accent. *He's not from Earth,* I reminded myself. The Enlisted Man's Empire had ceded this portion of the map to the people of Olympus Kri.

"You ever seen a shark out here?" I asked.

"We haven't been here very long," said the sailor.

Checking the surface of the water for fins, I said, "Tell you what. You stay out here, and I'll swim back to shore." There were no fins and probably no sharks. I couldn't be sure, though. The bottom was dark, probably thirty feet down.

I wanted to climb into the boat, but I didn't want to give in to my fears. How had I become afraid of the sea? Truth be told, I felt especially nervous when I swam at night, even if I was just in a swimming pool. Water made me nervous now, but it never had before. It wasn't like I had been chased by a shark or almost drowned; I couldn't think of anything that had caused this newfound fear. It didn't make sense.

"Would you like a ride into shore?" asked the sailor. They could take me right into the hotel—the architects who designed the hotel had carved a thirty-foot waterway that ended in the covered harbor they called the "Aqua Lobby."

"No thanks," I said. "I left my clothes on the beach."

I spun toward shore and started to stroke. In my mind's eye, I saw squid with tentacles as wide as telephone poles gliding along the bottom, watching me with basketball-sized eyes. They lazily waved their tentacles in my direction, waiting to wrap them around me and pull me apart.

The squid in my head were so big they could have snapped the shore-patrol boats apart like breadsticks—large enough to pull entire hotels into the sea.

I never spotted a writhing, snakelike tentacle or a shark's fin. After a minute or two, I saw sand ten feet beneath me, then I swam through the roil and waded onto the shore.

I didn't need to retrieve my shirt and shoes. A natural-born in a white uniform met me as I came out of the water. He'd gathered them for me.

"So you're my personal valet?" I asked.

He handed me my gear, and said, "If it pays better than a cop's salary, count me in."

"You'd need to call me 'sir,'" I said.

"Oh," he said. "Maybe I'll stick with police work."

Wet from head to toe, with white sand sticking to my feet and ankles, I pulled my T-shirt over my wet hair.

"Would you like a ride back to the hotel?" the man asked. I saw his car waiting along the street.

"Are there any sharks between here and the hotel?" I asked.

The man looked confused. He said, "No, sir."

I bent down and slipped on my shoes. "So long as the coast is clear, I think I'll walk," I said. The hotel was less than a quarter of a mile up the beach.

There might have been muggers waiting in the roadside bushes, but New Olympians didn't scare me as much as sharks. Take away the ocean with its hidden monsters, and my only phobias involved nuclear bombs and battles on naval ships. I considered my fear of nukes as I trotted along the beach toward the hotel. As far as I was concerned, having a healthy fear of nuclear bombs was a sign of intelligence.

By the time I stepped into the shower, I had run over eight miles, swum in the ocean, and done enough sit-ups to make my abs feel like they were folding. I turned up the heat until the water scalded my skin, turning the air in the bathroom into steam.

The New Olympians had placed me in a hotel suite befitting a bureaucrat, not an officer. I had a king-sized bed and guest rooms, a wet bar, a balcony overlooking the ocean, a media center, a fireplace, a dining area, and a hot tub. I'd lived quite comfortably in billets that were smaller than this bathroom. Truth be told, I preferred them.

At some point, living in luxury made me uncomfortable. I preferred the guest rooms to the master bedroom, never touched the wet bar, and went out to the balcony only to exercise. The hot showers, on the other hand, were the one luxury I enjoyed immensely.

The bioengineering geniuses behind the military cloning program saw no need for their progeny to grow beards. I might not have been a standard-issue clone, but the gene pool from which I emerged fed from the same trough. I could practically think my whiskers into nonexistence, but practically nonexistent didn't cut it for this Marine. I took a razor into the shower.

Pummeled by a steady stream of 108-degree water, I felt the sting vanish from my muscles while clouds of steam filled my thoughts. The familiar drowsy sensation turned my brains to mush. I used the soap stream to create lather, which I spread across my throat, cheeks, and chin, and then I shaved.

My shoulders relaxed. The muscles in my neck went soft. I braced my arm against the wall under the main showerhead and rested my forehead against my forearm.

How did I feel at that moment? How did I feel? I felt satisfied. I thought about stepping out of the shower and beginning my day, then I banished the thought.

I hadn't traveled to the New Olympian Territories on vacation, but the business I had come for would wait. *What would happen if I simply disappeared?* I asked myself. Would the summit go on without me?

Satisfied. Indulged. Placated. Satiated. I fantasized about staying in the shower for another hour, then drying off and walking away from everything. I could live a feral life in the desert and grow a wispy beard. The Enlisted Man's Empire didn't need me. I was the only clone left of my class, but I had a million distant cousins, all of them loyal to the empire. I was *satiated.* I was wasted and lazy, the energy in my body all burned out. My lethargy might have disgusted me had I not felt so damned relaxed.

My arm pressed against the shower wall, the hot water streaming down my head, back, and shoulders, my muscles a soggy mess. That was the position I was in when the assassins entered my hotel room.

I didn't feel a rush of cold air as they slipped into the steamy bathroom or hear their footsteps.

Had the first assailant used his gun, he could have killed me without a fight. With the condensation on the shower glass and steam in the air, I had no idea he was there at first. But then he stalked closer, close enough for me to catch the movement of his blurry silhouette in my peripheral vision.

The only reason I spotted the bastard was because he'd come dressed in the all-black uniform of a hotel bellboy, which stood out in my brightly lit, marble-lined bathroom. He was a shadow in a room full of white.

I remained in place, my forehead pressed into the back of my arm. If he'd pulled his gun, there would have been nothing I could do, not at this point. He stood too far away.

Still pretending not to see the man, I fiddled with the dial, heating the water from scalding to boiling, then I made a show of reaching for my razor and knocking it to the floor. As I bent over to retrieve it, I pushed a hand against the shower door, which swung open fast and hard, hitting a towel rack along the wall and shattering. Sharp gems of glass sprayed across the marble tile floor.

Even before the door hit the rack, I grabbed the assailant by his shirt and traded my balance for his. I used his high center of balance to pull myself to my feet and my low center to topple him to the ground. I added my weight to his as he smashed his head into the wall of the shower, then I spun him on his back so that the steaming water poured on his face, burning his eyes and filling his mouth and nose so that he could barely breathe.

He produced a pistol from wherever he'd been hiding it, but I batted it away. It clattered to the floor.

I drove my right fist into his face, a short-stroke blow, my hand traveling no more than four inches, but hitting hard enough to drive the back of his head into the marble floor. I pressed my left arm across his throat, hit him a second time when he started to struggle, and the bastard went limp.

I didn't have time to find out if he was dead or unconscious because his friend came running into the bathroom at that moment. Maybe he saw my bare ass sticking out of the shower, because he wasn't watching where he stepped and slipped as he ran over the broken glass.

Still on my knees, I spun, lashed out with my right leg, and caught the dumb speck's kneecap, sending him into a spontaneous collapse that ended with his forehead striking the corner of the toilet. Like his unconscious pal, this assailant decided to keep his gun concealed until it was too late. I spotted the handle protruding from his waistline holster, and that was when the third assassin appeared.

Like his pals, this one came dressed like the hotel help, black jacket with gold stripes on the sleeves, dark pants with a velvet stripe down the leg. Not until I spotted the third fellow did I realize that I'd been dealing with clones. Unlike his brothers in arms, this one came with his pistol drawn and his finger on the trigger.

Had I held on to the first guy's pistol instead of knocking it halfway across the bathroom, I could have shot the bastard. Now all I had was an unconscious stiff with a gash across his forehead. I lifted him to his feet and held him like a shield, placing him between me and the clone with the gun. As the third guy waved his pistol looking for a shot, I ran across the glass, tossed the stiff in his direction as if it were a medicine ball, and lunged.

Shards of glass carved deep slits in my feet, but I ignored the pain. I needed to get at this guy before he regained his balance. I needed to swarm him, to knock away his gun.

A long shard of glass embedded itself along my arch, digging deeper and deeper into my foot with every step. I tried to dart, but my lacerated feet slowed me down, and then the bastard fired his gun. I lurched forward, left foot down, right foot curled and in the air. We collided, my weight and momentum driving him back toward the wall. Already weak, I slammed my elbow into his jaw, brought my knee into his groin, and butted my skull into his nose. He had wounded me though I didn't yet know how badly.

My thoughts turned opaque. I needed to finish this bastard before I blacked out, so I drove the upper ridge of my forearm under his jaw and pressed my weight into it as I slowly went slack, one final thought still echoing in my brain—*If there's a fourth guy, I'm dead.*

PART II

THE INVESTIGATOR

CHAPTER SEVEN

Location: Mazatlán, New Olympian Territories
Date: July 17, 2519

"Where do you think you're going?" the policeman asked as he blocked the entrance into the hotel room.

Just over six feet tall, the policeman considered himself imposing. The man he stopped stood six-foot-five, nearly four inches taller, but something about him suggested he wouldn't put up a fight. He looked like someone who could be pushed around, the human version of a giant whale—big and strong but harmless.

The man said, "The Navy Office sent me." He held out his traveling workspace so that the policeman could see his ID.

Reading the big man as more bureaucratic than belligerent, the cop became more aggressive. He barked, "Put away the tablet, sir."

"What? I was just going to . . ."

"I don't care what you have on your tablet. My orders are to keep people out of this room."

Looking confused, the big man lowered the computer and took a step backward. Despite his size and his athletic build, the man had no fight in him. "I was trying to show you my identification. I'm here from the Pentagon. I have official orders. I . . ."

The cop cut him off. He said, "Sir, your orders don't mean a rat's right testicle to me." As the big man turned to leave, the cop smirked, and told himself, *Damn straight, I'm in charge.*

The stranger gave it one last try. He said, "I have clearance . . ."

"Then take it up with the police chief. I'll let you in when

Chief Story gives me a call. Until then, get your ass out of here."

That was when the second man stepped into view. This one was taller, easily seven feet tall, bald, and covered with muscle. The man's skin was the color of coffee and his eyes were black and spaced far apart. He glared down at the policeman, his expression impassive and yet menacing. He didn't speak a word.

Seeing the tall, dark man, the policeman knew the situation had changed and dropped his hand to the butt on his pistol. He started to call for backup.

The first intruder said, "The officer says we haven't been cleared. He wants us to go back to the police station."

Without speaking a word, the big man locked a hand the side of a catcher's mitt around the policeman's collar. With the ease of a chess player sliding a pawn into place, he pulled the policeman five inches forward, slammed him back against a wall, then gently lowered his unconscious form to the floor.

"Why did you do that?" asked Travis Watson.

Ray Freeman didn't answer. He stepped into the hotel room. Two more policemen stood just inside the entryway, their civilian pistols raised.

Freeman said, "The Pentagon sent us," and the policemen obediently lowered their guns.

One of the policemen asked, "I don't suppose you have some form of identification?"

Watson said, "I tried to show it to the fellow out there, but he wasn't interested." He held up his traveling workspace, waited while the policemen studied it, then asked, "Am I allowed . . . ?"

"Watson," one of the policemen said as he holstered his gun. "Why didn't you say so?"

"I tried. That guy out there . . ."

"Him? That's Garrett. They should have warned you about him. He's an asshole."

The second cop looked through the open door, spotted the body spread out on the rug, and said, "Maybe they should have warned Garrett about you guys."

Watson said, "This is Ray Freeman."

"Yeah, they said you guys were coming," said the second cop.

"Mind if we have a look around?" asked Freeman, his voice hinting that he didn't much care how they felt.

The policemen stepped aside.

The New Olympians hadn't yet formed their own local government. Gordon Hughes, their governor on Mars, had died a few months before the transfer to Earth began. The Enlisted Man's Empire appointed an interim governor, a lawyer named Jim Evans, to oversee the creation of a permanent government, but the New Olympians considered Evans a stopgap, not a governor.

Every town the New Olympians settled had established its own constabulary. The policeman in charge in Mazatlán was a man named Mark Story. He had come to the crime scene and already left.

Watson pointed to a stain and asked a nearby tech, "Whose blood is that? Is that Harris's?"

The tech looked at a palm-sized computer, tapped the screen, and said, "We don't have positive identification."

"Do you think it's his?" asked Watson.

"It came from a clone," said the tech.

"So it's his," Watson said.

"Could be," said the tech. "Could have come from any one of them."

"Any one of whom?" asked Watson.

Freeman did not waste time listening to the conversation. He meandered toward the bathroom, pausing to stare at the silhouette marking the location of a body just outside the bathroom door. The police called the silhouettes, "negs," short for negative image body models—three-dimensional holographic shadows that detectives used to mark both the locations and positions of corpses among other things.

The blood was still on the wall. A cleaning crew would clean the walls. By that time, the police would create negs showing the shape and depth of every drop and splatter on the walls and floor.

In his mind's eye, Freeman stretched out the body and measured it. *Less than six feet,* he thought. *Probably five-ten.*

He stopped a tech, and asked, "Were you here when they bagged him?"

"Bagged 'em myself."

"Was he a military clone?"

"All of them were," said the tech.

"How many were there?" asked Freeman.

"Three."

The tech looked at the neg on the floor, a shadow of a body, legs stretched, back curled, torso propped against the wall. He asked, "How'd you know?"

Freeman let a second pass before he answered, "Just a hunch." Normally he wouldn't have answered at all, but he suspected he'd have more questions and wanted to keep the techs friendly.

He walked into the bathroom and saw two more negs—one stretched out across the floor, one lying with its head in the shower and its feet on the marble floor. These two were laid out flat, more or less.

Freeman went to the water faucet. He asked, "Have you dusted for fingerprints?"

"Guess what we found," said the tech.

"Fingerprints from clones," said Freeman. "May I?" He pointed at the faucet.

"Yeah, we're done. Help yourself."

Freeman poured himself a glass of water, drank it dry, then set the glass beside the sink. He asked, "Were all three bodies general military clones?"

"None of them were Liberators, if that is what you are asking," said the tech.

"How about the blood?" asked Freeman.

"It's all clone blood."

"Can you tell Liberator blood from standard clone blood?"

"Not without lab equipment," the tech answered. "The DNA is almost identical. Somebody is going to need to analyze it right down to the nucleotides, and we don't have that kind of equipment."

"Have you checked the blood for adrenal levels?" asked Freeman.

"Why would we do that?" asked the tech.

"Harris is a Liberator. If these guys attacked him, his combat reflex would have activated."

"Adrenaline and testosterone," the tech said, sounding

impressed. "Easier to test for testosterone. From what I hear, Liberator testosterone levels are off the charts."

With Freeman following behind him, the tech scanned the walls, the bathroom floor, and the carpets. He knelt beside the neg lying in the shower and took more data. He took his equipment into the brightly lit dining area and read the results.

"There's plenty of adrenaline in this sample," said the tech. "This one's from the shower. The man in the shower was beaten to death; his jaw, nose, and neck were all broken. That probably accounts for the adrenaline level. His testosterone levels are fairly standard.

"At first glance, I'd say this blood came from the clone in the shower."

Freeman said nothing.

The tech played with his computer. He said, "This reading is from the bathroom floor. It's got fragments of glass in it."

Freeman had noticed the shattered shower door and assembled the sequence of events in his head. He imagined Harris showering as the assassins entered. Maybe he'd hit the first one with the shower door, then pulled him into the shower and killed him.

The second one, the one on the bathroom floor, Harris would have had to cross the broken glass to attack him. *The blood from the floor is Harris's,* Freeman decided. *It has to be Harris's.*

The tech looked at the computer readout and smiled. He said, "You know, I never really believed in Liberators. I knew about the Mogat Wars and all, but I always thought Liberator Clones were a myth. I mean, clone soldiers with glands that flood their blood with hormones during combat . . . how about unicorns and griffins?

"This blood came from a Liberator." He shook his head. "There's enough adrenaline to give a guy a heart attack. This bleeder had five times the testosterone level of a normal man."

He looked up at Freeman, and said, "Whoever bled this shit might be more comfortable dead than alive. Do you have any idea what he'd be going through if he was alive?"

CHAPTER EIGHT

Freeman and Watson sat in a small office in the transitional police station—a building that might once have been a cheap hotel. The chief had set up shop in the manager's office, giving himself more space but less privacy than he would have had in one of the rooms.

The makeshift station didn't have cells or interrogation rooms. It had a lobby, which the officers used as a cafeteria. They used guest rooms to store equipment. The New Olympian police had been issued very few guns, but they had plenty of computers, handcuffs, riot gear, and patrol cars.

Watson used his traveling workspace to catch up on messages. He placed it on the table and typed in a security code, then entered his communications address. Seeing he had a message from Major Alan Cardston, Watson tapped a key and called the major back.

As the head of Pentagon Security, Cardston carried a lot of authority for an officer of his rank. He lived in a world populated by colonels and generals, yet he seemed to carry as much clout as the men around him.

Watson didn't like dealing with Cardston; he considered the major a bigoted prick. Cardston referred to Freeman and Watson as "civilian contractors" and treated them as if they were lower than enlisted men.

When Cardston came on the line and saw Watson, he seemed to sit on his hands. Had it been a general on the line, Cardston would have saluted. Had it been a civilian politician, he would have asked a friendly question. Instead, he merely said, "Watson, what have you found?"

Having worked with Wayson Harris and Ray Freeman, Watson had learned not to give information easily. He said,

"They found three corpses in the hotel room. All three of them were clones."

"Yes, I saw that in the police report," Cardston replied.

"Two were beaten to death, one was shot."

"Yes, that was also in the report."

"They entered Harris's room at 08:05," said Watson.

"Oh-five?" asked Cardston. "Strange. The other attacks began precisely at 08:00, but this one was five minutes later. Are they sure they entered at 08:05?"

"The door lock automatically made a time stamp when it was opened at 08:05. It's part of the hotel's security protocol," said Watson. "They use it to prevent maids from robbing guests."

"Maybe the clock in the door was off," said Cardston.

"Freeman had the police check that. The clock is accurate."

"Interesting," said Cardston.

"We know Harris entered the room thirty-two minutes before the assailants," said Watson. "There's a security feed showing him entering the hotel lobby, and a security time stamp at 07:33.

"There is a lot of blood in the room. We know that some of it came from Harris," said Watson.

Cardston paused. He looked down, his eyes jetting back and forth. Watson thought he was probably looking over the report he had received, the one that seemed to have all the answers, the one generated by the New Olympian police.

"How do you know it was his?" asked Cardston.

"Freeman . . ." Watson began.

Freeman, who was in the room but out of the camera, put up a hand to stop him.

Watson changed in midsentence. "The police analyzed it for adrenal levels."

"The combat reflex," Cardston said. "Good thinking."

Liberator physiology was human, but it included a unique gland that dumped hormones into their blood when their systems hit high levels of stress. The hormone dumps were called the "combat reflex."

The reflex made them clearheaded and deadly in battle, but it also proved addictive, leading to massacres, some involving civilians. The engineers who had designed the current model of military clones had removed that gland and replaced it with a gland of a very different sort.

"Some of the blood was laced with adrenaline and testosterone, so we know Harris was there," Cardston said. "I'm not sure I would have thought of that."

Watson started to respond, but Freeman spoke over him. He said, "All we know is that Harris was there and that he lost a lot of blood."

Cardston said, "Freeman?"

"Yes."

"Do you think he was shot?" asked Cardston.

Freeman said, "Possibly."

"How about security feeds? Did you check with hotel security? Do they have anything?"

"We checked the video feed. It doesn't show how the clones entered the building or how Harris left."

After they ended the call to Cardston, Freeman and Watson met with Mark Story, the chief of the New Olympian police in Mazatlán, a white-haired man with the polished demeanor of a politician.

Story said, "I heard somebody attacked the Pentagon this morning. Obviously, if there is anything I can do, my entire department is at your service."

Freeman seemed content to let Watson do the talking.

Watson said, "We appreciate that, Chief Story."

"I heard about an attack on a prison."

"Sheridan Federal Correctional," said Watson.

"Both attacks happened at the exact same time that the clones attacked Harris. Do you think they're related?" asked Story.

Freeman remained silent.

Not the exact same time, thought Watson. He'd seen military precision. If it had been a synchronized attack, he had no doubt that Harris's door would have opened at the exact same time the grenade exploded in the Pentagon and the gunship fired in Oregon.

He said, "It's too early to tell."

"Can I get you coffee or tea?" Story asked, then he thought a moment, and added, "I can get you something stronger if you like."

"I'm fine," said Watson.

Freeman didn't answer. He seemed to have lost interest in the conversation.

They sat around Story's desk. The chief said, "Obviously, we will do everything in our power to find General Harris. We've set up security stations on roads in and out of town. We've blocked off the airport.

"You can leave, of course, but the runways are closed, and we're scanning for transports.

"Per Pentagon regulations, we haven't allowed extra-atmospheric travel in or out of the New Olympian Territories at all. We've got boats patrolling the coastline. If somebody has General Harris, they won't get far."

"Do you think it was a kidnapping?" asked Watson.

Freeman sat in his chair mute and menacing, a giant wedged into a chair meant for a normal-sized man. He kept his legs out front, arched up and bent at the knees. His hands, wrists, and half his forearms extended beyond the armrests. His thickly muscled legs and broad torso blocked any view of the chair on which he sat.

"Had to have been. You were there when my techs analyzed the blood samples. The general lost a lot of blood. Best-case scenario, General Harris was ambulatory when he left the hotel room. He might not have been conscious at all."

"What do you think happened?" Watson asked, pretending that he didn't consider Story an incompetent bureaucrat.

"It seems pretty clear. Somebody sent in a team of commandos. They waited until Harris was in the shower, then they tried to kidnap him. Harris put up a fight, but he lost.

"My guess is that they sent two men into the bathroom with two more waiting in the hotel room. Harris killed the first two in the bathroom. He killed the third outside the door, then the fourth one got him, probably shot him, judging by the blood. What happened next is anyone's guess."

"How would they have slipped him out of the hotel?" asked Watson.

Story leaned back in his chair, rested his hands on his chest, laced his fingers as if saying a prayer. He thought about the question for several seconds. "That's the big question, now, isn't it? How do you sneak a dying man out of a hotel?

"If he's dying or dead, or maybe just unconscious, you could place him in a case of some kind. That would conceal him. You could drop him in a laundry basket. You could shove him down a trash chute. We checked the trash. It was clean.

"We've searched the building, of course. The easiest answer is to hang a DO NOT DISTURB sign and leave your victim tucked into bed. We've checked every room in the hotel."

Watson smiled, and said, "It sounds as if you have all the bases covered."

"We're trying. We're giving this one everything we have."

"I guess that's everything for now," said Watson.

"Are you flying back to Washington?" asked Story.

Before Watson could answer, Freeman stood. Mark Story stood. Watson followed, realizing that the meeting had ended.

Story said, "We'll notify you the moment we find something."

One of the policemen appeared at the door and asked Story if he could speak to him. The police chief apologized and left the room.

"Why do you want them to think we're flying back to Washington?" Watson asked.

Speaking in a voice that was more reverberation than whisper, Freeman said, "Because smart cockroaches only come out when you leave the room."

CHAPTER NINE

As he and Freeman left the police station, Watson asked, "What do we do now?"

The sun still shone in the sky, but evening had begun, and the day's heat had turned mild. Night wouldn't come for a couple of hours, but the day had ended.

Ahead of them, the streets were nearly empty. The New Olympians had not come with fleets of cars or trucks. The only vehicles they had were the ones the Enlisted Man's Empire had given them.

Freeman said, "We're going to the spaceport."

"So we're leaving," said Watson.

"You're leaving," said Freeman.

"What about you?"

"I'm staying."

The police station was located in the center of what had been an abandoned downtown. Steel shutters covered the entrances of many of the buildings along the street. The New Olympians would open and populate the city, but the process would take time. They still hadn't restored power or water to much of the city. The people still lived in a relocation camp on the north edge of town. They lived in a prefab ghetto with communal dormitories and cafeterias, and they ate military rations for meals.

The only cars on the street were police cars.

Freeman said, "Keep walking."

As they passed the car that had chauffeured them from the spaceport, the driver—a policeman—stepped out.

Watson said, "Wait for us here. We'll just be a moment."

They walked to the end of the block, crossed the street, walked another block, then turned a corner. They were several blocks from the ocean, but the wind carried a hint of salt.

"Why am I leaving?" Watson asked.

"Because I work better alone," said Freeman.

"What's that supposed to mean?" Watson asked, though he already knew the answer and didn't want to be reminded.

Freeman obliged him. He said, "You went to law school; you're not trained for this."

"What are you planning to do?"

Freeman didn't answer immediately. They walked around another corner. The block ahead had been a storefront with tinted windows and a black marble frieze, a style of building that looked out of place in a coastal tourist town. Ahead of them, business buildings gave way to parks.

Freeman said, "I want them to see us board a shuttle, and I want them to see the shuttle leave. I want them to think we've gone home."

"You can't possibly think you can slip back here and blend in unseen," said Watson.

Freeman stood seven feet tall. He was a black man, a pure-blooded African-American living in a society that had outlawed races several centuries ago. His family had been part of an all-African-American Neo-Baptist colony that had not been touched by the Unified Authority's integration efforts.

Freeman and Harris had something in common: they were both the last of their kind. Harris had been minted decades after Congress had nixed the Liberator project. Freeman's Neo-Baptist relatives died when the Avatari incinerated a planet called New Copenhagen.

Freeman didn't respond to Watson's comment. In his mind, answering questions only invited further discussion, and Ray Freeman didn't like to chat. He said, "Harris is still here."

Watson stopped walking. He asked, "How do you know?"

"They didn't come here to capture him," Freeman said. "They came here to kill him."

"You don't know that."

They entered a park with overgrown hedges and an empty fountain riddled with bird droppings. The grass had grown knee high. Shrubs and palm trees lined the walkways.

Freeman said, "Let's cross the street."

"Don't you like parks?" asked Watson.

"Not as much as I like privacy," said Freeman. "If we step out of their line of sight, the New Olympians will send soldiers to keep an eye on us."

By this time, three police cars and a truckload of soldiers trailed behind them. Having lost the second-highest-ranking officer in the Enlisted Man's Empire, the New Olympians weren't taking any chances.

The police cars and troop transport waited in the distance as they crossed the street, then lingered a hundred yards back.

"How do you know they didn't come to kidnap Harris?" Watson asked, as they stepped onto the next sidewalk.

Freeman asked, "If you were going to kidnap a clone like Harris, would you shoot him?"

Watson thought for a moment. He said, "Not if I wanted him alive. I'd try to convert him, get him to walk out on his own."

"Did you smell any chlorine? Did you smell ammonia?" asked Freeman.

"It's been more than twenty-four hours; the smell might have gone away," said Watson.

Freeman shook his head. He said, "The police checked. They wrote about it in their report."

"So that's it? You're taking me out of the loop?" asked Watson.

"You'll be safer in Washington," Freeman said. "You wouldn't like the direction I'm headed out here." And that, as far as Freeman was concerned, was all that remained to be said. He steered Watson back to the police station in silence, and their driver took them out to the spaceport.

Gordon Hughes Spaceport was technically an "airport," not a spaceport. It was designed to handle atmosphere-only flights though its runway was long enough to handle fighters. The spaceport could easily accommodate military transports, which were vertical-landing crafts, but it lacked the upgraded equipment needed for fueling extra-atmospheric freighters and commuter crafts. Any space birds landing in Mazatlán would need to pack sufficient fuel to fly home.

Freeman considered the logistics of extra-atmospheric flights from Mazatlán as the caravan rolled onto the spaceport grounds. He saw cargo planes and atmospheric commuters, but no extra-atmospheric freight haulers.

Hughes Spaceport did have enough space for a fleet of transports, and those were extra-atmospheric birds that carried large amounts of fuel. Even if a ship's tanks were nearly empty, there were spaceports in California, Texas, and Utah where an extra-atmospheric ship could refuel.

Freeman mulled this over in silence.

Humiliated that he was being sent home, Watson remained quiet as the car approached the spaceport. He told himself he was angry, but he knew the truth. He was embarrassed.

The car caravan drove into the hangar in which the government shuttle was parked. While Watson thanked the New Olympian driver and policemen, Freeman entered the shuttle. The escort stayed to watch as the pilot powered up the shuttle's engines and taxied out of the hangar.

No one noticed that Freeman had already exited the plane. He had entered the main cabin, walked to the galley, and exited through the service hatch at the rear of the plane.

CHAPTER TEN

Returning to town meant a ten-mile hike, but Freeman didn't mind. Hiking back to town would give him time to piece together the information he had learned.

The airport was south and east of town, far from the beaches. It was late at night now, with a sky so purely black in which the stars looked ripe and ready to fall. Freeman drew in breaths of dry desert air. He didn't run and saw no reason to rush. Crossing parking lots, alleys, and fields, he shadowed the road. The few times that cars passed, he calmly ducked out of sight. Mostly, though, he had the country to himself, just him and the sounds of the wind and the insects.

He would need a gun, but that didn't worry him. He had money, both cash and credit, and a man could always find guns if he knew where and how to look, even in a newly formed territory. Black markets grew spontaneously. They were indigenous in all societies.

Freeman entered an open field, saw a dilapidated farmhouse three hundred yards away, and knew that the land had been out of use for centuries. Scabs of grass grew, but most of the ground remained bare, the soil modified to withhold nutrients from seeds that did not contain the proper genetic sourcing. Once the New Olympians established their territory, they would restore the farmhouse and plant the land.

The field had space for an armada of transports, and there were other fields nearby that were just as large. He asked himself if those clones could have come in transports, but gave the idea no credence.

The gunship that attacked Sheridan Federal Correctional Facility seemed to have appeared out of nowhere. EME radar had not picked up the bird until she had nearly reached the coast. There had been three transports as well. According to radar tracking, they materialized about one hundred miles off the Oregon coast. A mystery.

The same tracking system showed no unidentified aircraft entering New Olympian airspace—not near the sea, not leaving the atmosphere. The Enlisted Man's Navy had established a blockade around Earth. Transports penetrating that blockade would not go unnoticed.

Freeman jogged some of the distance, but mostly he walked. He walked up a hill, crested the rise, and saw Mazatlán in the near distance. A few lights glittered in buildings and along the streets, but mostly the city showed as a solid silhouette against the less absolute darkness of the night. On the other side of town, the lights of the relocation center glowed like a field of embers.

The scene before him sat silent in the desert air, heavy and dry. Freeman could see the sea from this spot as well. A nearly full moon hung above it, illuminating waters as black and shiny as obsidian, with gray breakers rolling into shore.

CHAPTER ELEVEN

Location: En route to Washington, D.C.
Date: July 17, 2519

Travis Watson called Emily, his fiancée, from the shuttle a few minutes after takeoff. He didn't worry about waking her. She was a night owl; call her anytime before three in the morning, and she would be alert and awake. Call her before noon, and she would sleep through the call.

She answered on the first ring, and said, "Baby, what is going on down there?"

Watson said, "I'm on my way home."

"Do they know what happened to Wayson?"

Though Harris's disappearance had not been released to the public, Emily knew about it. Gordon Hughes, the late governor of the New Olympian refugees, had been her grandfather. She didn't live or work with the New Olympians, but she kept up with news of the Territories, even when the news included classified information. Few EME generals or admirals had been informed about Harris, but Emily knew all about it, as if all people associated with New Olympia absorbed the information through the airwaves by osmosis.

Since he saw no point denying information that she already knew, he said, "No."

"Is he still missing?"

"Yes."

"Jeez," she said. "What a nightmare. It's like everything is happening all at once, the attack on the Pentagon, the one on the prison, and now Harris. Someone said they all happened at the exact same time, like it had all been synchronized."

Watson said, "I can't talk about that." Then he admitted, "It must have been."

"What does Don have to say about it?" "Don," the late Admiral Don Cutter, was Watson's boss.

"I haven't spoken with him," he said, trying to sound natural. Cutter had been killed in space. Only a small group knew about the assassination—the crew of the *Churchill*, a few select officers in the Pentagon, Freeman, and the people behind it.

"I don't get how the military works," said Emily. "I would have thought Harris's disappearance would be a top priority."

Hoping to prevent the conversation from evolving into a guessing game, Watson said, "Look, Emily, Sunny doesn't know about Wayson."

"You haven't told her anything?"

"I wanted to wait until we had something . . . something more than an empty hotel room." He wondered what he could tell Emily and what she already knew. As the late Gordon Hughes's granddaughter, Emily had well-placed friends in the New Olympian hierarchy.

He said, "I saw Harris's hotel room. If they got him, he didn't go down without a fight."

"Do you think they killed him?" Emily asked, the shock apparent in her voice.

"No. I don't think so," he said, remembering his final conversation with Freeman. "He killed three of theirs. There may have been a fourth, but I don't think they would have taken his body if they got him," said Watson. *They* left *Cutter sitting at his desk,* he added, but only in his thoughts.

"M, I'm going to call Sunny next," he said, trying again to take control of the conversation.

Silence. Then after several seconds, Emily said, "Oh, Trav, I don't know if that's a good idea. I mean, how is she going to take it? You know, she's kind of, I mean, she's kind of . . ."

"Pampered" was the first word that came to Watson's mind. Other words like "spoiled," "controlling," "clingy," and "needy" followed.

Emily didn't like her, either. Sunny Ferris was a smart, beautiful, well-educated lawyer who knew both how to turn on the charm and how to shut it off. Even when she smiled, and she normally only smiled for Harris, there was something unpleasant about her.

Emily, who had spotted it first, hadn't liked Sunny from the start. Watson fell for her charm in the beginning, but the pretty face and the witty banter soon wore thin for him as well.

He dismissed it as a consequence of her wealthy upbringing. Sunny had grown up in mansions, spending vacations in the best resorts around the galaxy. Neither the alien invasion nor the clone uprising had touched her family or their wealth. Her father's shoe-manufacturing company continued producing shoes, and his sports-gear business kept on selling sports gear. Over dinner, she sometimes talked about the trials of maintaining friendships on both coasts and of taking extravagant vacations.

"Look, M, I want you to go to her apartment . . ."

"Oh, Trav, no. Don't do this to me."

"M . . . M, somebody has to go sit with her. You know how she is. We can't let her go through this alone."

"Yes we can," said Emily.

"No we can't," said Watson.

"Call her when you get home, then you can sit with her."

"What if someone else tells her?" asked Watson.

"Who?"

They both knew who. The law firm that employed Sunny represented the New Olympians.

Emily changed her tactics. She said, "Send somebody else. Travis, she doesn't like me. She always ignores me when we go out with them. She only talks to you and Wayson. You know that. That's why I told you I didn't want to go out with them anymore."

"What if it was me who was missing?" asked Watson. "Wayson would send Sunny to help you . . . and she'd go." The words rang hollow in Watson's ears as he said them. He knew better, and so did Emily.

She said, "No he wouldn't. Harris? He wouldn't bother telling me. He'd wait until I found out on my own. And Sunny . . . Wayson never sends his little princess anywhere she doesn't want to go."

It was true. Watson didn't try to deny it. He said, "M."

"I don't like her, Travis. No, that's not true. I specking hate her. I do. I hate that bitch. I don't know why I hate her so much, but I hate her. I'm not going. Don't ask me again."

She remained silent for a few moments, then she sighed and asked, "What's her address?"

During the minutes between his call to Emily and the call he dreaded, Watson poured himself a drink, a half-filled tumbler of Scotch and ice. He didn't bother watering the Scotch, not on this night. He hoped the drink would take the edge out of the guilt he felt about sending Emily.

In his heart, Watson hoped Sunny would not pick up the phone, but she answered on the third ring. Sounding tired and confused, she said, "This is Sunny."

"Sunny, this is Travis Watson." The clock on the cabin wall showed the time as 10:23 P.M., but that would be Mazatlán time, which was two hours behind Washington, D.C. For Sunny, it would be just after midnight. He said, "Sorry to call so late."

"It's okay, Trav. I wasn't asleep."

A chime sounded on her end of the connection. She said, "That's strange, there's somebody downstairs. Can you hold for a second?"

The line went silent.

During the next few moments, Watson allowed his thoughts to meander. Sunny was Harris's girlfriend. At least, Harris had stopped seeing other women when he took up with her. Watson didn't know if Sunny shared the commitment.

"That's strange," she said, sounding more confused. "That was building security. Emily is downstairs. I told them to send her up. Did you send her?"

"Yes, I did," Watson admitted.

"Travis, is everything okay?" she asked.

"Fine . . . fine," he lied, too nervous to begin the explanation.

Sunny had read his silence. He heard it in the way she paused. Sounding both scared and suspicious, she asked, "Where are you?"

"I'm on a shuttle. I'm just flying in from the New Olympian Territories."

Another pause, then, "Wayson went there last week. Were you down there with him? Is he on the shuttle with you?"

"No, he isn't?"

The doorbell rang. Sunny ignored it. She swallowed loudly. Her voice quavered as she asked, "Is he all right?"

Watson said, "Maybe you should let Emily in."

"Travis, is Wayson all right?"

Watson sighed.

Sunny couldn't have known that someone had assassinated Don Cutter, but if she kept up with the news, she'd know about the other attacks. There had been no point trying to hide them, not when civilians were involved.

Emily rang the doorbell a second time.

"Travis?"

"Why don't you let Emily in?" he said.

"Is he alive? Will you at least tell me if he is alive?"

He couldn't. He didn't know himself. He said, "Sunny, this is classified information. I'm not supposed to tell you any of this."

"Please, Travis, give me that much. Is he alive?"

Watson sighed and gave the only answer he could. He said, "I don't know."

The phone went silent for several seconds. In a quiet,

defeated-sounding whisper, Sunny said, "I'd better get the door." He heard her set down the phone. It fell off the edge of the table and clattered to the floor. A moment later he heard Emily's voice. And then the crying began.

Watson was glad he had chosen an audio connection instead of a video feed. He wouldn't have wanted to watch Sunny cry. Crying women made him anxious.

He heard Sunny say, "Travis is on the phone. I better get back to him."

She already knows the worst of it, Watson told himself, giving himself permission to rush off.

Sunny picked the phone up from the floor. In a mechanical voice, she said, "Travis, Emily is here now. She's in the other room. Now, please tell me what has happened to Wayson." Her voice had a crushed quality to it. She sounded calm, but that calm was a thin veneer.

Thinking about how little he knew, Watson said, "I don't know what to tell you."

"Don't leave me hanging like this!" Now she sounded angry.

"Wayson is missing, that's all we know."

"'Missing'? 'Missing'? Does that mean he's alive?" she asked, now starting to sound frantic. "What does that mean?"

"People broke into his hotel room this morning. We don't know who they were or what they wanted. Wayson killed three of them. We think he may have been injured. That's all we know."

By the time he hung up, Sunny had become a screaming, sobbing wreck. She insisted Watson return to Mazatlán. She wanted the Marines to send a division. Emily had come into the bedroom by this time. The last thing Watson heard as he hung up was Sunny screaming at her.

Watson returned to the wet bar and poured himself another drink. He knew he shouldn't have told Sunny as much as he had; it was classified information.

Sunny was weak and pampered, and her connections with the New Olympians made her a security risk. Her law firm, Alexander Cross, had represented the New Olympians when they were on Mars. That was how she had first met Harris. She had gone to the Pentagon on behalf of a New Olympian client.

Maybe her friends can track Harris better than me or Freeman, he thought. He doubted it, though. Freeman was a one-man army.

Alone in the cabin, he sipped his Scotch, looked out the windows at the night sky, and turned down the lights. He would have gone to sleep if he could have. Sleep sounded good, but he couldn't even get himself to close his eyes.

The elephant in the room . . . the fact that everybody knew but no one wanted to address was who had launched the attacks. Everybody knew who wanted to kill Wayson Harris and Don Cutter. The prisoners in Sheridan had all been arrested for the same crime. There was a reason why the bomb had been placed on the third floor of the Pentagon. The Unified Authority was making its move. That much was obvious.

Freeman had quietly checked the hotel room for signs of ammonia and chlorine. *He's a butcher, but he knows what's what,* Watson reminded himself. Thinking about Freeman sent a shiver down his spine. Worrying about ammonia and chlorine left him empty and scared. He finished his drink.

Classified info, he thought. There were things he wished he'd never heard. The clones that made up the Enlisted Man's Empire had neural programming in their brains, programming that the insurgents had learned how to alter using combinations of common chemicals.

The year before, the entire Second Division went missing at Camp Lejeune, the only signs of trouble that the investigators found were traces of ammonia and chlorine in the air ducts—fumes from common chemicals, wafted in the right combination, the right sequence, and the right amounts. When the clones inhaled them, the programming caused their brains to reboot. Freeman was right. Had the men who entered Harris's hotel room pumped those chemicals into the bathroom, he would have fallen helpless and unconscious to the floor. They could have captured him without a fight.

He reminded himself that Harris wasn't the only clone on the scene. The three men he had killed had been clones as well.

Watson remained alone in the dimly lit cabin, drinking himself morose. He felt guilty and ashamed as thoughts flashed like news headlines in his head: Cutter dead. Harris missing.

Top Unified Authority war criminals sprung from jail. The Enlisted Man's Empire left without leadership.

The attack on the Pentagon didn't play into his thoughts. At least they'd caught that one in time. Alan Cardston was an officious prick, but nothing slipped past Pentagon Security with him in charge.

Watson wondered what would happen if the Enlisted Man's Empire collapsed. The clones had been benevolent conquerors. Once they shut down the Unified Authority military complex and arrested a few key politicians, life had returned to normal. The clones had left the U.A. legal system intact. Lawyers, judges, and policemen, most of whom were initially hostile toward the clones, kept their jobs.

Despite fears that the clones would use teachers to spread propaganda, the U.A. educational system continued unmolested. Since the clones had their own medical system, the civilian medical industry was left untouched. Rather than obliterating the U.A. government, the clones kept an eye on EME interests while the civilian government retained both its Senate and House of Representatives. Taxes had gone down, and the clones had successfully relocated New Olympians into the nearly unpopulated region of Central America.

And yet the people still resented the clones. They were conquerors, benevolent or not. They had waged war against Earth. Few people viewed clones as human, and antisynthetic sentiment ran deep.

It always had.

Watson remembered conversations he'd had with Harris over the two years he had worked with him. Harris. On the surface, Wayson Harris was the gung ho Marine, all "*Oorah* this" and "Semper fi that," but that layer of the man was little more than bullshit and polish. Sometimes, when he was alone, Harris's demons came out of hiding.

Harris's hate for the Unified Authority ran deep. He'd borne the brunt of the prejudice from the people he'd been created to protect his entire life. He was worn-out and angry. He'd seen brave men, clones, die willingly to protect the natural-born civilization that betrayed them time and time again.

He'd been sent into battles in which natural-born officers had calculated that every Marine and soldier would die. He'd known officers who placed a higher value on tanks and ships than the clones inside them. "Clones, boots, and bullets," he would say, meaning that the U.A. military placed the same approximate dollar value on all three.

For the last year, Watson had spent more time with Don Cutter than Harris, but his feelings toward Cutter were mostly ambivalent. Cutter was a newer make of clone, clones who had absolutely no idea of their origin. Instead of a combat reflex, later clones like Cutter had a gland that released deadly poison into their brains the moment they realized they were not naturally born. Clones like Cutter had complex sets of neural programming in their brains, one set of programs prevented excessive introspection. Another fooled them into ignoring clues about their origins.

Ask Don Cutter about clones, and he would tell you about growing up as a natural-born child in an orphanage filled with clones. Harris, on the other hand, knew the truth.

Watson tried to imagine Harris as a boy growing up in an orphanage. Like the other kids around him, he'd been told he was the one natural-born, and that his parents had died in an accident.

"Orphanage #553," Watson whispered, amused that he had heard Harris reference his orphanage so many times that the number had imprinted itself in his memory. He had no idea which orphanage Cutter had called home.

During the halcyon days of "manifest destiny," Unified Authority factories had stamped out slightly over a million infant clones every year and raised them in orphanages.

What was Harris like as a boy? Watson wondered. He tried to imagine him as a ten-year-old. Would he have been taller than the others, even back then? Mature Liberator clones stood six-foot-three. Standard-issue clones stood five-foot-ten. Did the height genes kick in when they were babies?

Even as an adult, Harris had not always known he was a clone. He'd found out about it after joining the Marines. An admiral had called him in one day and told him the news. Watson knew the story well. Harris had told him about it. The admiral had called him in and told him that he was a Liberator clone and that knowing he was a Liberator would not kill him.

Harris said he almost vomited on the admiral's floor he was so scared. He also said he went out and drank himself drunk that night.

Harris never gets drunk, Watson thought. Beer had no more effect on him than water, part of his Liberator makeup. *Harris never gets drunk,* Watson thought, choosing to believe the story about the admiral but not the story about the bar that came later the same night.

Watson looked down, realized he was on his fourth glass of Scotch, and that he had become quite morose indeed.

CHAPTER TWELVE

Location: Mazatlán, New Olympian Territories
Date: July 17, 2519

Freeman reached the outskirts of the city by 23:00. It would take him another two hours to reach the camp on the northern end of town.

As he stole closer to town, he moved more slowly and tried to keep to the shadows. The night air hummed in a few small, lit pockets. The New Olympians had placed standard-issue military generators to power high-priority projects so that workers could take round-the-clock shifts.

Freeman watched a team of workers from across a dark street. In the white glare of the arc lights, men with laser torches climbed in and out of a trench. Some of them joked and told stories along the ledge of the trench, their voices audible but not understandable above the sound of the generator. Others silently climbed down ladders, disappearing from view. They might have been working on the power grid or possibly the waterworks.

The project didn't interest Freeman. He moved on.

Freeman had the single-minded instincts of a shark. He noticed everything—sights, sounds, smells, vibrations—sifted them for valuable intel, and dismissed the dross. For Freeman, every stroll was recon and every chat an interrogation. He gathered information and filed it away in his mind.

His first stop was Harris's hotel. He wanted a chance to search it without cops looking over his shoulder.

The police had barricaded the drive that led onto the hotel grounds. Seven policemen manned the gate. A small generator purred in the background. Pods of lights showered glare around the area.

Had he come to kill these men, Freeman couldn't have engineered a better scenario. They stood in an island of light, blinding them to everything that happened in the darkness around them. A sniper could see them clearly and target them quickly with impunity.

Remaining in the shadows, Freeman slipped past the policemen. He spotted the motion sensors they had placed around the grounds, bargain-basement burglar alarms any thief, spy, or mercenary would spot and avoid. He adjusted his path so that it took him into the sensors' blind spots and beyond their range. He breathed slowly, stepped softly, did not brush against shrubs or leaves. He pressed tightly against walls, crawled between parked cars, and entered the building using the security pass he had swiped from the policeman he had knocked out earlier that morning.

The lights were out in the lobby, a crescent-shaped foyer with inch-deep carpets, elegant furniture, and a glass wall facing the sea and the moon. Freeman wished the windows faced inland instead. The light of the moon poured in through the glass, illuminating the floor, the walls, the furniture. He would look like a shadow to anyone peering in from outside, but an alert guard would notice his movement.

Without realizing he had done it, Freeman ran the odds in his head. Moving slowly and creeping behind furniture, it would take him nearly a minute to cross the lobby. He ducked behind the concierge's desk, then slipped behind a row of chairs, then a table. He moved slowly and methodically, his breathing nearly silent, then he scurried around a corner into the complete blackness of inner hallways; doors and elevators sat hidden in the darkness. Even here, hidden by the walls of the hotel, Freeman traveled with care.

He didn't step as he walked. Instead, he shuffled his feet in a C-pattern, barely lifting them off the ground. His footsteps made no noise. He traced his left hand along the wall to gauge his position, identifying doors by touch and trying their handles as he moved. It took him several minutes to find the stairs.

He climbed in total darkness. Darkness was an inconvenience but little more.

Even gentle steps would echo in the empty stairwell. Freeman wasn't nervous, but his senses were keen to stimulation. If he dropped a coin, he'd have counted the number of stairs it touched before it landed. He'd have known in his head how far it had traveled before it stopped.

Counting flights and doors, Freeman worked his way to the twenty-third floor. He opened the door a crack and did a visual sweep, finding no lights. A motion sensor would have tracked him opening the door, but he wasn't worried. This was a crime scene, not a military base. The violations had already taken place. The police had already searched. They were trying to keep people out, not tracking violators who let themselves in.

Silent as a shadow, Freeman slipped from the stairwell and counted doors until he found the entrance to Harris's suite. He didn't need to kick the door open or pick the lock. The police had sealed off the building and left the door open.

Pale moonlight shone into the room from the door to the balcony. The police must have left it as they found it, open. Curtains fluttered in the breeze.

Freeman stepped into the room, looked from side to side to be sure he was alone, and proceeded. He saw the patches of dried blood on the floor and wall, coin-sized drips and plate-sized puddles that looked black in the moonlight. Transmitters no bigger than bullet casings sat in the spots where the bodies had been, ready to project bodies on demand.

Freeman didn't care about negs. The police had come to investigate crimes and bodies, not him. He'd come looking for Harris.

Freeman didn't worry about leaving fingerprints. The police already knew he'd been in the room; they'd been in it when he arrived. He'd made a point of entering the bedrooms and the bathroom with them looking over his shoulder. So what if they found his fingerprints in the room? They'd seen him touch the furniture and the walls.

He went to the bed. It was made, the comforter wrinkled where someone had sat on it—probably a policeman. The pillows along the top ran in a perfectly straight row.

As a Marine, Harris would likely have made his own bed when he awoke. Harris didn't own a home. Freeman had visited him in different billets and had seen that he preferred orderly quarters.

He went to the closets. Harris had brought a pair of slacks and a couple of button-up shirts. In Freeman's experience, Harris practically lived in his Charlie service uniform and wore his Class-A uniform to formal events. Only a Class-A hung in the closet.

Freeman pulled the civilian shirts from their hangers and caught a faint whiff of flowery perfume. *A girl?* Freeman asked himself. Harris was no Puritan, but he wasn't enslaved by penile urges, and he had a girl he supposedly liked back in Washington, D.C.

But the scent on the shirt still lingered. It was weak, but unmistakable.

He went to the sliding door that led to the balcony outside. Heavy curtains hung across it, billowing as a strong breeze whistled through the partially opened glass. Freeman twisted the curtains so he could examine them in the moonlight. He searched them for traces of blood and found nothing.

There were no bloodstains on the carpet around the door to the balcony. Freeman stepped outside. He surveyed the floor and the waist-high railing, knowing that the police had done the same.

From twenty-three floors up, the roar of the waves sounded more like a whisper. Moonlight illuminated the scene below, making the landscape visible while hiding its colors. Freeman watched uneven rows of whitecaps rolling from the charcoal sea to the granite-colored shore.

Knowing the police had done this as well, Freeman

crawled along the balcony and checked the ledges for signs of blood or bullet casings. He found nothing.

Had Harris been shot? He'd lost a lot of blood. He'd been weak. Where would he have gone? In Freeman's experience, the simplest solution usually proved accurate. *Not even Harris could climb down from here,* he thought. *Harris had either walked out the door or somebody had carried him.*

Why hadn't anybody seen him? Simple enough, for the same reason no one had spotted Freeman. The hotel wasn't open for business; the only people on the premises were Harris, a few diplomats, a skeleton crew . . . and three general-issue clones.

Had any other high-ranking officers been sent, the entire floor would have been filled with aides and adjutants, but Harris eschewed entourages. He referred to the junior officers who rode the coattails of their superiors as "remora fish," and allowed no hangers-on.

Off in the distance, several miles away, the relocation camp glowed like a fire. It stood out from the black-and-gray landscape around it, its golden light transforming the ground around it.

Freeman gazed down at the camp. If there were answers to be had, he knew where to find them.

No barbed-wire fences surrounded the camp. The New Olympians didn't build gates or guard posts at the front. The residents could come and go as they pleased. So could Freeman.

He walked around the perimeter of the camp, hiding in the brush and scrawny trees, and the darkness. This was not a prison or fortress—the perimeter lights faced into the camp, illuminating the ground so that people could see where they were going, obscuring the world outside the perimeter. Freeman knelt in the scrub no more than twenty feet from men in a small cart collecting trash. The men driving the cart didn't notice him.

They dragged an empty Dumpster to a collection site, backed it into place, and unhitched it from their cart. Then they drove around the platform to the spot where a full Dumpster sat. They hooked it up to their cart and drove away, all the while gabbing about fishing.

Freeman moved around the outside of the camp until he found an unlit area. Once he entered the camp, he walked straight ahead. He no longer stuck to the shadows. Now that he had entered, his only camouflage was to pretend like he belonged.

With seventeen million refugees, the New Olympians had many camps beside many cities throughout the Territories. Freeman estimated the population of this camp to be between fifty and one hundred thousand people. He saw whole avenues of prefabricated housing that served as dorms for families and neighborhoods.

These people had just spent a year on Mars, living in a spaceport. They'd showered in communal showers. Those among them who needed sex more than privacy had learned to fill that need in crowded halls. For these people, privacy was a distant memory.

As he walked down a lane that ran between two three-story dormitories, Freeman heard couples chatting. He heard snoring. The sound of babies crying was loud, the occasional argument even louder.

The people Freeman wanted wouldn't linger around the dormitories at night. Like him, they would dislike the noise and clutter and bustle of families. They would find twilight zones in which they could quietly gather and whisper among themselves. He wasn't looking for citizens; he was looking for lurkers, the rats and roaches of society who flourished under the floorboards and lived a cancerous coexistence.

Freeman walked past a streetlamp under which two young lovers kissed. The boy spotted him, turned to get a better look at him, and stared.

"What is it?" asked the girl. She followed his gaze toward Freeman. Not saying a word, they stood and walked away, breaking into a jog as they got farther from him.

Freeman saw their fear as a confirmation. They had meandered into an unfamiliar neighborhood. They had chanced a murky, poorly lit lane, then, seeing someone strange and menacing, they had run to a safer place to hide.

There were plenty of streetlamps in this part of the camp, but some stood unlit. Fires burned in metal drums by an open shelter in which men sat on chairs.

The fires weren't for heat. It was nearly eighty degrees. A combined chorus of crickets and cicadas creaked.

Freeman felt more than heard the men following him. One might have bumped into a trash can. One might have scuffed his shoe. He might have heard them whispering. It didn't matter. Freeman didn't need audio cues to sense them. He didn't turn to look at them and did nothing to alert them as he walked to the shelter.

They closed in on him, standing no more than ten feet away.

The men chattering under the shelter went quiet. They turned to look at Freeman as he approached. He quietly returned their gaze.

"What do you want?" someone asked.

Freeman answered, "Information."

Someone asked, "Why the speck would we talk to you?"

Freeman got the sense that they knew who he was or at least why he had come. He'd spent time on Mars living among New Olympian refugees. He'd traveled in their underground circles. These people would have seen him as an ally back then, back when their only ambition was to relocate to Earth.

The men who had been tailing him made their move. Relying on his senses, Freeman knew their speeds and their positions. His instincts were accurate, his reflexes instantaneous. Just by the sound of their steps, he knew the one to his right would strike first, then the one to his left.

Timing his reactions to the last millisecond, he stared straight ahead as if unaware of the danger. He spun right, threw a short punch that hit the first man flush on the jaw, shattering it at the point of his chin and breaking it at the hinge. He turned to the left, caught the man's wrist and lifted it out of the way, then dug a hard right into the man's exposed ribs.

Freeman did not bother taking the man's knife. He knew precisely how much damage he'd dealt.

The second man was big, only a few inches shorter than Freeman. He grunted softly when the fist dug into his side, took a wobbling, shuffling step backward, and teetered in place. His knife slipped from his fingers. A moment later, he dropped to his knees. He knelt, silently struggling to breathe as the bubbles of blood escaped from his lips.

Freeman sensed that guns were now pointed at him, but he didn't know how many.

Somebody said, "That wasn't very nice."

Freeman said, "I'm looking for information."

A large man stood. He was six-foot-three, maybe taller, with beefy shoulders and a wide, solid girth. He stood silently and stared back at Freeman, an unconcerned expression on his face when his eyes locked with Freeman's. He had the solid chin of a fighter, short brown hair, and small dark eyes. Finally, he said, "You don't give the orders around here."

Freeman said, "I want to know about three dead clones and a missing Marine."

Somebody said, "Three dead clones and a missing Marine? Sounds like they canceled each other out."

Most of the men under the awning cackled, but not the big man. He continued staring at Freeman. The calm and quiet of his voice cut through the laughing. He said, "Jimmy, make yourself useful, take Frankie to the hospital."

Frankie now lay on his side, unconscious, blood streaming from his mouth. He'd need a very good doctor. Freeman's punch had shattered two ribs and ruptured his kidneys. The one with the broken jaw was ambulatory. Frankie would die.

Four men scraped Frankie off the ground, using his legs and arms like handles. Two more grabbed the other guy.

The man in charge said, "I could kill you right now if I wanted. You're a tough guy, but that doesn't make you bulletproof. Next time you come to my camp looking for trouble, you better be bulletproof . . . Mr. Freeman."

Then, pretending he could read Freeman's thoughts, he added, "Yeah, I know who you are."

Freeman said nothing.

The man asked, "What do you want to know?"

"I want to know what happened to Harris."

"You want to know what happened to Harris," the man repeated. "You want to know what happened. So do the police. So do a lot of people. That doesn't make you special. If you got business with us, say what you got, then get running."

"What happened to Harris?" Freeman repeated.

One of the thugs, not the man in charge, shouted, "How the speck should we know?" Another said, "Why don't you take it up with Story? I hear you're tight with the cops." A few of the men under the shelter laughed. Most remained silent.

The man in charge said, "No one here had anything to do with it."

"That wasn't what I asked," said Freeman.

The man said, "You're not winning friends here."

Freeman didn't answer. He wasn't looking for friends.

CHAPTER THIRTEEN

Location: Washington, D.C.
Date: July 18, 2519

"Why did he have to take our air-conditioning with him . . . in July? I'm as open to suicide bombers as the next guy," Cardston told Watson as he escorted him through the security station, "but why couldn't he have waited for November to off the air?"

Watson had been in the Pentagon on the day of the bombing. He'd been evacuated from the building with everybody else. Having left later that day for the New Olympian Territories, he hadn't been briefed about the aftermath of the provocateur's attack. He knew that the provocateur took dead MPs with him, but he didn't know that the grenade had destroyed the air-conditioning system.

He said, "If all the bomb did was blow up the air-condition—"

"Grenade," said Cardston. "He left a bomb on the third floor, then killed himself on a service floor with a grenade.

"I suppose we did get lucky. Now we know how to screen for burners."

"Burners?" asked Watson.

"Burn-a-bombs."

Watson had read the first few pages of the official report during his flight into Washington, D.C. He hadn't been drunk, at least he wouldn't have labeled himself "drunk." He'd certainly guzzled off any rough edge. None of the information he'd read had stayed with him.

He'd also been distracted. With Cutter dead and Harris missing, Watson wondered what would become of the Enlisted Man's Empire, a military regime run by clones who had been designed to take orders, not give them. Some of the clones made excellent commanders, but in his experiences, most of them failed miserably in command.

Watson said, "This Herman . . ."

"Leonard Herman," Cardston said.

"He came in through the main entrance?"

"Cleared the same security station you just passed."

They stood a few yards away, watching the station. A long queue of people, some military, some civilian, passed through the posts.

"The report said something about his having a weapon on him when he passed through the posts," said Watson.

"A ring with a poison-laden spike hidden under a gem . . . small but effective in the right situation. He only needed to kill one person to accomplish his objectives—to kill the guy he came to visit. Didn't even need the ring, not really, he could have strangled Day with a general-issue belt or stabbed him with a pen. Have you seen images of Herman?"

"Just what you included in the report. Not the most intimidating man I've seen," said Watson.

A steady line of people filed through the security station. They submitted their bags to be searched and scanned, then they walked between the posts, for metal detection and spectral detection.

"Do you know if Herman was his real name?" asked Watson. "Even his name sounds harmless."

"So far, his entire story checks out. Leonard Herman, resident of Chevy Chase, Maryland, owner of Rolenta Cleaning Supplies. We've been to his house and his factory. I've got teams investigating every angle.

"Would you like to see the security feed?" asked Cardston.

His eyes still on the line as it filtered through the posts, Watson said, "I better pass. Do I have time to speak with Tasman before the meeting?"

Cardston looked at the wall clock—07:21. He tapped his earpiece, and asked, "Has Tasman checked in?"

"Yes, sir. Came in early today. Security checked him in at 05:00."

Cardston told Watson, "He's in his lab. Keep it short."

Watson had not returned to Washington to meet with Howard Tasman—the Unified Authority scientist who had developed the neural programming used in the cloning program. Watson's official reason for returning was to hold a leadership summit—something akin to attending the conclave of cardinals who select the next pope.

In this case, only one cardinal qualified, and in everybody else's mind, he wasn't fit for command—Major General Pernell M. MacAvoy. With Cutter dead and Harris missing, MacAvoy was the highest-ranking officer in the Enlisted Man's military. Along with MacAvoy, the people attending the meeting would be Rear Admiral Thomas Hauser—captain of the EMN *Churchill* and the late Don Cutter's second-in-command—and Hunter Ritz, only a colonel in the Enlisted Man's Marines but Harris's most trusted officer.

Watson understood why Hauser, Ritz, and MacAvoy needed to meet. He had no idea why he'd been summoned to attend. He said, "I want a word with Tasman before the summit. We'd better get to the lab."

As they walked toward the elevator, Watson said, "It's not that bad in here. Maybe we can get by with the air-conditioning out."

Cardston laughed. "It's only 07:00. Stick around a while."

They joined the crowd beside the elevator door. The elevator opened. A couple of Army officers stepped out. Cardston and Watson waited their turn, then stepped onto the elevator. Once on, they stood in silence. Cardston watched the floor numbers flash above the door.

Pressed against the side of the elevator, towering over all the other passengers, both clone and natural-born alike, Watson watched the people around him. He had long ago noted the way clones fastidiously watched the floors flash by and wondered if it was part of their programming.

Cardston led them off the elevator on the third floor. He

pointed down an empty hall. "We found the burner in a closet down that hall."

"Were they after the lab?" asked Watson.

"I thought about that," said Cardston. "Could be, but if that's the case, we have a bigger problem than terrorists with burners. The lab's supposed to be a secret. I'd hate to think that the Unifieds know what floor our high-level security lab is on." He sighed, and added, "We have a leak. That much is certain.

"You know why we stuck Tasman on this floor, Watson? We stuck him here because nobody in his right mind sticks an operation like this on a middle floor. Your secrets become more secure when nobody knows about them, right? You come off the elevator on this floor, what do you see? You don't see guards and checkpoints, you see an open hall. We got plenty of security protecting the lab, but it's discreet. You put up a set of posts and a big security station, and you tell your enemies that this is the spot to hit."

Antiseptic, Watson thought. *Fluorescent lights, white floors, empty halls, we might as well be in a damn hospital.* As he thought this, he remembered the weeks Harris had been in the hospital after all the trouble on Mars.

Mars. Specking Mars, he thought. Watson had arrived on Mars just as the trouble began. He'd started working for Don Cutter when Harris and his entire regiment had been abducted on Mars; they'd simply vanished. When they resurfaced a week later, they acted as if nothing had happened. Believing Harris had been reprogrammed, Cutter relieved him of command. A short time later, everything started going to hell. Cutter, who sent Watson, a civilian advisor and untested in battle, to the Mars Spaceport. Watson arrived, and two days later . . . *two specking days later,* a U.A. thug nearly beat him to death. On the third day, he hiked ten miles across the Martian desert with a broken jaw, busted ribs, and not nearly enough pain medication. Freeman had been there. Watson would never have made it to safety without Freeman; no one would have.

Freeman had forced him to shoot an unarmed man that day. Whenever Watson thought about Mars—he avoided thinking about the red planet as much as possible—he always concluded that he had left most of his soul on the plains between the spaceport and the Air Force base.

Watson had returned with a poorly set jaw, a broken nose, four broken ribs, and a body so bruised that his doctor put him in a body cast. He'd looked better than Harris, though. The man who attacked Watson had gunned down Harris from behind, shooting him at nearly point-blank range with a shotgun. After pulling shot from his lungs, liver, and muscles, his doctors had had to restore his tissue and skin.

Tasman was on Mars, Watson thought. Since returning to Earth, Watson had purposely avoided the old man's lab. It wasn't the lab or the unpleasant old man that kept him away. He didn't want to deal with memories of Mars.

Cardston led him through the maze of nondescript doors and halls. Entering a suite of offices that looked like any other from the outside, they came to a bulletproof barricade behind which sat four Marines in combat armor. The glass that screened them was nearly two inches thick. Since taking up with Cutter, Watson had entered dozens of checkpoints with quarter-inch armored windows. This barricade wasn't just bulletproof; it was meant to stop bombs.

Even though he was with Major Cardston, the head of Pentagon Security, the guards asked Watson for his ID. Both Cardston and Watson passed through posts to be DNA-typed and scanned.

Watson commented, "You run a tight ship," meaning to congratulate Cardston on the way his security team protected Tasman's laboratory.

Cardston said, "This security station? This is just the part you see; sometime I'll show you what's behind the curtain.

"You know how we located that burner? It was hidden in a scan-proof case in the large closet in the Pentagon and we spotted it ten seconds after catalyzation began. I had six independent sensor arrays in that closet, and every one of them detected that bomb the moment Herman lit it up. He never even armed the damned bomb. My bomb removal team entered the closet forty-two seconds after catalyzation began."

As they waited for a very thick mechanical door to slide open, Watson asked, "Would the explosion have reached the lab?"

"Probably not. Then again, it wouldn't need to," said Cardston. "Demolish enough of the building and everything else comes down, right? If the first floor and the second floor collapse, the third floor comes down."

"Was the bomb big enough to do that?" asked Watson.

"No," said Cardston. "Not even close."

Once you got past the security station, entering the lab was like stepping into a bank vault. The door that cleared out before them was six inches thick with steel and chrome.

Six men in combat armor sat in a bulletproof booth on the other side of the door.

"More Marines?" asked Watson.

"Not Marines," said the old man in the wheelchair sitting beside them. It was Howard Tasman. Watson recognized the cantankerous old bastard's voice even before he saw him. As his motorized chair wheeled forward, he said, "However much time I have left, I wouldn't want to shorten it by entrusting it to clones."

Tasman was ninety-one years old, but he looked older. He had a full head of fine white hair, so fine that his scalp showed through it. His skin was white as paper, the blue veins running beneath it as visible as the streets on a city map. His eyes were clear and white though the rims had turned red. His head, neck, and arms were skeletal, bones held together by skin so thin that Watson suspected a strong wind might blow him apart.

He said, "How are you doing, Watson? It's been a long time. I would have thought you'd visit an old comrade in arms more often."

Watson didn't like to look at Tasman. He didn't like being reminded that men become decrepit before they die; seeing Tasman reminded him how cruel the years become. Watson didn't like Tasman's wrinkled, desiccated looks, and he didn't like the old man's odor, either. He smelled old and antiseptic, like the spleen of an ancient Egyptian pharaoh who has been washed, mummified, and stored for six thousand years in primitive formaldehyde. Watson thought, *"Comrade in arms" my ass, you old bastard.* He said, "These last few months have been spinning out of control."

Tasman turned to Cardston, and said, "Watson and I have some catching up to do, Major. Would you mind if we chatted alone?"

Not wanting to be alone with the living fossil, Watson hoped Cardston would hold his ground. He didn't know what he could tell Tasman.

Cardston said, "Keep it short, he has an important meeting coming up." He made a show of checking his wristwatch and left.

Tasman said, "Let's go to my office," and started rolling away at top speed, forcing Watson to trot. The scientist steered his chair to a door at the far end of a hundred-foot-long hallway. Like every door in the lab—*possibly even the toilet,* Watson suspected—the door to Tasman's office required DNA identification. Tasman touched a finger to it, and it opened.

The old scientist entered the office. Watson followed. When the door closed behind them, the scientist said, "If they exploded a thermonuclear bomb out there, it couldn't break these walls. We'd be killed, of course, but not by the explosion.

"Do you know what that means, Watson? It means that the people protecting me place more import on my work than my life. God help you, Watson, I hope you never live to see every world and person in your life turn to dust. My work, my home, my family. The only reason people bother with me is because of the things I got wrong."

The old man's complaining bored Watson. He said, "You've made more than your share of monumental mistakes."

Tasman glared at him. At first, anger and hate blazed in his clear green eyes. He laughed, an ugly sight that revealed teeth as gray as storm clouds. He said, "'Monumental'? Is that what my mistakes have been, 'monumental'? Why not 'cataclysmic'? You want to remember that, Travis. You're an important man, and important men make monumental mistakes."

"I couldn't make mistakes on your level if I tried," said Watson. "Your mistakes brought down the Unified Authority. They may bring down the Enlisted Man's Empire as well."

CHAPTER FOURTEEN

For the last seventy years, Howard Tasman had been the galaxy's leading authority on neural programming. When the Linear Committee, the executive branch of the U.A. government, began developing the Liberator cloning project, a very young Howard Tasman participated on the project.

He'd become a hero on his home world after the Liberators had made the galaxy safe. For a planet that had never produced an important politician, or a noted actor, or historic athlete, having a famous scientist had to do. Then things went wrong with the Liberators. They killed civilians and prisoners alike on a penal colony named Alcatraz Island. They massacred civilians on a planet named New Prague. In a chilling irony that ruined Tasman's life forever, the Liberators murdered most of the civilian population on his home planet of Volga as well.

Tasman told Watson, "The Enlisted Man's Empire never had a chance of survival. Clones are impotent. They can't reproduce without labs, and the Mogats destroyed the labs back in 2512." He smiled, a gracious, self-satisfied grin, "The clone empire didn't need my help to go bust."

Repulsed that Tasman's skin was whiter than his teeth, Watson averted his gaze from the old man's face.

"A one-generation empire isn't an empire at all," said Tasman. "It's a placeholder."

Watson looked up, and said, "Maybe, but you've brought down two empires. Your clones brought down the Unified Authority."

Tasman's smile vanished. He said, "They shouldn't have been able to do that. They shouldn't have been able to unite. Their programming . . ."

"The programming you created."

"Maybe their neural programming wasn't perfect," said Tasman, no longer exhibiting signs of his former humor. "It was the best we could do under the circumstances. I couldn't have anticipated the Unified Authority's dismantling of its own military. No one could have foreseen that. The military deciding to junk its own clones wasn't one of the contingencies the generals asked me to consider."

Watson wondered just how much information he should give up. Living on a military base and never going out in public, Tasman didn't pose much of a security threat. He didn't socialize with anyone outside the Pentagon, had no living relatives, and received no visitors.

He's a bitter old fool, Watson reminded himself. But who wouldn't be bitter. His attitude softening, he thought, *So late in life to be so alone*, and took pity on the old man. Tasman was unpleasant, but he was reaching the end of his existence. Even on Mars, when it looked like they would die, he'd irritated anyone who'd come near him.

Speaking softly, slowly, just loud enough to be sure that Tasman heard him clearly, Watson said, "Don Cutter is dead."

"Dead?" asked Tasman, leaning forward in his bulky wheelchair.

"Assassinated."

Tasman fell back on his chair, let his arms drop to his sides, sat slack and silent. It occurred to Watson that the old man might have suffered heart failure upon hearing the news. Several seconds passed, then Tasman said, "I knew about the prison in Oregon and I heard about Harris, but nobody told me about Cutter."

He mulled the situation over, then sat up and rubbed his chin. He scratched an eyebrow, folded his hands on his lap, then raised them and rubbed his nose before announcing, "That is quite a switch-up. Now the Unified Authority regained its leadership and the clones lost theirs all in the same day."

"All in the same minute," said Watson.

"What's that?" asked Tasman.

"All of the attacks took place at the exact same time."

"But I heard that the attack on the prison was at eight in the morning."

"Eight A.M. West Coast time," said Watson. "That was eleven o'clock here."

"Eleven? You mean, it happened at the same time that they tried to explode the bomb?" asked Tasman. As a citizen of Volga, then Olympus Kri, he wasn't entirely familiar with global time zones.

"The bomb, the prison break, and the attack on Cutter all took place at the exact same moment. They were a few minutes late attacking Harris . . . the best plans of mice and men, right?"

". . . a couple of minutes late with Harris," Tasman said, confirming the information.

"This is all classified information," Watson said, reassuring himself by reminding Tasman of the obvious.

"Then you're in the right place, Travis. This is the most classified operation in the Pentagon."

"There's something I wanted to ask you," Watson said, getting back to business. "I just got back from the Territories late last night. We don't know exactly what happened there, but the men who attacked Harris appear to have been clones."

"Clones?" Tasman repeated.

"Freeman thinks they were reprogrammed clones. Can you identify whether or not they were reprogrammed?"

Tasman didn't answer.

"If I brought the bodies, would you be able to perform an autopsy?"

Tasman shook his head. "What do you want me to look for?"

"I want to know if they were reprogrammed."

"And you think that will turn up in an autopsy?" asked Tasman.

"Reprogramming doesn't leave any physical traces. They inhale chemicals and pass out. The Unifieds run a few more chemicals past them, and their programming changes. It's not a lobotomy, Travis. There are no incisions and no scars. Nothing happens to their frontal lobes."

"I know that," said Watson, though he had only suspected it. "What about traces of the chemicals in their blood or tissue?"

"It's all olfaction, minor traces of chemicals taken in the

right proportions and the right sequence, but it's traces, just traces. Just because you walk by a barbecue and smell meat cooking doesn't mean we'll find a cow in your blood," said Tasman. "The Unifieds aren't injecting them with the chemicals. All it takes is a little whiff of the right chemicals in the right proportions in the right order.

"The trick isn't getting the chemicals in them, it's getting the chemicals to them. Did you ever look at the flask they used when they tried to attack Harris last year? The damned thing had a thousand chambers, aromatic release vents, and internal fans. It was a masterpieces of precision engineering."

Watson took in this information. He'd been sent a report about the flask but hadn't read it; now he wished that he had. He nodded and sighed.

Tasman changed the subject. He asked, "Are you still with Emily?"

Watson said, "We're engaged to be married." He didn't like doling out personal information to Tasman, worried that the old man might start dropping hints about them having him over for dinner.

"Married?" asked Tasman. He snickered, and added, "I wouldn't have thought that either of you was the marrying type."

"You were saying something about the chemicals," Watson prompted.

"Yes, I was. Does Emily wear perfume?"

"I'm not sure what brand," Watson said, starting to feel annoyed.

"Performing an autopsy on a clone to find out if he's been reprogrammed would be like performing an autopsy on you to discover Ms. Hughes's choice of perfume.

"I'd have more luck pumping your stomach on the off chance you'd swallowed the label from one of her perfume bottles."

Watson arrived at the summit.

He knew all of the officers in attendance except Major General MacAvoy. He'd first met Rear Admiral Hauser while working for Harris, then spent considerably more time with him while working for Admiral Cutter. Hauser was the captain of the *Churchill*, the flagship of the fleet.

Watson had only met Lieutenant Colonel Hunter Ritz of the EME Marines on a couple of occasions, one of those occasions being the battle on Mars. He liked Ritz.

Cardston had informed MacAvoy and Ritz about Cutter's death. Hauser already knew; the assassination took place on his ship. None of them knew about Harris.

Watson sat in the conference room silently listening, watching the three senior-most officers in the Enlisted Man's Empire. From the horror stories Harris had told him about officers wrangling for power, he expected the men to start attacking each other. He spotted a few cracks in the façade, but for the most part, they treated each other with respect.

Which one would I place in charge? Watson asked himself.

That was the purpose of the summit. Cutter might or might not have left a will, but he left absolutely no instructions concerning the chain of command.

Pernell MacAvoy, a major general in the Army, was next in line. He was the oldest of the three officers, a clone whose hair had turned mostly white. "It doesn't hardly seem like the Enlisted Man's Empire is a military operation anymore," he lamented. "I'm running out of privates and corporals. You have to give your boys promotions every so often so they know you aren't angry with 'em. The problem is, if I have too many sergeants and not enough grunts, the sergeants have nobody to push around. That's a problem. It's a big problem."

"Maybe you can give them bonuses instead of promotions," Admiral Hauser suggested.

"That may be the right way to run an empire, but it's no way to run an army. What's the good of making sergeants if you don't have grunts for them to bully?" asked MacAvoy. "There's no use putting torpedo tubes on ships that don't carry torpedoes, and there's no point having sergeants if they don't have privates they can push around. They can't shout at themselves, and I pity the sergeant who raises his voice at an officer."

Hauser smiled as he listened. Watson wondered if he had ever seen a more condescending smile.

MacAvoy stood, walked the length of the office as he thought how to respond, then said, "The Enlisted Man's Empire was a military organization. Military organizations are made up of soldiers. Once we captured Earth, we stopped being a military operation and became a wet nurse for civilians and refugees. We're beating our heads against walls trying to babysit the people who sent us into space. It's ridiculous.

"I'm sorry Cutter is gone. He was a fine officer, but he was out of his depth.

"He should have stepped down the moment we went from fighting wars to balancing budgets."

"Stepped down?" Hauser asked, looking and sounding outraged.

Starting to pace again, MacAvoy reaffirmed his position. "Stepped down. He was an admiral, not a senator. The man was out of his depth."

"What about General Harris?" asked Colonel Hunter Ritz. "Do you want him to step down?"

Ritz, the Marine, was twenty years younger than Hauser, who was at least ten years younger than MacAvoy. The older officers were of the spit-and-polish variety, dressed in crisp blouses and well-creased pants. Ritz attended the meeting in fatigues. He leaned back in his chair so he could rest his combat boots on the seat beside him. He had the petulant smile of a perpetual truant.

"Step down?" asked MacAvoy. "I want Harris to step up. The man doesn't want to run anything larger than a platoon. He keeps promoting everyone around him and letting them run the empire into the ground."

"Do you think he's out of his depth?" Ritz asked, his tone daring the old general to say something bad about Harris.

MacAvoy stopped pacing and faced Ritz. He said, "General Harris knows his limitations. That is why he put Cutter in charge. I only wish he'd been as aware of Cutter's limitations."

"Bullshit!" yelled Hauser.

"What's bullshit?" asked MacAvoy.

"Everything you just said is bullshit," said Hauser.

"So you don't think Harris knows his limitations?" asked MacAvoy.

"Okay, yeah, well, I agree; he knows his limitations."

"But you don't think Harris put Cutter in charge?"

"Well, yeah, he did."

"Then we agree," said MacAvoy.

"You said you wished Harris was aware of Cutter's limitations," said Hauser. He rose to his feet as he said this.

"Do you think he knew Cutter's limitations?"

Still on his feet, Hauser said, "Well, maybe not."

"Are you saying Cutter didn't have any limitations?"

Hauser sat back in his chair. "Obviously, he had limitations."

"Do you think Cutter was up to the task of running a civilian empire?"

Hauser didn't answer that question. Instead, he said, "The Navy runs the military. Cutter did a good job running the Navy."

"Who would you choose to run the empire?" asked Watson.

"Bull-specking-shit," MacAvoy grumbled. "Harris has been calling the shots from behind the shadows for years. It's high time he took over."

"Are you saying the Marines should run the show?" asked Ritz.

"The Marines can't run shit. Son, you're talking about a branch that can't even deliver its men to the battle. If there's a branch that should run things, it's the Army," said MacAvoy. "We're the largest branch."

"Oh, speck no!" said Hauser.

"Why the hell not?" asked MacAvoy.

"Your *boys* kill people and break stuff. That's what armies do. That's all armies do," said Hauser.

MacAvoy made a show of scratching his chin, then he brightened as if an idea had just occurred to him. He pointed a finger toward the ceiling, and said, "Hang on, now! I forgot; with Cutter assassinated, you're next in line. I bet you want the Navy to call the shots."

"I'm next in line to run the Navy . . . the Navy . . . the Navy. I manage ships and fleets. I command sailors. I don't give orders to civilians."

"You know your limitations," said MacAvoy.

"Don didn't want it either," said Hauser. "He agreed to run

the military. He agreed to run the empire back when the military was the empire. Once we took Earth, he locked himself on his ship. Now that he's gone, I think General Harris is the only man who can take the reins."

Ritz straightened in his chair, and said, "He gets my vote."

MacAvoy nodded.

Watson said, "Gentlemen, I think you should know that General Harris is missing."

"What do you mean by 'missing'?" Ritz growled, becoming as livid as a junkyard dog.

"Admiral Cutter sent him to the New Olympian Territories two weeks ago. He was attacked in his hotel room yesterday morning. We haven't found a body, but there was blood in his hotel room. The New Olympian Police have identified it as his."

"What are we going to do about that?" asked Ritz. "I need to get men down there. He's a Marine. This is a Marine operation. I could have a Fifth Regiment—

"Is that why we're here? Hauser interrupted. "You're looking for someone to run the show?"

MacAvoy returned to his chair. He sat silently for a moment, then said, "That's above my pay grade."

Watson said, "As I understand it, General, you're next in line."

MacAvoy shook his head. He said, "If Harris wasn't fit for the job, I sure as speck can't do it.

"I execute battle plans. I started as a rifle-toting grunt. I never attended officer training. I may not have mentioned this before, but I grew up in an orphanage."

Everyone in the room knew that MacAvoy had grown up in an orphanage. They could see that he was a clone even if he couldn't.

Watson said, "General MacAvoy, are you saying that you are unwilling to take command?"

"That depends on what you want me to command," said MacAvoy.

"Admiral Hauser?" asked Watson.

"I'm next in line to run the Navy. I can do that."

"How about the empire?" asked MacAvoy. "Are you ready to run the entire show?"

Hauser looked at Watson, and said, "I'm not sure I'm ready to run the fleet."

Watson nodded, jotted a note, and asked Colonel Ritz, "Are you prepared to run the Marines?"

Ritz said something inaudible; it might have been, "Yes, sir" or possibly, "Yeah. Sure." He met Watson's eyes, and said, "I suppose I am."

"And the empire?" asked Watson.

Ritz chuckled, and said, "Sure. I'll run this motherspecker."

Admiral Hauser gave Ritz a quick, desperate glance, then said, "Mr. Watson, I think the Enlisted Man's Empire might be more prosperous with civilian leadership at this juncture. You'd make a great interim president."

MacAvoy sneered at Ritz, and said, "That's exactly what every militaristic clone empire needs, a natural-born civilian as commander in chief."

"A civilian leading the Enlisted Man's Empire, what an interesting turn," said Hauser.

Ritz finally spoke up. Staring at Watson, their eyes locked, he said, "If you're looking for a natural-born president, I know who Harris would have elected."

CHAPTER FIFTEEN

Location: Mazatlán, New Olympian Territories
Date: July 18, 2519

Ray Freeman slept on a bed in one of the gangster-held dormitories; not that he trusted the gangsters. He slept with one of their M27s beside him; another lay on the floor beneath his cot. Freeman had a notion about when and how the guns had come into Pugh's possession. If he was right, they had a third M27 stashed somewhere near Pugh.

The dormitory was two stories tall, made with polymer walls that blocked the heat and the sunlight. The furnishings were sparse—folding cots for beds and cardboard boxes for dressers.

Freeman had slept soundly, but he'd organized his thoughts as he dreamed. He'd thought about Harris's apartment, the placement of the corpses, and the perfume on his shirt.

He woke to the sound of footsteps. The apartments inside the dormitory were ten-by-ten cubes, divided by clapboard partitions that were no more soundproof than rice-paper walls. The door didn't lock.

He had no illusions about the door or walls protecting him. If someone started firing Pugh's third M27 in his direction, those walls would do nothing to slow the bullets.

Freeman didn't waste time thinking about the person who walked past the door. Many people had come and gone during the night. He'd woken up and tracked their footfalls. As a mercenary, he'd spent weeks in enemy territory. For him, being at rest didn't include being unguarded.

Two men chatted in whispers as they approached Freeman's door. They didn't slow or try to quiet their steps. He remained on the cot, his eyes shut, his finger along the trigger guard of his gun.

One of the men knocked.

Freeman didn't answer. He lay on his back, his eyes still closed, his other senses alert.

"Freeman."

Recognizing the voice, he answered, "Yes."

"You want to know where those clones came from?"

Already dressed, Freeman sat up and stepped to the door. He opened it. The man on the other side was Brandon Pugh, the man whom Freeman had identified as the "thug in charge."

"You done with our guns yet?" Pugh asked as he walked through the door. The man was built like a retired football lineman, with a gut that was starting to go soft and massive shoulders that hadn't. He had one man with him and another down the hall. So much for the mystery about the third M27; the one down the hall was holding it.

Freeman handed Pugh the M27 he held in his hand.

"We loaned you two," said Pugh.

Freeman said, "I'm not done with the other one."

"Yeah? Well get done with it real soon, would you? I don't see why you need a gun. With my boys watching out for you, no one is going to touch you, not even Story."

"I'm not worried about the police," said Freeman.

Pugh gave him the crooked smile he normally reserved for bad bluffers in poker. He said, "You don't seem like the nervous type."

Freeman read the smile and didn't care. He said, "You said you knew where the clones came from."

"Yeah. They came from the beach. You want to go have a look?"

Freeman asked, "They came by boat?" He hadn't put much stock in that possibility.

The New Olympian government didn't have radar stations or satellites, but the Enlisted Man's Empire most certainly did. In this day of air freighters, water travel had mostly sailed into the sunset. Civilians kept small boats for fishing and other hobbies. A small boat like that could approach shore unnoticed, maybe even roll right up to shore undetected. It could carry five men. A pilot and three assassins: that would leave room for a wounded victim.

"And do you know where they landed?" asked Freeman.

"Yeah, I know where."

"Did your men see them come in?" Freeman asked. Knowing how many men the Unifieds sent would answer questions. Three clones meant an assassination, five or six meant an abduction. If they had five or six, they could have injured Harris and hauled him away.

"No. They slipped right by us," said Pugh. He rubbed his nostril with the side of his fist. "I don't have enough men to watch the water all night. My boys found out about them after the fact, if you see what I mean."

Pugh and his men didn't use cars. They had access to one, but driving attracted attention, something Pugh and his organization preferred to avoid. Under the cover of night, they walked from the camp to the beach.

The streets were dark, the night warm and dry. In the distance, waves rolled onto the beach, the crush of the water slapping the sand rang in the air.

As they walked past darkened buildings, Freeman asked, "Harris came here a week earlier. What was he doing here?"

"The speck would I know?" Pugh asked, his irritation showing.

"Because you were following him," said Freeman.

"Why would I do that? Harris didn't mean anything to me."

Freeman said nothing. They walked in silence for three blocks, Freeman at the front of the group, Pugh beside him, followed by five other men.

Pugh said, "Okay, maybe I want to know what's what in my territory."

Freeman remained silent. They crossed another block.

"I don't know why he came."

Freeman asked, "Who was the girl?"

"The speck would I know?" They continued walking. No one spoke until Pugh said, "None of your damn business, Freeman. That's who."

"Is she part of your organization?" asked Freeman.

Pugh didn't answer. He stopped to glare at Freeman, said nothing, then started walking again.

Freeman didn't ask the question a second time, didn't even consider asking again. He had the patience of a sniper.

"What are you saying? You think we went after Harris? You think I sent three clones into his hotel room? You think, maybe, I have my own army of loyal clones?

"Look, man, back on Olympus Kri I dealt in guns, girls, and gambling. You want to lude, I can arrange it, anything you want to lick, sniff, or shoot. The Unies didn't like me. The clones didn't know about me. I always did what I could to keep it that way. Enemies aren't so dangerous when they don't know you exist."

Pugh called citizens of the Unified Authority "Unies."

"How does the girl fit into this?" asked Freeman.

"The speck business is that of yours?" asked Pugh. That was all he said on the subject.

Mazatlán had a curfew and policemen patrolling the streets to enforce it.

The police rode on motorcycles and carts that moved slowly and silently along dark avenues. Searchlights shone from the carts, rolling across buildings, sidewalks, and muted streetlamps. The motorcycles were electric; the only sound they made came from their tires.

A police cart turned onto their street. Freeman heard the screech of its tires. Pugh and his men didn't, but they spotted the light long before the cops on the cart could have spotted them. The policemen shined their searchlight, filling the lane with a hard white glare. Shadows turned to crystal. Light bleached the color of the plants and stone and roofs so that everything appeared in shades of gray.

Freeman and the gangsters stepped behind a building and waited as the cop drove by.

Pugh and his men simply hid. Freeman analyzed. The cart had no armor except a low windshield. The cops wore helmets but no body armor. They could be neutralized, decapitated, by a neck-high wire stretched across the street.

The cart moved smoothly at a fifteen-mile-per-hour clip. Freeman asked himself if he could allow the cart to pass, then sprint fast enough to catch it from behind. He had his doubts. Maybe several years ago, when he been in his prime; now he relied on both strength and intelligence.

That was how Freeman evaluated every situation. Walking into a room filled with men, he determined whom he would kill first if it came to a fight, where he could duck for cover if his enemies had a gun, how he would escape if he found himself in trouble, and what advantage he might find by starting the violence himself.

In his mind, the difference between killing and preserving life was situational ethics; self-preservation came as automatically as breathing. Pugh was his ally for now, but Freeman didn't trust the man and suspected that the alliance would end in a death.

They crossed sand and walked beside a stone-and-cement pier that ran out past the waves. The pier was wide, and strong enough to support trucks or tanks.

"This is where they landed," said one of Pugh's men.

They walked along the side of the pier, ducking low so that no one would spot them in the moonlight. The soft roar of sea waves remained constant in the air.

Both Freeman, Pugh, and a third man carried M27s. In Freeman's and Pugh's hands, the guns looked like oversized pistols. In the other gangster's hand, it looked like the high-bred automatic weapon it was designed to be.

Pugh said, "They didn't come by boat. They swam in, SCUBA style."

"Have you gone through the gear?" asked Freeman.

"Sure we did," said Pugh.

The gear had been stacked into a pile. Before you could see it, you had to climb under the pier, wade through waves and knee-high water, and pick among the rocks. Here, the clones would have been hidden from view and hard to overhear. The sound of the waves slapping the rocks was loud.

Freeman examined the SCUBA gear. It was of a recent Unified Authority make, probably manufactured within the last two years. It was the kind of gear used for deep-sea operations; breathing harnesses that included saturation gear—bulky rebreathers that dispensed a calculated combination of gases instead of simple oxygen. They'd come in special armor that fitted around their heads and torsos and compensated for pressure . . . deep-water gear.

Three dead clones, three sets of deep-sea diving gear, thought Freeman. A trained diver could go down hundreds of feet in this gear, maybe even a thousand. The rebreathers included inboard screw systems that worked like underwater jetpacks. With rebreathers providing an unlimited air supply, the right mixture for breathing in deep water, and the propulsion systems doing the swimming, the clones could have come in from fifty miles out.

Freeman lifted a rebreather with one hand, spun it so he could look at the back, and opened the airtight compartment. It had enough room to hold a pair of M27s and spare ammunition as well.

He examined one of the masks. They had night-for-day lenses. With night-for-day lenses, the clones would be able to swim at night without using torches . . . without drawing attention to themselves. The lenses also allowed them to swim in deep water, where sunlight didn't show.

Three masks. Three rebreathers. Three sets of fins. Had there been a fourth? A fifth?

Freeman asked, "How much do you know about SCUBA gear?"

"None of us are deep-sea divers, if that's what you want to know," said Pugh. "You don't look like a SCUBA diver yourself."

Freeman said, "Your men didn't spot them because they came from a long way out." He held up a rebreather. The unit weighed nearly fifty pounds, but Freeman handled it as if it were a ten-pound toy. He showed them the venting along the sides.

"It's like having a submarine strapped to your back. The propulsion system pulls in water here," he said, pointing to the holes along the top. "The water comes out here.

"A trained diver can cover fifty miles per day with one of these."

"Sounds good," Pugh said, sounding unimpressed.

Freeman dropped the rebreather back onto the sand. It landed with a soft thud. He held up one of the face masks, and said, "This mask has all the same gear they put in Marine combat helmets. The clones who came here were able to see in the dark. They probably knew exactly where your men were sitting, and they might have been listening in on their communications."

"They got all of that in those little masks?" asked Pugh.

Freeman said, "You have no idea what you are up against."

CHAPTER SIXTEEN

"Do you think Harris knew these guys were coming for him?" Pugh asked, as they slipped back toward the camp.

Freeman thought about that question but did not answer immediately. Harris had been captured by the Unifieds once before. Now that the chemical was in play, every clone lived under the constant threat of capture or reprogramming. In the old days, the Unified Authority killed clones, and that was the end of it. Now, they *converted* prisoners, reprogramming them and sending them back as saboteurs.

Whatever they had done to Harris on Mars remained a mystery. Freeman doubted that Harris had any idea.

They returned to the camp, having spent three hours walking to the beach and back. Freeman said, "He didn't know when he got here. He might have suspected something near the end."

As they entered the suite of rooms Pugh had arranged for himself by removing clapboard partitions, Pugh asked, "What makes you so sure?"

Freeman said, "If Harris knew he was walking into a trap, he would have come armed."

The conversation slowed after that. Freeman said, "Three clones attacked him in his hotel room. He killed the first two, and the third one shot him."

"How do you know he was shot?" asked Pugh. "I heard there weren't any bullets."

Freeman seemed to ignore the question. He said, "Judging by the amount of blood he lost, he probably took the shot in the gut, maybe the chest."

"You lose a lot of blood taking one in the gut," Pugh agreed.

Freeman seemed to have entered his own isolated world. He seemed not to hear anything Pugh said. "If Harris was right on top of that third clone when he pulled his gun, he would have killed him quickly . . . and then he would need help.

"That's where the girl fits in."

"What girl?" asked Pugh.

"The one you're hiding."

"I told you, Freeman, there isn't any girl," said Pugh.

"Once the clones were down, Harris would have asked her for help."

"You aren't listening to me," said Pugh.

"She would have been the one who took his clothing. If she placed a towel over the wound, that would have stopped the blood." Silently, Freeman asked himself how she could have slipped Harris out of the hotel. Even a Liberator in the throes of a full combat reflex would have been too weak to walk out of the hotel with an M27 slug in his gut.

"I said there wasn't any girl," Pugh repeated.

Three clones, thought Freeman. *Three combat veterans. They break into his room, and they see the girl. Why not kill her?* He could only think of one reason for allowing the girl to live. He said, "Either the girl was working for the Unifieds, or . . ."

Pugh brought up his M27.

Freeman asked, "When was the last time you put in new rounds?"

"You specked with my bullets?" asked Pugh. "Bastard . . ." And then Freeman hit him. Pugh was already unconscious when Freeman pulled him up by his shirt and hit him a second time . . . to be sure.

CHAPTER SEVENTEEN

Location: Washington, D.C.

"Sunny."

"Oh. Hello, Travis. What are you doing here?"

"I came to see how you're doing. May I come in?"

He used the telephone by the security desk. There was no screen, just audio.

She did not answer, but she must have approved; the guards waved him through. He tried to thank her, but she had already disconnected.

The girl has money, he thought as he strolled through the lobby. The building was twenty stories taller than any of the buildings around it. It looked more like a hotel than a condominium. Other buildings had security doors; this one had a couple of armed guards sitting behind a long wood-and-brass balustrade. A chandelier with thousands of crystal tears hung from the ceiling.

This wasn't a young person's apartment complex. The tenants Watson passed on his way to the elevators looked to be in their late fifties. The lobby was silent and lifeless, like a wood-paneled, thick-carpeted museum . . . like a high-end old-folks home.

Watson took it all in with revulsion. Elegance mattered little to him; he preferred energy and chic.

He entered the elevator and selected the thirty-eighth floor, Sunny's floor. He'd been to her apartment a couple of times, Emily always in tow. Usually, they stopped by her place for double dates, Watson and Emily, Harris and Sunny. He felt exposed entering the building alone.

Like everything else in the building, the elevator was top-of-the-line, shiny, and substantial. The moment the doors closed, the elevator began a nimble ascent, moving from floor to floor. The highly conditioned air felt cooler than the air in other buildings. The silence in the elevator somehow seemed more profound.

Watson wished he hadn't come. By the time he admitted this to himself, however, the doors had already slid open. He looked at his watch, tried to think of excuses, then started down the hallway, a hallway that looked like it belonged in a luxury hotel.

Sunny's place, Number 3854, was halfway down the hall.

The carpeting was so thick that walking on it felt like walking on sand. That thought reminded Watson of Mazatlán, and Freeman, and Harris. Watson hissed, and said, "Bastard. You always have to stick yourself on the front line."

He knocked on the door, and told himself, *Travis, this day has already gone to the shits. Why the speck did you have to come here?*

Sunny opened the door and stood in the doorway.

She was beautiful, hair as brown and lustrous as mink, eyes that were blue and liquid. But the eyes were red from crying, and the hair had been left unbrushed and pulled back in a band, and her face was puffy from lack of sleep.

She wore no makeup. Watson, who'd lived a life of one-night stands, had seen women in various stages of what he once considered "unpresentability." Few did unpresentability as presentably as Sunny. Dressed in a long terry-cloth bath-robe, with her hair in a mess and her face undone, she looked good.

Not hiding her lack of enthusiasm about his dropping in, she said, "Hi, Travis. Do you want to come in?"

She reminded him of a mural on a crumbling wall—beautiful and disintegrating right before his eyes.

He asked, "Would that be okay?"

She stepped out of his way. "You want some coffee? I could brew some."

"No. I'm fine," he said, as she shut the door behind him. The apartment had the heavy atmosphere of a funeral home. Watson could feel the sense of grieving in the air.

Sunny's apartment faced west, giving her a panoramic view of George Washington University, the Potomac, and the afternoon sun. She generally kept the curtains open, bathing her apartment in daylight. On this day, she had the curtains drawn and most of the lights turned out.

What is it about people in mourning? Watson wondered. *What do they have against the sun?*

Three minibottles of whiskey or rum sat on the coffee table in the living room. There was an empty wine bottle on a nearby end table. Watson spotted more bottles and wine-glasses in the dining room.

Harris and Sunny had never been particularly affectionate, not that Watson could recall. He'd never seen them holding hands or kissing. Watson couldn't imagine Harris kissing a girl out of simple affection.

Sunny surprised Watson. He'd expected her to ask him for an update, but she didn't. He decided to answer the unasked question just the same. He started by repeating what he had told her before, that Harris's status was classified, then he said, "We still haven't heard anything."

"Did you expect to?" she asked, suddenly sounding cross. "What did you think, that you'd find him sunning on the beach?"

He let the moment pass, then said in a soft voice, "It looks like he's missing, not dead."

She stared at him, her liquid blue eyes boring into his. "He said this would happen. Right from the start he said he had enemies. He was such an idiot.

"No. No, I was the idiot! Everybody warned me about him. You did. Do you remember? You told me he always has to be in the middle of all the action, that's what you said. You said something about how he always puts himself on point."

Tears welled up in the corners of her eyes, but they didn't fall. She said, "I've never approved of wars and armies, never. So who do I end up dating, a clone . . . not just a clone, a Liberator, and a general in the Marines. He wasn't even in our Marines. He was in the Marines that conquered Earth!

"There was just something . . ." She sighed and stared down at her lap. When she looked up again, she seemed resigned. She asked, "Does Admiral Cutter know about it? What does he have to say? Has he sent people down to investigate?"

Watson said, "The local police are investigating. The Pentagon is sending men down as well. Look, Sunny, I've known Wayson for a couple of years now. The man is practically indestructible. If . . ."

Sunny cut him off, shouting, "Really? I've only known him for a couple of months, and this is the second time he's been given up for dead. The last time, some bastard shot him in the back with a shotgun."

"Yeah," was the only thing Watson could think to say. She had exaggerated. No one had given Harris up for dead when he was shot on Mars. Harris had been healed and walking by the time he started dating Sunny.

"Was he on point when he got shot?"

"I don't know. I wasn't there," Watson answered, very aware that he no longer had control of the conversation. He said, "Look, Sunny, if he's alive, we'll find him. I don't know what else I can tell you." He had a headache; his heart raced; he wanted to get away from Sunny.

Sunny was a Harvard-trained lawyer. Watson was a lawyer, too, but he'd gone to a less expensive, less prestigious school. He thought he might be able to keep up with her in a legal setting, but not here, not when she was the grieving lover. He felt obligated to extend her every courtesy, but he wanted to get away from her as quickly as he could.

She said, "I forgot your coffee."

He waved it off, saying, "I'm fine. It's a nice day outside. You should go for a walk, the fresh air could do you good."

She furrowed her brow, her blue eyes still piercing his. "What is happening at the Pentagon?"

"You mean the attack?" he asked.

"The bomber. I heard they got him before he could do anything."

"He killed himself," said Watson. "Blew himself up with a hand grenade. He took the air-conditioning system with him. It gets so hot in that building that I don't need to go to the gym; I just go to work and sweat off the pounds."

She laughed, but it was not a happy laugh. "All he got was the air conditioner?" Sunny asked, the look of passing amusement softening her eyes.

"Yeah; now it's like an oven in there."

"Are they going to fix it?" she asked.

He shook his head, and said, "They'd better."

CHAPTER EIGHTEEN

"We'll fix their air-conditioning," mumbled Franklin Nailor, hiding in the back room, listening carefully to everything Travis Watson and Sunny Ferris said. He had a gun, a small pistol, but he wouldn't have used it. He'd nearly beaten Watson to death three months earlier, having purposely kept the big slug alive as a message for Harris. Nailor had taken his message to Harris directly as well, shooting him from behind with a shotgun.

He would have liked to have killed them, but the choice wasn't his. Watson had been a little fish at the time, maybe he still was, and worth more as a message than as a martyr. And Harris . . . Franklin Nailor would have given anything for the pleasure of killing him, but U.A. Special Operations had spent a lot of time and effort reprogramming the bastard (an utter failure) and controlling him (a modest success).

With Sunny in place, the Unifieds knew when and where Harris was going before he boarded his transport. They knew his tactics. They knew his penchant for leading battles in person. Wayson Harris was a devil they not only knew, but whom they could manipulate. Screw food, the fastest way to a man's heart was through his crotch, and Sunny had that down pat.

Nailor remained in the bedroom, listening carefully, admiring the way Sunny fleeced Watson for information. She manipulated the big stiff with such grace. One moment she played the grieving girlfriend, and the next she glided into her sultry, almost angry, persona. She drew sympathy from Watson, all the while subtly jabbing at his confidence. When he left the apartment, he'd feel that he'd acted foolishly, but he wouldn't know what mistakes he had made.

She had a knack for making herself unpleasant in indistinct ways, ways that honest people couldn't quite identify. When Watson stepped out the door, he would dislike the bitch without knowing why, and he would berate himself for being unfair to her.

Watson said, "Oh, well, Sunny, it's already been a long day, and . . ."

"I could still brew some coffee."

Nailor smiled. Seeing that Watson wanted to leave, Sunny reeled him in for another swipe. First she grumbled about letting him in, then she flashed her anger, and now, as he prepared to leave, she offered him coffee. *Brilliant bitch,* thought Nailor.

He thought about the time he had attacked Watson. Watson was tall, six-five, a full foot taller than Nailor, but he'd been awkward, frightened, and unprepared. He'd tried to protect himself as Nailor had blackened both his eyes, broken his ribs and nose, and shattered his jaw. The fool didn't know how to defend himself. Now here he was with Sunny, still unable to defend himself. *Fool.*

Harris hadn't been as easy. He wasn't supposed to shoot Harris, but when it came to violence, Nailor had trouble saying, "No." For him, violence was the highest form of comedy, and murder was only mischief.

Peering through a crack in the doorway, he saw Watson hug Sunny.

What an ass, he thought. *They all believe her. They all think she is so specking sincere.* He smiled. He liked the way she hugged Watson, her back stiff as she maintained space between them, the way you hug a smelly child or an adult with a contagious cold.

Nailor was both homicidal and bitter. He had played an important role in the operation when they captured the clones and ran experiments on them. He had drugged them, tested chemical programming sequences on them, and watched dozens of them die when glitches in their neural programming caused them to have death reflexes.

He'd enjoyed watching the clones die. He got a kick out of the way they stiffened and collapsed. Seeing blood pool in their ears amused him.

Harris had been different. With him, Sunny and Franklin had resorted to classical brainwashing with a few chemical enhancements.

They'd put on a show for Harris. Nailor had tortured Harris physically and emotionally. Sunny had seduced him, pretended to protect him, and staged her own death. Once they had indelibly imprinted fear and attraction into his psyche, they rebooted his brain, wiping the memories from his mind, leaving stray impulses in their place.

The first time the recently released Harris saw Sunny, he fell in love with her without ever wondering why. Harris showed signs of stress whenever the name "Nailor" entered into the conversation.

Across the hall, Watson assured Sunny that he would look in on her. She thanked him for "being so thoughtful." He told her he would let her know the moment he heard anything. She told him he was "wonderful."

She played him.

Sunny walked Watson to the door, gave him another lifeless hug, then locked the door behind him as he left. She said, "He's gone."

Nailor stepped out from the bedroom.

At five-foot-five, he was slightly shorter than Sunny. He had movie-idol looks except for the perfectly round scar in the center of his forehead. The scar had come complements of Harris. They had staged an escape, planning for Harris to run from his cell and find Sunny's dead body. Harris had specked the entire show. He attacked when Nailor expected him to run. He had found a jagged pipe and driven it into Nailor's forehead.

Vain by nature, Nailor hated Harris for ruining his looks. He'd hated Harris before the escape, hated him because he was less than human. Killing Harris wouldn't satisfy the grudge; he wanted to make Harris suffer and beg.

He said, "Why didn't you ask if Freeman is in the New Olympian Territories?"

Sunny said, "That wouldn't be very smart. I've never met Ray Freeman. And how would I go about bringing that up? 'Oh, hey, Travis, how was the weather? Did you eat any good meals while you were there? Oh, and by the way, did you happen to run into Ray Freeman while you were there?'"

Nailor didn't enjoy receiving the same treatment he'd just seen Sunny lay on Watson. He pushed past Sunny, walked to the kitchen, and helped himself to her refrigerator.

She said, "You know, Franklin, I get the feeling that you're scared of Freeman."

Nailor, who had a pitcher in one hand and an apple in the other, went to a counter. He emptied his hands, and said in a voice so calm it could only have come from a lunatic, "Of course I'm scared of Ray Freeman. I'm scared of your boyfriend, too. Either one of them would kill me in a fair fight, that's why the odds are never even.

"I hope he scares you, too. Girls get hurt when they get comfortable."

"Scared of whom, Freeman or Wayson?"

"Both of them."

Sunny said, "Oh, don't worry about Wayson. If he scares you so much, I can fix it. That's why I keep that magic cartridge in my air vents." She walked over to the thermostat on the wall and tapped it. "If things go bad with Harris, I'll make sure he never wakes up again."

"Assuming he's alive enough for you to kill him," said Franklin.

"There is that," she conceded.

Franklin bit the apple. He smiled as he chewed. "What the speck happened down there? If it's one of ours who did that . . ."

"Gee, Franklin, that's touching," Sunny said, sounding impressed. "You almost sound concerned about him."

"We need your boy alive for now. Enemies become valuable assets once you've been inside their heads."

Sunny's eyes softened, and her face slipped into a sympathetic expression. She touched a finger to the scar on Franklin's forehead, and said, "You don't always know what he's planning."

"I got sloppy," he said. "I underestimated the bastard. Just you don't make the same mistake."

CHAPTER NINETEEN

Location: Mazatlán, New Olympian Territories

Brandon Pugh woke up to find something dirty in his mouth and a knife pointed at his throat. He said, "Better watch your back, Freeman. One way or another, you're going to pay for this." The words came out soft and garbled. Whatever Freeman had stuffed into his mouth, he'd rammed it back so far that some of it ran down the gangster's throat.

Freeman said, "Let's talk."

Pugh's hands were tied behind his back. He lay on the cot in his shirt and his underwear. Freeman had removed his pants. His feet were bare and tied to the bed.

For the first time in his adult life, "Big" Brandon Pugh felt panic setting in. He tried to look Freeman in the eyes but found himself unable. Freeman's eyes were spaced far apart and showed nothing resembling sympathy or mercy.

His face was pocked with small scars, possibly burns, nearly erased using a laser. The man's pores were as wide as pencil leads.

"Are you going to pull out the gag?" asked Pugh.

The words came out like choking sounds, but Freeman understood them. He said, "Not yet. Right now, I am going to do the talking."

Trying to mask his fear, Pugh said, "Get specked." It sounded like, "Whiff whecked."

Pugh couldn't tell if Freeman understood. The man's face showed no emotion. He leaned forward, as if preparing to untie Pugh or possibly to pull out the gag. Instead, he pinched Pugh's earlobe between his thumb and forefinger, flattening it against the knuckle.

Blazing pain filled Pugh's brain. He tried to scream and inhaled the gag deeper into his throat.

He screamed, "Son of a bitch! You motherspecking son of a bitch!" It came out, "Sum sum a bip. Ya muvaspepping sum sum a bip!"

Freeman squeezed the earlobe even harder. Pugh felt tears come to his eyes. He didn't know if they had been caused by the pain or the frustration. Even when he screamed his loudest, the gag muffled the sound, and now he could barely breathe.

Freeman released Pugh's earlobe, and said, "Three clones entered Harris's apartment. There was a girl in the apartment. They didn't kill her, and she didn't try to warn Harris."

First, Pugh struggled to breathe, then he inhaled through his nose, and screamed, "I don't know what you are talking about!" He was scared. Nothing and no one had ever scared him like this.

The words came out emphatic but indistinguishable.

Freeman said, "Here's my explanation. Tell me what you think.

"The way I see it, the reason the clones didn't kill the girl is because she was working for you, and you were working for the clones. Does that sound right?"

His head spinning, panicked by the difficulty of breathing and by the pain, Pugh said, "She doesn't work for me. She's my niece." Pugh could barely understand himself, but Freeman asked, "The girl in Harris's room was your niece?"

Pugh nodded. He hated himself for giving in. He hated Freeman and wanted to kill him. He felt ashamed of himself for being a coward.

Freeman recognized the signs of a broken man. Without warning Pugh about what would happen next or threatening him with consequences if he called for help, Freeman pulled the gag out of the gangster's mouth.

When he realized what Freeman had done, Pugh's feelings of fear and anger and shame increased. His mouth was so dry it hurt, and the gag had scratched his throat. He wanted to threaten Freeman, but he didn't dare. He wanted to swear at him. He wanted to scream in frustration. His throat would not obey him. His brain had divided. A very small part of it wanted to fight, but the rest of his psyche admitted defeat.

"How does Harris know your niece?" Freeman still held the knife, a large, serrated dagger that Pugh had kept strapped to one calf.

Pugh gulped in air. He said, "She met him before all this happened, before the civil war and the aliens and Mars space station. They met like ten years ago, back when Harris was still a private or a sergeant."

"Does she have a name?" asked Freeman.

Pugh tilted his head back so that his chin stuck up in the air. Had he been standing, the gesture would have shown defiance. With him lying on his back, it went unnoticed. He said, "Her name is Kasara."

There was a knock on the door.

The dormitory walls were prefabricated and flimsy, with doors so thin that Freeman could hear people breathe as well as talk. He looked at Pugh, and whispered, "Get rid of him."

Pugh said, "Look, Freeman, you already have a problem with Story and the police. Now you got a problem with me. You let me go now, and maybe you get out of this mess alive."

There was another knock. "Brandon, you in there?"

Pugh asked, "So why don't you do us all a favor and let me up?"

Freeman continued to point the knife at Pugh's throat. Without speaking, he raised his M27 and pointed it at the door.

Seeing that the mercenary would not release him, Pugh

said softly, "I bet you don't know what to do with yourself when you're not fighting a war." Then he shouted, "Hey, Leon, we're having a private conversation here. Can it, will you?"

The man at the door said, "Sorry, it's just that the cops are here. They're looking for you."

"Who is it, Story?"

"Yeah, Story and a couple of peons."

"See that, Freeman, you got all of your enemies in the same place. Convenient, eh?"

Ignoring all the distractions, Freeman asked, "Why didn't the clones kill your niece?"

Pugh didn't answer.

"Why didn't she warn Harris?" asked Freeman. "Was she working for them?"

"What do you want me to do about Story?" asked the man at the door.

"Tell Story I'll be down in five minutes." He glared up at Freeman, and said, "She didn't warn Harris because she thought they were his clones. She would have tried to help once the trouble started, but there was another person in the room keeping her quiet. There was another guest at the party."

Freeman ran the data through his head and said, "You were there."

"Right again," said Pugh. "That other person was me."

Freeman said "Where is Harris?"

"He's safe," said Pugh.

"Take me to him," said Freeman.

"He's safe, Freeman. That doesn't mean you are."

Freeman sat over Pugh and considered the information, not worried about Pugh's screaming for help; he'd already conquered the gangster. Freeman said, "Your men didn't spot the clones, they were waiting for them."

Pugh laughed. "You know, Freeman, you're a smart man. You're not just muscle. Tell you what; I'll take you to Harris. First things first, though, I got a favor I need done."

"How do you like that, the chief of police has come to chat with me in my humble abode. To what do I owe this honor, Officer Story?" asked Pugh as he came down the stairs.

"You tell me, Pugh," said Story.

"If I had to guess, I would assume this was a social call. I can't think of any other reason for you to be here."

"What about a missing Marine?" asked Story.

They stood in a foyer, just inside one of the dormitory entrances. With two of Story's policemen stationed outside the door and three of Pugh's men guarding the halls, no stragglers would disturb them.

Story wore a suit and tie. Pugh wore a short-sleeved button-up. Both men were tall, heavy, in their forties. Both men exuded confidence. They met each other's gazes and toyed with each other's patience.

"Harris, right? Wasn't that his name?" asked Pugh.

"That's the one," said Story. "He's a three-star general. The Pentagon sent a few guys down here. They'll send a whole lot more if we can't find him . . . or if he turns up dead."

They sat together on a couch in a foyer. A moment later, one of Pugh's men brought them each a cup of coffee. Pugh said, "I heard you found dead clones in his hotel room."

Story asked, "How did you hear that?"

"We're in a relocation camp. Most of your officers live here. You snuck one of them in this very building, a policeman living on the first floor; imagine that. You didn't really think you could keep that a secret did you?"

Story said, "I hoped I could." He asked, "What do you know about Harris?"

"How would I know anything?" Pugh asked, inwardly hoping the policeman accepted this answer more readily than Freeman had.

"The same way you know about the clones," said Story. "Mazatlán may be a small town in a big territory, but you control it. Not much happens around here without your hearing about it."

What do I want Freeman to hear me say? Pugh wondered. Freeman was hiding in the next room. He wouldn't know if Pugh passed notes to Story as they spoke. The big merc had two M27s, but the police had guns as well.

The son of a bitch hit me, Pugh reminded himself. *He deserves whatever he gets.*

But Pugh knew that he would not hand Freeman over to the police if for no other reason than because he was scared.

He tried to tell himself that he didn't trust the police any more than he trusted Freeman, but it wasn't true. He had spies among the police.

Story drained his coffee, and said, "Your coffee isn't any better than ours."

"You expected something better?" asked Pugh.

"Of course."

"How would we get good coffee? We're living on the same rations as you."

Story didn't answer. Instead, he said, "You should have seen the guy who came looking for that Marine. They sent a giant."

"I heard about him. A black man, right?" In his imagination, Pugh saw Freeman listening in, cocking his M27s as he heard these words and preparing to fight. He hoped that was the case. He wanted to send Freeman the message that he wasn't scared even if it wasn't true.

"How did you know that?" Story asked as he placed the empty coffee cup on the floor beside his chair. One of Pugh's "friends" trotted over and took the cup away.

"I hear he knocked one of your boys flat on his ass."

"That got out, too?" asked Story.

"Yeah, well, what happens at the scene of the crime doesn't necessarily stay at the scene of the crime."

"What do you know about the crime itself?" asked Story.

Pugh put up his hands and shrugged his shoulders. He said, "Nothing."

"You knew about the clones."

"Okay, as I understand it, there were dead clones at the scene."

"Anything else?"

"Yeah, the Pentagon sent a giant black man down to investigate it. That's it. That's everything I know."

CHAPTER TWENTY

They went to the sitting area in which Freeman had first introduced himself to the gangsters. Pugh said, "I hope you don't mind having this discussion in the open with my boys around. The last time I had a private meeting with you, I ended up with a sore jaw."

Freeman, who sat with an M27 on his lap, had already evaluated the situation. Pugh had five of his men, big, beefy guys, most of whom would not think twice about attacking a smaller, unarmed enemy. Pugh hadn't come to fight. If the discussion went violent, he would back away and let his men handle the action.

Two of the men were scared. Freeman saw it in the way they insisted on looking him in the eye, in their overly corrected deadpan stares, and in the way they hid their hands. Another of Pugh's men looked like the type who ran, two of them would fight and die.

These weren't Pugh's best men. Watching the way that Pugh regarded them, Freeman saw that they were expendable.

Lights blazed under the awning, illuminating everything and everyone beneath it, shrouding the surrounding grounds in shadow. Freeman could not be certain, but he would operate under the assumption that Pugh had an assassin in the shadows holding an M27.

He hoped it was the M27. If Pugh went to his former allies, the ones who'd left those SCUBA tanks on the beach, there might well be a trained military sniper behind that trigger.

Showing no nervousness, Freeman said, "You mentioned a deal."

"Yeah," said Pugh. "I got somebody I want you to visit."

"Who?" asked Freeman. While he listened, he watched the

men around him for clues about the assassin. Did they become more restless? Did they look ready to duck for cover?

Pugh sat near the edge of the tent. He would run. He would hide in the darkness. Anyone coming after him would make an easy target.

Pugh said, "This may come as a shock, but I don't necessarily get along with my competitors.

"I'm a big fish here in Mazatlán, but every city has its own big fish, see, and some big fish want to nest in other fish's ponds. Over in the mountains, there's a shark named Petrie. He's the biggest fish in the Territories. Back on Olympus Kri, he was the big fish there as well."

"What kind of business does he do?" asked Freeman.

"Same as me, girls, gambling, guns, drugs. The difference between him and me is that he kept it up on Mars. I wanted to hang my shingle, too. There was plenty of demand at the spaceport, but I couldn't get my hands on the merchandise."

Seventeen million people living in lawless squalor, Freeman reminded himself. Anyone with drugs to sell or private rooms for sex would make a fortune.

"How did he do it?" asked Freeman. All the cargo coming into Mars Spaceport was shipped in by the government. The spaceport was so crowded that the only uninhabited areas were high-security ones.

"Simple enough," said Pugh. "Ryan has friends in high places."

"Who does he know?" asked Freeman.

"Riley."

"Martin Riley?" asked Freeman. He knew the name. Colonel Martin Riley had been the head of Spaceport Security when the New Olympians lived in it. He was also one of the first "converts," one of the first clones that the Unifieds captured and reprogrammed. They'd reprogrammed Riley and all his men. After their "conversion," Spaceport Security clones joined forces with the Unified Authority.

Pugh said, "Petrie had another ally, a guy named Franklin Nailor. You heard of him?"

Freeman nodded.

"I figured."

Nailor was a mystery. The things that some people knew about him, everyone knew. Everybody knew that Nailor was an important player and that he worked for the Unified Authority Intelligence Agency during the war, but nobody knew anything else.

"Yeah, well, Petrie is the reason I hooked up with those clones. Petrie has the Unies watching his back. He's bigger than me already, having the Unies on his side makes him much too big to live with if you see what I mean."

Freeman asked, "Why would the Unified Authority bother with a New Olympian gangster?"

"I don't know if the entire Unified Authority is buddying up with Petrie, but Franklin Nailor is."

"So the clones that came to get Harris weren't working for Nailor?" asked Freeman. That explained why they were late. If the attack on Harris wasn't part of the Unified's plans, maybe it was in reaction to it.

Pugh said, "They weren't working for Nailor, and they sure as hell weren't working for the Unies. And they sure as hell weren't working for Harris. You should have seen the way they went after him.

"They never said who they were working for, just who they were working against."

"And the girl?" asked Freeman.

"She didn't have anything to do with it. I told you that. I said I'd help them hit Harris so long as Kasara walked out without any new holes."

"Your men met them on the beach?"

"Just like you said," Pugh admitted.

Freeman looked at the men around him. The talking had gone on long enough for four of them to have relaxed; one still looked ready to spring. If he pulled the M27 off his lap, Freeman could have hit all five of them and left Pugh breathing . . . and he knew which one he'd have to hit first.

And the assassin? he wondered. By this time Freeman had determined that Pugh had brought along the assassin for protection rather than an ambush. He was the ace Pugh had hidden up his sleeve.

"You let them into Harris's hotel room," said Freeman.

"Yeah. I waited until Harris went into the shower, then I let them in. Kasara thought they were his men right up until the third guy shot him. The first two went into the bathroom, and we never saw them again. They had guns, M27s. You're holding one of them."

Pugh paused, looked Freeman in the eye for just a moment, then looked away. He said, "Harris put those first two out of their misery like he was doing them a favor. Something crashed in the bathroom. The water was still running. It sounded like somebody dropped a glass or something. Kasara said something about making sure he was okay, and I told her, 'Jeez, the man is in the specking shower.' That was enough for her up to that point because it all happened so fast.

"Another moment, and the third clone peeks into the bathroom. He fired a shot, and that was everything I saw. I mean, that did it. Kasara started screaming and shrieking and trying to run to help him. My niece and Harris are . . . um, attached at the hip, if you know what I mean; she would have done whatever it took to save him. Can you believe it? Three trained commandos attacking a Liberator clone, and my skinny little niece wants to run to the rescue.

"I had to grab her and wrestle her to the bed. She barely weighs a hundred pounds, that little girl, but she put up a fight that time.

"When I heard the shot, I figured it was over, then Harris came charging out of that bathroom like he'd been fired from a cannon. He was like a rocket, like a missile, and he flew into that last clone and snapped his neck as neatly as you please. I tell you what, at that point I'm thinking, 'Shit, I put my money on the wrong horse.'

"But he was hurt. His feet were all shredded and the blood leaking from his gut . . . you could have floated a yacht in it.

"By this time, Kasara was crying and punching me and begging me to help him. I made a snap decision. Snap decisions always bite you on the ass, you know that?

"I rolled Harris up in a blanket and carried him out of there. I took him to a secure place; somewhere we could hide him. That's where he is right now, hidden."

Freeman thought about the hotel room, how it had looked that morning, and later that evening when he broke in. He thought about the blood on the floor in the bathroom and the huge stain just outside it. There hadn't been any blood anywhere else. The story fit.

"You had your men clean the room?" asked Freeman.

"If you mean sweep up the shells and remake the bed, yeah, my men cleaned the room. We had the room clean before the police arrived."

At the moment, Ryan Petrie didn't matter, neither did the dead clones or the girl named Kasara. Freeman had come for Harris, not to take sides in a gang war, but he was a patient man. Having spent his life working with generals and politicians, Freeman understood the gangster's mind. Favors, bribes, and power bought allies.

He said, "Tell me what I need to know about Petrie."

CHAPTER TWENTY-ONE

Location: Washington, D.C.
Date: July 20, 2519

The clones around the Pentagon accepted Travis Watson's authority. Obeying authority figures was hardwired into their genes. Clones had trouble ascending to power, even those who wanted to, but accepting authority came naturally because they had been designed to take orders.

Only a select circle of officers knew that Watson had replaced Cutter as the leader of the empire. Alan Cardston knew, and so did the top officers in Pentagon Security. They didn't refer to Watson as "Mr. President" though. They simply called him "sir."

Military clones referred to all natural-born males over the age of eighteen as "sir." When they became nervous, enlisted clones sometimes referred to authoritative women as "sirs" as well.

As the "transitional president," Watson had become the

temporary head of the Enlisted Man's Empire even though he had never served in the military. He had permission to run the Empire, but not to become a true citizen. The clones around him, officers and enlisted men alike, treated him like an outsider.

He watched the officers who served under him. They guarded him and obeyed him, but they did little to hide their resentment. Why should they? They had liberated themselves from natural-born rule and conquered the nation of natural-borns that had created and abandoned them only to wind up with a natural-born ruler.

Watson had many reasons for hoping Harris was alive—handing over the reins ranked high among the top.

He wasn't nervous of assassination. As far as he knew, the only clone who had killed his superiors was Harris, and Harris was missing. Outside of Hauser, MacAvoy, Ritz, Cardston, and Pentagon Security, no one knew about Watson's coronation. Few people even knew about Don Cutter's death. The assassin who had committed the crime was dead; Hauser's MPs caught him trying to steal a transport. Once he'd known he was caught, he locked himself in the cockpit and killed himself.

Freeman called on an official line. The receptionist said, "Sir, Ray Freeman is on the line." Watson's receptionist had always called him "sir." He didn't know about Watson's recent job promotion.

Watson nodded and took the call, wondering what Freeman would say about his becoming king of the clones.

As soon as Watson identified himself, Freeman said, "I've located Harris."

"Is he alive?" asked Watson.

"I haven't seen him yet," said Freeman. "From what I hear, he is alive and convalescing."

"I'll send a medical transport and doctors," said Watson.

"Not just yet," said Freeman. "The locals say they aren't ready to turn him over."

"I can send troops."

"Not yet."

"Not yet? If they have Harris . . ."

"I want to work with them."

"Work with the people who abducted Harris?"

"They didn't take him, not by force."

"I was in that room; he didn't go willingly."

Freeman asked, "Do you know Harris's girlfriend?"

Watson asked, "You mean Sunny? Sure. I know her. What does she have to do with this?"

"How well do you know her?"

Watson started to say that he knew her well, then stopped to reconsider. He and Emily had doubled with Harris and Sunny on three, maybe four dates. She chatted mostly with Harris when they went out, asked Watson a few questions, and ignored Emily entirely.

"I've talked with her."

"What about Harris?"

"What about him?"

"How serious is Harris about her?"

Watson didn't know how to answer the question. He started to say something about Harris loving her and stopped. *Does he love her?* he asked himself. He knew about Ava Gardner and Harris. She'd been a Hollywood screen goddess, then word got out that she was a clone. The timing couldn't have been worse. The news of her origins broke about the same time that the Pentagon decided to abandon its military-cloning project. She was an innocent swept up in a time of fear and anger.

Harris and Ava had fallen in love during the days when all clones were banished from Earth. She died during the second wave of the alien invasion. He never spoke of her. Cutter had talked about her, though. So did Colonel Ritz. Listening to them, Watson got the feeling that Harris would have married her.

If the rumors were true, she had been unfaithful to Harris. She had taken up with a natural-born. Ritz and Cutter agreed about that much. They did not agree about what came next. Ritz thought Harris left her on a planet that the aliens were about to incinerate. He said Harris left her there to burn.

Cutter said that something had happened, that seeing all the devastation, Ava Gardner had given up on life. He believed she had asked Harris to leave her behind.

Watson said, "I think Harris was . . . is committed to Sunny. I'm not sure he loves her."

Freeman asked, "Have you ever heard about Ava Gardner?"

Watson perked up. He said, "Yes. I heard she died when the Avatari burned Providence Kri."

Freeman didn't respond. Instead, he said, "No one ever wondered if Harris loved Ava; the answer was obvious."

Watson asked, "Why are you asking about Sunny?"

Freeman told him about Brandon Pugh, his involvement with the clones, and that Harris was sleeping with Pugh's niece, Kasara. After he finished, Watson whistled. He said, "Another girl. That doesn't sound like Harris."

"From what Pugh says, they knew each other already."

"Do you believe him?" asked Watson.

"Yes. Even if I didn't, I want Pugh on our side. If he's telling the truth, something is going on in the Unifieds. We may need an ally in the Territories."

Freeman explained what he knew about Ryan Petrie and his rival organization. When he finished, Watson said, "It sounds like he needs us more than we need him."

"It's not a question of needing him more," said Freeman. "Having an ally behind enemy lines is useful."

"Even if he's a gangster?"

"Especially if he's a gangster."

"Can you trust him?" asked Watson.

"I don't trust him, but I am going to do this favor for him," said Freeman. "I'm going to need some equipment."

"What do you need?" asked Watson.

Freeman had the list ready. He said, "A sniper rifle and Special-Forces-grade demolitions gear for openers. You'll find everything I need in a little Bandit I have hidden just outside of town."

CHAPTER TWENTY-TWO

A team of Army engineers began work on the new air-conditioning system later that afternoon. Because it was too big to fit in an elevator, the only way they could deliver the new equipment was by helicopter. Watson didn't watch the delivery though most of his staff went to see the spectacle.

So did Major Cardston and his security team. They inspected the equipment for bombs and pronounced it clean. They only allowed clones from the Army Corps of Engineers to work on the project.

The engineers used a crane to remove a section of roof from the Pentagon, then a team of helicopters lifted the destroyed HVAC equipment and delivered its replacement. The helicopters delivered enormous canisters of the compressed-oxygen refrigerant, then the cranes replaced the roof. The entire operation took nearly three hours.

While his secretaries and staff went out to watch the spectacle, Watson remained in his office. He was still there ten hours later when the air-conditioning units finally began pumping cool air into the vents, but it would be hours more before the atmosphere in the building felt comfortable.

"Yes, sir. This is Major Cardston from Pentagon Security." Now that Watson was an interim president, Cardston began every conversation by identifying himself as if they had never before met.

Programming, thought Watson. He looked away from the communications screen and gazed out the window. It was early in the afternoon. The air in the Pentagon now had an October chill. Watson looked out his window and was surprised to see a bright sun and a few scattered clouds.

He asked, "Have your men found Freeman's warehouse?"

"It's like an armory. If this guy declared war . . ."

"Let's just make sure he doesn't," said Watson.

"Doesn't what?" asked Cardston.

"Let's make sure he never declares war on us."

"Sir, I think we should confiscate—" Cardston began.

"He's an ally, Major. Just ship his plane and his gear to the New Olympian Territories. I promised Freeman he'd have them to him by this time tomorrow."

"Sir, yes, sir," said Cardston. He was assigned to the Pentagon, but he was an officer in the Enlisted Man's Army. When he received new orders, he sometimes responded with the term Harris dismissively referred to as a "sir sandwich."

Watson signed off.

He stared out the window at the river and the marble monuments just beyond its banks. The needle of the Washington Monument stood above the city like a giant steeple on a church. Beyond that ancient monument, the marble-walled buildings of the National Mall seemed to stretch out forever. The capitol itself, the largest building in the galaxy, loomed like a distant mountain.

The day was bright but hazy. Watson could see the capitol building, but its shape blended into the sky behind it. Harris loomed in the back of Watson's thoughts, an overshadowing concern that made it hard to concentrate.

Alive . . . wounded . . . unfaithful to Sunny. Did he love her? Watson asked himself. The indestructible Harris he thought he'd known didn't match the one Freeman described on the telephone.

Harris had occasionally alluded to the pleasures of sex with Sunny. He often spoke about her beauty. *She is nice to look at,* Watson admitted to himself. *So is Emily,* he reminded himself. *And Emily isn't such a bitch.*

Watson loved Emily. He knew he loved her, and he knew why he loved her. Why would anyone love a woman like Sunny? Sure, she was beautiful, but underneath the beauty, she was toxic.

From what he could tell, Harris had only slept with a handful of women before meeting Sunny. Ask him about fighting or killing, and he sounded confident. Talk to him about women, and the deadly Liberator ran out of things to say. Was that why he stayed with Sunny?

Sunny was intelligent and rich and elegant and beautiful. From what Harris had said, she gave herself to him easily.

Could Harris have cheated on her? Watson wondered. *What about "Semper fi"?* he wondered. "Always faithful." Did it extend beyond his brothers in the Corps?

Watson's private phone rang. Cardston wanted him to jettison the phone for security reasons. He said it was easy to trace, easy to target, easy to booby-trap, but Watson had owned the phone long before Harris hired him as an aide, and he planned to keep on carrying it long after he finished his term as the interim president.

Besides, if he stopped carrying the phone and answering it, people would ask questions. No one outside the Pentagon knew that he was the acting president of the fledgling empire; he wanted to keep it that way.

He pulled the phone from his coat pocket, saw the call was from Emily, and answered. She said, "Travis, you'd better get home quickly."

"What's the matter?" asked Watson.

"Sunny is here."

"Sunny?" He remembered how she'd looked the last time he'd seen her. She'd been drunk and disheveled. He asked, "How does she look?"

"How do you think she looks? She looks like a beauty queen. Why don't you ask me how she's acting? Why doesn't anybody ever care about how she behaves?"

"How is she behaving?" asked Watson.

"Like she owns the place," said Emily. "She came in, asked for a drink, and said, 'Where's Travis?'"

"What did you do?" Watson asked. One of the things he loved about Emily was that she stood up for herself.

"I told her I'd call you. I also told her I had to go to a meeting off base."

"Where are you going?"

"I don't know yet, but I am not going to hang around with her. I'll wait till you get here, Travis, but after that . . ."

"I love you, M," he said.

"You better." She hung up.

Watson and Emily lived on Joint Base Anacostia-Bolling, in the southern corner of the District. The late Admiral Don Cutter had ordered him to move there just after the attack on Mars Spaceport.

He and Emily both hated the place.

He also hated riding in a chauffeured limousine and living with bodyguards. The limousine, driver, and three bodyguards came with the house because the Empire's enemies were now Watson's enemies. Two of Watson's bodyguards had died protecting him a few months back. He didn't like having bodyguards or living on a military base, but knew he needed them. Had the bodyguards not been with him at the Unified Authority Archive building, he would have been killed. The bodyguards would be a fact of life for the rest of his life. Even if he quit his job and went into hiding, he would never be safe again.

He called his aide, and asked, "Is my car ready?"

"Waiting for you, sir."

"Thank you," said Watson. "I'll be out for the rest of the day."

"Yes, sir."

Watson placed his traveling workspace in his bag and slung the bag over his shoulder. The computer weighed less than a pound. He hurried out of his office.

His bodyguards waited for him by the elevator. The doors were open. The two guards standing outside the elevator were military clones. The third guard, waiting in the lift, was natural-born.

All three dressed like civilians. Their uniform included black suits, dark glasses, discreet earpieces, and pistols. Their jackets were bulletproof, technically, but in an age with explosive bullets and bullets made of a third-generation uranium alloy, the term "bulletproof" described a nebulous concept.

The natural-born bodyguard asked, "Where are we going, sir?" as Watson stepped onto the lift.

"Home, Mark," said Watson. "Home."

Watson now made it a point to learn his bodyguards'

names. At the time, he'd jokingly referred to the ones who'd died protecting him as "B1" and "B2." Looking back, he decided the joke had been disrespectful.

The bodyguards referred to him as "sir" or "Mr. Watson." Even before he'd become the acting president, he'd been "sir" or "Watson." When he wasn't around, they referred to him as "MTW," short for "Mr. Travis Watson." Creativity was not a talent cultivated by bodyguards.

When the elevator's doors opened three floors below street level, in the secured garage, two more bodyguards were there to meet them. So were three limousines. A natural-born bodyguard and two more clones joined the entourage that escorted Watson to his car. Some of the bodyguards climbed in his car with him. Some stepped into the other cars. As they drove off, Watson thought about clone programming. A natural-born bodyguard and two clones escorted him at all times. Why hadn't the clones ever noticed that they weren't the natural-born?

Watson sat in the back, poured himself a drink, and managed a few sips before the car pulled up to the front gate of Bolling Air Force Base. The guards at the gate saluted and let his caravan through. For security purposes, the car had been cleared from the Pentagon.

The limo pulled up to his home, a building that had once been reserved for admirals and generals reporting in from outer colonies. Watson hated the lawn, with its manicured hedges and the beds of wildflowers that lined the walkway. He loathed the bright blue façade of the home, with its white trim and faux shutters.

Until Cutter had moved him into this place, he'd lived in the city. He'd gone bar hopping every night and never slept with the same girl twice. First came the house, then Emily had entered his life. Was he transforming into his parents?

Emily met him at the door. She let him in, kissed him on the mouth, and said, "I better get going, Trav, I'm already late."

She was beautiful as ever. He felt a pang whenever he saw her. She had shoulder-length honey blond hair, blue eyes, and a nice figure. A natural athlete, she had a graceful walk, but she also had the swagger of a woman who had made the rounds. Emily wouldn't have interested him had she come across like a virgin.

He barely managed to say, "See you when you get back," before she had swept past the bodyguards and into her car.

Sunny sat in the living room, gazing out the window, looking as if Harris had never disappeared. She said, "Wow, Travis, I didn't know you had bodyguards. Did you tell them to wait outside while you were in my apartment the other night?"

"They're used to it."

She did not stand to greet him. She remained on the couch, legs crossed, holding a tall glass of iced tea. He walked to her, kissed her on the cheek, and asked, "How are you doing?"

Her eyes were clear, no red at all. The puffiness had gone from her face. She looked good. She looked beautiful. Her hair was brushed back, the soft, shiny brown hair that always made Watson think of mink and chinchilla.

She said, "I spoke to my boss about Wayson." Her boss was Alexander Cross, one of the biggest, noisiest, most successful ambulance-chasing lawyers in the capital.

"That was classified information," Watson said. He'd always lived by a simple rule—*Don't expect people to keep secrets you don't keep yourself.* For some reason, he had decided to tell Sunny classified information, and, of course, it had backfired on him. He was mad at her and even angrier at himself.

"It was classified?" she asked, sounding more curious than sorry. "I'll try to keep it quiet."

Sunny said, "My boss offered to send some of our investigators down to look for him; our firm represents the New Olympians. The New Olympian government will cooperate with us; it always does. He said I could go to help with the investigation."

"To look for Wayson?" *Am I angry or embarrassed?* he asked himself. The answer was, *Yes.*

Watson wanted to tell her not to go, but he didn't know how he could stop her without giving her more information, and he didn't want to tell her anything more. Telling her as much as he had had been a mistake.

She put her drink down on an end table. Emily had given her a coaster, but Sunny didn't bother placing the glass on the it.

Watson noticed this but said nothing. He hated the bland

wood and leather furniture in the house every bit as much as he hated the house. He debated within himself about telling her that Freeman had found Harris. He might have found Harris, but Harris wasn't out of the woods. From what Freeman had said, he could be in bad shape. *Even the great Wayson Harris can die,* he reminded himself. *He's a killer, but that doesn't make him immortal.*

She interrupted his thoughts. She said, "You don't look happy."

"I don't think you should go."

"Why wouldn't I go? It's not like I'm going down there by myself. I'm going with our investigators."

Watson said, "They're only going to get in the way."

"Are you saying you already have people down there?" she asked.

"Of course we do. The highest-ranking officer in the Enlisted Man's Marines is missing; of course we're investigating."

"Are they making any progress?" she asked. "Maybe we can work together, you know, you tell us what you know, and we'll tell you what we find out."

"Sunny, this is a government operation."

"And it doesn't seem to be going anywhere. Travis, he's been missing for over a week."

He looked at her, noticed how she pursed her lips. *She does that too much,* he thought. *Did it get on Harris's nerves?* It got on his nerves. These days, everything about her got on his nerves.

"Sunny, we have a full investigation under way. We're making progress."

"That's not what I hear," said Sunny.

"What?" Travis Watson, the acting president of the all-clone empire found himself stunned. He asked, "What have you heard?"

"I heard that you and some other guy went down, some giant named Freeman. That's what the police said, that there were only two of you . . . you and Freeman. They said you looked at the crime scene and asked a few questions, then you flew home.

"Is that it? Is that your big investigation? It doesn't sound like much."

"What are your detectives going to find that the New Olympian Police and my Marines haven't found?"

"Your Marines? The police told me that your Marines aren't down there," she said. "According to the police, you left the matter in their hands."

"Sunny, I shouldn't have told you as much as I have. I gave you classified information . . . and you told it to your boss. I shouldn't . . ."

She interrupted him, shouting, "What would you do if Emily was missing? What would you do? Would you go after her? Would you talk to people who could help you? Would you spend a lot of time worrying if the information you learned was classified?

"We're talking about Wayson. He may be a *Marine Killing Machine*, but I love him. What would you do if Emily disappeared down there? Wouldn't you go after her?

"My boss talked to Mark Story. He said he met with you and a man named Freeman. He says you gave up and flew home. What do you expect me to do?"

"Did he tell you there were three dead clones on the scene?" asked Watson. "We think Harris killed them. Your detectives probably won't find anything if they go, or if they do, they might just find something that gets them killed.

"Whoever went after Harris meant business, Sunny. They didn't send those Marines to talk to Harris; they sent them to kill him."

"Have you given up on him?" asked Sunny.

"No, of course not."

"What about Freeman, the other guy. What does he think?"

Watson paused, weighed the pros and cons in his head and decided he needed to stop Sunny. He said, "Look, this is classified information. What I am going to tell you is for you only. Don't go running to your boss. Do I have your word?"

Sunny said nothing.

Watson didn't trust her, but he didn't want her to go to the Territories. If she got herself killed, he'd answer to Harris, and that thought terrified him. He said, "Freeman is still down there. He's located Harris."

Sunny smiled. She asked, "Is he okay? Was he hurt?"

Already regretting his decision to tell her, he sighed, and

said, "I've already told you too much. Now, just . . . go back to your apartment, okay? Just go home and sit tight. I'll let you know when we have him."

Sunny stood and took Watson's hand. She said, "Okay, thank you for telling me. Trust me on this one, Travis. I'll keep it to myself."

CHAPTER TWENTY-THREE

Location: Guanajuato, New Olympian Territories
Date: July 22, 2519

Freeman fit into his Piper Bandit the way a size-twelve foot fits into a size-eleven boot. For a man of his size and bulk, the little plane was entirely impractical, but it had its virtues. This particular Bandit had been redesigned by the Unified Authority Intelligence Agency for smuggling infiltrators onto EME-held planets. It had a rudimentary broadcast engine and a stealth shield.

Viewing the mountainous territory through night-for-day technology built into the glass of the windshield, he saw barren peaks and jungle-covered slopes. He saw rivers and deserts.

He flew slowly, letting his onboard computer chart possible landing sites, hoping to touch down no more than five miles from the city, from his target.

The Bandit would need a runway to land, but that runway wouldn't need to be long or wide. A hundred-foot stretch of open dirt road would do.

Landing, it turned out, would be the only part of the operation that came easily. As Freeman approached the city, he found a spider's web of paved roads and abandoned towns. He chose a site eight miles north and west of the city, a small farm town that looked dark and afflicted. Using the heat-tracking equipment in the Bandit's cockpit, Freeman scanned the streets and houses for heat signatures. He found wild dogs, pigs, rats, and birds, but no people.

He touched down on the old country road that ran through the center of the ghost town, a better runway facility than he had expected to find. He landed smoothly and taxied past the edge of civilization, rolling silently through the moonlit landscape until he found the ruins of an old brick wall. He hid his plane behind the wall. The ground around him must have been farmland at some point, maybe hundreds of years ago. It was still flat, but overgrown with scrawny trees and knee-high grass that had dried to gold. Copses of cactus peered out from behind scrub.

Freeman opened the cockpit and pried himself free. He stretched his arms, legs, and back, encouraging blood into limbs that had first gone numb, then fallen asleep. Circulation returned slowly, burning as it did. He did not care about the ache in his arms; it didn't matter.

He reached back into the cockpit and pulled out his rifle, patrol pack, and satchel. The satchel held a change of clothes, BDUs designed for mountainous terrain and jungle boots. He could have worn the BDUs for the flight, but the thick cloth would have made fitting into the cockpit even more difficult.

He stripped down to boxers and a tank top, stuffed his discards into the cockpit, and sealed it, knowing that he might not return for days.

The morning had not yet begun as he started the hike to the town that his navigational computer identified as Leone. Moonlight shone down on the road, on the barrens, and on the wispy trees that covered the slopes. He jogged a mile, but mostly he walked. The air was thin, and he had sixty pounds of gear on his back. At 350 pounds, Ray Freeman would never run a marathon.

He owned a complete set of Marine combat armor, but he didn't want it for this mission. Instead, he wore a set of goggles with sensors that tracked his path and laid virtual beacons, gave him night-for-day vision and heat vision.

He traveled six miles before spotting the first guard. Using the scope on his rifle, he spied the man patrolling the top of a distant ridge. Freeman searched the ridge for more guards, but the man was alone, an easy target. Freeman didn't fire. Dead men attract attention. Corpses don't answer calls or report in at the end of their patrols. Even when you kill them silently without anybody noticing, dead men tell tales.

Freeman would leave corpses behind when the time came; Pugh had sent him to kill Ryan Petrie, but he would do nothing to draw attention until the moment presented itself.

Skirting that guard would add an extra half mile to his hike, but Freeman chose to add it. Unlike Pugh's organization, Petrie's seemed ready for company.

Freeman's BDUs masked much of his body heat, and it included a hood of the same material that he pulled over his head. Seen through heat-vision goggles, he would look rust-colored, instead of red or yellow. A trained soldier might spot him; he'd need to be alert.

Skirting that first guard had been a waste of time. As he neared the vacated city of Leone, where Petrie had established his base, Freeman found men guarding every ledge and ridge. Two guards here, one guard there, he could pick them off if he had to, but he he'd come to kill the gangster, not the men guarding him.

Too damn many guards. Someone tipped him off, thought Freeman.

Pugh had placed a few guards around the Mazatlán relocation camp as well, but nothing like this. Then again, Pugh was a smaller player. He was a bottom-feeder who'd tried to buy his way back into the game by cashing in on his niece. He was still cashing in on his niece.

It was possible that Pugh had set him up, but Freeman dismissed it. Maybe Pugh was a bit player trying to buy a seat at a table for high rollers, but he was scared of the other players.

Freeman still felt like he had stumbled into a trap. There were too many guards. This was supposed to be a backwater operation, but the gangsters were on alert. Freeman asked himself who else knew his plans and came up with only one answer, Travis Watson. He had told Watson where he was going and what he planned to accomplish. Freeman trusted Watson; they'd fought together on Mars.

In another hour, dawn would break. The sun would rise, lighting the flats between the mountains. Like a vampire fleeing the daylight, Freeman would need to find a hiding place before dawn. He needed one question answered before he hid for the day. He would take a closer look at the guards.

Natural-born or clone? That question needed answering. If those guards were natural-born, Freeman could still run his operation as planned. If the stories Pugh told were true, Petrie ran a large organization, but Freeman had seen New Olympian thugs in action, and he wasn't impressed. If Petrie's guards came from the same gene pool as Pugh's, Freeman had little to worry about.

On the other hand, Petrie supposedly had made a pact with the Unified Authority, an alliance that could include equipment and trained personnel.

Freeman knelt and removed his backpack. Silently flipping through the contents, he located a SCOOTER (Subautonomous Control Optical Observation Terrain Exploration Robot), a ground-scuttling spy probe that contained a self-preservation routine in its programming.

The SCOOTER was a disc, six inches in diameter, and its entire surface worked like a fish-eye lens. Freeman had modified the unit so that it sent its signal directly to his goggle. Using optical commands, he could assign the SCOOTER targets and territories to investigate. He would be able to see through the robot's lens.

Using an optical command, he powered the SCOOTER's motor and placed it on the ground, then he marked the sentries for recon and watched as the robot slipped into the darkness, making no more noise than an ant.

Freeman sealed his backpack and headed west, away from the guards and the city. He would find a better hiding place, one from which he couldn't see the guards, and they absolutely would not see him. The robot would find its own way back. That was part of its programming.

Freeman crossed a gulch. Seeing that he'd left footprints, he kicked the top of the bank, causing a small cave-in that covered most of his tracks. If trained trackers came looking, they would spot his partial footprints, but that couldn't be helped.

Traveling slowly, Freeman pushed into the brush. When he checked on the SCOOTER, he saw that it had made slow progress as well. That was the problem with self-preservation programming: it turned robots into cowards.

He found a dry divot hidden behind a gnarly, nine-foot tree and stepped into it. He checked the ground around him for snakes and kept an eye out for wolves and coyotes as well. Wolves made noise. On this night, with the silence broken only by the buzz of insects and the gentle breeze, the growl of a wolf would carry. It would draw attention.

Freeman checked the area for heat signatures, saw nothing. He settled back and kept his rifle ready.

The SCOOTER circled the ridge, looking for ruts and hollows, approaching the guards with all the confidence of a gazelle sneaking up on a lion. In a little corner of his goggles, the signal showed Freeman the world as the robot saw it. He saw trees and scrub from just above their roots and the night sky as seen through tall grass. In the clear, dark heavens, a million million stars sparkled.

The robot jiggled over tiny rocks and past clusters of salsola that would soon detach from their roots and become tumbleweeds. Along with the lens on its back, the SCOOTER had eyes—powerful cameras that adjusted to darkness and zoomed in on distant objects. Still hundreds of yards from the sentries, its microphones listened for voices. Its eyes searched through grass and branches, then focused on the targets.

Freemen groaned inwardly. The first guard the SCOOTER found wore combat armor. He might have been natural-born or clone. It didn't matter; either way, Petrie had properly trained men around him.

Maybe Petrie was naturally careful, or maybe someone had warned him. Freeman asked himself a second time if he trusted Watson and no longer knew how to answer. He had the patience of a sniper, though. He could wait a day, a week, or a year, time spent hiding, watching, and planning.

CHAPTER TWENTY-FOUR

Location: Pentagon, Washington, D.C.
Date: July 23, 2519

Watson took the call at 08:00. It came on a secure line.

He said, "Freeman, where are you?"

Ray Freeman's voice, so low that Watson might have mistaken it for sound distortion, concealed emotion the way a black hole conceals light. When he said, "The Unifieds knew I was coming. They sent troops," his voice betrayed neither anger nor suspicion. He might just as well have been describing the weather.

"Are you still going to kill the guy?" asked Watson.

Freeman didn't respond, and Watson understood. He wouldn't have remained had he not planned to hit Petrie. Watson asked, "How did they know you were going after Petrie?"

Freeman answered with a question of his own. "Who have you talked to?"

"Nobody," said Watson. "I don't know anybody in the Territories." He could feel tension rising like bile in his throat. "What about Pugh? He was the one who sent you. Maybe he wants you killed."

Freeman said nothing.

Watson thought about it. Why send an assassin to kill an enemy and then warn the enemy? You might get the assassin killed. The enemy and the assassin could also end up as allies.

He said, "Maybe Petrie has spies in Pugh's camp."

"He might," said Freeman. "Did you tell anyone I was down here?"

Hoping to make the question go away, Watson said, "Cardston knows you're down there."

"Anybody else?"

Watson paused. He rubbed a hand across his forehead, and

his gaze naturally sank to the floor as he said, "I told Harris's girlfriend."

Freeman said nothing.

"She's a lawyer. Her firm represents the New Olympians; that was how Harris met her in the first place. When I told her that Harris was missing, she took it to her boss."

In his head, he rephrased his words. *I told her classified information and she told it to her boss. Her boss has friends in the Territories, friends all over the Territories. Shit, I specked up. Lord Almighty, did I ever speck this one.*

Freeman asked, "Do you trust her?"

"Yes . . . No," he said. "I'm not sure. She isn't connected to the Unified Authority. She's a lawyer, a young lawyer. Her boss is Alexander Cross. He's another story. For all I know, Petrie could be his favorite client."

Anxious to change the subject, Watson added, "Mark Story told Cross about our visit."

"Yes. He and a couple of cops came sniffing around Pugh's dormitory."

"Story told Cross that you and I came, had a look around, and pretty much abandoned Harris. Sunny said that Cross offered to send investigators down to the Territories to look for Harris."

"You ever had a boss offer to do anything like that for you?" asked Freeman.

Watson thought about it. "No."

"And you told her that I was down here," Freeman extrapolated.

"She asked if I had somebody down here. When I said, 'Yes,' she asked if it was you. Apparently, you made quite an impression on Story."

"Petrie has the New U.A. in his pocket. Pugh allied himself with those clones because he was scared of Petrie.

"It looks like the Unifieds want inroads with the New Olympians."

"Even if he's a gangster?" asked Watson.

"Gangsters make good allies; they're ruthless, they run tight organizations, their customers depend on them, and the general population is scared of them. Petrie is exactly the kind of ally the Unifieds would want."

Watson played with that thought. "So the Unifieds are with

Petrie. Okay, that works, but you said the clones who attacked Harris were working against the Unified Authority."

"They must have gone rogue," Freeman agreed.

"Okay, but who did they work for before they went rogue? They can't have been ours, or they wouldn't have tried to kill Harris." Coming at the conundrum from another direction, he said, "I could see the Unifieds sending converts to kill Harris. They'd want him out of the way."

Harris must have had thousands of enemies, maybe even tens of thousands of enemies. He'd killed superior officers, waged a massive war against the Unified Authority, and led men into battles that few had survived. He probably had enemies inside the EME Marines. Watson asked, "Could they have been ours, maybe disgruntled Marines?"

"Their programming wouldn't permit them to attack him," said Freeman. "You need to take this to Tasman; maybe he can figure it out."

"What are you going to do?" asked Watson. "If the Unifieds have Marines guarding Petrie, maybe this isn't such a good idea."

"Nothing has changed down here as far I'm concerned. The deal hasn't changed. I hit Petrie and Pugh gives us Harris."

CHAPTER TWENTY-FIVE

Location: Guanajuato, New Olympian Territories
Date: July 23, 2519

Freeman watched the U.A. transport as it floated across the sky. It flew like a bumblebee. In space, where gravity and wind currents didn't exist, transports flew as well as any other craft. In Earth's atmosphere, dealing with wind shears and air pockets, transports fumbled as they relied on thrusters instead of riding air currents to stay aloft. With their bloated hulls and distended wings, transports were anything but aerodynamic. Cut their thrusters, and they dropped like boulders.

That transport meant more guards. Hiding on a distant ridge, using his powerful rifle scope like a telescope, he counted the troops as they left the ship. Fifteen men. The transport had room for one hundred men. *Maybe the Unifieds are calling off the alert,* he thought.

Freeman took that as a good sign. If the Unifieds had known he was there, they would have sent a full company, one hundred men.

Unlike Pugh, whose organization was attached to a larger population, Petrie had Leone, a vacated mountain city, all to himself. He and his men lived in a relocation camp about two miles south of the abandoned city.

They didn't only have the city to themselves, they had the entire area. The Enlisted Man's Empire had sent men and equipment to help reestablish Mazatlán. The Unified Authority might one day do the same for Leone, but it would draw attention if they did that now, so Petrie and his men made camp. From a strategic point of view, they'd picked badly—low ground surrounded by ridges on almost every side. As long as he avoided sentries, Freeman could move around freely, able to observe the camp from nearly every angle. Once the shooting began, he'd have a high-ground advantage, meaning he could hit anywhere in the camp.

As he circled the perimeter, Freeman heard the soft percussion of distant gunfire. It was sporadic—a shot every few seconds with an occasional burst, the rhythm never quite repeating itself. Target practice. Gunfights came in frenetic bursts instead of interludes.

It was midday, and Freeman generally preferred to do recon at night, but he could adjust. The trees and rocks offered good cover. Petrie had the numbers, but Freeman had the high ground. For recon, high ground was better than numbers. But when it came to a fight, numbers were the better advantage.

The day was getting hotter, well over eighty, and the air was dry. Freeman strapped on his backpack and carried his rifle by the forestock. He climbed to the top of a thirty-foot ridge and found a natural nest from which he could observe the camp hidden behind rocks. He settled in, pulled the scope from his rifle, and inspected the camp.

Looking around the facilities, Freeman did not see women or children. He scouted men eating out of aluminum pouches, U.A.-supplied MREs. He saw men driving jeeps and trucks. It was just an estimate, and Freeman placed no faith in uneducated guesses, but he thought Petrie might have somewhere between three and five hundred men.

Freeman left his rifle and backpack in the nest. Using spindly trees for cover, he walked to the crest of the ridge, looked back toward the camp, and saw nothing of interest.

He went back to the nest, retrieved his gear, and continued circling, checking the camp from every visible angle. He found a vantage point from which he could see straight into the heart of the camp, dropped to his stomach, and remained as still as an alligator waiting for prey.

Though he could not see the size of the drop, he could see that the ledge ahead of him ended with a vertical wall—a good spot for sniping or to launch a rocket attack. Using his scope, he peered down into the camp and saw that he was near the motor pool. He counted five jeeps, three trucks, two motorcycles.

Petrie's fleet was hand-me-downs of the worst variety, outdated military supplies covered with dents and welds. His fuel supply was stored in aboveground tanks, twenty-foot metallic cylinders that no saboteur could ignore. Freeman had rockets and automatic launchers; the depot would definitely go.

A half dozen men guarded the area, all of them carrying M27s. Petrie had his own men here, men who carried their weapons with the casual indifference of the severely untrained. One guy stood leaning against a fence. He held his M27 by its muzzle.

The other men displayed signs of slightly better intelligence. One had his rifle laying flat in the dirt beside him, but he'd had the good sense to point the shooting end away from himself.

Freeman moved on, working slowly, hiding just below the crests of the ridges. The sound of the shooting grew louder. He belly-crawled to the top of a ridge and peered out from between two trees, staying low so that his body was hidden in shadow, his heat signature distorted by sun-heated rocks and mounds.

He spotted a potential point of entry, a dirt road that ran along the edge of the camp, bending and winding around the fence before finally entering. A dry creek bed ran along one side of the road, the banks waist high, offering a measure of concealment. These features had not gone unnoticed. Either Petrie or his benefactors had strung razor wire along the banks of that creek. If the Unifieds placed that wire there, they'd probably electrified it.

As he scouted the area, Freeman finally spotted the shooting range. A dozen men stood near the fence targeting holographic figures of commandos that ran and dodged across the creek. Petrie's men guarded and trained at the same time—an efficient but worthless use of manpower. They didn't take either task seriously. Freeman could have performed jumping jacks with yellow flags tied to his arms without their noticing, but their target practice was equally unimpressive. They missed the target most of the time and made jokes about each other's accuracy like hunters more interested in drinking beer than killing game.

As he watched them, Freeman spotted sensors along the fence, three hundred yards from the fence and hidden behind trees and rocks. Freeman didn't need to worry about tripping the sensors, but they would detect him long before he could reach the camp.

From this purchase, he could see deep into the camp. Looking between buildings and down alleyways, he could see both the road that led to the motor pool and the one that led out of the camp.

He climbed back up to the crest of the ridge. Beyond this point, there were semibarren fields, some overgrown with grass, some almost bare. He surveyed the peaks and ridges that ran to the horizon. Escape would be impossible in a land like this, but this mountain terrain also meant a single man could fight a small army.

By this time, Freeman had already scraped together the first elements of his plan. He knew where he would attack and how he would distract the enemy. He still needed to find and identify Petrie. Destroying the entire camp would mean nothing if Petrie survived.

And then, as if by magic, the target presented himself. A flock of men walked into view. Freeman tracked them using the scope from his rifle. He sighted the men at the front of the pack, stooges, big men with big muscles and pistols hanging from shoulder holsters.

Most of the men were thugs, but Freeman spotted a team of natural-born soldiers in their shadows. They wore fatigues, not armor, and carried M27s. Freeman counted five of them. He noted the way they ignored the men around them.

In the center of the herd walked a tall man with brown hair, brown eyes, and an angular, narrow face. He had the confident smile of a man who finds himself the center of attention. *Petrie. Not a dangerous man,* Freeman decided. *Not on his own.* Surrounded by armed friends, anyone would be dangerous.

Freeman recognized the man standing beside Petrie—a short man with blond hair and a snigger instead of a smile. The thugs belonged to Petrie, but the soldiers belonged to the other man. Freeman knew this because he knew the man. It was Franklin Nailor.

By reflex, Freeman pulled his rifle and attached the scope. He tripped the safety, becoming aware of himself only as he wrapped his finger across the trigger. He would not fire, not yet.

Freeman targeted Franklin. He trained the crosshairs a few inches ahead of Nailor's ear. The bullet in the chamber had a hollowed ballistic point filled with enough explosive gel to split an oak tree. A well-aimed shot might flip a jeep. If he hit Nailor, the only parts of the man not destroyed would be below his navel.

Tracing their path, Freeman spotted the waiting transport in the distance. Nailor's bird had landed deep in the middle of the camp, in an area protected from snipers.

Freeman ran the calculations automatically. He doubted he could shoot Nailor and escape with his life. Which mattered more to him, preserving his own life or ending Nailor's?

Freeman didn't cling to life. Fear didn't enter his calculations.

What would he accomplish by killing Nailor? That Nailor tortured and killed without remorse did not figure into Freeman's calculations. His concerns were strategic, not moral. If Nailor died, it would take the Unified Authority a long time to find another sadist of Nailor's caliber. They would find one, though. Sooner or later, they would find one.

In another five steps, they would pass behind a row of buildings, and Freeman would lose his shot.

He had come to kill Petrie. If he arranged things properly, he thought he might be able to kill Petrie and walk away with his life. Survival played a very small part in his calculations, however; success mattered more.

But Freeman admitted to himself that he wanted to kill Nailor, and allowed that desire to figure into his calculations. Nailor was a bastard. Keeping his scope trained on Nailor's head, Freeman tracked him as he moved toward the transport. The entourage turned a corner and Freeman lost his bead. Buildings blocked his view. Freeman caught one last momentary glimpse of Nailor as he strode up the ramp of his transport.

Still hidden in his blind, Freeman watched the transport rise into the air. Cradling his rifle against his body, he slipped between the rocks and the trees, hiding himself from the pilot's view as he watched the transport float into the hazy distance.

He would make his move in the early evening, under the cover of night.

CHAPTER TWENTY-SIX

Location: Pentagon, Washington, D.C.
Date: July 23, 2519

"Franklin Nailor was here."

Watson recognized the name and instinctively his pulse jumped. The specter of Nailor lurked like a ghost in his nightmares—both waking and sleeping.

He asked, "Did you shoot him?"

Freeman said, "No."

"You should have shot that bastard," said Watson.

"That's not what I came for."

"Who cares why you went. Look, Freeman, if you bent down to pick up a nickel and you saw a hundred-dollar bill, you'd grab it. Speck Petrie; Nailor's the enemy."

Freeman said, "Nailor flew here in a transport. I need to know if our satellites tracked the transport and where they first detected it."

"It had to have come in from space," said Watson. "The Unifieds have spy ships. They probably broadcasted in a few million miles out, crept up to the atmosphere, and released the transport."

"That's one possibility," said Freeman.

"Do you have another?" asked Watson.

Freeman didn't answer the question. Instead, he said, "Does Naval Intelligence have tracking data on the gunship that attacked the jail in Oregon?"

"I'm sure they do," said Watson. "That's Cardston's area; I don't have much to do with it."

Freeman said, "Have him find out where that gunship first appeared and tell him to keep a watch on the area. Traffic could pick up once I make my move."

Irritated that Freeman was giving him orders, Watson, the acting president of the Enlisted Man's Empire, asked, "Is there anything else I can do for you?"

"Ask Tasman about clone factions," said Freeman.

He'd asked the question as a sarcastic jab meant to put Freeman in his place, but the jab had gone unnoticed. Now, hating himself for acting like an office assistant, Watson switched on his pad and jotted notes. "Clone factions? Anything else?"

"Yes," said Freeman. "Once I hit Petrie, things might get hot down here. I'll make a run for my plane, but I might not make it."

"I can have Ritz send some Marines," Watson offered.

"Not yet. I don't want to draw attention until I make my move."

"I'll have him send them to Mazatlán. They'll be close by, armed and waiting for your call," said Watson.

"That will work," said Freeman.

Watson nodded to himself, and repeated his message, "They'll be ready."

Watson called Colonel Ritz. He said, "How soon can you get men to the New Olympian Territories?"

"Down to Mars? Depends how many and what you need 'em for."

Frustrated by Ritz's attitude, Watson said, "They might need to fight."

"Fight who?" asked Ritz. "Are we talking Unifieds or Martians?"

"I don't know," said Watson. Ritz was beginning to irritate him. The worst part about him was that he seemed to enjoy getting under other people's skins.

"When you say 'the Territories,' which part are we talking about? It's a big place."

"Do you have a map in front of you?"

"I do."

"Why don't you stage in Mazatlán?"

"Isn't that where Harris disappeared?"

"Yes," said Watson.

"Does this have anything to do with Harris?" asked Ritz.

"Indirectly. It has more to do with a man named Ray Freeman."

"Freeman? I know him," said Ritz.

"So how quickly can you get men down there?"

"That depends. Do you want me to send a squad, a platoon, or a division?"

"How many men are in a squad?" asked Watson.

"Twelve."

"Not enough."

"Next step up is a platoon."

"How many men is that?"

"That's three squads plus a few additional hands."

"More. You're going to need more men."

"A company? That's three platoons."

"How many men?"

"A hundred men more or less," said Ritz.

"Anything bigger?"

"I can send a battalion. That's three companies."

"Three hundred men?"

"Now see, that depends on their element. I have companies with over five hundred men."

"How soon can you get a battalion down to the Territories?" asked Watson.

"What kind of battalion are you looking for? I have battalions that specialize in everything from heavy artillery to dental hygiene. It just so happens that the Second Dental Battalion is on alert right here in Camp Lejeune as we speak. If the problem down there is gingivitis, I got the perfect battalion."

Watson felt himself losing his temper and went silent. He took a deep breath and reined himself in. Speaking in a stiff voice, he said, "I'm not interested in the dental situation of your Marines, Colonel."

Ritz said, "President, I got recon battalions, tank battalions, armor battalions, and a whole lot of infantry. What is the mission, sir? You tell me what you want us to do, and I'll tell you who I think we should send."

"Freeman is about to attack . . ."

"You have a civilian leading a Marine assault?" asked Ritz. "The Second Dental maybe . . ."

"Do you consider Freeman a civilian?" Watson asked. The notion surprised him.

Ritz stopped to consider the question. "Is he attacking a Unified Authority location?"

"New Olympian, but there are . . ."

"You know, sir, them boys in the Second Dental do have combat experience, Mr. Watson."

"Freeman says the Unifieds are guarding it."

"There must be a bunch of them if Freeman is calling for backup."

"What kind of troops would you use?" asked Watson.

"Infantry . . . maybe light armor," said Ritz, "but I'd hold some tanks and fighters in reserve."

"Tanks and fighters? Are you serious?" asked Watson.

"Mr. Watson, those bastards nearly beat us on Mars. If we're really talking about the Unified Authority, we might want a fleet of fighter carriers in ready reserve."

CHAPTER TWENTY-SEVEN

Watson entered Tasman's lab at 19:30 that evening, with three bodyguards in tow.

Acting president or not, he submitted to the voice-and-eye security procedures as well as passing through the posts for a DNA scan.

Tasman waited in his motorized wheelchair just beyond the posts, an amused grin on his wrinkled-linen face. He asked, "Do you have a problem with the posts?"

Watson said, "I'm tired. It's been a long day."

Tasman smiled all the more. "Perhaps you weren't built for running empires."

"I didn't ask for the job," said Watson.

"And yet, you have it. Interesting that a natural-born with no ambition has become the president of a synthetic empire."

Several of Tasman's assistants remained in the lab. They were scientists, but they behaved more like mathematicians, relying on computers more than microscopes.

Watson said, "Maybe we should go to your office."

"Travis, this is the most secure area in the most secure building in the Enlisted Man's Empire. What could possibly be so important that we can't discuss it here?" asked Tasman.

"It's about Freeman."

"Maybe we should go to my office," said Tasman. He led the way, steering his wheelchair with the little joy lever built into the right armrest. Tasman's chair rode on six free-axle wheels, almost like a tank running on treads. Tasman's wheelchair weighed nearly three hundred pounds.

As they moved toward the office, Tasman looked back, and said, "I've never understood why you and Harris place so much faith in Ray Freeman."

He steered through the door, waited for Watson, then sealed the door by pressing a button on the armrest of his wheelchair.

Watson said, "Hold it."

"What?"

"I'm keeping my security with me."

He said, "You're bringing bodyguards into my office for a chat? Travis, I'm flattered. A big man like you, I shouldn't think you'd need protection from an old man like me."

Knowing he should ignore the comment, Watson took the bait. He said, "They go with me wherever I go."

Then Watson changed the subject, and said, "Freeman saved your ass on Mars. You'd be dead or working for the Unifieds if he hadn't saved you."

"Ray Freeman is a wealthy man. Did you know that?" Tasman didn't leave Watson time to respond. "He's one of the wealthiest men alive. The Unified Authority paid him one billion dollars for his participation in the war against the aliens. He made millions killing Morgan Atkins's believers before the Avatari arrived."

"How do you know the Unifieds didn't take their money back when Freeman joined the clones?" asked Watson, not that he thought it mattered. He didn't care if Freeman was rich; more power to him. He would let Tasman play his mental games for another minute or two, then he would ask about factions. He had come at Freeman's direction, but he had questions of his own. He wondered if possibly there might come a day when the converted clones would return to the Enlisted Man's Empire.

Tasman said, "I looked into that. It's amazing what you can find out using Pentagon computers.

"The Unifieds haven't touched Freeman's money. He's still a billionaire, so the question remains, Why would a mercenary like Freeman risk his life fighting for clones?

"Why did he come to Mars? At first I thought that the clones had hired him, but they didn't know he was there."

Watson confessed, "I thought you hired him?"

"Me? I didn't know he existed."

Watson searched for explanations, but none came to mind. "How did he know about you?" Watson asked. "You're highly classified."

"Good question," said Tasman. "Harris and Cutter didn't

know about me. They didn't send him. Unless you know something I don't, I think we can both agree that no one but Harris and Cutter had the authority to hire him. That means that Freeman decided to go to Mars on his own."

Watson thought about it and saw the logic. *If nobody sent him, he must have gone to Mars on his own,* he agreed. "What's your point?"

"He's not in this for the money."

"Probably not," Watson conceded.

"If he's not after money, then perhaps he's doing this for sport," suggested Tasman.

Watson dismissed the idea. "Maybe it's his moral compass. Harris told me he joined the EME because they were evacuating planets that the Unifieds abandoned to the aliens. Harris used to call him a 'homicidal humanitarian.'"

"Did he go to the New Olympian Territories to save lives?" asked Tasman. He smiled as he asked this, his teeth the color of a stormy sky.

"He went to look for Harris."

"And what is he doing now?"

Watson felt cornered. Rather than lie, he changed the subject. He said, "Freeman heard something about converted clones fighting against the Unified Authority. He says that the clones who attacked Harris were reprogrammed clones who were fighting against the Unifieds."

Tasman knitted his fingers and furrowed his brow. He asked, "Wouldn't they have been working for the Unified Authority? I mean, if anything, wouldn't the Unifieds want Harris dead?"

"Freeman says they were working against the Unifieds."

"Working against the Unifieds . . . and they weren't working for us, not if they attacked Harris. Their programming would have prevented them from attacking Harris," said Tasman.

"This is an unexpected turn."

Tasman placed a bony white hand across his pale lips and stroked his cheek with fingers so gnarled that his knuckles looked like the burls of an ancient tree. "Ours could not have attempted the murder, not without tripping a death reflex."

"They weren't ours," said Watson.

"Factions within factions," Tasman whispered. "I always wondered what would happen. I don't know if this is good news, but it certainly could work out for the best."

"What?" Watson demanded.

"Neural programming is an immature science, something we developed as we went along. Apparently, our successors face similar problems.

"Whenever they've reprogrammed clones, they've left bodies behind. Do you know what that means?"

"They've triggered death reflexes," said Watson.

"Yes . . . yes. Watson, clones die when they discover they are clones. That is why we program them so carefully to avoid killing them.

"When the politicians called for new clones to replace the Liberators, they wanted extensive programming . . . sometimes the programs caused conflict. They wanted fighting machines that would never attack their makers unless their makers declared independence. They weren't meant to kill humans; they were created to attack aliens if we ever found any. By the time we finally encountered aliens, the clones had been fighting nothing but humans for decades.

"They have programming in their brains that forces them to follow orders, right? They also have programming in their brains that tells them they are natural-born. What would happen if an officer ordered a clone to acknowledge he was synthetic?"

Watson thought about this. Conundrums. He'd enjoyed playing with paradoxes as a boy. One of his favorite paradoxes had been, "If God can do anything, can he create a rock that is too big for him to lift?" Those had been juvenile mental masturbations. Now he faced a conundrum that could bring down an empire.

He looked through the office window. The aides outside working at their computers were all clones. *What if I went out and told those aides that they are clones?* Watson asked himself.

"What happens if you tell a computer to shut down and to do a mathematical equation at the same time?" asked Tasman.

"It tells you it has a program running and asks you if you still want it to shut down."

"And if you do?" asked Tasman.

"It shuts down," said Watson. "It shuts down without finishing the equation."

"Which is precisely what happens when you reprogram a clone," said Tasman.

"What are you talking about?" asked Watson.

"Those clones have hundreds of programs etched into their brains, some active, some dormant, some complementary and others conflicting. Some programs carry priority scripting that makes them able to override other programs. The way we designed their brains, their minds work just like computers.

"Think about it. What would happen if somebody tried to override the programming in a computer by introducing a random protocol? What if you told the computer, replace all programs written in a certain language with programs written in another language? You might not disable all of the programs that you wanted to disable, and the surviving programs might override the programs from the second language."

Tasman picked up a notepad and scanned over files. He mumbled, "So many programs . . . so many things that can go wrong." The man seemed energized.

"But they're clones. They're all exactly alike. Wouldn't they all have the same reaction?" Watson asked as he turned to watch the clones outside the window. To him, they looked as indistinguishable as ants.

"There is a colonel in the Marines; I believe his name is Hunter Ritz. Have you met Ritz?" asked Tasman.

"I've met him," Watson said, turning to face Tasman again. "He's the ranking officer in the Corps right now if you can believe it. Harris was negligent about promoting officers. He didn't spend time on administrative functions like promotions."

"And you worked for Admiral Cutter?"

Watson nodded. "Sure."

"How would you have described Cutter?"

"Stiff, formal, a by-the-book sort of officer."

"And Ritz? Is he a by-the-book-type Marine?"

Watson laughed. "He's like a kid who never grows up. Everything is a game to him, even war."

"What about General MacAvoy?"

"Not the brightest man I've ever met."

"Is he as smart as Cutter?"

Watson laughed. "MacAvoy? The man's a hammerhead. I've seen blocks of wood that were brighter."

"And yet he and Cutter started out with identical brains created out of the exact same DNA. They have the same programming, too," said Tasman. "We didn't create Marine clones and Navy clones. We created military clones."

"So why did MacAvoy come out like MacAvoy and Cutter come out like Cutter?" asked Watson. "That doesn't make sense." He asked the question though, in the back of his mind, he jokingly wrote MacAvoy off as a product of brain damage.

"That's what happens with low-priority programming," said Tasman. "We arranged their brains so that experience would override low-priority programming. We needed some clones to become Marines and some to become soldiers and others to become sailors, right? We needed them to think differently, to act differently, to develop different skills.

"I expected their programming to be more stable. I thought they would all have similar personalities, but their experiences began overriding the low-level scripts right from the start. Some clones showed signs of aggression by the time they were three. Some were more studious.

"If the scientists that the Unifieds have assigned to this task still have a one-size-fits-all mentality, they're going to kill more clones than they convert," said Tasman. "During the alien war, a number of clones acted out against higher-priority programs. There were acts of vandalism and insubordination. The vandalism, that's a midlevel programming problem, but it's associated with insubordination . . . they're not supposed to be able to act up under any circumstances.

"I'd need a few live specimens and a team of psychologists to pinpoint the problems. We both know I will never have an opportunity like that.

"You know, Watson, I was already retired by the time the Avatari came, but I heard about New Copenhagen. I always wondered how it was that clones came to ignore their programming. Until this moment, I never figured it out."

Watson said, "From what you are telling me, it sounds like the Unifieds have a problem on their hands."

The chilled air carried a chemical scent. Watson noticed,

but didn't bother think about it. Tasman sniffed, and muttered, "The new air conditioner." Using his arms to brace himself, he managed to stand in his wheelchair so that he could peer over Watson's shoulder. He looked, dropped back into the chair, then motored around Watson for a closer look.

The scent smelled like chemicals. *Janitors?* Watson asked himself. *Is that smell cleaning supplies?*

The clones in the office had all collapsed without a struggle. Tasman, who had programmed this reaction into their brains, had never seen it put to the test. He stared across his laboratory fascinated and terrified.

One of Watson's bodyguards, the natural-born, opened the door. He said, "We need to go."

Watson started to ask what had happened, but he knew. He saw the lab workers lying on the ground and slumped across their computers.

The bodyguard looked at Tasman, and asked, "You created their programming, is that right?"

"I did," Tasman answered, still staring at the fallen clones.

"How much information will they remember when they wake up?" asked the bodyguard. When Tasman didn't answer, he grabbed the old scientist by his collar, and repeated, "Will they remember names and addresses when they wake up?"

Tasman shrugged his shoulders, and said, "Everything."

"Will the bodyguards remember they were bodyguards?"

"Yes."

"Will they remember briefings?" the bodyguard asked, now holding a pistol in one hand.

"Yes. Yes, they will remember their names and their missions and their orders . . . everything," said Tasman. "They will remember what they were doing in this lab and what they discovered. The only thing they won't remember is the reboot itself."

Without saying a word, the bodyguard stepped out the door and fired bullets into the skulls of the two clone bodyguards.

Watson jumped as if startled from a deep sleep.

"We need to go," said the bodyguard.

"Go?" asked Watson.

"Now!" shouted the bodyguard.

"Howard, you need to come with us," said Watson.

"We're not dragging that chair," said the bodyguard. He swept the room with his pistol, looking for any sign of movement. Outside the door, the two dead bodyguards lay in bright red puddles of their own blood. The other clones would soon wake, but not the clones on Watson's security team.

The natural-born bodyguard asked, "How long before they wake up?"

"I don't know," said Tasman. "A scientist got doped last summer. He woke up five minutes later."

"We'll have to carry him," said Watson.

"That's not my job. He's not my job," said the bodyguard. "If you want to bring him, you carry him. My job is getting you out." As he said this, he knelt beside the dead bodyguards and took their guns. He handed one to Watson, who dropped it into his jacket pocket.

"You want to keep that out," said the bodyguard. "That gun won't do you any good if it gets stuck inside your pocket."

Watson pulled the pistol out and held it in his right hand.

"They'll kill me," Tasman said, looking right and left, desperation showing on his face. "You can't leave me here!"

Without saying a word, Watson bent down and flipped the old man onto his left shoulder. He was old and brittle, with balsa-wood bones and kite-string muscles. As Watson started for the door, Tasman groaned, a dry and pained sound that emanated from his core.

The bodyguard trotted ahead, his own pistol out, the other in his holster. Without looking back, he said, "Old man, if you slow us down, I will shoot you."

"You'd shoot a crippled old man?" Watson asked.

"Whatever it takes to accomplish my mission."

Tasman couldn't have weighed a full hundred pounds. Watson placed him at eighty, maybe less. At eighty pounds, Tasman was easy to lift, but he slowed Watson, and he made it clumsy to step over the bodies that covered the floor.

They left the lab and entered the hallway. Nothing had changed. The lights burned as brightly as ever. The air-conditioned air was cool and had the lingering scents of ammonia and chlorine.

The bodyguard didn't run. He stayed eight feet ahead of Watson, purposely slowing himself down to match Watson's pace. His expression remained impassive. Not looking back, he growled, "We need to hurry, sir."

Watson said, "I'll be there by the time the elevator arrives." Even as he said that, the elevator opened.

"You can't take Tasman, sir," said the bodyguard. "We don't have time."

"I'm not leaving him," said Watson as he sprang over two unconscious soldiers and stepped onto the elevator.

The doors closed.

"Do you have the car ready?" the bodyguard asked into the discreet microphone in his collar. He nodded, apparently pleased by the answer. Looking at Watson, he said, "It's going to be messy in the garage. Be ready for some blood."

Tasman, folded over Watson's shoulder like an old-fashioned mailbag, his hands and head dangling down Watson's back, labored for breath. He twitched and rolled to take the weight off his stomach. His breath rattled in his throat.

The elevator passed the lobby without stopping and went directly to the fourth floor of the underground parking lot. *How long has it been?* Watson wondered. *Have they started waking up?*

The doors to the elevator slid open revealing the bodies of the clones that Watson's natural-born bodyguards had shot—six men lying with arms and legs spread, pools of blood expanding on the marble floor beneath them. They wore military uniforms.

Seeing the blood, Watson was not unmoved, though he had seen enough blood and killing on Mars that the sight of death no longer sickened. He saw the bodies, breathed deep to steel himself, and tasted the last remnant of the chemicals in the air. Realizing that the air was almost clean, he wondered how long it would take before the clones awoke.

Beyond the clones, a long black sedan sat, its doors hanging open.

One of the bodyguards screamed, "Everybody into the car! Into the car, now!"

Tasman, still draped over Watson's shoulder, continued to fight for every breath. The bodyguards held their pistols out and ready.

"Who's the old guy?" asked one of the bodyguards.

"Scientist," said another.
"Why'd you bring him?"
"POTEME wouldn't leave him."
"Speck," said the first bodyguard.
Watson saw two clone officers sitting in a car. He said, "We need to warn them."
"We're not here for them," said a bodyguard. He growled like a dog, grabbed Tasman from Watson's shoulder, and tossed the old man into the backseat of the car.
"Hey! Hey! Don't go in the building! Chemicals in the air . . ." Watson shouted to the clones in the car as his bodyguards shoved him into the backseat.
The clone officers heard the shouting and turned to look, but they clearly hadn't understood. One of them seemed to have recognized Watson. He took three steps toward the car.
Watson asked, "Whose car is this?" as the bodyguards sat in the front seats.
"You passed him," said the driver.
"Dead?"
They were moving now, screeching around the corner, dashing up ramps.
"Sure. I killed him," said the driver. "I didn't want him reporting his missing car." He floored the gas pedal, and the car lurched forward. "Alan Cardston is going to wake up any minute now. He has the license and make of every car in your fleet. We needed a new set of wheels he doesn't know about, and we needed to make sure he didn't hear about a stolen vehicle."
"What about security cameras?" asked the natural-born bodyguard who had shepherded Watson down the elevator.
"Out of commission," said the second bodyguard.
To Watson, the escape felt more like a kidnapping than a rescue. Looking out the back window, he saw clones racing out of doors . . . and then the gunfire began. The car sped on.
A second sedan followed them. Watson looked at the driver, a natural-born, maybe an off-duty bodyguard.
"What about the gate?" asked the bodyguard in the passenger's seat.
"Don't worry about that. We got a couple of ours at the gate."
Cardston an enemy, Watson thought. An unpleasant man,

but one of the most competent officers Watson had met. Alan Cardston had once saved Watson's life. *Cardston the enemy?* The world had just turned over on its head.

Three clones appeared at the top of the ramp, more poured out of the building. They wore security bands and carried M27s. They didn't wait to fire. The last streaks of daylight still shone in the sky, a calming dim. The thick windows muffled the gunfire as bullets struck the car. Looking up between the seats, Watson watched the windshield crack into a thousand shards without shattering. He could no longer see what was in front of the car. All he could see was that the world ahead was brighter than the world he had left behind.

The car skidded, scraped, and bounced up the ramp, hitting a human and careening off another car as it dashed onto the road.

PART III

THE AGGRESSOR

CHAPTER TWENTY-EIGHT

Location: Guanajuato, New Olympian Territories
Date: July 25, 2519

Night, in the mountains in a drizzling rain. There was no wind, and the water evaporated from the air as quickly as it disappeared from the rocks.

Freeman could see stars through the gauzy clouds. He didn't bother with his goggles; in another minute, visibility wouldn't be an issue. During daylight hours, this was the side of the camp that the guards had used as a firing range.

He sat on an inaccessible spot on the ridge, about two hundred yards from the edge of the camp. If he ran straight ahead, he would fall down a sheer twenty-foot drop. If he survived the fall, he would cross bare ground, leaving him an easy target, then he would need to contend with the electrified fence.

Freeman didn't intend to enter the camp.

From the perch he had chosen, he had an unqualified view down the central lane that led from the motor pool to the dormitories. Once the action began, he would have a clear shot.

Freeman had already killed the six guards at the entrance to the camp. They were the first to die. He didn't bother with the guards by the motor pool. Their time would arrive soon enough.

After giving his gear one last pass, Freeman pulled the remote from his satchel and pressed the button.

Five hundred yards away, two rockets fired, the hoarse cough of their engines sounding soft and low. The first rocket arced over the fence and struck a jeep, knocking it over on its side, causing the gas tank to explode and sending a ten-foot pillar of smoke and flame into the air.

The second rocket, an incendiary weapon that sprayed thermite on impact, struck the fuel depot. Exposed to oxygen and aluminum filings, the thermite ignited, rapidly reaching forty-five hundred degrees, instantly melting the sides of the tank so that it leaked fuel and fumes that exploded in the heat. The flames and the reaction traveled into the fuel tank, causing a greater explosion that shot a knotting, twisting, fist-shaped fireball 150 feet in the air.

From his perch, Freeman saw the fireball rise above the buildings and dissolve. He watched the chaos below. No alarms or Klaxons sounded in the camp, just men running, grabbing guns and rocket launchers, racing toward flames. One side of the camp was bathed in quavering orange light, the other the steady white glare of halcyon.

Freeman sat and watched, a nonparticipant, a spectator witnessing a disaster of his own creation.

The big explosion set off a chain reaction. Twisted pipes and fragmented walls marked spots where the buildings closest to the motor pool had stood. Flames covered the ground and the overturned vehicles.

Petrie appeared, surrounded by bodyguards. Freeman had hoped he'd run to the motor pool, into his line of fire, but the gangster didn't cooperate. He seemed content to let the motor pool burn. He let his men run ahead and stayed behind, surrounded by his bodyguards. An army of men with guns and fire extinguishers swarmed at the edge of the fire, but Petrie did not approach it.

He'd made the mistake Freeman had angled for. Since the explosion was at the motor pool, Petrie expected Freeman to be on that side of the camp, somewhere hiding behind the flames and the devastation. Had Freeman approached from the east, from behind the motor pool, he would never have seen Petrie emerge from his dorm. But Freeman had hidden on a ridge overlooking the southwestern end of the camp. There, he only saw a glimpse of Petrie as he emerged from the dorms. As Petrie shuffled away from the motor pool, however, he moved into Freeman's sights.

Dressed like a man shaken out of his bed, letting his safari shirt hang open as he buttoned his pants, Petrie searched the street for a saboteur. His brown hair was messy, his whiskers had grown halfway to a beard. Freeman was about to shoot, but then he saw something that caused him to pause. An old jeep rolled into the camp dragging a trailer. On the trailer sat his modified Bandit, his ride.

Freeman put the plane out of his mind and fired his rifle. The bullet struck Petrie's right temple, flattened, and took the cheekbone with it as it exited on the other side of his head. The force of the bullet caused most of his skull to splinter so that everything above his grimacing upper lip splashed like thick soup against the wall.

Ray Freeman didn't bother confirming the kill. He threw his pack over his back and carried the rifle in his right hand. Without looking back, he trotted up the ridge.

The question was not "if"; it was "when."

They would come for him. Petrie's army would come first. When they failed, Nailor's soldiers would follow. Petrie's men would come on foot, the attack on the motor pool had seen to that. They would hike up roads and walk blindly into caves because they were gangsters, not soldiers, and they knew nothing about mountain warfare and insurgency tactics. Mountain warfare favored small units that moved quickly and used concealment. In the mountains, snipers could take out entire platoons, and grenadiers could cancel companies . . . as long as the fighting stayed on the ground.

Petrie's men didn't worry Freeman. They would come with guns and rockets, unable to defend themselves. Freeman would hit them from far ridges and withdraw, attack and withdraw. He would hit them from the higher ground, and when he did not have the high-ground advantage, he would wait. Unprepared and undisciplined, the gangsters would fire blindly when they should duck. They were unused to dealing with snipers.

Freeman wanted to call in the Marines in Mazatlán. For the third time since he'd pulled the trigger on Petrie, he tried to reach Watson. When no one answered, he knew he would need to dig in for the long haul.

It was late at night. Wearing his goggles, Freeman could see clearly.

The mountains in the near west were taller and partially overgrown with scattered trees, tall grass, and cactus. He'd be able to hide from Petrie's men on those ridges. Jungles would offer better cover and cities more protection, but a man could hide indefinitely in the mountains, depending on his foe. When the Unifieds arrived, they'd come with gunships. They would scan the mountains for heat signatures and search the caves with metal detectors.

Freeman covered ground as quickly as he could. He ran down one slope, entering the elbow between two steep rises. The moon showed above him. A few wisps of cloud floated in the sky. For Freeman, this was familiar territory—running from a larger force while preparing to kill their scouts. He'd introduced Watson to these tactics on Mars.

He wanted to stop and try the call again, but he knew no one would answer. Where was Watson?

He came to a steep climb and turned west, tracing the slope upward, farther into the mountains. He entered a dry patch with no trees or grass, just a few cactuses.

Freeman saw the bird before he heard it. Too large to be a star, too bright to be the moon, a searchlight stabbed through the darkness. The gunship floated through the darkness as smoothly as a train crossing a track. Freeman saw it and knew things had gone from bad to worse.

Not wanting to be caught in the open, he sprinted to the nearest ridge and hoped he'd find a cave.

CHAPTER TWENTY-NINE

Location: Mazatlán, New Olympian Territories
Date: July 27, 2519

I knew who I was and where I was and what I was doing there. What I didn't know was how I had gotten there, but I had a good notion about who had brought me and what condition I had been in when I arrived.

The doctor said, "We prolonged your coma to help you recover more quickly."

I asked, "Didn't it also make me easier to guard?"

The doctor was a young man, not even in his thirties. But he had an old man's face, wrinkles, pale skin, and all. He was skinny, too. In short, he was a New Olympian who had not entirely recovered from his time on Mars.

He gave me a good-humored smile, and said, "I kept you unconscious to help you heal. If your girlfriend had ulterior motives, you'll need to take that up with her."

I sat up on the bed. The movement made my head spin. I looked down at my right arm and saw twin tubes running into it.

"Blood?" I asked.

The doctor stood. He said, "No, no, no. Not blood. That's saline. We needed it to keep you hydrated.

"The air is dry here, and you weren't in a position to drink for yourself."

I squeezed my right hand into a fist, felt the needles dig into veins, and liked the feeling. "Am I a prisoner?" I asked.

The doctor laughed, and said, "Oh, Lord no. You can walk out of here right now if you can stand without fainting."

"You think I'll faint?" I asked. I pulled the sheet off my legs and swung my feet over the edge of the bed. My temples throbbed, and I felt bile rising up in my throat. Whether or not I fainted, I would puke if I tried to stand—and then I might fall.

"You might want to disconnect those tubes from your arm before you stand up. You'll save yourself a few stitches," the doctor said, the humor showing in his face. "If you prefer, I can find you a wheelchair."

"I can just walk out?" I asked.

"You will get farther if you wheel yourself out."

That calmed me down. I asked, "How long have I been here?"

"Should I send for your wheelchair?"

I put up my hands in surrender, and said, "I can be reasonable."

The doctor said, "Eleven days. Do you remember what happened?"

I looked down at my gut. The doctor must have dressed me recently, the bandages around my waist were gleaming white and perfect. "I was shot," I said.

Finding humor where only a doctor might, he said, "Your feet needed more stitches than the gunshot wound. Next time you step out of the shower, I suggest you keep an eye out for broken glass."

I prodded the area where I had been shot, and asked, "In the stomach?"

"Well below the stomach. The bullet went through your smaller intestines, but it wasn't the bullet that would have killed you. No, you almost died from an infection.

"We've cleaned the wounds, fixed up the damage, strained the bacteria from your blood, and pretty much set you right. Considering you almost died, I'd say you're pretty healthy."

I didn't feel very healthy. I felt weak and dizzy. When I told the doctor how I felt, he said, "That, my friend, has more to do with the cure than the disease. We got the bacteria out of your system, but there's still a lot of medicine in your blood.

"Like I said before, if you want to leave, be sure to take a wheelchair."

Feeling like I had no alternative, I lowered myself back onto my pillow and fell asleep.

* * *

The building might even have been a hospital eons ago. It was very old, with stucco walls and heavy arches. I suspected it once had something to do with treating patients, a hospital, maybe an asylum, maybe a rehab center. The walls were white and bare. The windows overlooked an overgrown garden and a backdrop of taller buildings. The floor was white.

I wasn't in a room; it was more like a ward, a long and loaf-shaped room with a rounded ceiling and a floor the size of a basketball court.

I seemed to be the only patient but not the only person. There were guards outside my room. They didn't have guns, not that I could see. They didn't enter my room; they waited outside by the door. I got the feeling they had come to protect me. The only time I got a good look at them was between shifts, when new men would arrive.

They weren't clones, and they didn't dress like soldiers.

The day after I woke up, Brandon Pugh came to visit me. I knew him, but not well. Had it not been for him, I would have died in my hotel room, but I suspected he was the one who let the clone commandos in to kill me.

I played dumb. I asked, "Are you the person I should thank for this?"

He smiled. He had small eyes and a prominent jaw. He was heavy and strong, and tall . . . easily six feet and five inches. He said, "I arranged for the facilities, but you had better thank Kasara for bringing you here. I think she would have attacked those clones if you didn't kill them first."

"Where is Kasara?" I asked.

"She's safe."

"Where am I?"

"You're safe, too," he said.

"What about the summit?" I asked.

Pugh picked up a chair and moved it beside my bed. He said, "It didn't happen."

"Because of this?" I said, looking at my surroundings.

"Assassinations make people nervous," Pugh explained.

"They also draw attention," I said. "This place should be lousy with EME Marines."

Before answering me, Pugh paused to think about what he should say. He finally said, "The local police are looking for you. They've searched the beaches and the camp. Mazatlán is a big, empty city. Hiding one guy in a big, empty city doesn't take brains or effort. You find an empty building in an empty neighborhood, and there you are.

"The best-kept secrets are the ones that nobody knows. When nobody knows, nobody blabs."

I asked, "What about the doctor?"

"On permanent call until you leave. You may have noticed how eager he is to discharge you. He doesn't go home until you walk out."

"He has a family, doesn't he?" I asked.

"I suspect he does."

"And they haven't reported him missing?"

"As far as they know, he died. That's what the police reported. Poor man was beaten to death on the beach."

"By three Marines," I guessed.

"As a matter of fact. His family is in for a happy surprise."

"So who died?"

"Doesn't matter," said Pugh. "One of mine. He ran into an accident the day you disappeared."

"No one came looking for me?" I sat up. The drugs had mostly worn off. I still felt weak—eleven days in a coma wreaks havoc on your muscles and equilibrium. Blood still rushed to my head when I sat up, but I didn't feel sick this time.

Pugh watched. He didn't reach out to steady me though concern showed in his eyes. For him, I was an investment. "Two people came looking for you. They met with the police, had a brief look around town, and decided the police had it under control. That's what they told the police.

"One of them left. The other one beat one of my guys to death. You know that stiff they found on the beach? One of your pals did that."

"Ray Freeman," I said.

"Yeah. Big guy . . . not especially pleasant."

"Where is he?" I asked.

"Now that is an interesting question," said Pugh. "Freeman found me his first night here. He stole into camp and identified me as a man in the know."

I interrupted him. "But he only killed one of your men?"

"One dead, one still recovering."

"You got off light," I said. "Did you tell him about Kasara?" I asked, not caring much either way.

"He figured that out on his own. Smart guy." Pugh paused again. He no longer smiled. Now he fidgeted and looked uncomfortable.

"You had a deal with the clones who came to kill me," I said. "I bet Ray figured that out."

"Something like that," he admitted. "My guys got them to the hotel. I let them into your room."

"Was Kasara in on it?" I asked.

"No, sir. No, sir, not that girl. I had her convinced they were your guys right up until she heard the shower door shatter. She tried to run in when she heard the gunshot. Then you were down and they were dead and she was screaming at me to help you."

"And you changed sides," I said.

"Yeah . . . maybe. I guess I changed sides; maybe, it depends on whether or not you're willing to work with me." He didn't meet my gaze as he said that. He stared down at the floor.

"Let's see . . . you made a pact to get me killed. You stashed me in a hospital and kidnapped a doctor to take care of me. You lied to the police so you could hide me. I'm going to go out on a limb and guess that you're a criminal."

"A businessman," said Pugh.

"Girls, guns, and gambling?" I asked. "Are those your enterprises of choice?"

Pugh said nothing.

"Where is Freeman?" I asked.

"Interesting story," said Pugh.

"Where is he?" I swung my legs from the bed. A little push, and I would be standing. I had no doubt that I had the strength to stand. I also had enough strength to fight, assuming I was fighting a child or maybe a newborn kitten. For the first time since I woke up, I felt the stirrings of a combat reflex. The will was there, but so was the atrophy in my muscles.

Pugh said, "He went to run an errand for me."

"Who did you want him to kill?"

"A criminal, a man not unlike myself."

"Only more powerful than you . . . you wanted him to kill the competition," I said. I wanted to say that Freeman wouldn't do that, that he didn't get involved in domestic disputes. He would, though. He'd made a fortune dabbling in the Unified Authority's disputes.

By this time I was standing. I hadn't exactly sprung to my feet, but I was up.

"You and I have a mutual enemy, Harris, a guy named Ryan Petrie," Pugh said, sounding scared and defensive. "He made a pact with the Unifieds. That was why I gave you to the clones; I was looking for an ally."

I didn't care about Pugh's selling me out; I had already dealt with it. *So I was his price,* I thought. *Freeman accepted a job as a favor for me.*

"He left a couple of days ago. We haven't seen him since."

CHAPTER THIRTY

Pugh might not have been forthright when I asked about Freeman, but he rose to the occasion when I asked about getting home. He had a couple of lackeys drive me out to the airport at the edge of town, where I found 460 Marines and six transports.

My Marines had built a twenty-foot fence surrounding the airfield. Six Marines in combat armor met our sedan as we approached the gate. They pointed M27s at our windows and told us to get out.

As I climbed out of the car, I looked through the fence and saw three Jackals—particularly agile jeeps with armored turrets and stealth technology for confusing radars and missiles. The Marines manning those turrets had their guns trained on us. Something had happened while I was away.

One of the guards pointed his M27 at the guy next to me, and asked, "What business do you have here?"

I asked, "What's your name and rank, Marine?"

He answered out of reflex. "Shek, Arthur, Corporal, sir." The "sir" didn't necessarily mean that he recognized me.

I said, "Corporal Arthur Shek . . . good to meet you. Who is in charge of this operation?"

He said, "Colonel Ritz."

"Colonel Ritz," I said. Ritz and I were old friends. I promoted him to colonel. "Okay, Corporal Shek, why don't you place a call to Colonel Ritz and tell him that Lieutenant General Wayson Harris is here to see him."

Shek was wearing armor, Marine armor; that meant he had an interLink connection. The interLink was a local communications network that connected Marines in combat armor. As the man in charge, Ritz wouldn't only have an interLink connection, he'd have a commandLink that would enable him to look through his men's visors and listen in on their conversation.

Now that I had identified myself, I had no doubt that Ritz was watching me at that very moment.

Shek said, "Colonel Ritz would like to speak with you."

"That's convenient. I would like to speak with him," I said.

"Sir, you are cleared. He wants the car to return to town immediately."

"You okay with that?" I asked my driver.

The men shrugged and climbed back in their car. Without a handshake or a good-bye, they drove off without me.

It was a warm day and a particularly bright one. My mouth was dry. Four of the sentries fell in around me as I passed through the gate. I stopped to watch the car back up. It rumbled onto the road and sped away.

Until Ritz or another senior officer cleared me, these clones wouldn't see me as a superior officer. At this point, I was simply an intruder.

They all wore the dark green camouflaged armor of the Marines. The armor was very light, a full suit weighing about ten pounds. It wasn't bulletproof or shrapnel-proof, but I couldn't punch through it. It offered that much protection. Its chief virtue was that it was light, and it didn't slow your movement. Heat waves rose up on the runway ahead of us, making it look like a puddle had settled on the tarmac, but that wasn't possible. Six transports sat on the runway.

I had a low-grade headache. A week and a half had passed since I had last stood out in the sun. I didn't have sunglasses, and the glare hurt my eyes. As I said before, my mouth was dry.

Five more Marines came to join us, four of them wearing complete armor, helmet and all. The fifth had removed his helmet. His face should have been identical to that of any of any other clone, but I recognized him. I always recognized my friends.

Stopping about fifteen feet from me, he said, "I just received orders to shoot you on sight."

This was Lieutenant Colonel Hunter Ritz. If he'd been meaning to shoot me, he would have done it already. He generally shot first and didn't bother with the questions.

"Who issued those orders?" I asked.

"They came from the top," he said.

"What are the charges?" I asked.

Ritz considered the question. He said, "Orders don't generally come with explanations, sir."

"So you have orders to shoot me on sight, but no charges?" I asked. "Are they from Cutter?" I asked.

"Admiral Cutter? He's not exactly issuing orders these days. These orders came from the Pentagon."

"The Pentagon is a big place," I said. "Anyone in particular?"

"Come to think of it, I didn't see any names. Maybe I should ask about that when I head back. I have a meeting there tomorrow morning."

We stood there a moment longer, Ritz sizing me up, four armed and armored men standing behind him, four more surrounding me. He said, "I came here looking for Ray Freeman. Do you know where he is?"

"He came here looking for me, and you came here looking for him," I said. "And now you have orders to shoot me. I don't suppose you have orders to shoot him as well?"

"Nope."

I said, "That's 'No, sir.'"

Ritz's crooked smile started on one corner of his mouth and worked its way to the other. He said, "General Harris, sir, it's a specking pleasure to have you back. We have a lot to talk about."

Then he turned to his posse, and said, "That will be all." Then he added, "Get this man some armor, some bullets, and some MREs. He looks like he could use a bad meal."

According to Ritz, the acting commandant of the Marines, the world had changed in my absence. Never realizing that the promotion would place him in line to command the Corps, I had promoted Ritz to lieutenant colonel. He was smart and resourceful, a good leader in battle, but he didn't have a reverent bone in his body.

If I'd been thinking, I would have made him a general a long time ago. Hell, I should have given him all three of my stars.

We sat alone in the kettle of a transport—the cargo area. Transports were winged warehouses with badly clipped wings at that. They had a cathedral-like cargo hold called a kettle—"kettle" because it was all metal except for the wooden bench that ran along its outer walls. The kettle had no windows and no comforts, just harnesses for standing passengers, a wooden bench, and a head so small that men in combat armor could not use it.

I sat on the bench. Ritz stood.

Like the old-fashioned teakettles from which these holds took their name, they were dark as a cave on the inside. It was broad daylight outside. There were plenty of lights in the cockpit. In the kettle, there were red lights for night operations but no white lights.

The rear hatch was open. A blade of light shone on the gray metal wall.

I said, "Freeman is supposed to be here, somewhere. He came looking for me."

"Yeah, I came down here looking for him. Last I heard, he was going to kick some anthill filled with Martian gangsters, then the Unifieds showed up." Ritz used more derisive names than any other Marine I ever knew. He referred to the New Olympians as "Martians." Other Marines referred to reprogrammed Marines as "converts." He called them "Repromen."

"Did Admiral Cutter send him?" I asked.

"General, sir, a lot has happened over the last two weeks."

"What kinds of things?" I asked.

"Classified things," said Ritz.

"Such as?"

Ritz looked around the kettle as if checking for eavesdroppers. There were none, of course. He stared down the deck and out the hatch. "Cutter is dead. He was assassinated the same day they hit you.

"And they didn't stop with you and Cutter. They attacked the Pentagon and some prison called Sheridan."

I'd heard of Sheridan and knew who'd been held there. A sinking feeling in my gut, I asked, "Who's running the empire?"

"Travis Watson. He's temporary. Once Hauser and MacAvoy see that you're still around, I bet Watson's back to playing secretary."

"Watson running the clone empire," I said. "We live in an age of wonders."

Watson running the Enlisted Man's Empire, I thought. I liked the sound of it.

"He's an interim leader, I assume," I said.

Ritz nodded.

"Isn't Tom Hauser next in line?" I asked.

"Actually, General MacAvoy was next in line. He didn't want it."

"What about Hauser?" I asked.

"Same."

"With me out of the way, weren't you . . ."

"You don't really consider me a good candidate to rule the world?

"Watson was MacAvoy's idea. He wanted a political figurehead, somebody more acceptable for the natural-borns. Now that you're back, I guess you're king. That ought to give the natural-borns a boner."

"Thanks," I said. I had always ducked when people talked about *playing king*. I didn't like commanding troops, and I really dislike politics, especially politics involving civilians. I said, "I think I prefer the standing arrangement."

Ritz said, "It may not be standing much longer."

I was about to ask about the attack on the Pentagon, but his last comment placed that on hold. "What do you mean?" I asked.

"Watson is missing."

"Missing?" I asked. "Missing like I was missing?"

"That remains to be seen. He could be dead, he could be in hiding, or maybe he just needs a new phone," said Ritz. "I can't reach him."

"But he called a summit?" I asked.

"Yeah. Cardston called us in, but he said it was Watson's idea."

"Alan Cardston? Last time I checked, he was still a major." Okay, when it came to chain of command, the Enlisted Man's Empire was no more predictable than a well-shuffled deck of cards. The ranks were filled by clones who'd been programmed to take orders, not give them. Some clones rose to the challenge, most fell far short of the mark.

"It's Watson's show," said Ritz. "Cardston is just sending out the invitations."

"So Cardston is in communication with Watson?" I asked.

"That's what he says."

"Have you asked him to put you through to Watson?" I asked.

"I have. He says Watson isn't available."

"Has he said why?"

Ritz shook his head. He said, "I've tried calling Watson on his private line, too. No one answers."

"That summit has a bad smell about it," I said.

I thought about calling Emily Hughes, Watson's financée. If he was in trouble, she'd know about it. Then again, maybe she wouldn't. What if someone called Sunny to ask about me? I hoped that they didn't call Sunny. What a speck-up that would be.

I said, "I don't suppose you can reach Hauser from here."

"No, sir," said Ritz.

I hadn't thought he would have that ability. Transports sometimes came equipped for planetwide communications—if the signal could tap into a satellite network, that is.

Back in the day, the Unified Authority had three fleets in every arm of the galaxy—some of them a full hundred thousand light-years away. The Unifieds also had a working broadcast system that enabled instantaneous communications and travel. Using the network, I could communicate with officers on the other side of the Milky Way as easily as I could speak to people in the room next to me.

Now, all our ships patrolled between Earth and Mars, few of them ever straying farther than eighty million miles from home, but communications moved at the speed of a game of chess. It took several minutes for messages to cross the chasm from Earth to Mars. I would speak my piece, wait five to ten minutes, then the person on the other end would hear it and answer, and his answer would take five to ten minutes to reach me.

Watson missing, Freeman lost somewhere in the Territories, Cardston calling a summit on behalf of the missing president, a prison escape at Sheridan, and Cutter murdered . . . I realized that I had left an important piece out of the mix: Three clones had tried to kill me.

"So we can't reach Hauser, but we can sure as speck chat with MacAvoy," I said.

"I've called him," said Ritz.

That was Ritz, a competent officer who didn't care whether or not people credited him for his competence. He was glad to be an officer, but he hadn't kissed any asses to arrange the promotion.

"What does he think about all of this?"

"He thinks the summit is a trap, but he says the only way to expose the trap is to step into it. You know MacAvoy—doesn't bust his hump looking for alternatives."

I'd seen the way MacAvoy ran his troops. He didn't bust his hump looking for alternatives in battle, either. He was a "run 'em up their asses" type of officer whose columns marched straight and true.

MacAvoy was stationed at Fort Benning, our largest operational Army base, a site that would certainly have the equipment we needed to reach Admiral Hauser.

I wanted to find Freeman, but that would need to wait. The first thing on my agenda was holding a summit of my own.

CHAPTER THIRTY-ONE

Location: Guanajuato, New Olympian Territories
Date: July 27, 2519

The men tracking Freeman had sealed their own fate when they brought the dogs.

Twelve men with five dogs had followed Freeman into the valley. They hiked slowly, methodically, the dogs smelling for clues, the men looking for footprints. Watching them through the scope of his rifle, Freeman decided they were better trackers than hunters.

The Unifieds had sent a gunship as well, and that was the problem. Freeman could pick off the tracking team easily enough, but then the gunship would come. At this point, the Unifieds weren't sure which route Freeman had taken. They'd sent ground teams across three different ridges; who knew how far and wide the gunship had searched.

Once Freeman shot the dogs and their handlers, the Unifieds would know his route. Shooting the dogs would buy him a little time, but it was a fool's trade. That gunship would follow him like a cat shadowing a mouse.

There would be caves in the bare rock ledges ahead, though, places in which a man could hide from gunships. Even killing the dogs and escaping the gunship might not be enough. Given another two days, water would become a problem. Freeman could go days without food. He might get lucky and catch a snake, a rat, or a rabbit. If he found the right cave, he could build a fire and cook any dogs the Unifieds sent in after him. He'd wind up killing the dogs either way, it seemed a shame to waste their meat on coyotes.

The late-afternoon sun hung low and bright. The air was warm and thin. Freeman found himself breathing heavily, taking in mouthfuls of air instead of breathing through his nose. He knelt on the rocky soil, hiding behind thin brush.

He sensed something and lowered his rifle. A scorpion scuttled across the ground, its pincers up and its tail curled. Not knowing if the creature was posturing or ready to attack, he pulled his knife from his knee scabbard and slashed it in half with a motion so smooth that the scorpion reacted only in death, its tail lashing at empty air.

Guessing how long he had before nightfall, Freeman thought maybe four hours. Four hours to find a cave and hide. If he located it quickly, he'd have time enough to strike. He was two miles ahead of the hunting party. He could hit them from this distance, but he'd waste a lot of shots. He'd hit the first target, that would be the gimme. After that, one in three shots at best.

They wouldn't spot him from this distance, though. He was well out of the range of their heat vision. The sun was behind him, shining down on them. He didn't need to worry about light reflecting off the lens of his scope.

He watched the hounds loping and pulling, straining against the electronic leashes that kept them within a one-hundred-foot orbit of their handlers. The handlers should have trusted them more. Even if they gave the dogs free rein, they could have summoned them back using the impulses in their collars.

Freeman could see that the dogs had picked up his scent. He had walked and slept on rock shelves when possible and had left few footprints and no trash behind. The dogs still found him.

Freeman carried his rifle strapped to his back. He stood, chose a path that would leave minimal prints and evidence, and continued along the ridge. In two hours, he would reach the rock wall and hunt for caves.

He had to be careful. Freeman was no naturalist, but he'd had some training. He knew that bats lived in caves, a dangerous situation. He knew about coyotes and that some snakes slept in caves during the day to avoid the heated ground.

He climbed higher, finding it harder and harder to breathe as he went. The men in the hunting party would have the same problem. The dogs might, too, but they'd be too excited to notice.

Freeman hated dogs. He admired their ability to track, but he'd always preferred robot trackers.

A rock slid from under Freeman's foot. He started to fall but caught himself, twisting his ankle in the process. For a moment, just a moment, he thought he'd dodged a bullet, then he felt the familiar ache around the top of his foot. The sprain didn't hurt, but the ankle would seize during the night.

The cliffs hadn't moved, but now they were farther just the same. He glanced back down the ridge, but without his scope, he couldn't find the party. Freeman moved on.

He smelled the air as he breathed it, searching for smoke and fumes. He listened for the wind to carry sounds, the thud of helicopter rotors, the rumble of gunfire, even the shriek of a hawk. Two miles back, the dogs probably yapped and whined, but he couldn't hear them.

He pushed ahead, less mobile now. He stepped on the twisted right foot, placed weight on it, testing the joint. It wasn't a sharp pain yet, but soon the foot would swell. He stepped quickly, shifting his weight to his left foot, leaving a blurred footprint in his wake. Knowing he no longer had the ability to cover his tracks, he moved on.

The sun slipped lower in the sky. To the east, hidden by the mountains, the sky had turned red. Darkness would follow.

Freeman had goggles that let him see in the dark. Night would favor Freeman.

Two more hours passed before he reached the stone wall that rose out of the ridge. The ground was rocky here, and lifeless. There were no plants, not even brush.

The side of the peak was rough and covered with indentations but no caves. Freeman moved on, stepping with his left foot, planting his right and rolling over it, aware that his breathing had become labored. His ankle hurt. When he stood, he placed his weight on his left foot and balanced with the ball of his right.

Somewhere below him, hidden by the mountain, the hunting party would stop for the night. Freeman wondered if they had found his footprints. If so, he hoped they didn't report them. He didn't know how he could deal with that gunship.

He needed to find a place to hide. Peering through the scope on his rifle, he counted the heads in the hunting party.

Twelve men. Five dogs. He might be able pick them off as they climbed the next steep ridge, but then the gunship would follow. *How fast?* he wondered. *How fast could it get here?*

Freeman found a five-foot-deep alcove in the side of the wall. He crawled into it and unslung his backpack. He fumbled through until he found his water bottle, and then he took three deep pulls from the water in slow succession. He drank, held the water in his mouth until his throat absorbed it, then took another, and, finally, a third.

He would not remove his boot that night. If he did, he would not be able to put it on again in the morning.

CHAPTER THIRTY-TWO

Location: Fort Benning, Georgia
Date: July 28, 2519

The dynamics of meetings with clones. When the topic of General Pernell MacAvoy arose in conversation, Admiral Thomas Hauser often rolled his eyes, and asked, "Why did they stuff his head with sawdust instead of brains?"

MacAvoy considered Admiral Hauser a coward and a snob. Speaking of the admiral, MacAvoy told me, "I have buck privates who have seen more combat than that bastard."

Ritz, by the way, agreed with both of them. He considered MacAvoy an idiot and Hauser a "glorified civilian."

On this occasion, though, both MacAvoy and Ritz smiled as they watched Hauser in action.

It was an informal meeting, organized by Hauser, who was still on the *Churchill*. MacAvoy participated from his office in Fort Benning. I sat in the office as well, hiding just out of the range of the camera. I had a little screen that let me watch the meeting, but I attended as a fly on a wall.

Ritz, who took the call from the cockpit of a transport, routed his signal through the Pentagon. His transport sat in a Fort Benning hangar. If Cardston traced Ritz's signal, he'd have no trouble locating the point of origin. That couldn't be helped. The Major Alan Cardston I'd known in the past would have traced that signal. He was a thorough officer who left little to chance.

I didn't want to believe that the Unified Authority could have gotten to Cardston, but it appeared that they had. Hauser took the lead, speaking as smoothly and confidently as a caller at a carnival midway. "Oh, Major, I was trying to reach President Watson, are you fielding his calls now?"

Sitting at his desk in the security office, Cardston looked unchanged. He acted as he normally would, stiff and bureaucratic. "We're still on alert, Admiral."

General MacAvoy wanted to join the conversation. He cleared his throat and shifted in his seat. This was liar's poker, though. He wasn't fit to play. His "ram it up their ass" style made him a lousy liar.

Hauser kept the ball. He said, "I can't make the summit tomorrow, that's why I called this confab."

Cardston asked, "You're too busy to meet with the president?"

"You mean the acting president," said Hauser, not missing a beat. "You will recall that Perry was next in line, and I'm in line after him, then Colonel Ritz . . ." He paused, turned to Ritz and asked, "Are you really just a colonel? How the hell did a colonel make third in line?"

Ritz said, "Yeah, Harris should have made me a two-star."

"A colonel in charge. What a *clusterspeck*! I'll have to fix that," said Hauser.

"You gonna bust him down?" asked MacAvoy. "Maybe you should make him a private, that's about as far as he would get in this man's Army."

"Get specked," said Ritz.

"Watch it, Ritz; you're speaking to a superior officer," warned MacAvoy. Both of them were playing. Neither one of them had much in the way of respect for the other, but they knew how to work together.

Listening to Hauser throw his weight around, I had to stop myself from laughing. He played his role so brilliantly that

Cardston only offered token resistance. He asked, "How can you be too busy to come to the summit? What's more important than the future of the empire?"

Hauser asked, "Major, are you having problems with your equipment? How about you, MacAvoy? Do you read me?"

"Loud and clear, Admiral."

"So the summit is off?" asked Ritz.

"There's no need to cancel it, let's just relocate that damn thing," said Hauser, who seldom swore. He was trying to talk like the old natural-born admirals who ran the Navy in the days before the Enlisted Men declared independence, and was doing a pretty good job. "We can still hold a summit; we'll just hold it on the *Churchill* instead."

"Sounds good to me," said Ritz.

"I'm in," said MacAvoy.

"Wait," said Cardston. "You just said you don't have time for a summit, now you're saying you do have time?"

"I have time for a meeting; I don't have time to fly to Earth," said Hauser. "I just checked the orbital charts; I'd be flying five hours each way. I'd spend more time en route than attending the meeting. Tell you what. I'll send my personal shuttle to collect you three . . . by three, I mean Watson, MacAvoy, and Ritz. No offense, Major, but you're in way over your pay grade."

"I doubt President Watson has ten hours to spare," said Cardston.

"You may be right," said Hauser. "Why don't you patch me through, and I'll ask him."

"He's not available at the moment," said Cardston.

"Is he using the head or something?" asked Ritz. Someone had to ask that question. It did not surprise me that Ritz asked first.

"He's in meetings," said Cardston.

"Major, I am the highest-ranking officer in the Enlisted Man's Navy. You see these other men on the screen, the one in olive drab with the crew cut is the highest-ranking officer in the Enlisted Man's Army. Now, you see that young guy with the nonregulation haircut, the one in the tan-colored shirt; he is the highest-ranking officer in the Enlisted Man's

Marines. Who in the hell could that civilian appointee be speaking with that is more important than the three of us?"

Cardston looked troubled. His eyes leaped to each of the men on the screen as he said, "I am sorry, sir. President Watson is not available."

"I see," said Hauser. "If he is too busy to get on the horn with us today, is there any reason we should not expect him to make an appearance at the summit?"

Remaining entirely calm, Cardston attempted to change the subject. He asked, "Will Harris be at the summit?"

Ritz's smile faded ever so slightly. For a moment, I was afraid he would play it dumb and try to slip the momentary lapse past Cardston, the Enlisted Man's Empire's most effective interrogator. I could see the hawk in the major's glare, as his eyes narrowed while the rest of his face remained impassive. He didn't stare at any one officer; he watched all three of them.

Ritz, sticking as close to the truth as possible, said, "Freeman said something about locating Harris. That's why I came down here. Now I can't find Freeman."

Hauser played the peacemaker. He said, "Major, all three of us have tried to reach Watson. We're becoming concerned."

"Well, I have spoken to him, and he wants to know if you've found Harris," Cardston said, making no effort to hide the suspicion in his voice.

"No such luck," Ritz repeated.

"What about Freeman. How do I reach him?" asked Cardston.

"Freeman? He's that mercenary, right?" asked MacAvoy. "Why are we talking about a mercenary?"

"Because he is in the New Olympian Territories, and he might have found General Harris," said Cardston.

"Let me get this straight. Harris is missing in the Territories, and Freeman is missing in the Territories. It's starting to sound like the New Olympian Territories are dangerous. Maybe we should invade them," said MacAvoy.

"An invasion seems so extreme," said Hauser.

"How about a benevolent occupation?" asked MacAvoy.

"What would that accomplish?" asked Cardston, responding precisely as Hauser had predicted he would.

Flinging his words as precisely a knife thrower tosses daggers, Hauser said, "Major, that is a topic for the president and his senior-most officers to discuss. I see no point explaining myself to a junior officer."

For the first time, the anger showed in Cardston's eyes. He winced. He glared. He somehow managed to hold his tongue, but hate seethed in his expression.

Pretending not to notice, Hauser said, "Well, unless any of the rest of you object, perhaps we should take up this discussion again tomorrow . . . at the summit on my ship."

CHAPTER THIRTY-THREE

"You don't really think Watson is coming to your summit tomorrow?" asked MacAvoy.

"Sure he will," said Ritz. "I bet he rides out to Mars on Genghis Khan's horse with good old 'Honest Abe' Lincoln holding the reins."

MacAvoy, Ritz, and I now sat in the same office, facing a screen on which Thomas Hauser appeared. He was the officer in charge. He had control. Technically, MacAvoy and I outranked him, but I had long since learned my place as a Marine, and MacAvoy was a simple soldier. We had an unspoken agreement among us that the Navy would run the show.

Hauser was a good man for the job, smart and crafty, and he listened to what the rest of us had to say. He said, "I'll send a shuttle to Bolling tonight . . . just in case; but I'm sending Marines in combat armor to guard it."

"Good idea," said Ritz. "I'll have a full company guarding the spaceport."

"Do you think they got to him?" asked MacAvoy. "Do you think they got to Cardston?"

"Obviously," said Hauser.

They all turned to me for some reason, so I nodded and said, "Looks like it. The question is, did they get to all of them?"

"All of who?" asked MacAvoy.

"Everyone in the Pentagon," said Hauser.

"How could they have gotten everyone in the Pentagon? It's not like they gassed the building," said MacAvoy. Seeing Hauser's expression on the screen, he turned to me, and asked, "How the speck could they do that?"

Hauser said, "I don't know, but that seems to be exactly what they did."

I said, "It all fits together pretty neatly, doesn't it. The only two natural-borns I knew in that building were Watson and Tasman. Now I can't reach either of them.

"Travis Watson, the acting president of the Empire, is missing, and no one in the Pentagon seems to have raised an eyebrow."

"We'll need to circumvent standard channels for the time being," said Hauser. "We can keep Cardston pretty much out of the loop if we run all intelligence operations from my ships. Do any of you have a problem with that?"

"Good with me," I said.

"Intelligence doesn't matter to me," said MacAvoy. I took this comment in stride, but Ritz and Hauser couldn't keep from laughing.

"What if he produces Watson?" I asked.

"Can they reprogram Watson?" asked MacAvoy.

"He's a natural-born," said Hauser. "Natural-born brains don't have programming."

"That doesn't mean shit, and you know it," said MacAvoy. "They could still control him. He's got a fiancée, right? I heard he was engaged. They could catch her and blackmail him. I like Watson, but he doesn't strike me as the kind of guy who puts up a fight."

"And what about Tasman?" asked Hauser.

"He's a scrappy old geezer," I said. "He'll break before he bends."

"Who the hell is Tasman?" asked MacAvoy.

MacAvoy hadn't been on Mars during the fighting, and, as he said, "intelligence didn't matter to him." The dumb speck had probably skipped out or slept through every briefing he'd ever attended.

"He's a scientist," said Hauser. "He was the U.A. genius who invented clone programming. He's working for us now."

"If he's still alive," I said.

Now that he was no longer the commandant of the Marines, Ritz remained silent as a church mouse through most of our meeting, but hearing the name Tasman, he flew into a rage. He said, "There is no way in speck that that old specker is still alive. That old boy is so dry, I bet he shits dust!"

Ignoring Ritz, Hauser asked, "So what do you suggest?" The question was directed at me. He didn't care what Ritz or MacAvoy had in mind.

I said, "First things first—we need to contain the Pentagon. We need to know if anyone in the building is still on our side. We need to know who's friends with Cardston and who's still with us."

"I can do that," said MacAvoy. "Shut down the Pentagon, hooah! Just thinking about is giving me a woody."

"Don't get too erect, General," I warned. "However they gassed Cardston, you know they're going to try to get you the same way."

"I hope they do," he said. "I like it when my targets come to me."

"We need somebody to find Watson," I said.

"Since I'll be in the neighborhood, I got that, too," said MacAvoy. He added, "Harris, I've been looking for an excuse to run some combat scenarios around Capitol Hill."

"What about me?" asked Ritz.

"You and I have a friend to find in the New Olympian Territories."

CHAPTER THIRTY-FOUR

Location: Guanajuato, New Olympian Territories
Date: July 29, 2519

The boot kept Freeman's ankle from swelling out of control, but it didn't fix the sprain. Placing weight on the foot sent a shock up his leg. Freeman ignored the throbbing altogether, but the stab that ran through him when he placed weight on the foot was another story.

He anchored his mind on the present, not allowing himself to analyze the past or worry about the future. He listened to the rhythm of his breathing, slowed it, and let it carry him as he huddled in a blind, surrounded by rocks, high up on a cliff. He breathed slowly, rhythmically, taking the thin air deep into his gut. His stomach rose and collapsed with each breath. He breathed in through his nostrils, held the air for five seconds, and exhaled through his mouth. He drew in a breath and spooled it in his lungs as he selected his first target, aimed his rifle, and tightened his finger across the trigger.

Twelve men and five dogs, slightly more than a mile away. He had planned to shoot the dogs first. Now, as he examined the posse, he changed his priorities. Two of the men wore combat armor. If they were reprogrammed clones, the armor wouldn't matter, but if they were natural-borns, their armor would be shielded. Once the shields went up, Freeman's bullets wouldn't hurt them.

He had to shoot the Marines first, hit them fast before they got their armor up, then shoot the dogs and the others.

Breathe in . . . feel the oxygen spreading through your body, the air brings strength, serenity, peace, he told himself. In Freeman's twisted Zen, murder and meditation were sometimes one.

Freeman pointed his rifle first without using the scope, then fine-tuned his aim with the scope. The men in the armor stayed toward the back of the pack, away from the dogs. He targeted one, the reticle of his scope resting in the middle of the man's head.

He inhaled, felt the air cooling his insides, held the breath for five seconds, and exhaled. His breathing was even and regular and calm as waves rolling in to shore.

At 09:00, the day was already bright and warm.

Freeman's foot and ankle throbbed, but pain became a distant sensation . . . a fire on a faraway island. He could see the smoke. He knew it was there, but it was far away and he was at peace and the air washed in and out of his lungs like waves on a gentle sea.

Freeman didn't care if the man he was targeting was kind or evil. Freeman didn't wonder if the man had children or if his parents were yet alive. He didn't let sympathy about wives or pets or burial arrangements enter his mind as he first centered the reticle on the man's combat helmet, then slightly forward and high to compensate for distance and wind. The scope had circuits designed specifically to calculate wind, temperature, and distance, but Freeman trusted his instincts more than the circuits.

Working almost of its own volition, his finger pulled back on the trigger.

He fired the first shot, switched to the next target, then fired again. He was a mile away; his bullets would strike a moment before the sound of the gunfire caught up to them.

The men in the armor had no idea that death had come for them. They stood at the back of the pack chatting happily, letting the dogs and the men around them worry about Freeman.

The first bullet struck, hitting the man in the face, shattering his visor, the flattened slug dragging splinters of glass and filament behind it as it smashed into the front of his skull, passed through his brain, and exploded through the back of his head. The second Marine didn't realize what had happened for an instant. Had he listened carefully during that instant, he would have heard the rumble of the report from Freeman's rifle, but he wouldn't have had time to digest what he'd heard before Freeman's second bullet struck the side of his head.

The pack reacted, scattering like billiard balls after a break.

Still breathing slowly, his mind calmly in the present, his brain still in a Zen-like meditative state, Freeman went after the dogs. The hunters had kept them on electronic leashes, magnetic connections that allowed the animals to run freely around trees and rocks so long as they stayed within range.

With the electronic leashes restricting them, the dogs could not stray more than one hundred feet from their handlers. They darted quickly, springing unpredictably in every direction, but their leashes limited and confused them.

Freeman "dispatched them with extreme prejudice." In his mind, the dogs were threats, not living creatures.

Once he was sure that the dogs were neutralized, he went after their handlers. A man threw the controls for an electronic leash aside and tried to dash down the path. Freeman fired, hitting him in the back, his bullet shoving the corpse like a wave washing a wreck in to shore.

Freeman didn't waste time watching to see if his targets stayed dead. He didn't care. They were no different than the dogs; wounded or dead, they no longer posed a threat.

One of the men crouched behind a rock holding a pistol in one hand and touching the pointer finger of the other against the communications device clipped to his ear. Freeman shot him. The bullet cut a crease across the top of the man's shaved head, leaving a gouge and burned skin. He dived into a shallow dent in the ground. Thinking no more clearly than a scared rabbit with nowhere to run, he'd left a good hiding place for a bad one. Freeman killed him with his second shot.

Two men tried to run to safety. Freeman hit both, then paused to reload. He dropped the clip from his rifle and replaced it with a preloaded spare. He hadn't reloaded to continue the ambush, however. He could have hit some. Instead, he watched as posse survivors ran down the ridge. Now, having dissolved the hunting party, he slung the rifle over his shoulder and limped toward his sanctuary, his cave.

Far away, at the foot of the mountain, a U.A. gunship slid through the air.

The gunship no longer worried Freeman. He'd found the opening to a large mineshaft that would take him deep into the mountain. Once he entered the shaft, the gunship would no longer matter.

Freeman had surveyed the mineshaft during the night. The path he chose would take him through unstable caverns laced by timbers so old and dry they crumbled at his touch. If the Unifieds sealed the entrance behind him, he would find alternate tunnels, air vents, and caved-in areas through which he could escape. They could send an entire battalion to hunt him if they liked. One man or a thousand, it wouldn't matter, not in that old mineshaft. In there, a grenade or bomb would kill a thousand men as likely as one.

CHAPTER THIRTY-FIVE

Location: Washington, D.C.
Date: July 30, 2519

The transports flew in before dawn.

Having been left to his own devices, General Pernell "Perry" MacAvoy decided to deal with the search and the Pentagon "the Army way." He flew in the 3rd Corps, complete with its armor, cavalry, and two infantry divisions.

At 05:00, one thousand transports and dozens of larger, cargo-hauling aircraft appeared in the skies over Washington, D.C. The transports landed in metro-area spaceports, parking lots, military installations, civilian shopping malls, with a few stragglers touching down in public parks.

Forty landed on the expansive ground-level parking areas surrounding the Pentagon. MacAvoy waited in the first transport, watching as his officers deployed men and equipment under the steel-colored skies of dawn.

Each transport had room for one hundred men, or ten

jeeps, or some combination. Twenty of MacAvoy's transports carried infantry—men, rifles, and the occasional jeep. Ten of his transports carried heavy armor—two tanks and two crews. Five of his transports carried cavalry. MacAvoy preferred jeeps to Jackals. They were slower and not as well armored, but MacAvoy believed that men in jeeps remained alert while men in Jackals enjoyed the ride.

"General, I have an incoming message," said the pilot.

"Put it on the squawk," said MacAvoy. He leaned back in the copilot's chair, pulled a cigar from his pocket, and lit it. He said, "MacAvoy here."

"General, this is Major Alan Cardston from Pentagon Security."

"Yes, Major. We spoke yesterday," MacAvoy said.

"General, what exactly are you doing, sir?" asked Cardston. His face remained calm, but he raised his voice. "Why exactly have you landed an invasion force outside the Pentagon?"

MacAvoy pulled the cigar from his mouth. He blew out a long stream of smoke that formed into curling ribbons in the air around him. He waved the cigar in the air and admired the glowing orange ember of its tip. "Major," he said, "I am declaring martial law in this burg. As of this moment, Washington, D.C. is officially under Army control."

Cardston looked like he might have a heart attack. He said, "Martial law! Martial law! General, how the speck can you declare martial law? This is the Pentagon . . . we're the military!"

"You know, son, I don't see it that way," said MacAvoy. "The way I see it, you've changed sides. Now if you were to produce President Watson, I'd be willing to listen to his side of the story."

"General, as the head of Pentagon Security—" said Cardston.

"See now, you're not listening, son. Last I heard, you were only a major. Did someone give you a promotion last night?"

"No, sir."

"That right? So you're still just a major in a building filled with colonels and generals and an acting president. I don't know why I always end up chatting with you, Major. The head of building security . . ." He laughed. "Next time, they'll give me the head of the Janitorial Squad."

"General, my duties extend to EME Intelligence. I am . . .

MacAvoy interrupted him. He asked, "Does the Pentagon use civilian janitors?"

"Look, sir, I'll come out, and we can discuss this . . ."

"Oh, I wouldn't do that," said MacAvoy. "I have sharpshooters trained on every door of that building, son. They won't care if you come out carrying a white flag, a nuclear bomb, or a bowl of wonton soup; anyone leaving that building will be shot. Even if my sharpshooters miss you, my tanks sure as shit won't. They have orders to clean up anything that gets past my sharpshooters, Major. Step out that door, and they'll juice you into a puddle of blood."

"General, you're making a colossal mistake. Have you spoken to Admiral . . ."

MacAvoy interrupted him again. "See now, son, they probably don't talk about these things in security school, but in infantry terms, this here is what we call a 'siege.' You might want to learn that term. A siege is where we surround your building and cut off your food and support."

"Unless we surrender," said Cardston.

"Damn it, son! What the speck happened to your esprit de corps? You're supposed to be a soldier. Haven't you ever heard of holding out to the last man? You don't just give up and surrender; you don't ever surrender, and you sure as elephant speck don't surrender before we make our demands.

"What did you do after basic training, son? Did you specialize in butterfly catching or bird watching?"

By midafternoon, MacAvoy had surrounded the Pentagon with twenty-five hundred soldiers, thirty tanks, and forty jeeps, a daring move. More than seventeen thousand trained soldiers, sailors, and Marines worked in the building. Assuming the Unifieds had converted every man in the building, he was outnumbered but not outgunned. Only security personnel carried arms in the building.

MacAvoy had three additional battalions in the vicinity. If he needed support, he would have it in ten minutes. He also had another entire corps on deck. When the shooting started,

MacAvoy could call in forty thousand additional troops; their equipment had already been loaded onto transports.

Sitting in a mobile nerve center, the general watched with satisfaction the way his men scrambled into position. "That's some erection they got going on," he mumbled as he watched men in BDUs set up gun nests, barricades, and a command post. They erected security stops at the entrances of every road leading into the parking lots.

A few hundred yards away, a team of soldiers sealed the ramps that led into the underground parking structure. They stretched razor wire across the ground, aimed laser barriers across the ramps, and assembled bulletproof barricades in which guards could sit. The men worked quickly.

At the top of the food chain, their main guns aimed at the Pentagon, two Schwarzkopf tanks oversaw the operation.

MacAvoy wanted the Schwarzkopfs front and center; they were the key. Minted at the very end of the war, Schwarzkopfs were the finest tanks ever built. Designed for optimal performance at speeds of up to one hundred miles per hour, they had superb antiaircraft capabilities and hardened armor that was impervious to missiles, mines, and radiation. With their powerful engines and oxygen-regeneration systems, they could plow through water twenty feet deep. They could even hide underwater.

When they see those Schwarzkopfs, MacAvoy thought, *they'll know that I came to win.*

God bless the man who invented those specking tanks, MacAvoy thought with warm, generous satisfaction. *I hope he wasn't an asshole.* With disappointment, MacAvoy realized that he must have been working for the Unified Authority and decided he probably was.

A captain appeared on one of the communications consoles. He said, "General, sir, there are converts forming an unauthorized congregation inside the west entrance."

"Damn straight it's unauthorized, son. I told them specifically to keep their arms, legs, and asses inside the bus," said MacAvoy.

"Yes, sir."

"West entrance, you say?" asked MacAvoy.

"Yes, sir."

"What's the matter with you, boy? There's a screen right in front of you. Punch in the code and let's have a look."

The screen showed the lobby and the west entrance. As MacAvoy watched, the camera zoomed in, showing men wearing bulletproof vests and helmets, carrying shields and M27s. Men from every branch—they wore blue, green, tan, and white uniforms under black protective vests. All of the men were clones.

"General MacAvoy, sir, it appears that they want to challenge your quarantine order, sir," said a colonel as he stepped into the picture on the screen.

Unlike Marines, who wore visors with cameras and interLink signals, only MacAvoy's radiomen carried mikes and cameras. Many of his officers acted like mediaLink reporters, posing in front of cameras so that their faces would appear in the action. At the moment, the camera was on the colonel and not on the lobby. He asked, "Do you want me to send them a warning?"

"We already warned them," said MacAvoy. "Any more warning would be a waste of breath."

Another monitor winked to life, this one showing a ramp to the underground parking area. "Sir, there are cars coming up the ramp," said the colonel in command of the area. His radioman had his camera pointed down the ramp. MacAvoy didn't see any cars, but he heard tires squealing.

Whenever he led his men into combat situations, MacAvoy carried a lit cigar. He'd once swore that he'd keep a cigar lit until his last man returned to base. It was a rash vow and not always convenient to keep. He'd been involved in the siege of Safe Harbor, a twelve-week battle in which his fingers went numb and his lungs turned black.

MacAvoy still preferred to wade into battle with a cigar in his mouth, but since Safe Harbor, he'd smoked for pleasure, not to make a point. He took a long drag from his cigar, and said, "Boys, it appears that they want to test our resolve."

The colonel at the south entrance asked, "Permission to engage?"

MacAvoy laughed, and said, "Son, the engagement began the moment we landed on their parking lot."

The colonel said, "Yes, sir. Do I have permission to fire at them?"

MacAvoy said, "Hell yes. This is a military engagement, son. That's how we engage folks in the Army; we shoot at them."

Hoping that his entire command staff was listening, he said, "Now hear this! This is General Pernell MacAvoy. I have given the enemy strict instructions to remain in the building. You have my complete and unquestioned permission to dispatch any and every clone, dog, and civilian that sticks his, her, or its head, arms, or ass out a specking door. I want their mudholes muddied and their pieholes on pikes.

"Are there any questions?"

MacAvoy's men knew better than to respond.

Unaware that he was on a live mike, the colonel in charge of the underground parking area said, "Damn, I love it when he talks dirty."

"General, where are you going?" asked one of the staff officers as MacAvoy climbed out of his chair.

The general turned and smiled, but surprise showed in his eyes. He said, "The shooting's about to start. You don't honestly think I'm going to sit this dance out. We're about to send these converts back to their maker."

"To God?" asked a particularly brown-nosing major.

"They're clones, son. God never had anything to do with them."

He put on his cover, grabbed an M27, and trotted out of the transport. With the cigar hanging from his mouth, he held his weapon in his left hand and pressed down his hat with his right. Most of his twenty-man staff followed in a line behind him, though a few stayed back to keep the nerve center alive.

They jogged down the metal ramp and onto the asphalt. It was still early morning, with only a few traces of sunlight breaking up the eastern sky. Cars with lit headlights buzzed along on distant roadways. Traffic would slow as the cars reached town; MacAvoy's 3rd Corps had the city in lockdown.

Old, but still in fighting shape, MacAvoy cantered across the parking lot to the west entrance into the Pentagon. Surrounded by acres and acres of asphalt, the squat black building looked like the silhouette of a giant mesa against the morning sky.

Streetlamps lit up small patches of parking lot. Jeeps buzzed back and forth, their headlights no more significant than fireflies from a distance. MacAvoy watched men scurrying into position.

Inside the Pentagon lobby, lights blazed, revealing the men and furnishings normally hidden behind the walls of heavily tinted glass. As he approached his troops, MacAvoy slowed to a walk. He ambled behind the barricade, breathing in Washington's languid morning air.

Fifty soldiers guarded this position, with a few hundred more manning positions nearby. The general mood was tense, ready for a fight. One of MacAvoy's staff officers handed him a pair of binoculars. He took them without a word and surveyed the lobby.

The lights in the lobby were bright but muted by the black glass exterior of the building. From this distance, the men inside the building looked small and indistinct.

"General, are you sure you want to be here?" asked the captain in charge of the company.

"Here?" he asked. "Do you mean the Pentagon or the front line of the fighting?"

"On the front line?" asked the captain.

"Hell yes, son," said MacAvoy. "This is precisely where I want to be." He pulled out his cigar, examined it, and placed it back in his mouth.

Ten minutes passed before the shooting started. The entrance doors slid open, then men rushed out of the building.

The sharpshooters went to work. The crack of sniper rifles echoed across the parking lot. Single shots rang out, shattering the morning silence. It was a symphony of kettledrums played a single note at a time.

Ten men ran out of the doorway. Not one of them reached the sidewalk. The first clone darted out like an Olympic sprinter. A heartbeat later, he toppled backward as if his feet were slipping on ice. He fell on his ass, and his feet were the last part of his body to hit the ground.

He'd been wearing a bulletproof helmet, but MacAvoy's snipers fired bullets made specifically for penetrating body armor. A hardened pin in the bullet's tip penetrated armor plating, and a dab of explosive jelly detonated behind the pin.

"More bullets than brains," muttered MacAvoy.

One of MacAvoy's officers heard this, and added, "That last boy doesn't have any brains at all. Not anymore."

Reports came in about other escape attempts around the building. When a car had come careening up one of the underground parking ramps, one of the Schwarzkopfs fired, sending the smoldering wreckage skittering back down the ramp in a cloud of sparks and concrete.

MacAvoy tossed his old cigar away and pulled another from his pocket. He turned to one of his aides, and barked, "You, get Cardston on the horn."

"Yes, sir, General, sir. Sir, you won't have a visual . . ."

"I don't need a damned video feed, son. I already know what he looks like. He's a clone. He's five-ten, has brown hair and brown eyes, sound familiar?"

"Yes, sir." A moment later the man passed MacAvoy a handheld.

MacAvoy asked, "This Cardston? You figured out the term 'siege' yet?"

Sounding as if he was speaking through gritted teeth, Cardston said, "Yes, General, I understand the term 'siege.'"

"Glad to hear it, son. So why don't you stop wasting our bullets and keep your damn men in the coop?"

"General, what do you hope to accomplish with this attack?" Cardston asked, sounding surly and annoyed.

"You know, Major, anything I might want is above your pay grade. Now, I would be willing to discuss my commands with Watson if he's around."

"I'm sorry, General. President Watson is not in the building."

"He's not likely to enter the building as things stand now, is he? Tell me where to find Watson, and maybe we can do business."

Cardston let out a long, exasperated sigh. He said, "I'm not sure where he is at this time."

MacAvoy laughed, and said, "Things are looking up, Major. I believe you this time."

Contradictory orders.

The soldiers of 3rd Corps had two objectives—"Locate Watson" and "Business as usual for civilians."

The first objective included instructions to "search government buildings, businesses, and residences as necessary." The second directed soldiers to "avoid direct interaction with civilians if at all possible."

It wouldn't be possible, and MacAvoy knew it.

Reporters and bystanders gathered around the Pentagon parking lot to watch the confrontation. MacAvoy and his soldiers neither ignored nor acknowledged the observers; they simply went about their business.

Around the capital, jeeps and troop carriers traveled the streets. Soldiers wearing disc-shaped gas masks set up security stops outside government buildings and transit centers. They didn't stop pedestrians or civilians in cars, not yet, but they left the option open.

On behalf of Harris and Hauser, MacAvoy contacted every military base in the empire to inform the commanders that the Pentagon was officially off-line. Until further notice, all directives would come from the EMN *Churchill*.

CHAPTER THIRTY-SIX

Location: Mazatlán, New Olympian Territories
Date: July 30, 2519

Around the city, things changed on a daily basis. When I had first arrived in the New Olympian Territories, the only building that had power and running water was the hotel in which we planned to hold the summit. Now the city had a working waste-disposal system, streetlamps, and traffic lights. The only thing those traffic lights ever stopped were the trucks used by the engineers who installed them and the occasional police car, but that would change soon enough. The camp to the north of town sat mostly abandoned.

I returned with the "First of the First," the First Battalion First Marines, seventeen hundred barbed-wire-chewing, bullet-spitting seasoned infantrymen. You could fight a world war with these sons of bitches and they wouldn't quibble. The New Unified Authority had trapped and reprogrammed their brothers, and these boys wanted a little "specking revenge."

"What exactly is that Marine doing?" I asked Ritz as we prepared to load the troops into their transports. Ritz walked over to have a look. Seeing Ritz, the man jumped to his feet and saluted. The man had been using his combat knife to whittle his bullets.

Ritz, freshly promoted to the rank of two-star general, spoke to the master gunnery sergeant. They traded a few words, then the master gunnery sergeant saluted, and Ritz responded. He said, "He's carving nipples into the points of his bullets."

"Nipples?" I asked.

"Yes, sir."

"Did he explain why?" I asked.

"He says he 'wants to give them something to chew on,' sir."

Nipples, I thought, then I remembered another man's doing something similar, carving a horizontal line and a . . . Penises.

"Are they all that sick?" I asked.

"Sick, sir?" Ritz asked, feigning a naïveté he'd probably lost by the time he turned five.

The local police drove out in force to greet us, twelve jeeps forming a wall of cars along the landing strip. A tall, white-haired man led the way, followed by policemen in civilian garb. I suppose they didn't yet have uniforms. They'd barely moved into the city. *City first, then uniforms, then paychecks,* I told myself.

The white-haired police chief counted the stars on my collar before extending his hand. Apparently he knew something about ranks, pay grades, and chains of command. He said, "Three stars. Does that make you General Harris?"

I said, "The stars don't make the man."

"But you are Harris?" he asked.

"I am."

He shook my hand, and said, "You gave us quite a scare a few weeks ago. I'm Mark Story. I'm the chief of police in these parts."

I said, "Good to meet you," then I introduced Ritz. They knew each other. Apparently Story had come out to visit Ritz before I turned up.

Story looked past me, and said, "That's a pretty big army you have in there, General. Are you expecting trouble?"

I had come with twenty-seven transports, some artillery, and a lot of men. I looked back out of reflex, then pretended to take a mental inventory of my forces. I said, "I ran into difficulties the last time I visited."

Story nodded, and said, "Yes, sir, General, I know exactly what you mean. I expected you to be dead after I saw your hotel room. What exactly happened in there?"

I didn't have anything against Story, but I didn't have time for him. He could only get in the way of my current operation. I had come to see Brandon Pugh. Pugh and Story knew each other, of course, but they probably weren't friends.

I chatted with Story, but I kept my answers terse. "What happened in the hotel room? Not sure."

"Why would my Marines attack me? Good question."

"Why did I have so many men with me? Marines, too much is never enough."

Story eventually cottoned on and excused himself. He left, then the mission began.

We'd have no problem finding Pugh. I knew where to find him. He'd made sure of that before he delivered me to Ritz. I could have sent Ritz or some of my men to fetch him, but I hoped to run into someone else along with the gangster. I did bring Ritz with me.

Along with a full battalion of Marines, I'd returned to Mazatlán equipped with jeeps, Jackals, and gear. Now we put some of the Jackals to use.

In my opinion, Jackals were little more than jeeps with a face-lift. They had turrets on the back for combat, a little extra plating, and souped-up engines that more than made up for the extra weight, but those were the superficial modifications. Jackals had stealth gear that did a moderately decent job of blocking radar. They also packed enough communications equipment to serve as a command center, but they were meant for combat.

Story and his police would have us under surveillance.

That was fine. We sent out a convoy of ten cars that reached downtown Mazatlán and scattered in ten separate directions.

Even if the police had tracked us with satellite surveillance, they wouldn't have known which Jackal was on an errand and which ones ran interference.

Two Jackals went to the north edge of the city, and they didn't stop there. One continued north along the coast, and the other headed inland. Several units drove circuits in the center of town. One went to the beach, another went off road in the wilds just east of town.

Ritz and I were in one of three cars that entered a southern peninsula. The others split away, but we continued on, crossing the bridge that spanned the harbor, then entering a mountainous island that rose like a knuckle out of the sea. We followed a winding road that took us to the top of the mountain, and there we found a lighthouse.

The lighthouse was primordial, a relic from days when men and goods traveled on water-bound ships because commerce relied on the ocean. When men first turned their attention to the stars, terms like "ship" and "shipping" lost their nautical origins. Now, neither the Unified Authority Navy nor the Enlisted Man's Navy maintained oceangoing vessels.

The lighthouse was a stubby, three-story missile at the top of the island. It wasn't the sleek spike I had expected, and not entirely round, either, but a nearly round structure made up of narrow, flat facets. Decagonal.

I climbed out of my Jackal and looked back toward town. The view stretched from the harbor to the north end of town. I saw so many hues of blue, tan, and white that I felt like I was staring into a kaleidoscope. The air was clear and hot and dry. Sand and rock pulsed with heat while the open waters sparkled like stained glass.

A pelican glided overhead. With its beak out and its wings spread, it created a jagged profile like a piece from a puzzle or maybe a shard of glass. The big bird dipped and glided toward the rocks along the base of the mountain, where a disorganized flock of seagulls mingled.

A few long weeks ago, I had jogged along that shore. Had I appreciated the sights at that time?

Time and the salt in the air had left their mark on the walls of the lighthouse. Pockets of cement had crumbled. A word about General Hunter Ritz—he was not the kind of man who appreciates nature. He climbed out of the jackal, removed his sunglasses, and asked, "Do you think they have snipers in that tower?"

"It's a lighthouse," I said.

"Yeah, right, a lighthouse. Should I be worried about snipers?"

"I doubt they have rifles. They might have a guy with a slingshot."

"You must be specking joking, Harris. You said this guy was a big-time gang leader."

"Was," I said. "He had something going on Olympia Kri, then we evacuated the planet. Now he's trying to rebuild his organization."

Ritz nodded and smiled. He nurtured some snide remark in the back of his head but kept it to himself.

He said, "Cardston mentioned something about a girl."

"Did he say that before or after they converted him?" I asked.

He laughed, and said, "Of all the officers I've ever known, I can't believe Alan Cardston is a Reproman." He shook his head, and added, "I believe we spoke before they *reprocessed* him. I guess that means there was a girl."

"There was a girl," I agreed.

Pugh and his men came out from behind the lighthouse, still fifty or sixty yards away. Kasara stood with them.

Ritz asked, "Which one is Pugh?"

"Third to the left."

He looked at Kasara, and said, "Cardston said that the girl was his niece."

Pugh and his five thugs led the way. Kasara walked a few paces behind them. They wore suits and swung their arms like apes as they walked. They were big men who wanted to tread like dinosaurs.

"I met her when I was fresh out of boot," I said. That wasn't exactly true; I'd been out a couple of years and had already been promoted to sergeant.

"What about your girlfriend?" Ritz asked. He didn't know Sunny, but I'd told him about her.

"Good question," I said. "She doesn't hear about anything that happens here."

"Unfaithful bastard," he muttered. He said the words under his breath because Pugh and his friends were now close enough to hear us. From him, the term came with a tone of admiration.

Pugh's jacket flapped in the wind. He could have tucked a gun in the back of his waistband, but he had probably come unarmed. In the real world, people don't like to tuck guns into their waistbands where they are hard to reach and the barrel digs into your ass.

Pugh stopped three yards ahead of us, his friends forming a wedge behind him. He stood silent for a moment.

Kasara didn't stop. She walked around Pugh and his formation and hugged me.

As she approached, I saw surprise in Hunter Ritz's eyes. I don't know if he had ever actually seen Sunny, but word gets around, and Sunny Ferris was a beauty. Ritz had met Ava, the former Hollywood goddess I'd dated in another lifetime . . . my one true love.

Kasara had been pretty back when I first met her, which was back in 2510 . . . nine years earlier. She'd had silky blond hair and the last traces of baby fat still in her cheeks. She'd been athletic back then, swimming like an otter in the ocean and jogging for exercise.

Over the last nine years, she'd married and divorced, seen her planet conquered then incinerated by aliens, and spent a year as a refugee in an overcrowded spaceport on Mars. Kasara's body was the right length for her sundress, but it rode on her bony shoulders as if she were a wire hanger. Wind blew the loose fabric of her dress as if it were a flag. Her eyes and mouth looked slightly large for her face.

She was still pretty by New Olympian standards. With few exceptions, these people had starved and suffered. Pugh still had some excess poundage. So did a few of his boys.

As Kasara wrapped her arms around my neck, the bones in her wrist and forearm pressed softly into my skin. She whispered, "I'm glad to see you."

Pushing gently through the cascade of dress around her, I

found her waist and placed my hand on it. My fingers touched pelvis and hollow and rib. I said, "You look beautiful."

She laughed, hugged me tighter for just a moment, then stepped back. She knew she was an unattractive shade of her former self. Her smile might have been in gratitude for my lie, or it might have been simply because she was glad to see me. She said, "Harris, you're so full of shit."

Then she turned to Ritz, and she said, "Is he like this on base, too?"

"Like what, ma'am?" asked Ritz.

Skinny as she was, with her long, bony arms and skeletal body, Kasara must have looked like a cross between a human woman and a preying mantis to Ritz. And yet . . . and yet she still had an air of mischief about her. Given a few months of good food and walks on the beach, life would return to Kasara. She'd never again be the shallow, attention-loving nymph she'd been; you can't erase experience—at least you can't erase them from the minds of natural-borns.

When I first met her, she'd been a cocktail waitress sharing an apartment and saving her dimes for an annual vacation on Earth. When she came to Earth, she squeezed life out of every minute of her time, swimming, sunning, dancing, drinking, and doing whatever she pleased. One-night stands had pleased. She was "scrub," that was what Marines called party girls. Most girls got mad when they found out that was what we thought of them; Kasara wore the moniker with pride.

She asked Ritz, "Does he tell you things you want to hear? Has he ever told you 'nice shot' when you missed the target?"

Neither easily intimidated nor easily impressed, Ritz said, "I wouldn't allow myself to miss the target in front of the general, ma'am, not unless I had a surgeon handy."

"To remove your gun from your ass?" she asked.

His punch line stolen, Ritz said, "Something like that."

Pugh interrupted our friendly conclave. He cleared his throat to attract our attention, and said, "I noticed you brought half the Enlisted Man's Marines with you."

I said, "The smaller half. The other half comes with tanks and missile launchers."

"Is there a reason you have so many men?" he asked. He maintained his distance, about ten feet from me. It occurred to me that a ten-foot clearing was more than enough space for a sniper, even a bad one, to hit his target without taking collateral damage.

"I may need them," I said. "I'm going after Freeman."

The chill in the air suddenly vanished. He must have thought I wanted revenge for the scene at the hotel. Now that he knew my plans, he shook my hand and introduced himself to Ritz. He said, "Ritz? I heard you were a colonel."

Ritz said, "I was."

Pugh said, "Good thing you got your name on your uniform. I couldn't tell you from anyone else without it."

Kasara froze when she heard that. As a former cocktail waitress, she knew what to say and what not to say around clones. Most people did. One of Pugh's thugs sprang over to him and whispered in his ear, no doubt informing him that he had broken the cardinal rule of dealing with military clones—don't tell them that they're clones.

I didn't worry, though. Ritz wouldn't take the comment seriously. He'd been programmed to disregard such comments, and his lackadaisical nature insulated him beyond his programming.

Apparently anxious to change the subject, Pugh asked, "Have you heard from Freeman?"

Freeman scared him; I could see it in his expression and I could hear it in his voice. Pugh was a big man, but Freeman was bigger. Neither man would likely give an inch, but if there had been trouble, Freeman would have emerged on top. A man like Pugh would remember that. He might have cut a deal with Freeman, but the scar would always remain.

I shook my head.

"We're in the same boat," said Pugh. "I expect he'd call you before coming to me. You're the one with the tanks and the missile launchers."

"Last he heard, I was in a coma," I said.

"Now look at you," said Kasara. "It's like nothing ever happened."

She was wrong though I tried to hide it. I was weak and stiff, and I didn't stand like a Marine with my back straight and my head high. I had started playing with sit-ups and calisthenics, but I wasn't ready for weights or running.

"Maybe we should go inside," Pugh said. "No need to pose for prying eyes."

"So is this yours?" I asked, as we walked toward the lighthouse.

"Men in my line of work don't move into the lone house on the hill," said Pugh. "I need to live someplace comfortable and inconspicuous. This isn't it."

"But you can't beat the view," said Kasara.

The inside of the lighthouse was empty except for shadows. As this was not his living space, Pugh hadn't bothered furnishing it.

Whenever he thought no one would catch him, Ritz stole glances at Kasara. Whether he found her pretty or hideous, she clearly fascinated him.

"There's not much I can tell you about Freeman," said Pugh. "I'll show you where we sent him and who he was up against, but I don't think that's what got him in trouble."

Ritz said, "I heard he went into the mountains to kill a guy named Petrie. Is that right? He's like you, right, a Martian thug?"

Kasara, who moved away from us as we started talking business, giggled when Ritz called her scary gangster uncle a "Martian thug."

Pugh glared at her, then he turned his glare on Ritz.

Pugh stood more than half a foot taller than Ritz and outweighed him by a hundred pounds. He had a small army of goons at his command. Depending on which rackets he controlled on Olympus Kri, Pugh had undoubtedly been involved in killings. Hell, he'd sent Freeman out to kill someone and let three clones into my hotel room to kill me. That much I knew.

He didn't scare Ritz, though, not in the slightest. If anything, he seemed to irritate Ritz, and Ritz generously made sure he shared in the pleasure.

Pugh thought for a moment, swallowed down his anger, and said, "Ryan Petrie ran the largest criminal organization on the third most populated planet in the Unified Authority. He had operations on other planets as well. Think of him as a *Martian thug* if you like, General Ritz. By all means, think of him as a *Martian thug*. I'm anxious to see where it gets you.

"Maybe Freeman thought of him as a *Martian thug* as well."

I said, "Doesn't matter if he's a gangster or the patron saint of warlords. He wouldn't—he couldn't—have survived a visit from Freeman without organized help."

"Ah, well, on that we agree." That was when Pugh told me everything . . . including things that Freeman didn't know. Petrie had run the docks on Mars. His men ate and worked while everyone else sat and festered.

The Unifieds had allied themselves with the biggest thug, I thought. They would have supplied him with weapons and bodies when he needed them.

Ritz said, "He's still just a local thug."

"He doesn't scare me, either, but the Unifieds do," I said. "If they think they've got a shot at Freeman, this is going to be an all-out war."

CHAPTER THIRTY-SEVEN

Location: Guanajuato, New Olympian Territories
Date: July 30, 2519

When he shined a light instead of using the night-for-day vision in his goggles, the walls of the mine were mostly tan and yellow, approximately the same the color of sawdust. Little clusters of crystals sparkled from the rock. Rough-hewn, with rounded ceilings, a thin skin of dirt and dust on the ground, stairs carved out of the same rock that formed the walls, shafts that dropped straight down to unseen depths, and darkness—seeing his surroundings, Freeman knew that fear would paralyze him if he let his thoughts wander, so he tightened his grip on his thoughts.

Some parts of the mine looked a thousand years old, crumbling knee-high offshoots that Freeman couldn't possibly have entered even if he stripped off his clothes and slathered himself with grease. Some of the newer tributaries looked wide enough and strong enough to accommodate a tank.

The main hub of the mine was as wide and as tall as a gymnasium, with walls that shot twenty feet straight up. In one corner, shrouded in dust and cobwebs, sat an abandoned office, its door hanging open, its picture-window walls so covered in dust that they were the same color as the ground below them. A skein of cables and wires ran from the top of the office and disappeared into a pipe that had been driven into the ceiling.

Freeman harbored no doubts that men had died here, maybe even hundreds of them. He suspected that a thousand workers had watched their minds erode as they spent day after day trapped in the darkness and claustrophobia. He would not allow himself to become the mine's latest victim.

Not far from the office, Freeman found racks of ancient equipment, and farther still, an enormous generator. The machinery was a snarl of pipes and motors, seven feet tall and twenty feet long, and covered in dust. Exhaust pipes as straight and thick as Grecian columns rose from the heart of the contraption and vanished into the ceiling.

He placed a sensor under the large cylinder, which must have held fuel sometime in the past. The sensor noted motion and lumen fluctuation; it also included a chip that recorded and analyzed audio and intercepted radio signals.

Freeman reached an arm through a gap in the machinery. He placed a remote charge against the side of a heavy motor. Walking around the generator, he placed two more charges deep inside the tangle of pipes and wires. The generator might have weighed six tons, it might have weighed eight; Freeman hoped the force of his charges would ricochet against the solid rock wall, launching the generator across the chamber. Depending on the condition of the structure, it might even blow the generator apart, sending pipes and bolts and fragments of ancient metal through the air like shrapnel.

The charges might bring down the house, but Freeman doubted it. The walls and ceiling were solid.

Freeman moved on. His goggles let him see through the

darkness, but they did nothing more. The Unifieds, if they sent their Marines, would have combat visors—smart equipment that, in Freeman's experience, was often smarter than the men using it. If they utilized all the tools in their helmets, they would be able to run sonar scans to find weak spots in the floors and hollow pockets in the walls. They'd find his charges and detect his sensors.

In this empty old mine, every floor, ceiling, and doorway was a risk. If the Unifieds brought all the right equipment, they would be able to analyze the tunnels to see where they led. They wouldn't even need to enter the mine. They could send hunter drones that would locate Freeman by the noise of his breathing and his heartbeat.

Weak walls and crumbling floors wouldn't bother the drones; some flew through the air, and others weighed less than a pound. Freeman hoped the Unifieds would start out by sending drones. Seeing their drones destroyed sometimes scared the humans out of following.

He walked down a staircase that had been carved into a solid rock floor. Reasoning that the floors would be weakest in their center, Freeman pressed against the walls.

A message appeared in his goggles, warning him that the motion sensors he had placed up near the entrance had detected motion and sound. Before he checked the findings, the message flashed and went dead.

The Unifieds might have destroyed the sensors, or they might have blocked all communications frequencies as a precaution.

The ceiling became lower as Freeman pressed ahead. By this time, his sprained ankle had seized so badly that instead of stepping, he now dragged the foot. He felt dizzy and slightly nauseated, and his breathing grew heavier.

In the opening days of the war between the clones and the Unified Authority, the Unifieds had tried to crush the rebellion by sending Marines to a planet called Terraneau. The U.A. Marines had hoped to fight Harris and his Marines in a traditional battle, but Harris outsmarted them. He lured their force into an underground parking lot attached to a subway station. Once he and his men had exited the structure through the station, he detonated the charges he had hidden in the parking lot, burying the U.A. troops under three stories of rubble.

That maneuver had stayed with Freeman, had influenced him to place the charges in the generator. If the Unifieds were sludging the airwaves, however, the charges would no longer work.

Using the gear in his goggles, Freeman sent the signal to detonate the charges. Nothing happened. The ground did not shake, the air remained still and silent, no flash disturbed the absolute darkness.

If a hunting party had entered the mines, they could no longer use drones. The same equipment that blocked the signals from his sensors would render the drones useless.

Here in the mine, Freeman had lost his sense of time. He didn't know if he had been underground for an hour or a day. There was no sun, no sky, no shadows, just the variations of tan and yellow that formed into images in his goggles. The tunnel ahead was black. The walls were a bluish white. He passed posts and braces along the walls, some made of wood and others of metal. He looked for snake tracks on the ground but saw nothing. This deep in the mines, there would be little for snakes to eat. Sometimes he smelled ammonia and must in the air. Bats.

The smell of guano had made it hard to breathe in the first caverns he'd crossed. Now, though, he just caught a brief whiff of the bat shit. Bats wouldn't venture this far into the mine unless they found a nearby exit.

He had no idea how long he had been in the mine or how far he had traveled when he heard the ground crack. As he limped forward looking for a safe spot, the floor disintegrated beneath him. Dust rose, and he plummeted, falling so quickly he wouldn't have had time to reach for a railing if there had been one to grab. He fell backward, and his backpack struck a post or a wooden beam, something that splintered under his weight.

The fall lasted two or three seconds. He had no idea how far he had fallen. All he knew was that he landed on dust and rock, feetfirst, his legs buckled, and his knees struck the ground. Pain he could not ignore radiated up his thighs and into his spine. He grimaced but made no noise.

He was blind. The goggles had toppled from his head.

Taking a deep breath, he rolled into a crawling position and ran his fingers across the ground in search of his goggles. Freeman, who had never acknowledged his fears, now had to deal with rage and insanity. Neither would help him, but they might overwhelm him if he allowed it.

When he moved his leg, searing pain shot up from the ankle. The boot had become too tight, so tight that it now cut off any circulation into the foot. Soon he would need to cut the boot off his foot. If he didn't, infection would set in, possibly gangrenous infection. Freeman had brought guns, goggles, charges, and a knife, but he hadn't brought medicine or painkillers. Those, he had always believed, were the necessities of smaller men.

Freeman didn't second-guess his decisions and mistakes as he searched the ground for his goggles. Patting the ground around him in an ever-expanding circle, he finally located the goggles laying with their eyepieces pointing up.

He brought the goggles to his mouth and blew the dust off them, then he slipped them over his eyes and realized that the worst had happened. They had broken when they hit the ground. Concentrating on what needed to be done instead of what had been lost, he tossed the goggles aside and forced himself to focus.

He started to pull the hand torch from the shoulder strap of his backpack, but he heard distant voices and let his hand drop. These would be the scouts, the stool pigeons. They would see the hole and most likely come to investigate. Would they drop down the hole? He wasn't ready to make his stand, but if two men came, or three, or even five, Freeman would attack them.

For him, though, the darkness remained complete at that moment. He held a hand against the wall, limped forward as fast as he could, and hoped he had chosen a direction that would offer him cover. He couldn't tell if he was walking deeper into the mines or toward stairs.

He grunted softly with each step. The ankle presented a problem. It was no longer just a sprain—bones had broken when he hit the ground. That much he could tell. He limped on another twenty feet before he found a ledge behind which he could hide. He discovered a deep alcove carved into the wall and stuffed himself in, stumbling over a pile of helmet-sized rocks, and there he sat. He pulled the flashlight from the shoulder strap, then shrugged off his backpack and felt inside it for his pistol.

He planned to save his rifle, his most favored weapon, for later. These were the scouts, he could handle them with a pistol, but he needed the scope from his rifle. He was blind without his goggles, and his options were few. He could start a fire or use the flashlight, but the glow would alert the enemy. His only other option was to remove the scope from his rifle.

As he tinkered with the bindings that held the scope in place, Freeman listened for the hunting party. He heard nothing but his own breathing. The acoustics in the mine stifled sound, drowning it the way a gallon of water would douse the flame on a match.

Time crawled on, and then he heard men speaking. The same sludging technology that blocked the signal from Freeman's sensors and stopped him from detonating the charges now worked against the Unifieds. It blocked all interLink and radio signals. The only way they could communicate was by speaking. Apparently, a few of the men felt they had to shout to be heard.

One of the men said, "He went down that hole."

His friend shouted the answer, "That's a cave-in. If he went down there, he fell down."

"Maybe he died."

The scouts' rappel tools purred softly as they paid out line.

Freeman gave up on removing the scope. It was a smart scope, a device that communicated with the rifle's inner workings. To remove the scope, he would need to disconnect circuits as well as stanchion screws. Now that the hunters had arrived, he couldn't risk giving his position away with a click or a scratch. Instead of removing the scope, he aimed the rifle in the direction from which he had come.

Looking through the scope, he could see the spot where he had landed, then tilted the rifle toward the roof of the cavern and spotted the hole through which he fell. He had fallen twenty feet, striking an old wooden crossbeam on his way down.

As he watched, three rappel lines rolled from the ceiling, looking like giant fishing lines. Keeping his scope trained on the lines, Freeman took a deep breath and tried to clear the pain from his thoughts. He had a harder time focusing now. It wasn't just the pain; his mind kept drifting.

Removing his eye from the scope, he stared up at the ceiling, hoping the hunters would use flashlights. Nothing. Darkness. Total darkness.

It these men were Marines, they wouldn't need flashlights. They'd have night-for-day lenses built into the visors.

He pressed his eye to the scope once more and waited until he saw three pairs of armored boots lower from the ceiling, then he leaned his back against the wall of the alcove. He drew in a deep breath and waited.

He would kill the scouts. With the airwaves sludged, they couldn't call for assistance. The most they could do was leave a beacon to mark their path.

If they were Marines with Marine combat armor, Freeman would take one of their helmets. He would cut a groove in the back of the helmet so that he could fit it over his head. He'd done it before. With a working combat helmet, he would be able to see.

"Hey, check this out; there's blood on the ground here!"

"Yeah, and a pair of goggles."

"Hey, Sarge, there's no doubt the speck came this way," one of the Marines called in a loud voice. "He left some gear behind, there's a whole lot of blood."

Freeman considered the risks and the options. Three men had come down into the tunnel with him. He had no idea how many more watched from overhead. The clip in his rifle held twenty-five rounds, but the weapon was too slow and cumbersome for a close-range shoot-out.

"Man, that speck is bleeding like a stuck pig."

"I don't see blood."

"Yeah. It's hard to see it with night-for-day vision," said one of the Marines. "Shine your light."

By the time the light appeared, Freeman had already switched from his rifle to his pistol. Shining through the dusty dry air, the cone of illumination looked like an object, like a silver arrow, the broad end poised at the floor and the narrow end pointing at the target. Freeman fired his pistol.

The Marine dropped his flashlight as he died. It hit the

ground, rolled a lazy half revolution, and inside its beam stood two Marines in combat armor. Freeman shot them, then waited in absolute silence to see what would follow. No more lines dropped from the ceiling; no one returned fire. Ten seconds passed. Twenty.

Willing himself to ignore the pain, Freeman gimp-stepped to the dead Marine and the fallen flashlight as quickly as he could. As he approached, he looked up at the ceiling and spotted a Marine staring down at him. Freeman shot him. He might have grazed the man or merely scared him away, but he didn't think he had killed the bastard.

After one last look to make sure no one would shoot him from the ceiling, he grabbed one of the dead Marines by the foot and dragged him into the darkness.

CHAPTER THIRTY-EIGHT

Location: Flying from Mazatlán to Guanajuato, New Olympian Territories
Date: July 30, 2519

"Harris, nine transports appeared directly over the Territories. There's only one way they got there. The Unifieds are using a spy ship," said Admiral Hauser.

"A cruiser?" I asked.

"That's my guess," said Hauser. "The cruisers they were using at the end of the war had three landing bays. Each bay had room for three transports.

"The Unifieds landed nine transports a couple of hours ago. I'm no mathematician, but three bays holding three transports . . ."

"Do you think they're using our spy ship?" asked Ritz.

In the early days of the war between the Enlisted Man's

Empire and the Unified Authority, we captured a U.A. cruiser that had been equipped with a stealth generator. That ship quickly became the crown jewel of our fleet, but it vanished shortly after the battle for Earth. One thing about stealth ships—once you lose track of them, they stay lost.

"I have no way of knowing," said Admiral Hauser.

I said, "If it's ours, I want it back."

We were already in the air, already winging our way east, toward the mountains. Ritz and I sat in the cockpit of the lead transport. The sun set behind us as we flew forward into a blue-black sky.

Wanting to oversee his global blockade, Hauser had moved the *Churchill* to an Earth orbit. He had sixty ships forming a tight net around the planet. We might not have had the tools we needed to stop spy ships from parking outside the atmosphere, but the Unifieds knew better than to send conventional ships.

Hauser said, "Harris, our radar picked up a gunship circling the area, a TR-40. You better watch yourself down there. If the Unifieds smell a shot at Freeman, they'll throw everything they have at him. If they figure out you're there . . ."

Gunships were every Marine's worst nightmare. Shoulder-fired rockets barely dented their armor. Ritz had once knocked a whole flock of them out of the sky with a mortar, but he'd attached an EMP to that shell. No one had packed EMPs for this op.

"How long has it been there?" I asked.

"That's the problem," said Hauser. "We didn't notice it until after you asked us to scan the area. For all we know, they could have an air base somewhere nearby."

Transports carried one hundred men. If the Unifieds had nine transports outside Petrie's camp, that gave them a maximum nine hundred troops unless that spy ship returned to deliver another load. How the speck they smuggled a gunship into the area was another question.

"Did Cardston ever get back to you about the summit?" asked Ritz.

Speck, I thought. *The summit.* Cardston and the summit had completely slipped my mind.

"Oh, I've heard from Cardston," said Hauser. "Did you hear what MacAvoy is up to?"

I was almost afraid to ask . . . almost.

"He declared martial law in Washington."

"He did what?" I asked.

Ritz went silent for a moment, then laughed. He said, "We're a military empire; the only kinds of laws we have are martial laws."

Hauser ignored him. He said, "He landed an entire corps and declared martial law. I swear I've eaten MREs with more brains than that clone."

"Martial law?" I asked. "Are we talking checkpoints and guard stations?"

Hauser groaned and nodded. "He's quarantined the Pentagon . . . has troops and tanks surrounding the building. He also put out a general call informing every Army, Navy, Air Force, and Marine base that the Pentagon is currently off-line. That's how he put it, 'off-line.'"

I said, "I really wish he had discussed this strategy with us before pulling the trigger."

Ritz disagreed. He said, "You got to love MacAvoy. I bet the Unifieds didn't see that coming."

I realized that I should have known that a hammerhead like MacAvoy would launch an undeclared war when I told him to watch the Pentagon. The Navy and the Marines had fine, sharp tools for surgical strikes. The Army specialized in blunt-force trauma.

"What's he doing about the gas?" I asked.

"Gas masks," said Hauser.

There was a time when Army gas masks had involved large, cumbersome hoods that covered the soldier's entire head. Newer, sleeker models had replaced those primeval relics. They were now clear plastic discs that covered the mouth, nose, and eyes with filters so powerful they could strain breathable oxygen out of mud.

"He's forcing them to make their move," said Ritz. "They're either going to act fast or lose the Pentagon."

"Assuming they really did gas the place," I said. "Maybe they just gassed Cardston."

Nine transports sat in one long row along an ancient highway. Beyond the birds, the remains of a relocation camp smoldered.

The flames had died, but the ruins of the buildings still looked hot.

Ritz saw the wreckage from the cockpit, and asked, "Freeman?"

I said, "My pal Ray."

We were deep in a mountainous area with ridges climbing toward the sky in every direction. I asked the pilot, "Can you scan the location for enemy troops?"

"Sure. They're over there," said Lieutenant Chris Nobles, the man who played pilot on most of my missions. He pointed out the cockpit.

The world was dark around us. Looking out the cockpit, I saw slopes that were rocky and steep, leading up to stony cliffs. Though I could not see the army that had gathered on the distant cliff, I saw the lights of their encampment, a tiny bubble of white light in a world otherwise given to darkness. We were too far away to see the men themselves.

"Any sign of the gunship?" I asked.

Nobles looked at his radar and shook his head. We could survive a gunship in this bird though it would be a bumpy ride. Transports were floating bunkers, defenseless but covered with armor and surrounded by powerful shields.

"Get us as close as you can," I said.

Nobles said, "Aye, sir, but I wouldn't want to set her down on that trail. Those slopes weren't meant for transports."

He was right. The rise was too steep for the skids, our bird would slide as she touched down, maybe even roll. Shields or no shields, I didn't like the idea of rolling down a mountain.

"How close is the nearest landing area?" I asked.

Nobles said, "General Harris, I think the Unifieds are using it. I can park us next to them if you like."

I didn't like. Somewhere deep inside me, I had a gnawing feeling that Freeman needed help. We'd be able to unload our Jackals and light armor if we parked, but we'd lose a lot of time traipsing back up the hill. We needed to jump.

I said, "Ritz, prepare your men."

"Aye, sir," said Ritz.

A voice I had forgotten asked, "What's the situation, Harris?" I turned back to the communications console and saw Admiral Hauser. He looked concerned.

"They have nine transports, which probably means they have nine hundred men with a high-ground advantage and time to dig in," I said.

"You have twice as many men," said Hauser, who, as a sailor, had never actually had to deal with tactical advantages of this sort. He had never fought on land. He asked, "How important is the high ground?"

I asked, "How important is having twice as many men?"

Why whine? Why tell him that an assassin on a ledge above our heads could move with complete impunity. Our helmets prevented us from looking straight up.

CHAPTER THIRTY-NINE

As we approached the jump site, the communications gear in my helmet went dead. The stupid bastards were sludging the area, and I was glad. That would inconvenience us now, but cause them significant problems once the fighting started. We had twice as many men as they did, and the sludging meant that they couldn't call the gunship for backup.

The transport dropped to no more than four feet off the ground, and there it hovered, the churn from its jump-jet thrusters blowing dust and doing unknown damage to the rock shelf beneath it. We jumped out quickly and cleared the way for the next transport.

Emptying the transports took ten minutes, a well-organized maneuver.

It was night, but that didn't matter. We all wore combat armor. We saw the world around us clearly enough, though depth and color were a problem. The night sky was so clear and cloudless that I saw layers of stars when I stared up into the void.

Barren slopes of rock and dirt awaited us.

The enemy couldn't have missed our noisy arrival.

Transports are loud and clumsy birds with glowing shields. Wherever the Unifieds had hidden their gunship, their pilots might well have noticed our landing as well.

"Move out!" I shouted at my company commanders. This was the part where the sludging would get in our way. It forced me to shout orders rather than speak them over the interLink.

"Move out!" they relayed my orders to their platoon leaders.

The First of the First moved out, seventeen hundred well-oiled killing machines. My infantry men carried M27s and grenades, RPGs and the combat skills of experienced Marines.

My squads had fought together in many battles, giving the men confidence in the men beside them. Give a Marine armor he knows, a gun he has stripped and fired, and confidence that the men on his team have got his back, and you turn a fighting man into a force of nature.

We started up the slope. Ahead of us, peaks stood out in dull relief against the night sky like shadows on a dark gray wall. Seen through the night-for-day lenses in my visor, the jagged edges of the cliffs and peaks reminded me of broken glass. Sagebrush and a few spindly trees grew along the slopes, but mostly they were barren.

About a mile up, we passed a saddle from which peaks rose in opposite directions. A platoon leader whose team was on point sent a runner to tell me that his men had found something.

"What?" I asked, feeling annoyed that the messenger told me they'd found something rather than what they had found.

"It used to be a dog, sir," said the corporal.

I went to have a look. Ritz tagged along.

There, on open ground, the headless carcass of a dead dog lay on its side.

I'd never owned a dog, though I supposed I would have preferred a dog to a cat or a fish. Seeing this animal left me unmoved.

The corporal said, "There's another one over there and a few more down there." He pointed as he spoke.

"Think Freeman did this?" asked Ritz.

I said, "Shooting a dog wouldn't bother him."

Ritz looked around the scene, then said, "I don't see any bodies. Do you think he shot the dogs and left the people?"

"If he shot the dogs, he shot the men that were using them," I said. "If they were natural-borns, they probably left the dogs to rot and buried the corpses of their men."

Now that I was alert to it, I saw blood on boulders and on the sheer rock face. Freeman must have ambushed them.

The platoon captain drifted over to join us. Ritz asked him, "Have you found any bodies?"

"We found a section of a visor from a combat helmet," the captain offered. He held up a shiny, curved puzzle piece, about four inches long and three inches wide. I recognized it. Hell, all the men around me were wearing visors made of the same stuff.

Our combat visors were half window/half video screen. They had instant tinting for blocking out blinding light, and the inside of the glass was coated with a transparent film that worked as a visual display.

I put out the word to my company commanders. "Keep alert, Marines. One ambush is as good as another. A battalion marching uphill makes a tempting target."

The Unifieds allowed us to travel several miles before they followed Freeman's example. They started with snipers. The men on point reached a narrow rise, a natural bottleneck pinched between a rocky shelf and a steep drop that only four or possibly five men could pass at one time. There were no trees or boulders to use for cover, and the ridge at the top of the rise was equally devoid of cover.

I could have predicted what would happen, but I wasn't paying attention. I had fallen back to the rear, leaving a couple of company commanders to lead the march while I conferred with my colonels. At the moment, we stood in a circle, all viewing the same section of map on our visors. The map displayed the terrain around us with multicolored rings showing elevation.

A fire team scampered up the rise. I reviewed the record later, and they had done everything right. They held their M27s ready, jogged fast, and spread quickly so that others could follow. They scanned the ridges above them for enemy emplacements.

"Situation?" called their platoon leader.

"Clear."

The next team scurried up. To this point, their procedure remained flawless. The next team ascended quickly. They were alert enough to fan out, no point standing in a tight cluster that an enemy can take out with a single grenade.

So far, so good.

Moving quickly, securing the position, and clearing the way for more troops, we sent two entire companies up that thirty-foot rise. Just a thirty-foot rise. Child's play.

Fire teams and squads continued up the slope. The men at the base of that bottleneck started to gather, then the shooting began.

The Unifieds' snipers had been patient. They waited for my men to cluster at the top of the rise, then they fired at the larger group waiting down below. The shooting began like a rainstorm—one drop, then a few more, then the barrage began.

There was a crack, and one of my Marines toppled off a ridge and rolled a few feet along the ground. Suddenly, the sound of rifle shots filled the air. Every specking shot hit one of my men. They couldn't miss. They had waited until we had clumped together like fish in a barrel.

The men at the top of the ridge hit the ground. Trained men take cover in shallow pits or behind a tank when they don't have a wall or a bunker. Anything is better than standing in the open or offering a sniper your back.

Men returned fired shooting blindly at first. They knew which direction the bullets had come from, and that was enough. They didn't know how far or how high to shoot, but when fifteen hundred men return fire at a handful of snipers, distance and trajectory often take care of themselves.

We sprayed the ridges liberally, and the distant ridge went silent.

Then another sound cut through the night, the *lop lop lop* of rotor blades accompanied by the hiss of a jet engine. The gunship cut across the night sky, shooting out of the darkness like a tracer round. She slid through the air as smoothly as a puck traveling on ice.

I barely had time to think, *Oh shit, here she comes*, before she fired her first rocket. Like the sharpshooters hidden somewhere up the trail, the pilot in that gunship went after the tight cluster of men at the bottom of the rise.

My men reacted quickly. Companies split. Riflemen and automatic riflemen, knowing they were as good as unarmed against a gunship, scattered and searched for cover. The ridge offered little.

My grenadiers did me proud.

The gunship came in with her lights off and her chain guns glowing. It did not have glowing shields giving away her position, but we could see the orange plume from her jet engine. She was big. She was loud. She was a black silhouette in a moonlit sky, relying on speed over invisibility as she bore down upon us.

A hundred rocket-propelled grenades flew at her like a swarm of fireflies. At that moment, I thought to myself, *You can't kill a man with a spit wad no matter how many wads you shoot at him.* But after seeing what happened next, I changed my mind. Hit a guy at the top of a staircase with enough spit wads, and maybe one goes in his eye or flies in his mouth, causing him to stumble backward.

It might have been that the force of the explosion, or perhaps the simultaneous explosions, created an air pocket, or maybe a lucky splinter of shrapnel clipped a wire or flew into a vulnerable crevice. At any rate, something happened. It happened in the dark, and it happened fast.

One moment the gunship hovered in the air above us. The first wave of rocket-propelled grenades exploded, and a second wave began to streak toward the gunship. For no apparent reason that I could see, the big bird dropped a couple of hundred yards, then she crashed into the lap of a mountain. The fuel, the missiles, or the engines . . . something erupted in a fireball that shot into the air and dissolved.

CHAPTER FORTY

We marched another two miles through passes, up slopes, along ridges. The higher we climbed, the more the Unifieds hit us.

We crested a particularly winding slope and found ourselves entering an exposed ridge. I called the battalion to a halt and asked my officers in for a confab.

"General, once we cross this line, that is when the shooting begins," said Ritz. "We'll have their asses pinned once we cross this ridge, and they know it."

I agreed. This was the part of the battle I always hated most, the part in which the enemy throws everything he has at you to stop you from getting into position . . . the part in which you lose men you didn't need to lose.

One of my colonels said, "Looks pretty obvious, sir. Either we nuke the entire mountain or we march straight ahead."

I said, "We're not nuking this mountain."

He smiled, and said, "Then we march straight ahead."

The First of the First was a battalion that prided itself on being the roughest and the most ready battalion in the Corps. On my command, they would charge ahead, fully knowing some of them would likely die. Once again, the night was still except for the clatter of men in armor. I looked around at my Marines.

The natural-borns in the Unified Authority Marines wore shield combat armor, suits with a force field that would protect them from bullets and missiles and grenades, until the power source ran out. Every time we hit them, whether we hit them with a bullet or a pebble, the batteries that powered the shields upped the juice and drained more quickly. If we kept the pressure ongoing, the batteries went dry after forty-five minutes, and their armor would be no better than ours.

From what we had learned by surveying the slopes ahead, we had maybe eight hundred yards to go. Once we crossed this ridge, we would reach another rise, then the slender ridge that the Unifieds now occupied. Once we reached that final rim, we would face the enemy at close quarters, maybe even hand to hand. We had to make damn sure their armor ran out of batteries before we got that close.

Looking across the sheer face ahead, I saw a path that ran under the cliff. The path was little more than an eight-inch patch of washboard rocks covered with a dusting of loose soil, but it led beneath the enemy and came up behind them. The little ledge it followed was so narrow, you'd dig your toes into the side of the mountain, and your heels would be hanging in the air, but there were rocks and handholds in the face of the mountain for balance. Once we crossed that face, we'd have the enemy surrounded with nowhere to go. I said, "This assault would be a whole lot safer if we sent a company to flank them."

That has always been the way of the Marines. One team moves straight ahead; one team flanks. The first team keeps the enemy pinned while the second team cuts them down.

Ritz turned to look in the direction I was looking. I heard a dubious tone in his voice when he asked, "You want to send men across down there? It's suicide, you know."

He had a point. The ground didn't look stable. There was no cover. Anyone who tripped would fall straight down, and the drop was over a thousand feet. If the Unifieds started an avalanche above us, they'd wash us right off the slope. If they spotted us and shot, there would be no way to return fire.

"Was Hannibal committing suicide when he crossed the Alps?" I asked, not sure whether or not Ritz knew about Hannibal or the Second Punic War. I added, "And the subject isn't open for debate, Ritz."

We were down two hundred men by this time. We'd started out with seventeen hundred, and now we had somewhere in the vicinity of fifteen hundred.

"Yes, sir. General, do you think maybe we should send someone other than a four-star general and the commandant of the Marines to lead this maneuver?"

Every answer I considered sounded canned, so I simply said, "Pick out a company I can take with me."

Ritz said, "Harris, this is the specking First of the First; every one of these bastards will follow you to Hell."

So he gave me a hundred men, and we started down an unmarked trail that led along the face of a cliff. Soon, we were scaling the wall, digging our boots into dirt, and feeling for rock purchases, ignoring the thousand-foot drop beneath our feet. This wasn't Mount Everest or some other glorious mountain; this was an overgrown pile of crumbling desert rock, a mound of dirt and limestone pebbles.

Ritz didn't wait for us to hike to safety. He gave us a ten-minute lead, then he began shooting.

Since the Unifieds were still sludging, I had no contact with Ritz or any of my men. I had one hundred Marines trapped with me as we hugged our way around a curve. We heard gunshots and explosions above us, but the mountain hid the fighting from our sight.

I held my M27 in one hand and squeezed handholds with the other. Looking through my visor, using night-for-day lenses, I saw the soil as a bluish gray. I saw the night sky as black, and the stars had vanished.

The ground on which I stood seemed to dissolve under my left foot when I took a step. My breathing stopped. I pressed my face into the mountain and grabbed at rocks and outcrops. *Breathe!* I reminded myself. *Breathe!*

I closed my fingers around a knob of rocks that turned to dust. Dug into the slope as I was, my boots stabbed into shifting soil, and I kept my weight pinned into place.

Somewhere, in the blind spot that was everything straight up above my head, the enemy had spotted me. Bullets zinged past me. Some hit above my head.

Between Ritz and the uneven scarp, it would take a trained marksman to hit us. The battle on the ridge would unravel slowly. If the Unifieds used their shields, Ritz would hit them with guns and grenades while he waited for the batteries to give out, and the U.A. troops would advance on Ritz's position if they powered up. With their shields up, the only weapon the Unifieds could use were the fléchette cannons on their wrists, a short-range weapon.

I listened more closely to the sounds around me and heard bullets plow into dirt with a thud and the *zing* of slugs ricocheting off rocks. Someone got lucky and hit the Marine two places behind me, a shot to the shoulder that sprayed blood on rocks and dirt. The bullet didn't kill him, but he lost his concentration, then his balance. He tried to steady himself, but it's hard to grab holds in armored gloves.

The man didn't fall straight down. The face we'd been crossing was not set at a ninety-degree angle; it was more like seventy or seventy-five degrees. I watched him as he rolled and bounced down the mountain, hitting a boulder or a shelf, pieces of armor falling from his body with every hit he took.

Another man fell, then a third. We'd lost three.

By this time, most of the Unifieds had their shields up or they would have pelted us with grenades. They might have eradicated the entire company with a well-timed pill.

"Move it. Get your ass in gear," I told myself. I shared the message with the man beside me. Since we didn't have an interLink connection, everything had to be communicated from mouth to ear.

We pushed farther, digging our boots into footholds, looking for rocks and outcroppings we could grab with our hands, and trying to balance ourselves on a narrow ledge that kept becoming narrower.

I started to look down toward the base of the mountain and caught myself. When I read the Old Testament of the Bible, I was struck by the story of a woman who looked back toward the destruction of Sodom and Gomorrah and turned into a pillar of salt. If I looked down and lost my balance, I'd turn into a puddle of blood.

I distracted myself by thinking about Freeman. Nine hundred men they had sent out here, nine hundred men to track down one lone assassin. They wanted Freeman. They wanted Ray Freeman as much as they wanted me. Maybe more. They had captured me on Mars. They caught me, they mucked with my brain, giving me fears and trying to reprogram me, then they set me free, like a fish you catch and release.

Not Freeman. If they caught him, they would kill him. No reprogramming for him, that only worked on clones. *Was he on a ledge, in a cave, or on the run?* I wondered.

I looked up and saw that the night sky had begun to fade. Fingers of light showed in the distance. Up ahead, no more than fifty feet away, the slant of the mountain twisted, giving us more ledge to stand on. Up there, the slope became gradual, and the rocks and rifts formed a steep and stable trail. We'd be able to walk instead of hugging the mountain. We'd still have a climb after that, but we wouldn't need to worry about U.A. Marines dropping grenades from overhead.

I felt my heart racing, my mood lightening, my pace speeding up. *We made it,* I thought, and that thought, of course, offended the gods of war. Fifty feet to the path. Forty feet. Thirty feet. Twenty. I was less than ten feet away when thunder shook the mountain. Rocks and pebbles rained down on us. Stones of all sizes cascaded from above us like hail.

I jumped to the trail, my feet digging into a solid ledge, pressing my face into the side of the mountain, hoping the ridge above didn't come down on top of me. Rocks the size of a man's fist rained down, and I ducked my head. I felt bumps and bashes, most light, but some of the blows were heavy.

More thunder. More avalanche.

Mortars had struck the ridge above us. It wasn't the Unifieds firing those mortars, it was my men.

Mortars are powerful weapons, indispensable in mountain fighting, when adjusting to elevation means the difference between killing the enemy or dying with no way to strike back. Bullets, rockets, and RPGs are line-of-sight weapons; mortars let you fire at the enemy on the other side of the mountain. Depending on the shells you fire, they can be powerful, powerful weapons. The ones my men were firing shook the entire ridge, and that was dangerous.

I looked back along the slope and saw that I had lost at least ten Marines, maybe twenty.

Another mortar shell. Trying to hold on to the shaking rock face was like hugging an erupting volcano. I could have run to safety at this point, but if this kept up, I would lose every last one of my men.

But this was the First of the First. This was the First Battalion of the First Marines. These men didn't flinch. They kept pushing forward. There were holes where men had been. We'd taken casualties. One man had lost his footing and dropped fifteen feet before he'd stopped himself. Now he scratched and clawed his way back up the steep face, clubbing rocks and clods to dig his fist into the mountain, kicking his boot into the side of the mountain. He'd lost his M27, but he refused to fall.

The man's name was Lance Corporal Ian Minter, I read it as I watched him climb. If the interLink had been up, I'd have promoted Minter on the spot. Instead, all I could do was read his name from the label his smart gear projected, and soon enough, I didn't even have that much.

Minter found a spot where he felt safe, and he did something very intelligent. He tore off his helmet and let it drop. With his helmet off, he could turn his head and see what was above him. He could search for handholds and watch for men trying to help him.

The mortars stopped. I thanked God for silence and pulled men onto my ledge.

It only took Minter another minute to climb those last few feet. With his helmet off and his eyes wild with rage, he found places to step and nubs to grab, then two men pulled him up by his shoulders.

Someone asked, "You good?" and he said, "Damn straight."

If the fighting went the way that I expected on the ridge, Lance Corporal Ian Minter might find that he had only earned himself a brief reprieve.

I'd started out with a hundred men and lost twenty-six of them. Twenty-six men, one helmet, and one M27, a small down payment in a battle like this one. The Romans were undoubtedly surprised to see Hannibal climbing down the mountains with his elephants and his cavalry, but that doesn't mean they surrendered. Neither would the Unifieds.

The air rang with gunfire and the occasional grenade. If I'd been able to access the interLink, I would have radioed Ritz and told him to start firing mortars again, but communications stayed down. I'd checked again and again.

I listened to the battle, trying to read its sounds as we ran. The trail switched back and forth, tracing along the rock precipice in pendulum-like swings that led us closer to the fighting, and then farther away, then closer than before. I jumped over a rise and saw the battle spread out ahead of me.

We crested a peak overlooking two ridges. The men on the closer ridge, Unified Authority Marines, had a slight high-ground advantage. They had dug in, too, but that was their undoing. Instead of digging in, they should have attacked while the batteries in their armor were still fresh. Now, most of them had run out of battery life.

Hiding behind a boulder on a ridge above and behind the Unifieds, I saw where the three mortar shells had landed, great divots that were both black with soot and red with blood. By this time, the morning was in full bloom. Stripes of white and peach and ice blue filled the sky. The men of the First of the First were on the next ridge over, huddled like barbarians at the base of a parapet.

My men and I had pulled a Hannibal, having crossed our own personal Alps. We had a momentary element of surprise. It would not last long. In fact . . .

I announced our arrival with a grenade.

While my men took cover, I pulled the pill from my belt. I set the yield to maximum, slipped the pin out, and tossed the grenade toward the spot on the ridge where the Unifieds pressed together like sheep in a pen.

My grenade hit the ground and the officers leaped in every direction. Most of them made it to safety. The grenade splattered those who didn't all over those who did.

The mountain formed a wall behind me, a craggy, rust-colored rise with a wide, straight-edged opening that must have led into a mine. I understood the mysteries of this battle the moment I saw that entrance. This was where Freeman had chosen to make his stand. Maybe he'd been wounded; maybe the Unifieds had overwhelmed him with their numbers. He'd ducked into the mine, and they'd sent men in after him.

As I ran for cover, the Unifieds turned their sights on me. Most of them had used up the power in their shields and fired M27s, but a few fired fléchettes from their wrist cannons. I dived behind a boulder and hoped no one would throw a grenade.

About fifty feet away from me, Lance Corporal Ian Minter—the guy who had lost his helmet and his weapon—knelt behind a row of rocks, his left hand tense and empty and ready to grab anyone unfortunate enough to pass nearby, his right hand wrapped around a combat knife. I could see his face, his mouth turned down in an angry grimace, his eyes staring straight ahead as he waited for the opportunity to strike.

Even as I watched, a trio of U.A. Marines came looking for me. The one on the right had an M27. He stepped within a foot or two of Minter—and then he was dead. Minter wrestled him to the ground, pried his twelve-inch blade under the rim of the man's helmet, and blood splashed out.

The man's partners were slow to react. They turned to see what had happened, and one of my automatic riflemen cut them down.

Minter pulled his knife out of the dead man's throat. He wiped the blade on the ground then replaced it in his scabbard. Minter also took the dead man's M27.

The First of the First, I thought to myself. *They always get it done.*

I didn't have time to linger on warm thoughts. We were seventy-three men, flanking the remainder of what had once been nine hundred men. I now estimated their strength at below five hundred.

A few of them shot at me, their bullets and fléchettes scraping the rocks around me, kicking up dust, spitting chips in the air. They were unorganized. Now was when their sludging would hamper their efforts more than ours. They couldn't warn their men in the mine. They were flanked and outnumbered and unable to organize.

A wave of U.A. Marines rushed my position, firing a steady barrage of bullets meant to drive me and my men behind the rocks. They had us pinned, but they stood in the open. I looked out from behind my cover, fired three shots, then ducked as bullets tore into the wall behind. Lance Corporal Minter, who still had not replaced his helmet, stood and fired three shots, then dropped back.

While we abused the Unifieds from the rear, Ritz and his men advanced up the ridge. Almost certainly taking heavy casualties, they fired M27s and threw grenades as they forged ahead. Mortars would have been more effective if they could have used them, but without the interLink, they had no way of knowing where we were and how to avoid hitting us.

Their attention split and their options running dry, the Unifieds didn't back down. They fired at us. They fired at

Ritz. Bullets scraping above my head, I leaped from behind my cover, fired six shots, hit the six nearest Marines, and darted into their ranks.

Yes, in my armor I looked exactly identical to the men I was attacking, but my instincts no longer cared what my brain had to say. I had been nursing the mother of all combat reflexes. It had started as we crossed the cliffs, continued as we ducked for cover, and now I needed to kill enemies before my head exploded.

Two men turned to face me. I shot them. A Marine ran at me, stopped to aim his M27, and I smashed the butt of my M27 into his visor, shattering it like a mirror. I struck a second time as well, battering shards of broken visor in cheeks and eyes, and blood sprayed in a halo around his face.

Somewhere in my body, a gland rewarded my every act of violence with an addicting dose of adrenaline and endorphins. My testosterone levels had spiked to unreadable levels; my heart beat so hard it felt like it might claw its way out of my chest, yet my breathing was calm and my brain at peace.

A Marine ran at me. I stabbed the butt of my M27 into his visor, knocking him back into another man, then I shot them both. The euphoria was damn near orgasmic, but I needed to shut it down. I was about to lose control, and I knew it.

No that wasn't true. I had entered the abyss. By the time I came to my senses, I stood thirty feet deep in enemy territory surrounded by hundreds of enemy Marines, shooting men at point-blank range, clubbing them, kicking their legs from under them and shooting them as they fell.

Fall back, I told myself. *Fall back.*

If I stayed here, ahead of either line, my own men would shoot me.

The fighting continued. A U.A. Marine ran past me. I grabbed his M27 from his hands, spun him, and threw him, using his own momentum against him. He hit the ground hard and slid another few feet. I could have shot him as he rose, but I didn't. By denying the kill, I hoped to make myself calm down.

Someone else shot the bastard. He made it to one knee, then a bullet crashed through the side of his helmet in a wave of blood and chunks.

As the adrenal rush of the combat reflex ended, a sense of melancholy followed. The man's M27 still in my hands, I watched him crumble. Stray bullets hit the ground around me. I looked at the gun, then I looked at the tiny cattails of dust kicked up by bullets. If anybody had actually tried to shoot me at that moment, they couldn't have missed. Apparently, neither side did.

Of all the people who could have saved me, it was Lance Corporal Minter who knocked me out of my stupor. He flew at me like an attack dog, leaping through the air and slamming into my chest with all of his weight and his momentum. I toppled backward and hit the ground hard. The corporal remained on top of me, his weight on my chest.

He must have been shadowing me from the moment I began my charge. Sometimes Marines do that in combat, they select a buddy and shadow them like a guardian angel.

Minter fired his gun again and again while other Marines closed in around us. I watched the scene, feeling strangely bemused. I didn't want to kill. I wanted the Unifieds to surrender. I wanted them to surrender, and to end their war, and to live.

I wanted to die. That was it. Boiled down to its truest essence, I was done with it. I no longer cared. I had been living on hate, and now it was eating me. Clones created for war cannot allow themselves to become battle-weary.

The men of the First Battalion kept me safe. I felt bad about the risks they took and the effort they wasted. They closed around me. Some knelt; some stood. A few fell. More blood on my hands. More damage on my account. If only they'd known the thoughts in my head, they might have turned their guns on me.

The First of the First, I thought. *You boys deserve better.*

Moments later, Ritz and his men came storming in.

Some U.A. Marines handed over their weapons; most died fighting.

CHAPTER FORTY-ONE

With Ritz and his men pressing the front flank, the fighting eased toward the rear. Corporal Minter grabbed my hand and pulled me to my feet.

I said, "Thank you, Corporal."

He said, "Looks like your gun jammed, General. Would you like me to fetch you another?"

We both knew better.

I said, "That's a hell of a trick you did with your knife, Corporal. Did you learn that in boot camp?" No one had shown me that move, and there had been many times when it might have come in handy.

"No, sir, I improvised." With that, he gave me the old macho nod and went to rejoin his company.

Don't spoil him, I told myself, but I knew I would. Nothing ruins an enlisted man more quickly than giving him a lieutenant's bars.

General Ritz found me as I assembled my men. He said, "It's almost sewed up. There are a few holdouts, sir."

I asked, "How many men have you captured?"

He discussed this with the man next to him, and answered, "Three hundred."

"How many did we kill?" I asked.

"Four hundred."

Neither answer was meant to be specific. Still, Unifieds had come in nine transports which supposedly gave them a maximum of nine hundred men, seven hundred of whom were now accounted for. That meant that the Unifieds might have sent as many as two hundred Marines after Freeman, an absurd amount to take into an enclosed and possibly unstable environment like an abandoned mine. There comes a time when adding more men isn't just overkill, it endangers your operation.

I said, "I want two platoons of your best."

"Ready and waiting, General," said Ritz. Damn if he hadn't known my orders before I gave them. Maybe he'd performed the same math as I had and had come up with the same solution—fifty men stood just beyond the mine.

Generals don't lead assault teams into subterranean mines, which was precisely what I planned to do.

I realized Ritz might have planned to go after Freeman as well. I said, "General, we may have won the battle, or we may only have defeated the first wave."

He said, "Aye."

I said, "We're going to need to guard this ridge."

He nodded, and said, "General, I know your tactics."

He'd been with me when I liberated Terraneau and when I led the invasion of Earth. He did indeed know my tactics. Neither of us had anything more to say, so we traded salutes.

He said, "Good luck, sir. We'll hold the ridge until you get back."

I took my men and entered the tunnel. Maybe I should say, we entered the *funnel.* We were fifty men, a light force, rushing down an all-rock corridor with barely enough room for us to travel ten abreast.

If I'd come in with a larger force, we'd have been bogged down in a clusterspeck.

The sky outside was bright, but we lost the sun the moment we entered the shaft. Here, we had entered an eternal darkness. I imagined Freeman passing this way, chased by an army and feeling claustrophobic. I felt a sense of urgency, one I couldn't quite explain away. Maybe it was just jitters, but I couldn't shake the feeling that Freeman was dangling at the end of a rope.

A few hundred feet in, we found the equipment the Unifieds were using to sludge the airwaves. It was a small machine with batwing antennae, a brightly lit dial, and two meters that checked for radio signals. I wasn't sure which switch would shut the machine down, but if worse came to worst, I figured I could always shut down the transmitter with my M27.

I knelt beside the machine, found the power switch, and I asked myself a question. *Why would Unified Authority Marines want to sludge themselves?*

I knew why Freeman would want the interLink down—shut down the interLink and men in armor go deaf and dumb. But why would the Unifieds want it down? The answer was obvious; Freeman was a skilled demolitions man. Hell, my transport had flown past the charred remains of a camp as we flew in.

Son of a bitch, he mined the mine, I said to myself. Of course he had. With the enemy on his ass, outnumbered and alone, he'd probably planted sensors and charges all over these shafts. Feeling that I had just dodged a bullet, I stood up and left the equipment untouched.

That turned out to be a good choice. A few hundred yards farther into the mountain, we found an abandoned office with lamps with prehistoric bulbs that probably had not produced light for multiple centuries. Beside the office stood an ancient generator.

The technology of the time favored ironworks—pumps, generators, and motors built to be as durable as combat equipment. The pipes and vents leading into this primeval fixture were thick and sturdy, the motor compartment, practically armor-plated.

Already knowing what I would find, I took a closer look and spotted a charge connected to a transmitter. If I'd harbored any doubts about whether we'd find Freeman in this mine, they evaporated.

I motioned my platoon leaders over and showed them my find. They looked and nodded. We were all wearing combat armor and visors, so I couldn't see their faces.

We ran into our first U.A. Marines no more then fifty yards past the office. Two of them stood guarding the entrance of an offshoot hallway. I peered around a corner and saw them standing idle and inattentive. *Like Hansel and Gretel's breadcrumbs,* I thought as I switched from my M27 to my S9 stealth pistol. *Disposable landmarks, marking the way.*

The darkness was almost suffocating. I watched it all through night-for-day lenses, so I saw everything around me, but the darkness still pressed on me, like an oppressive specter.

The hall was long and straight and narrow, with rough walls. The entrances to tributary crawlways formed shadow designs along the walls. Someone had strung a line of old electric lights along the ceiling, fixtures with rounded bulbs set in wire cages. Most of the bulbs had shattered over the years, but a few remained, coated in dust so thick their light could never have shown through.

The next set of guards was more alert. They spotted us before we spotted them. If not for the sludging, they could have called for support, and the fight might have lasted longer. My scouts spotted them and dispatched them in the same instant.

There were a few flashes, a few muffled claps of thunder, and we moved on.

We hiked another half mile before we ran into more Unified Authority Marines. As I rounded the corner, I saw a dozen Unifieds, and they saw me. One of my men did the unthinkable, he threw a grenade, only it was a flashbang that exploded in a brilliant flash of white, neither blinding me nor the men who were shooting at me because we all wore visors with tint shields.

Seeing the grenade, the U.A. Marines dashed for cover. Two members of my fire teams ran in behind the grenade, gunning the enemy Marines before they could return fire. First Battalion must have practiced this maneuver. They picked off the Unifieds without losing a man.

We moved ahead.

I monitored my breathing—keeping rhythmic and silent. I kept my finger along the trigger of my M27 instead of across it as I played with sonar and heat vision, anything to detect the enemy before he detected me.

However many men the Unifieds had sent into this mine, they hadn't sent enough. We'd caught them in a killing bottle, the same bottle they had meant for Freeman. Even if they found a way around us, they'd run into Ritz at the front door.

My sonar scan of the path ahead didn't uncover enemy Marines, but it revealed something interesting. We had come down a shaft carved out of solid rock with no pits or cavities hiding beneath the floor. The walls had been solid. The ground had been solid. But beyond this point, the area below us was hollow, and the floor was little more than a layer between excavations. Using a sonar signal, I pinged the floor ahead. The signal came back, superimposing itself in a radar-like image that flashed over the area in front of me. *Three feet here. Four feet here. Three feet here.* The floor looked solid, but it was a crumbling roof. A grenade would cave it in. High-caliber bullets would drill right through it. If Freeman placed a charge on these floors . . .

We came to a dogleg, and I had my men wait while I checked ahead. I searched for traces of heat and found nothing. I pinged the walls and floor with sonar. The walls were solid, the floor was thinner still, mostly two feet thick. I couldn't tell what hid beneath.

My sonar showed me a spot where the ground had worn away to inches of dirt spread across a wooden floor. Using hand signals, I warned my men to avoid that spot and prodded the ground with the toe of my boot.

And then there was an explosion.

CHAPTER FORTY-TWO

I heard the chatter in my helmet and immediately knew what had happened. I heard: "Speck! What was that?" "Major, how'd you get through? I thought the Link was down. Oh, speck."

Hoping the men outside hadn't removed their helmets, I used a command frequency to reach Ritz. When he responded, I said, "Ritz, there are some escapees headed your way."

As I ran the events through my head, there was only one possible answer. The Unifieds must have found a parallel tunnel and doubled back. They would have made their way to the front of the mine, then cleared the airwaves and set off Freeman's charges to seal us in.

Ritz said, "General, we've got all the guests we can handle out here."

"What are you up against?" I asked. I was in a cave surrounded by darkness, stillness, and silence. Had it not been for my helmet, I would have been blind. Maybe all of my enemies had fled this subterranean world. Maybe some had stayed behind.

But a mile away, Ritz's world was filled with sunlight and chaos. We might have stood on opposite ends of the universe.

I continued walking as we spoke, moving ahead slowly, watchful for traps, enemies, and holes in the floor.

"We have three U.A. gunships out here, sir."

Gunships, I thought. My grenadiers had downed one before entering the mines. It had taken everything they had to swat one gunship, and we'd had all our grenadiers alive and present at that time. We'd lost many advancing up the ridge, and some of the survivors had entered the mines with my company . . . and even then, shooting down that gunship had seemed like luck.

Without telling Ritz, I flipped some virtual switches in my visor so that I could view the world through his eyes. The tiny camera built into the framework of his visor now showed me what he saw in a tiny window.

I wouldn't describe what I saw as a battle. Ritz and his men stood on a ridge with little in the way of cover. They might have had enough grenades and grenadiers to knock down one of the gunships, assuming the other two stayed out of the way.

Some of Ritz's men had run to the mine for shelter. Once enough of my boys entered the mines, those gunships would pipe a missile into the entrance and kill every last one of them.

The gunships were herding my men. Even as I watched, one of the gunships floated in like a cloud, her gunners firing chain guns at men trying to escape down the ridge, grinding them into pulp. A few Marines found shelter and hid. More died. This was First Battalion; when they saw they couldn't escape the gunship, many of the men stood their ground and fired M27s as the chain guns bore down. The last great act of defiance is to die like a Marine. As the dust cleared, I saw armor and blood.

Swearing under his breath, absolutely unaware that I was watching through his eyes, Ritz ripped an RPG from his belt and sprinted toward the cliff and the hovering gunship.

"Ritz, you're not going to accomplish anything," I said, trying to sound calm even though I wasn't.

"Get specked, Harris," he growled, not even giving the words a second thought.

Looking through his eyes, I saw the edge of the cliff coming closer and closer, but he didn't slow down. As he neared the endless drop, he looked down at the grenade in his right hand and pulled a second grenade to hold in his left. Two gunships hovered just past the ledge, their chain guns flashing. One fired a rocket. Ritz didn't stop to see where the rocket hit; he focused on the closest gunship as he tossed one grenade, then the other.

One of the gunships turned so that she faced Ritz. She rose maybe a yard so that it hovered slightly higher than the ridge, and she moved forward. Ritz didn't flinch. He did not turn away. From my vantage point, inside Ritz's visor, it looked like he intended to play chicken with the big bird.

Less than ten feet from the ledge, he kept running. He looked down and snagged an RPG from his belt, then, still charging toward the drop, he raised his hand and prepared to fire . . .

I was drifting ahead, paying enough attention to stop myself from walking into a wall or stepping into a hole, but not thinking about what I was doing, and my carelessness damn near cost me my life.

When the first bullet struck the ceiling above my head, I barely noticed the *zing* it made as it careened off the rocks. I wouldn't have thought about it had the second bullet not grazed my right shoulder. It cut through the edge of my armor, nicking me, but the force of the bullet twisted me around and sent me to the floor.

My mind reeled.

Unbelievable! I was miles deep in an abandoned mineshaft, which was dangerous enough, but I had forgotten that the Unified Authority Marines had sent armed men into this shaft. That is one of the dangers of combat—given a long enough break in the action, men are often lulled into lethargy.

Let your mind wander during the slow moments, and the last thing that goes through your brain is generally a bullet.

I was watching Ritz when I should have been worrying about my own ass. At first I only felt the impact, then the pain started. It wasn't severe, just a stitch along my deltoid, but it burned.

Switching off all distractions in my visor, I searched the darkness. A fire team paused behind me, all four Marines with their weapons ready. With the sludging gone, I now could speak to them. I said, "Sniper. Stay put."

Searching the corridor ahead with heat vision and sonar, I found nothing, then I realized that the shot had hit me just below my shoulder and traveled upward.

I looked down and saw where the floor had caved in along a wall. *Specking idiot,* I told myself. Only an idiot could have missed it, or an officer stupid enough to voyeur his men when he should be watching for enemies. I was lucky the shooter missed my head.

Staying low, I approached the hole. Fifteen rappel cords hung from its edges.

Specking idiot, I thought, angry at myself now for overlooking a hole . . . literally, a gaping hole. Once I placed myself on point, I no longer had any excuses. I was the eyes; the lives of every man on this mission depended on me. If I walked past the hole, they would dismiss it as well.

Okay, yes, the hole looked like a shadow through night-for-day lenses. I tried to give myself a pardon, but I wasn't having any of it. *Asshole,* I thought. *You're going to get your men killed.*

My wounded shoulder still stung by this time. That's how combat wounds work; they give you a few moments to realize you've been injured, then they send signals about their severity. Sometimes the pain incapacitates you. Sometimes the fear and embarrassment hurt more than the injury itself. The gouge along my deltoid was shallow, like a slit from a knife. Blood ran down my arm, bunching around my wrist.

The notion that the Unifieds might have left a sniper behind finally occurred to me. As I remembered the noise I'd heard moments before the bullet struck me, I realized that two shots had been fired, the second shot fired one or two seconds after the first. *A lone gunman,* I reassured myself.

I thought about dropping a grenade down the chute. One of the men beside me had the same impulse. He reached for a pill. Like me, he thought again and changed his mind. The floor beneath us had already worn away. Drop a grenade, even on a low-yield setting, and those of us who survived would end up one deck down, buried in dust and rock.

I thought, *If the Unifieds sent fifteen men down that hole, Freeman must have passed that way as well.* "Freeman, you down there?" I called out, using one of the interLink frequencies he haunted. No response.

"Ray?" Nothing.

The shooter on the deck beneath us had gone silent as well. I kept low, out of his line of sight. He might pick up my heat signature if he used the right lens in his visor; he could hit me through the floor with the right armor-piercing ammunition.

Using the sonar equipment in my visor, I took a reading of the area around the hole. I risked moving closer, dropping on my ass and sliding within a foot of it. I edged closer, stopped, then slithered closer again.

I wanted to take a sonar reading to see how far I would need to drop to hit the next floor down, but to do that, I would need to look straight down the hole. Rather than make myself a target, I fished one of the rappel cords out of the hole and ran it through my fingers. I estimated the length at twenty-five feet.

I didn't want to climb down, and it was too far to jump. A man on a rope is an easy and defenseless target.

"Ray, you down there?" I called out on several frequencies.

No answer. He almost certainly had gone down that hole, and the Unifieds had followed him. Dead or alive, he was somewhere in the shaft below.

I gathered my men closer and positioned men around the hole. On my signal, they opened fire, shooting blindly into the deck below, and I took the cord. Instead of attaching it to my armor for a controlled and safe drop, I held it tight in my right hand and dived in like a swimmer in a race.

I fell down, down into the blackness, my momentum still carrying me forward as I fell. I had hoped to land on my feet, but I hit a post, then another, knocking me off balance. Instead of surfing to the ground, I slammed on my back, the air bursting from my lungs when I struck bottom. My head hurt. My neck went numb. Forcing myself to go through the motions, I rolled along the ground, sweeping the area with my S9.

I had landed on a junk pile of sorts, a heap of abandoned U.A. Marine combat armor. Only, I instinctively knew that it hadn't been abandoned. An entire squad had made a stand and lost on this very spot, and I had landed on their remains.

"General, are you . . ."

"I'm fine," I said, not even bothering to ID the officer. "Wait for my orders."

Then I shouted across all frequencies, "Freeman! Ray, are you here?" When that didn't work, I switched to my external speaker. I said, "Freeman, you miserable bastard, you shot me."

Silence. I was alone, just me and fifteen dead Marines. Pushing on helmets and chest plates, I worked my way to my feet.

I took no joy in wading through a pile of massacred natural-borns. They were stacked two and three high like dead trees on a forest floor.

"Freeman," I shouted, using the external speaker.

Once I had forced my way out of the pile, I found stragglers, lying still on the ground like scattered stones. About forty feet away, Freeman sat with his back propped against a wall and his rifle across his lap. I spotted the glow of his scope. And then I saw him.

He looked bad. He'd gone mostly limp. If not for the wall, he would not have been able to support himself. He'd removed his right shoe. His right leg was so swollen that I couldn't tell where his calf ended and his ankle began. I watched him through my night-for-day lenses. So much blood covered his face that he looked like he'd been carved out of wet stone. He sat there, eyes shut, face tilted toward the stars, and he drew in a deep breath, which he held in his lungs for several seconds. He couldn't see me, not in this darkness, not without a visor or his rifle scope.

Approaching Freeman, I stepped over the body of a dead Marine. I took two more paces, then someone spoke to me over the interLink. "There you are, Harris. I knew you'd come." The man spoke softly, a taunt instead of a threat.

Who the specking hell are you? I thought, though on some level, I must have recognized the speaker. A cold chill ran through me. I froze in place, just a few feet from Freeman. Standing in the darkness, feeling as vulnerable and alone as a newborn in a crib, I tried to sound brave. I asked, "Who the speck am I speaking to?"

"The name is Nailor; we met on Mars."

We sure as speck had met on Mars. The bastard shot me in the back and left me there for dead. He'd shot me, then knelt over me, so I could see his face.

"Are you down here, Franklin?" I asked. "I'd love to see you again, maybe give you my regards."

"No need to shit yourself, Harris. I can't touch you. I can see you, but you're out of reach."

I stopped and turned to look at the dead Marines. One lay on his stomach at the edge of the pile, his face turned toward Freeman, toward me. Freeman had shot him in the chest, leaving his visor intact.

Nailor watched me as I approached the corpse. He said, "Yes, that's right."

Like me, he had a commandLink. He could look through his men's visors the same way I had peered through Ritz's.

I pulled my S9 and fired into the dead Marine's visor. It took five fléchettes to shatter the visor, Nailor laughing at me the entire time. I should have kicked it.

I felt this sense of dreaded déjà vu, as if I'd heard him laugh at me before. Maybe he'd laughed at me as I lay bleeding on Mars. I wasn't sure.

He said, "I can't kill you, not in that hole. I wouldn't hit you if I detonated a nuke on that mountain. You're buried alive for now, but you'll dig your way out.

"In the meantime, Harris, I wanted you to know just how badly you have failed. The clones you left to guard the cave are dead. Unlike you, they couldn't hide under the rocks until it was safe."

Bastard, I thought.

He continued speaking, his voice in my ear, in my head. He said, "You'll dig your way out, but before you do, I'll hit

Washington, D.C. I'll kill Watson. I'll kill the soldiers you sent. Take too long digging yourself out, Harris, and by the time you wiggle out from the dirt, your Clone Empire will be gone for good."

Once he'd delivered his message, he disappeared. Maybe he was just outside the mine, surveying my dead Marines and laughing at my failures. Maybe he'd called from one of the gunships. Either way, he couldn't wait around. Hauser, who was supposedly monitoring the battle from the *Churchill*, would have sent fighters.

I didn't know how many ships the New Unifieds had in their fleet or how many of my clones they had chemically converted to their cause, but Nailor couldn't trade jabs with the Enlisted Man's Navy. Hauser's Navy had to have a ten-to-one advantage over the Unified Authority's fleet.

As I knelt beside Freeman, I called to Ritz. "Ritz, you there?"

Silence.

His name had vanished from the registry. Almost all the names had. When Marines die in action, their names disappear to show they are inactive. I remembered him running toward the ledge and pulling the rocket-propelled grenade. Was that when he died?

I called to the men who had entered the mine. Speaking on an open frequency, I said, "This deck is secure. Get your asses down here."

Then I said to Freeman, "You shot me, you piece of shit."

The cave was dark except for the glow from his rifle scope. Though he could not see anything, Freeman opened his right eye and stared in my direction. His head remained perfectly still as he said, "I wouldn't have shot you if you'd reacted the first time I shot. Next time, learn to take a hint."

CHAPTER FORTY-THREE

Location: Washington, D.C.
Date: July 31, 2519

The soldiers in the First Infantry Division of the 3rd Corps proudly wore THE BIG RED ONE as their shoulder patch. They also called themselves "The Fighting First."

On this mission, however, they had become "The *Finding* First." MacAvoy had assigned them the task of searching the city for Travis Watson. They hadn't found him so far, but at 03:00, they located an abandoned car in an unlit alley, in a ritzy downtown district called Mount Vernon Square. The vehicle had extensive body damage. Its front end was partially caved in, several of the windows were shattered, and bullet holes dotted the hood.

The make and the model matched a car that Major Alan Cardston had reported as "stolen from the Pentagon parking complex." The captain commanding the company wanted to call in the information, but MacAvoy was still sludging the airwaves. He hopped in a jeep and drove to the Pentagon, where he met with the full-bird colonel who was running the show at that late hour.

"Any blood in the vehicle?" asked the colonel.

The captain frowned, and said, "Urine."

"Say again?"

"Urine."

"I'm in what?"

"Piss, sir. Somebody pissed in the car."

"No blood, but those bullet holes must mean something. Search the area," said the officer in charge,

The company commander saluted and left, hating the forty-five minutes he'd just wasted because he could not call in his findings on the horn. *Specking sludging,* he thought as he drove back to Mount Vernon Square.

And so, at 04:23, with the sky dark and the streets empty, First Infantry 3rd Corps started searching Mount Vernon Square.

At 05:03, a squad of First Infantry soldiers began searching a street lined by luxury apartment complexes. The first cars of morning had just appeared as the sky brightened and the streetlamps faded to darkness. Sunrise reflected on the windows of tall buildings. The morning air felt cool against the soldiers' arms and faces.

Not realizing they had entered enemy territory, the soldiers let their attention slip. They didn't walk in formation. They left the safeties engaged on their M27s and traded jokes and stories.

Two women jogged toward them. The women were in their twenties and slender, their tops drenched with sweat. When the soldiers stepped into their path and asked them to look at a photograph, the women stopped, examined it, then shook their heads.

Nobody recognized Watson. He had not been elected; he was a military aide promoted to leadership. The soldiers stopped deliverymen, joggers, and commuters. A few people asked who he was.

The soldiers entered a wide avenue with trees and redbrick walkways and expensive tenements that no enlisted man could ever afford. Fancy sedans passed them on the street. They saw a few more joggers. The traffic remained sparse.

Sensing something out of place, the platoon sergeant led his men across a street. He looked up one side of the block and down the other, moving ahead slowly, releasing the safety on his M27, and allowing his left hand to drift to the compartment that held his grenades.

Two sets of storm drains faced each other on opposite sides of the street. Still not seeing anything, but trusting his instincts, the sergeant turned and aimed his M27 at the seemingly empty storm drain and fired a burst. Someone in the seemingly empty storm drain fired back.

A quick burst of shots, three maybe four, and one of the

soldiers fell clutching his bloodied knee. The sergeant responded, snatching a grenade and shucking it side-handed toward the storm drain. He yelled, “Fire in the hole!” followed by “Get your asses off the street!”

His men scattering in every direction, the sergeant dragged his fallen soldier to the sidewalk and ducked behind a car.

For a moment, he found himself under fire. Men with rifles fired at him. Bullets riddled the cars around him. His grenade exploded, a loud and percussive clap of thunder that spit smoke out of one storm drain and water from another. A manhole cover flipped askew but remained mostly in place. Screaming, yelling, and wailing echoed from the storm drains.

“Call HQ! Call HQ!” the sergeant shouted as he lowered his wounded soldier to the ground. “We need B Company here rapid, quick, and pronto!”

MacAvoy’s sludging had closed down the airwaves around the Pentagon and southwest suburbs, but interLink communications remained alive and well in the city itself.

The soldier the sergeant had rescued had twin wounds in his right thigh. He lay on his back squirming and groaning, his eyes closed tight against the pain. He cursed quietly, then let out a scream of frustration. “Specking hurts!” he moaned.

The sergeant counted the manholes along the street. Between the street and sidewalks, there were twelve manholes. A block away, there were another twelve from which a pack of U.A. soldiers slowly emerged. The sergeant yelled, “In the buildings. Move! Move!”

Ignoring the injured clone’s screams, the sergeant slung the man over his shoulder a second time. He fired two bursts down the street and loped into the nearest doorway.

“Thompson, get to the top floor. Tell me what you see!

“Martin, call this in! We need support. Tell Battalion Command the Unifieds are in the sewers! Tell them it’s the specking all-naturals.

“You, Galloway, make sure there’s no side entrance into the building. Gopher, Marks, cover the rear door.

“Martin, what do you see?”

A civilian, a chubby woman in a bathrobe and slippers,

came shambling down the stairs. She gazed at the sergeant, saw the squirming, bleeding soldier, and screamed.

The sergeant yelled, "Get to your room, ma'am. We're under attack."

She showed no sign of hearing the soldier over her shrieks.

Bullets and shards of glass flew in from the front window of the building. One of the soldiers stood, fired his gun, and took a bullet in the forehead. His helmet flew off, so did the top of his head. Blood splashed all over the carpet behind him. He dropped to a knee, then to the ground, his M27 still in his hands.

The woman screamed and ran. The sound of doors slamming rang through the halls.

A U.A. soldier neared the window. Seeing the grenade in his hand, the sergeant sprang from behind the couch he'd been using for cover. He shot the soldier in the arm, chest, and head, and that was how he died, with the grenade still in his hand. When it exploded, the force of the blast caused the front of the building to cave in.

News of this attack did not reach MacAvoy until the following day. By that time, the war had begun.

CHAPTER FORTY-FOUR

The destroyer entered the solar system unnoticed, broadcasting in two hundred and fifty million miles away, on the opposite side of the sun.

She had a stealth generator, an experimental prototype that had never been tested in battle, the only one of its kind. As long as she did not fire weapons or send messages, the destroyer would remain invisible. The moment she fired her weapons, the "sleeping clones" would be able to track her, and the fun would begin.

None of the EMN ships detected her as she glided silently into their net.

Invisible to their radar and tracking equipment, she slid into an orbit that placed her directly above Washington, D.C. Working quickly and efficiently, the crew selected their targets—Joint Base Anacostia-Bolling, the Archive Building, and the Pentagon. The destroyer was a lone ship in an enemy stronghold; she wouldn't survive in a battle, so her captain charged her broadcast engine before powering her weapons.

She fired at all three targets simultaneously, then she broadcasted out.

The Unified Authority assault began with instantaneous and successful bombardment.

At 05:30, three missiles struck Joint Base Anacostia-Bolling. The first struck the hangars, dissolving them in flames. The second missile hit the fuel supplies, creating a fireball that spiraled three hundred feet in the air. The third missile destroyed the communications building.

The first and third had been unnecessary. The force and heat from the burning fuel killed every man on base and destroyed every building.

In the heart of the capital, a missile struck the Archive Building, eradicating brick and mortar and classified files all at the same time. A security mechanism dropped the few computers that survived that first assault into an underground vault designed to withstand earthquakes. The destroyer hit the ruins with particle-beam cannons, obliterating the vault.

Across the Potomac from Anacostia-Bolling, a single missile struck the Pentagon. MacAvoy caught a glimpse of it as it dropped through the clouds. Standing with a group of junior officers at the outer edge of the parking lot, he glanced up and saw what looked like the finger of God bearing down on humanity, and said, "Shit, now they've gone and done it."

The missile struck the building. It bored into the Pentagon like a bullet to the head, and the building exploded, spraying glass, cement, steel, bits of furniture, wood, and pipe a full half mile in every direction. A whirlwind of dust rose from the wreckage.

The explosion sent a shock wave across the parking lot that flipped cars, trucks, and tanks with the same ease.

MacAvoy rose from the ground and dug a finger into his right ear, which had gone deaf and numb. Rivulets of blood poured down his cheeks and the side of his nose. When he looked at the finger he'd placed in his ear, he saw blood.

The first person he saw was a corporal with a communications insignia. He said, "No point sludging the airwaves now, not anymore."

The corporal said, "No, sir."

The bones in the boy's right shin were badly broken and no longer formed a straight line. One side of that broken line must have punctured the skin; his shoes were covered with blood.

In a soft voice, MacAvoy asked, "You all right, son?"

"Yes, sir."

"Do you need a ride to the dustoff?" The term "dustoff" referred to the medical evacuation center.

The soldier said, "No, sir. No, sir. I belong right here."

"Good boy," MacAvoy said, sounding tender. "We've been sludging their communications, but I don't think they're communicating with much of anybody now. Think you can clear the airwaves, son?"

"Yes, sir," said the corporal. He hopped to the mobile communications trailer, sat on the stairs, and pulled himself in, his injured leg dangling down the stairs.

"Once you got communications up, report to the dustoff, son. That's an order."

"Yes, sir."

MacAvoy watched the corporal with a measure of satisfaction. He walked over to a major who lay squirming on the ground, slapped him hard across the face, and asked, "Son, are you still alive?"

The major blinked and stared up at MacAvoy. Seeing he was conscious, but not necessarily lucid, the general slapped him a second time and said, "Get your ass in that jeep. You hear me, Major?

"There is an injured corporal in that communications nest over there. When that boy comes out, you load him in this jeep, then the two of you report to the nearest hospital. Do you read me, son?"

The fear and confusion in the major's eyes resolved into recognition and MacAvoy helped him climb to his feet.

A handful of good Samaritans headed to the Pentagon to look for survivors. MacAvoy caught their attention by firing a machine gun at their feet. He walked over, bawling, "Which specking, shit-for-brains fool officer gave you permission to approach my building?"

"Sir? We just . . ."

MacAvoy pointed his machine gun at the soldier to shut him up. He said, "You, Private, take that jeep and drive around the building." The soldier ran to the jeep and hopped behind the wheel. He was a lieutenant, not a private, and he hoped he could keep his commission.

MacAvoy said, "Private, you take a lap around the building. If you see any more morons trying to enter the building, you stop 'em. Yell at 'em to stop. If they don't stop, shoot 'em.

"You see any converts trying to get out, you shoot them, too. Do you read me, son?"

"Yes, sir."

He turned to the officers who had been walking with the lieutenant, and said, "You boys follow the private. If you see him do anything stupid, you shoot him. You got that?"

He sent the men to a truck with only half a salute.

The soldiers stumbled over to a jeep that lay on its side. Watching them, MacAvoy muttered, "Damn, son, did you lose your brains or your testicles?" Raising his voice, he shouted, "What's the matter with you boys! That jeep ain't going nowhere. Take that truck over there!" He pointed at a troop carrier that had remained on its wheels.

Watching the truck drive away, MacAvoy muttered, "We need a better class of clone."

An aide carrying a mobile communications rig ran over to MacAvoy. He said, "General, reports are coming in. They hit Bolling."

"No shit, son! I can see the smoke from here," said MacAvoy. He pointed south and east. Three miles away and across the Potomac, the joint base wasn't visible from the parking lot of the Pentagon.

The missile attack on the Pentagon had been clean, sending up dust and a winding plume of white smoke. The hit on Bolling had been another story. Thick ropes of black smoke rose into the air, forming a knot that looked like a storm cloud. A veteran of many battles, MacAvoy read the smoke and knew it came from burning fuel. He asked, "What's the damage?"

The aide, a lieutenant, hadn't noticed the smoke until MacAvoy pointed to it. He stood staring, hypnotized.

"Son! Son, I need you to stay with me here," said MacAvoy, his patience thinning. "What . . . is . . . the . . . specking . . . damage . . . at . . . Bolling?"

"Third Corps sent in the cavalry to investigate."

"What . . . did . . . we . . . lose?" MacAvoy shouted, his patience worn out.

"Everything, sir."

"Everything? What the specking hell is that supposed to mean! Bolling is a big base. It's got jets. It's got helicopters. It's got a post exchange and more latrines than a beer factory. Bolling Field has its own specking shit-treatment facility, son. Now, you get on the squawk and tell me which of those things are missing."

The lieutenant turned white as MacAvoy berated him. He gulped in air, nodded, and said, "General, they've all been destroyed. The base is a total loss."

"That so?" asked MacAvoy, suddenly sounding contrite.

The lieutenant knew better than to answer.

MacAvoy said, "Lieutenant, see if you can reach Admiral Hauser on the *Churchill*." He knew already that communications with the fleet had been disrupted, but he had the lieutenant try just the same. The Pentagon and Joint Base Anacostia-Bolling housed all the equipment for signaling space in the area. That equipment no longer existed.

A moment later, when the lieutenant said communications were down, MacAvoy told him, "Son, find a way to reach Hauser. I don't care if you have to run a kite string all the way to his ship, find a way to reach Hauser and inform him of the attack."

"Yes, sir," the lieutenant answered, sounding confused.

MacAvoy said, "That will be all," and turned to walk away. He pretended not to notice when the lieutenant saluted.

MacAvoy went to one of his colonels, and said, "Get on the horn. Tell every last soldier in Third Corps to be on alert, Colonel. You let them know we are under attack."

"Do you want me to call them in, sir?" asked the colonel.

MacAvoy didn't mind giving orders, but he didn't like discussing them. He said, "Colonel, pick up your gun and report to the farthest security post you can find from here."

"Yes, sir," the colonel said, and he ran, glad to escape with his life. MacAvoy's tirades were legend among his men.

The general pointed to the next closest officer, and said, "You, get over here. Yes, I mean you. Do we really need this discussion? If my nose is pointed at you and my eyes are staring at you, who the speck would I be talking to except for you, Major?"

He pointed to the mobile communications center, and said, "Major, do you know how to use the horn?"

"No, sir."

"How hard can it be? I've seen privates do this fresh out of basic. Listen here, you walk right up to the console and you find the button marked 'speak,' then you put your face in front of the screen and talk. Do you think you can handle that?"

"Yes, sir."

"Well hallelujah, son, the age of miracles has not ceased. Now listen up. You get on that horn and you tell every officer in Third Corps that we are under attack."

"Yes, sir. Do you mean the attack here at the Pentagon, sir?"

"SPECK! Listen to me, son. If you're too damn stupid to grasp this, I may just shoot you to put you out of my misery. Ah, shit, never mind. Get out of my way."

MacAvoy pushed past the major and entered his mobile communications center—an armored trailer covered with an array of antennae. He stomped up the stairs, shoved the hobbled corporal with the broken leg out of the chair, and spoke into the screen. He said, "Third Corps, dig in, prepare for attack. That'll be all."

Looking back at no one in particular, he asked, "Now how specking hard was that?"

Later that afternoon, MacAvoy held a conference that reached every military base on the planet. As officers started to appear on the screen, he said, "This is General Pernell MacAvoy. If you have any questions, keep 'em to yourself.

"I'm in Washington, D.C., with Third Corps, and we are under attack. I want men. I want machinery. I want every specking base in this man's Army placed on alert.

"You, General Glover, relay my situation to Admiral Hauser. You got that? Tell him Third Corps is under attack . . . *Under attack*, you got that? Good. While you're at it, ask him, 'Who the speck shot at us?' and 'How'd they get through his specked-up excuse of a blockade?'

"I don't know what the U.A.'s got planned for us, but it's going to be big."

CHAPTER FORTY-FIVE

The first U.A. fighter wing had forty jets. The jets flew fast, stayed low, employed radar-disrupting technology, and filtered their engine streams through heat-disbursement gear. They came from a new generation of Tomcats. They were slightly larger than the fighters flown by clone pilots and slightly slower, but more maneuverable and covered with a light-refracting skin that disrupted laser targeting.

The jets traveled halfway up the Potomac before anyone spotted them. They flew in ten-bird formations, tight together, low against the water, the draft from their aerodynamic slipstreams barely churning the river in their wake. They flew three thousand miles per hour, nearly four times the speed of sound, covering the 150-mile distance in three minutes.

Admiral Hauser's men spotted them halfway across the Potomac; by the time they informed the admiral, the U.A. fighters had already reached Washington, D.C., and no longer mattered.

As the Tomcats approached the junction where the Anacostia River splits off from the Potomac, they crossed the East

Potomac Golf Course, where MacAvoy had stationed two Z Battery units in case of an air attack.

Z Battery units were armored vehicles with chain guns that fired grenades instead of bullets. Each battery fired twenty grenades per second, pulling its ammunition from a chamber that held fifteen thousand grenades.

Flying at three thousand miles per hour, the fighters zipped past the burning ruins of Bolling Air Force Base and dashed into air saturated with grenade shrapnel. The flak shredded the fighters' armor, and they exploded as if they'd slammed into a wall. Traveling at three thousand miles per hour, the last pilots didn't have time to see what happened to their leaders before they went up in flames as well.

MacAvoy watched the fighters from several views. One showed them as they entered the mouth of the Potomac. Another showed them as charcoal gray streaks tearing past a checkpoint fifty miles north. The last screen showed the fighters as they flew in range of the Z Batteries.

Looking from this view, he saw the slow dawn of a summer morning, the white horizon, the clearing sky. He heard the *POPOPOPOPOPOPOPOPOPOPOP* of the batteries as they spat out thousands of exploding grenades. The air turned translucent, then almost opaque, with the silver of shrapnel and the thin white smoke of a million tiny explosions. Even watching carefully, MacAvoy never actually saw the enemy fighters.

His standard grimace worked its way into a smile. He muttered, "And saints and angels sing," under his breath. "Christmas came in August this year."

When one of his men gave him a congratulatory clap on the back, General MacAvoy turned to sneer. The officer quietly slipped from the truck, hoping to hide for the rest of his career.

CHAPTER FORTY-SIX

Three Schwarzkopf tanks from the Seventy-seventh Armor Brigade rumbled past the triangle junction where Constitution Avenue met 6th Street and Pennsylvania Avenue. A company of infantrymen surrounded the tanks, creating a perfect symbiosis, a martial partnership that had remained unchanged for nearly one thousand years—the tanks protecting the men from armor and light armor attacks while the men protected the tanks from infantry.

Weathering the early afternoon in Washington, D.C., with its high temperatures and its humidity, the soldiers' faces glistened with sweat. Glaring sunlight reflected off windows, and rays of heat rose out of the street.

Washington, D.C., wasn't a single city; it was three. The forgotten face of the city, the one forced to the outskirts, housed workers and bureaucrats. This was a bedroom community with average homes and lots of minimalls. The second face of the capital was filled with glitzy bars, expensive restaurants, and luxury hotels—a place where businessmen went to bribe politicians. The third and most famous face was the pangalactic government seat. Even now, with all the colonies lost and the clones in control, this part of the city remained resplendent, a living, breathing museum exhibit filled with monuments, marble palaces, and modern towers of metal, glass, and stone.

The triangle junction sat in the heart of monument boulevard.

To the left, a circular fountain sat hidden beneath a copse of trees. A large three-sided plaza filled the next block, its marble façade adorned with enormous columns that served no practical function except to help the building fit into the capital's Greek-temple motif. One block farther, the ruins of the

Archive Building smoldered, its granite-and-marble rubble still glowing orange, like coals in a fire.

A few walls of the once-glorious temple still stood, geometric planes that highlighted the differences between the symmetry of architecture and the entropy of destruction. A quarter section of the domed roof poked out of the twenty-foot-tall pile, covering it like a shield.

By this time, reinforcements had arrived. Fighters streaked over the city. Helicopter gunships hovered over neighborhoods. Above the atmosphere, fighter carriers and battleships circled.

Pockets of fighting had broken out all over the city—lightning assaults. The Unifieds attacked smaller units, nothing bigger than squads and the occasional platoon. Everyone had heard that a squad of soldiers from the Big Red One had gotten their noses bloodied near Mount Vernon Square. They'd gotten themselves trapped in a building until 3rd Corps Command sent a battalion to dig them out.

The patrol continued on, moving away from the National Mall, continuing down Pennsylvania Avenue toward the Linear Committee Building, the structure that had represented the ultimate seat of power under the Unified Authority, the one government building in all of Washington, D.C., that remained vacant.

The patrol passed the giant circular pool erected as a monument to the old Navy, the "Wet Navy." The building on the next block was a seven-story latticework of concrete and glass. Across the street stood a clunky marble fortress, a federal edifice that had remained in place for centuries on end.

Three Schwarzkopf tanks and 150 infantry men patrolled the lane. They were looking for Watson. They were hunting the enemy. They were looking for survivors. They were on patrol. Patrols don't require reasons.

The enemy fired rockets first, then machine guns. Shoulder-fired rockets streaked out of windows on either side of the street, striking each of the Schwarzkopfs several times. The heavy tanks didn't bounce or cartwheel, they bobbed and burst into flames, and their crews were incinerated inside them.

One moment, the tanks were rumbling ahead, the next their

turrets lit up like torches. A rocket struck one of the tanks directly below the main gun, causing the ceiling of the driver's compartment to melt under the heat of the flames. The soldiers standing outside the tank heard the screams of the men riding inside.

Gunfire and grenades poured out of the building.

Caught in a cross fire, some soldiers ran straight ahead. Some dropped, seeking cover between the burning tanks. A radioman called for support. A sergeant fired three RPGs into the building on the south side of the street. Glass shattered. Walls crumbled. Fine plumes of white smoke mixed with large clouds of dust rising out of the building, and the shooting continued.

A corporal stood and fired his M27, shooting at the building, not at the men inside of it. A sniper hit him in the throat, nearly decapitating him. Bullets hit him in the shoulder and chest.

The first EME gunship to respond came from two miles away. It chased up the block, dual chain guns carving the buildings from which the assault had begun. Bullets as long as pointer fingers drilled through windows and walls alike. Glass shattered into the building. Shards of marble dropped down its façade, and splinters of rock sprayed across the sidewalk.

A Unified Authority solider on the third floor of the southern building fired an L-19 rocket, a bulky-but-portable weapon specifically designed for damaging gunships. The rocket traveled less than one hundred yards before hitting its mark, leaving behind a fluffy white streak of smoke.

The rocket, a foot-long harpoon, struck the gunship in a dazzling flash of flame, chemicals, and electricity, incapacitating the floating fortress much the same way that a wasp's sting paralyzes its prey. The electricity short-circuited the gunship's computerized brain while heat and acid tore at her mechanical functions. The blast knocked the gunship to the side, and the pulse caused her engines to flutter, but the pilot maintained control of his ship, returning fire with a missile of his own.

The gunship was slowly dying. Smoke rose from her engines. The pilot would need to land shortly, but at the moment, he still had time to return fire for fire.

On the ground below, soldiers saw the struggling helicopter

and cleared out from beneath her. In the building, the assailants turned their attention to the soldiers. With the tanks destroyed and the gunship struggling, they nearly had the battle won. When a Unified Authority soldier appeared on the top of the building carrying a rocket, a gunner on the dying gunship spotted him and immediately turned his chain guns on the man.

To the west, three more EME gunships flew into view. The pilot of the first gunship saw them, flashed a distress signal, then fired a rocket cluster at the building on the northern side of the street. Grenade-sized explosions, a great bunch of them condensed into a fifty-foot space, flashed and dissolved across the face of the building, causing it to sag, then to collapse.

A standard rocket-propelled grenade struck the belly of the injured gunship, bouncing her skyward. It was a glancing blow that caused no damage though one of the gunners felt his sphincter clench as he rode an invisible elevator up three stories on the bounce. The pilot glanced at his radar, saw the other birds closing behind him, and radioed, "Can you take this one?"

"Affirmative," answered one of the pilots. "Specking HOOOOAH!" said the other.

The first pilot allowed the hit from the RPG to carry his bird up another few feet, then he used his pedals to turn her around as he crossed over the top of the battle and flew back to base.

CHAPTER FORTY-SEVEN

At 16:00, Pernell MacAvoy arrived in a mobile nerve center (MNC) to oversee the operation on Pennsylvania Avenue. Unlike General Harris, who always seemed so anxious to die with his Marines, MacAvoy had every intention of surviving the day.

Watching the scene on a monitor, he spoke to Major Max Jensen, the officer leading the operation. He said, "Son, what's it look like in there? Is that old bitch going to fall down on you?"

The soldiers in Special Forces didn't wear the same gear as Marines. Jensen and his commandos wore open-faced helmets with cameras attached above their foreheads. Sitting in the MNC, MacAvoy and other officers directing the show went along for the ride vicariously, watching every move through those cameras.

Major Jensen said, "The engineers say the back half of the building is safe, General. We should be fine as long as we stay away from the wreckage."

"Can you do that, son? Is that going to get in your way" asked MacAvoy.

The major pointed his camera across an undamaged lobby and down a mostly solid-looking hall. Glass shimmered on the floor at the far side of the hall.

"Have you checked for traps, son?" asked MacAvoy.

"Mines, wires, sensors, and infrared, sir," said Jensen.

"Did you scan for enemies?"

"Yes, sir. The building appears empty."

MacAvoy's adjutant had read him a report that said as much, but the general wanted to make sure. Jensen and his company were Special Forces, a type of soldier that commanded a unique place in Pernell MacAvoy's olive drab heart.

The major and his men were from the First Special Forces Operational Detachment. They were Deltas. They were tough, highly trained, and careful. They were the Army's best.

Jensen said, "General, I hope to hell there is someone in there. I'd hate to think you flew me here for sightseeing, sir."

MacAvoy said, "Son, I flew you out to the capital because I like your attitude. Watching you kill some Unified Authority speck, well, that would be just like finding chipped beef in the gravy on my biscuits. Now, seeing you interrogate one, son . . . you do that, and I'll retire a happy man."

The major called out to his men. He yelled, "Move out, Deltas."

They moved out.

Civilians had died during the fighting. Most had escaped,

but a few employees with offices facing Pennsylvania Avenue were caught in the cross fire.

The major sent a few scouts upstairs to search the building, but it was more of a perfunctory search for survivors than anything else. The Deltas had scanned the building with listening equipment that could pick up a rabbit's heartbeat from a mile away.

Jensen and the rest of his men headed into the darkness. As they left the sunlight behind them, lenses folded down out of their helmets and covered their right eyes. Unlike Marines, who "hid their pieholes behind a visor," Deltas used a discrete eyepiece that gave them a night-for-day lens and heat vision. Like Marines, they used an interLink connection. But, while Marines wrapped their heads in an audiovisual display, soldiers heard through earpieces and spoke into microphones.

Jensen sent four men down two different elevator shafts. The soldiers would rappel down to the dormant elevators and jimmy the doors.

As the rest of his men entered a stairwell, Major Jensen quietly groaned. The air smelled of sulfur and spoilage, like swamp gas and shit. One of his men whispered, "Speck, who flappered that one?"

"Stow it," hissed Jensen.

He looked at the stairs and saw tiny puddles of water on the concrete. Speaking to MacAvoy, he said, "It smells like a sewer down here, sir."

"A sewer," the general echoed, and disappeared from his mike. A moment later, he returned. Sounding authoritative, he said "Major, head down two floors. Tell me what you see."

"Yes, sir," said Jensen. MacAvoy didn't tell him to send men to search the first level of the underground parking structure or the lower levels, but he sent teams to each level just the same. Jensen also assigned men to guard the stairwell. He was a Delta, and Deltas left nothing to chance.

MacAvoy had risen through the ranks of infantry and armor, never having spent time in Special Forces. He knew how to bulldoze enemies and how to hold locations. This was a different kind of mission, and it required a different set of skills.

After sending men to investigate the lower levels and

guard the stairs, the major brought a single squad with him as he entered the second level of the underground parking structure—ten men, including himself. He didn't inform General MacAvoy about his precautions. On special operations such as this mission, the boots on the ground were given more room for discretion. They were specialists carrying out highly technical operations; they understood the inner workings of their world better than the officers on the other end of the mike.

The sulfurlike smell became stronger as they entered the parking area. Lights still shone from the ceiling, illuminating an underground garage filled with cars. Major Jensen and his squad entered the level and spread, each man finding cover, scanning for enemies, holding his place.

A thin layer of silt covered the floor, and tawny-colored water splashed beneath their boots as they walked.

"Are you getting this, sir?" asked Major Jensen. He took in a breath that smelled of rotten eggs and stepped ahead into the mud.

Jensen signaled for his men to stop. Speaking softly to the general, he said, "I suggest scanning this area again before we proceed, sir."

The sound of sloshing water echoed through the level. It sounded as if it was far away. The major heard it and wondered if it had something to do with air-conditioning.

MacAvoy asked, "Are you wearing a gas mask, son?"

"Yes, sir."

"Then you're good to go. Do you know what you are smelling?"

"Yes, sir," said the major. "We're knee deep in shit."

The masks filtered chemicals out of the air, but they did not eradicate smells entirely. Along with the rotten-eggs smell of sewage, the soldiers now imbibed the sharp odor of ozone.

Jensen gave the hand signal for the men in his squad to remain in wedge formation as they moved ahead. They trudged slowly, passing the ramp that led up to the first deck of the parking structure before they stopped.

He radioed General MacAvoy, and said, "Sir, we found their point of entry."

MacAvoy said, "And . . ."

Not knowing what else to say, Jensen said, ". . . and they entered through this point."

Sounding irritable, MacAvoy snapped, "Is it clear, son? Can you secure the location?"

Observing the scene through the major's head-mount, MacAvoy saw the twenty-foot section that the Unified had blasted out of the cement wall. Their charges had destroyed more than cement and structure; a yard-wide pipe had been blown in two. A steady trickle of mud dribbled out of either end of the pipe, but most of the sewage had poured out earlier. A pile of fecal matter had gathered below the pipes.

Beyond the broken pipes, the break in the wall presented a morbid landscape of underground tunnels with wedges of light that streamed in through street-level storm drains. This was Washington, D.C., through the looking glass.

Son of a bitch, thought MacAvoy. *No wonder nobody spotted the bastards, they came in through the waterworks.*

Soldiers used handheld meters to scan for the same information that Marines read through their visors. Army instruments were clumsy and inconvenient but generally more precise than Marine gear.

Jensen had his men test for explosives. He scanned for voices and electronic signals. Deciding to ignore the ontological meter's warning about high nitrogen levels and the increased probability of improvised organic-based explosives, the major determined the area was secure.

With his men behind him, he approached the wall.

The underground parking structure they were leaving wasn't particularly bright, but it looked like a sunlit field compared to the tunnel on the other side. A ten-foot-wide water trough ran down the center of the tunnel. Fortunately, the trough conveyed drainage, not sewage. Below the water, jade-colored moss grew like seaweed. Concrete walkways ran along the trough. The tunnel itself was semicircular, twenty feet in diameter, with flat spots along its otherwise curved walls on which spokes poled out like the rungs of a ladder, leading to manholes.

Jensen looked up one side of the tunnel and down the other. Large, thick pipes ran its length. The pipes looked like the twin strands of a helix. One held drinking water, the other, sewage. The major had an interior dialogue in which he joked about the effects of switching the pipes.

The underground tunnel system made him nervous, but fear was an emotion he'd been taught to ignore. He said, "Do you want us to go in?"

MacAvoy didn't hesitate a moment before answering. He said, "Hell yes. Son, enter that tunnel, but do not engage; this is purely recon. If you so much as smell anything larger than a rat, you and your men hightail out. You read me, Major?"

"Yes, sir, General. I do."

CHAPTER FORTY-EIGHT

Every step took the squad farther into a world that soldiers do not want to enter.

Afternoon slowly gave way to dawn. The light that filtered in through the manholes degraded from white-gold shafts to a pale glow. When they looked up through the storm drains, the Deltas saw shadowy buildings and darkening skies.

The tunnel was long, and they followed it in silence. Thorough by training, Deltas don't rush. They moved ahead slowly, methodically, leapfrogging positions, scanning tributaries, searching for traps, sensors, and mines. Deltas took the toughest assignments the Army had to offer and prided themselves in returning home with every man.

The tunnel ran flat and straight with tributaries that traced perpendicular routes. The traffic on the street above them ran constant and slow. Wheels rumbled, their noise cascading down through the storm drains. During a silent moment, the Deltas heard the clatter of shoes and the occasional voice, but the aboveground world seemed like a distant galaxy from under the street.

They didn't find enemy soldiers hiding in the tunnels.

Aside from pipes and cables, the only things running through the tunnel were rats. Locked panels and doorways had been built into the walls. Mounds of garbage piled up along the trough. And everywhere, rats rooted through the garbage.

One of the soldiers carried a GPS tracking device that showed their position in relation to the city. They had traveled south and west, the tunnel becoming darker the farther they went. Five blocks from where they started, the squad of Deltas came across a place where another hole and been blown into the wall. Major Jensen approached the opening, pressed a hand against the jagged edge of the concrete, and muttered, "Anybody home."

Then he signaled MacAvoy.

The general wasn't there to take the call. One of his aides, a colonel, responded. He asked, "What can I do for you, Major."

Jensen said, "We found another entry point."

Clearly not briefed on the mission, the colonel asked, "Entry point to what?"

Jensen wanted to say, "The entry to your ass, dumb shit, now put the general on the horn," but the protocol hardwired into his brain kept him silent. He couldn't bring himself to show disrespect to a superior.

He said, "Colonel, the general sent us into the sewers to track down the Unifieds."

"I am aware of that," the colonel said with ruthless officiousness.

Bullshit, thought the major. He said, "They entered two buildings along Pennsylvania Avenue through underground tunnels. We've found an entrance to a third building on H Street."

"H Street? Why would they give a speck about H Street?" the colonel asked himself.

Jensen didn't respond. He thought he knew the colonel's type—a do-nothing political climber. Clones like the colonel hid intel in their wallets and spent it to buy themselves promotions.

"Should we go in?" asked Jensen, though he'd already decided that this asshole of a colonel was incapable of making decisions for which he might later be blamed.

Jensen was wrong.

The colonel asked, "How many men do you have with you, Major?"

"I have a squad."

Not hesitating to consider the danger, the colonel said, "Search the building."

The colonel was a do-nothing climber, but hearing the word "squad" helped him decide. He measured risks and weighed possibilities by calculating the harm bad decisions could do to his career against the benefits an unlikely success could bring while factoring in the plausibility of blaming mistakes on junior officers. Win a battle, and your star rises; lose a squad, and you can blame your aides.

Even before they reached the lobby, the Deltas could tell that civilians had died. They found blood and bullet holes in the basement hallway.

The major opened the janitorial closet and found a man in a business suit sprawled on the floor. He'd been executed—told to lie facedown and killed with a single, well-centered shot in the back of his head. Jensen gathered his men, showed them the body, and told them, "We're not looking for clones in combat armor here. This was done by the Unified Authority Army, natural-borns. They might still be in uniform, but they also might be dressed like civilians. You see a civilian, I want your guns locked and loaded. If he reaches for his pocket, you shoot. Do you read me, Deltas?"

They found four bodies in a men's room and two in the women's. They found dozens of bodies stacked in the service area, men and women who had been locked in an airtight refrigeration unit and left to suffocate. The skin of their faces was pale and slightly blue, their eyes closed, their lips discolored.

Killing unarmed civilians is easy as long as you have the stomach for it, Jensen reminded himself. *Let's see how you bastards do against people who return fire.*

Sick and angry, Jensen and his men waited while his scouts checked for traps and alarms. They took several minutes. When they returned, they reported that the building was hot. They'd found sensors and spotted men with machine guns.

That was the only time Major Jensen doubted himself. He sent a man to radio the information in. Because he didn't know the address of the building, the corporal used a satellite to scan his location and set a beacon. Then he rejoined the squad.

Before leaving the basement, the Deltas found a gated storage area, practically a warehouse. The cages inside the storage area were packed tight with boxes. When Jensen opened one of those boxes, he knew that he and his squad were in over their heads.

Having just finished his MRE dinner, MacAvoy entered his mobile headquarters. He found the colonel sitting in his chair, and said, "'Scuse me, sir. I didn't mean to walk in on you."

The colonel swung around, saw the stars and the glare, and just about unloaded on the spot. He said, "Pardon me, General. I thought you were out."

"I was out, son; now I'm back and wondering what the hell your nonstar keister is doing in my three-star seat." He didn't raise his voice, not yet. That might come in a moment.

Pernell MacAvoy's tirades were legend throughout the Army. Once angered, MacAvoy behaved like a bear. If you ran, he attacked. If you attacked, he became more vicious. If you played dead, sometimes he lost interest and moved along. The trick for the colonel was to slowly climb out of the chair, pretend nothing had happened, and avoid eye contact. The trick for the rest of the general's staff was to show no sign of enjoying the show. At this point, a giggle or smirk could end an officer's career.

MacAvoy asked, "Were you warming the leather, son, or did you have a reason for sitting in my seat?"

"Ummm," said the colonel, weighing every possible answer before speaking.

"I just want to know if maybe I should change the lock on my bathroom before I catch you warming my toilet as well."

"The Delta team we sent to investigate the Pennsylvania Avenue shooting reported in," said the colonel.

"Did the major ask for you?" asked MacAvoy.

"No, sir."

"Did he ask to speak to me?"

"Yes, sir."

"But you took it upon yourself to hear his report?"

"Yes, sir."

Giving off the same vibrations as a nuclear warhead, the general calmly asked, "Did the major say anything of interest?"

Everyone in the mobile center knew that the moment had come, even MacAvoy. They could feel it in the air. He might scream until spit flew from his lips. He might even pull the ceremonial pearl-gripped sidearm from its holster and shoot the colonel; rumor had it that he had done that before.

"They followed the Unifieds into a building on H Street," said the colonel.

"H Street?" asked MacAvoy. Unlike the colonel, he didn't pretend to know the geography of Washington, D.C. The term "H Street" held no more meaning for him than "Dupont Circle," "Crystal City," or "Foxhall Grill." He mumbled something no one could decipher, though the words "incompetent," "firing squad," and "ass-first on a flagpole" rang clear enough.

MacAvoy turned to the only man in the mobile command whom he trusted, a sergeant major who had served with him back when he was an enlisted man. He barked, "Do I know H Street?"

The sergeant major located the street on a map on a wall and showed it to MacAvoy.

Though it ended and restarted a few times, H Street stretched nearly all the way across the map. Without saying a word, MacAvoy walked over to the map, tapped it, and said, "H Street has a shopping mall on one end and hotel on the other with five miles of buildings in between. I don't suppose you happen to know which building you told my Delta team to enter."

Thinking maybe he had dodged a bullet, the colonel said, "I had them set up a beacon before they went in."

"A beacon?" asked MacAvoy. He knew the term but had no idea how to access it.

The sergeant major tapped a button on the side of the map and the beacon appeared.

MacAvoy studied the location. It was about four miles away. He smiled as he asked the colonel, "Son, do you have any infantry experience?"

"Umm, yes, sir."

"Glad to hear it, son; the next life you save might just be your own."

CHAPTER FORTY-NINE

Army squads are small units, generally nine or ten men. When all of its members are Delta-trained, however, a squad becomes a tactical force. Trained for counterterrorism, Deltas hit hard, hit fast, and seldom miss.

Instead of entering the lobby as a group, the Deltas spread out, approaching it along four different paths. They moved as silently as mice, the riflemen spreading and looking for cover as they approached the lobby.

The three businessmen they found in the lobby wore suits and ties with loose-fitting jackets. They stood beside the reception desk apparently lost in a quiet conversation. But scanning them with the X-ray function built into the drop-down lens of his helmet, Major Jensen spotted the M27s hidden near their arms. He saw the knives they had strapped to their legs, and identified them as Unified agents.

The Delta riflemen selected their targets by proximity. At the major's signal, they would shoot. Every Delta carried an M27 with a custom suppressor, but, for this shot, the riflemen used S9 pistols—accurate at close range, silent, and clean. Shoot a man with an M27, and the bullet will likely blow out the back of his head. Hit him with an S9, and the fléchette passes through his skull, leaving through a pinpoint-sized hole.

A master sergeant placed a hand on the major's shoulder to get his attention, then pointed to the three security cameras perched on the lobby walls.

Jensen shrugged and nodded. He'd noticed the cameras as well. If the Unifieds had men in the security office, they might catch a quick glimpse of corpses or Deltas. The only other option would be to disable the cameras, and that would take time.

At Jensen's signal, three Deltas fired, making no more noise than a flag fluttering in a gentle breeze. The fléchettes entered each man at the base of his skull and exited through his forehead. Had they been hit with bullets, the targets would have splattered all the way across the room. Shot with fléchettes, only fine streams of blood were spilled. The Deltas quickly hid the corpses behind a counter. They stripped a jacket from one of the dead men and used it to mop up the mess.

Anyone entering the lobby would simply dismiss it as deserted.

Jensen didn't like nebulous missions with undefined objectives. He saw no point investigating an area that should be attacked. The problem was that the colonel had given him orders to investigate. Max Jensen, a general-issue clone, couldn't ignore orders even when he recognized them as *dumb-ass orders from a dumb-ass officer who belonged in a stockade.*

He sent three men to check the loading dock, giving them the order to kill any Unifieds on sight. He left three men to guard the lobby and gave them the same orders. At this point, the entire mission would be left to his discretion. Radio contact was out of the question, it would be too easy for the Unifieds to overhear them. The Unifieds and Enlisted Men used the same radio equipment.

Jensen took his remaining Deltas to go search the first floor. They found bodies hidden in offices. They found and killed five armed men dressed in business suits.

Jensen climbed the stairs to the second floor, where he found more bodies and killed six more *businessmen.*

He took his men to the third floor, and there they died.

CHAPTER FIFTY

The faint glow that shone through the lobby windows was too dim to have come from an office light. Sitting in his MNC, MacAvoy saw the building and recognized the glow of the shield armor. Having heard what happened when Harris's Marines engaged enemies in shielded armor, the general had no interest in fighting clean.

He tapped the microphone, and said, "Bring down the building."

The one-star on the other end knew better than to argue. He relayed the message to a colonel, who asked, "Clean or dirty?"

"What's the difference?" asked the general.

"Clean, we place charges around the base of the building and make it implode, sir. Could take an hour or two, but we could bring that baby down without scratching the cars parked around it."

"And dirty?" asked the one-star.

"Hell, I could pop her right now if you don't mind bricks flying through the neighbors' windows. The locals won't thank us."

The one-star general touched the microphone, and said, "General MacAvoy, sir, we'll have her down in ten minutes."

The troop carriers parked two blocks up the street, hidden from the Unifieds by buildings and trees. It was already nighttime, and this part of H Street sat mostly empty.

Globes burned in the streetlights, brightening the otherwise dark landscape below. A few dedicated employees still worked in the offices of the various buildings. The janitorial crowd cleaned around them, leaving scattered lights in office buildings and storefronts. The road traffic had died away hours ago.

Each team of soldiers included a guard, a trained grenadier, and two engineers. The guard would guide the rest of the team to their spots and keep them safe. The engineers would evaluate the target and locate soft spots. The grenadiers would pull triggers.

MacAvoy spoke to the general, and said, "I sent a colonel to watch this area a couple of hours ago."

"Yes, sir. That would be Colonel Dickens, sir."

"Dickens, yeah, Dickens," said MacAvoy, hoping he was the right man. He said, "Send him into the sewers. Tell him to watch the basement . . . make sure no one gets out."

"How many men should I send down with him?" asked the general.

MacAvoy didn't want to give the man a company, not a platoon, not even a squad. He said, "Send him on his own. Tell him we'll send a squad down as soon as we find one."

"Are you trying to get him killed, sir?" asked the general.

"General, I don't see how that is your business," said MacAvoy.

"Yes, sir."

"No. I am not trying to get him killed," said MacAvoy. "Just tell him to keep clear of the explosion; he'll be all right."

"Yes, sir."

Under the cover of darkness, the four teams took up positions across the street from the target. They wore dark gear and dark hats; they had black paint on their faces.

They hid behind gates and under awnings, invisible to the naked eye. If the enemy bothered to search the streets with heat vision, they would see the men and rockets, but that couldn't be helped.

H Street was silent. No sounds floated on the warm, languid air. Across the street, the lowest level of the building glowed pale gold. The shining forms of men milled within the lobby, their shapes visible, the glow of their individual shields mingling. Formations of men stood just inside the doors.

If the Marines in the shielded armor exited the building, MacAvoy's infantrymen wouldn't stand a chance against them.

"Our teams are in place, sir."

MacAvoy asked, "Are you sure my Deltas are out of commission?"

"They're not responding."

"Damn," MacAvoy muttered. "Specking hell." He loved his Deltas; they were the boys who did things no one else could do. He watched the scene through a pair of binoculars. "Those Unified sons of bitches look ready to pick. Light 'em up."

"Fire on my mark," said the general.

Across the street, the doors slid open. Beyond one of the doors stood columns of men in glowing armor. The soldiers could see them clearly. Had the Marines in the shielded armor used heat vision or night-for-day lenses, they would have spotted the soldiers as well.

"Three," said the general.

Marines started marching out of the building.

"Two."

Looking through laser sights, the grenadiers focused reticles on the spots that the engineers had painted with lasers.

A Marine stepping out of the east face of the building spotted the soldier across the street and shot his wrist cannon, firing fléchettes from the tube mounted along the top his arm. He hit all three soldiers before they could respond. The fléchettes, fragments of depleted uranium, hit the soldiers' arms and chests. They fell to the ground still alive, writhing and wounded as the neurotoxin coating the fragments spread quickly through their bodies.

More U.A. Marines ran through the door looking for targets, sprinting out to the street, their right arms out, their arm cannons ready to shoot.

"Fire."

The remaining grenadiers launched their shoulder-fired rockets. Any one of the rockets would have had enough power to demolish the building; three rockets struck, hitting central spots that supported the weight of the building.

The smoke from the rockets still hung in the air as they exploded in flashes of white and yellow and red. Shaken down to its foundation, the building fell apart. Its outer walls toppled; its insides collapsed deck upon deck. Alarms roared in the night, and a tide of rubble washed into the street. No fire, no flames, but an eerie orange glow showed through the rubble.

It just never gets old, General MacAvoy thought as he surveyed the aftermath. The building, now a hill of concrete and broken glass, glowed. The demolition had not been neat, but it had been thorough.

He walked around the foot of the mountain and listened to trapped Unifieds crying for help through his earpiece. Some begged for their lives. Some bargained.

MacAvoy was not the man who invented the tactic of demolishing buildings on top of troops in impervious armor; that had been Harris. MacAvoy admired the initiative and creativity of Harris's idea. *If you can't hurt the enemy, bury him.*

On his earpiece, he heard an officer shout, "Who is in charge out there? Who is your commanding officer? I want to speak to him."

MacAvoy chuckled. Back on Terraneau, where Harris had first employed this tactic, the Marines had referred to the voices as "ghosts." It made sense. They were calling from their graves. One thing was certain—no one under his command would dig these bastards out.

MacAvoy thought he had turned the tide of battle. He didn't know that the H Street building was one of ten buildings that the Unifieds had selected as launch points of a major assault. Sometimes, what you don't know can kill you.

CHAPTER FIFTY-ONE

Location: Guanajuato, New Olympian Territories
Date: August 3, 2519

We didn't have food, and our only liquid was the recycled hydration inside our armor. It wasn't much.

We were trapped deep in the mountain. As far as I could tell, Freeman's charges had collapsed the section of the mine stretching from the office complex to the entrance. There might have been some hollow pockets along the way. We couldn't be sure since we ran into a wall of rock that blocked both ends of the path.

And then there was Freeman. He'd always struck me as an indestructible man, but it looked like a badly infected leg might kill the man who bullets, knives, and bombs never seemed to stop. He didn't have enough strength to stand, so he lay on the ground beside the little campfire we'd built out of desiccated posts and studs. He slept mostly, shivering as if we'd laid him on ice.

I wished I could have stretched my body suit around him. It would have sensed his temperature fluctuations and kept him warm. But my body suit was a snug-fitting unitard that couldn't possibly stretch across his thick, seven-foot mass.

I stripped out of my armor so I could rig the hydration wire to keep his mouth moist. If he'd been conscious, he might not have allowed me to do that. Drinking another man's sweat and urine was an unappetizing thought, filtered or not.

We had no medicine for his leg. His foot was so swollen that we had to cut a slit around the ankle before the skin burst. His skin had turned slate gray.

Not all of the news was bad. The fire we'd started with desiccated wood burned so steadily you'd think we'd built it inside a furnace. At least we weren't hurting for oxygen.

And Hunter Ritz had survived along with 156 of my men. The last time I had seen Ritz, he was leaping from a ridge while attacking a gunship. I'd figured he'd died. I was wrong. He landed on the same lower ledge that I had used when I flanked the U.A. Marines. The men flying the gunships were so busy chasing down groups of men, they paid no attention to stragglers.

And then our reinforcements arrived. The sludging might have prevented us from contacting Admiral Hauser, but it didn't stop the admiral from watching the fight outside the atmosphere. Hauser sent fighters, and the fighters destroyed all three U.A. gunships.

Hauser also sent swarms of engineers to help dig us out. They scratched at the mountainside with lasers and drills, but they were miles away. They spoke to us, giving us progress reports as they spent hours reclaiming every yard.

I watched the reflection of the fire on the office's dusty

windows. The flames and embers cast a glow that seemed to fill the entire chamber.

I had time to think, to consider the day. I thought about Freeman, who had entered the New Olympian Territories to rescue me. He had walked into a trap. I told myself that he would survive this though I had my doubts. He was no longer lucid. There he was, lying beside the fire, I couldn't speak to him, couldn't warm him, couldn't feed him, couldn't cure his infection. If he lived, he might spend the rest of his life on one leg. If he died, the fault would be mine.

The Unifieds had killed most of First Battalion. The rescue crew found bodies everywhere. My grenadiers had knocked down one gunship; against three, they'd never stood a chance, and the Unifieds had showed them no quarter. A skirmish, right? The loss of a single brigade means little over the course of a war, but they'd been my men, damn it! They'd come under my command, depending on me to keep them safe, and when the shooting started, it was my specking responsibility to make their deaths count for something. I'd failed.

Should have been you, I told myself. Here in the mine, in the silence, with hungry men sitting around me and the smell of our existence fouling the air, I decided I wasn't such a great commandant.

In truth, I wanted to die, and now, thanks to the Unifieds, I had the ability to make it happen, but there was an account I needed to settle before anything else. This wasn't an emotional decision. I made it by the light of the cold, clear, unemotional logic of hate. Among Marines, hate isn't considered emotion, it's religion.

Franklin Nailor had made this personal. He had tried to kill me and the friend who'd come to rescue me. I had a reason to live, and that reason was an overwhelming desire to watch Nailor die. I would find him and I would kill him. Okay, yes, I had bought into a personal vendetta. I no longer thought of Nailor as an officer in a hostile army; he had officially graduated to a personal demon. Still, killing the bastard could result in dividends for the entire Enlisted Man's Empire. Fry his evil ass and maybe the Unifieds would get scared and run. The rest of them didn't seem nearly as homicidal.

Freeman moaned softly. His body was two feet from a

crackling fire, but he still shivered. His skin had a pallor. When I examined him using heat vision, his signature was almost yellow instead of bright orange. His body heat was feverish.

My men and I sat in silence. I didn't know if they blamed me. They probably did, but there was nothing I could do about it.

Only Nailor mattered. I would find him, and I would end him.

Outside this mine, in the mythical world of light and fresh air, things had happened, big things, important things, but no one would tell me what they were. Officers chimed in on the interLink. They asked about Freeman's condition. They asked how I and my men were doing. When I asked about the Unifieds or Travis Watson, they went temporarily silent, then said they would brief me once I escaped from the mine.

So I sat and reevaluated everything. I thought about leaving the Corps, resigning my commission, and killing Nailor. No one else mattered. Not anymore. Not even Freeman.

I thought about Sunny and knew that I didn't love her. I wasn't sure I ever had. My feelings for her had had a spontaneous quality, as if I fell in love with her every time I saw her, but the feelings disappeared when she went away. I would see her and feel an overwhelming need to touch her, to sleep with her . . . and I would feel a strange need to protect her, but I hated her as well. Once we'd had sex, I couldn't wait to get away from her. I went through the same emotional cycle every time I saw her, and I always left her apartment trying to sort out my feelings.

Sunny was pretty. She was smart. She was great in bed. If love entered into that equation, I failed to see where.

I thought about Kasara and knew that at some point I had loved her. But I had no room for love anymore. Not anymore.

"General Harris?"

I had lost track of time. My visor had a clock and a calendar, but I wasn't wearing it. Nothing slows the passage of time as effectively as having a clock right in front of your eyes.

I had no idea how long we had been trapped inside the mine when the call came in. I put on my helmet, and answered, "Yeah."

"General, the civilian engineers think they can pull you out through an air shaft."

"An air shaft?" I asked.

A passel of old pipes ran along one of the walls in this chamber. The bore of the largest pipe looked to be about two feet in diameter. Even stripped and greased, I doubted I could survive a trip through that pipe. Fitting Freeman, the only one of us with a pending expiration date, into that pipe would have been like stuffing a bowling ball into a syringe.

I said, "If you're talking about the pipes running up through the ceiling, I think I'll pass."

I didn't recognize the voice of the man who answered me. He said, "Not pipes, shafts. There is an alternate system of ventilation shafts running along the length of the mine."

Judging by the fact that the man neither called me "sir" nor cowered, I decided he was probably a member of Hauser's Corps of Engineers.

I later learned that the pipes in the ceiling had nothing to do with ventilation. When the engineer finally reached us, he identified them as having been part of a water system.

The vent was linked to ducts on every level of the mine. It spilled out on a lower ridge. This was the system that brought air to miners when the main system failed.

Once I knew that help was on the way, I began watching the clock. Three hours, twelve minutes, and twenty-seven seconds later, somebody poked a hole in the ceiling above us.

The first man down was a medic. He knelt beside Freeman, ran sensors over his body, and shined a light in his eyes. "This man is in bad shape," he said as if pronouncing an insightful diagnosis.

"Will he be able to keep his leg?" I asked. The doctor shook his head, and answered, "I'm not sure this man will survive the trip out."

He did, though. The medic loaded Freeman on a travois and strapped him tight, then used a winch to raise him into the ventilation shaft. Not wanting to let Freeman out of my sight, I came up next and insisted on helping with the travois.

Men always look smaller to me when they are injured, and even Freeman did. Lying on that travois, he looked no larger than a normal man. Dragging him out that vent with its twists and uphill slopes strained my back and arms. I tried to pull my side of the travois the entire way, but I didn't have the strength. How long had it been since I'd been shot?

Freeman had come to the Territories to pull my ass out of the fire. It wouldn't have been the first time he'd saved my ass, either. I went to the front of the travois and pulled as long as I could, but I had been shot in the gut a few weeks earlier, and my strength gave out. The Marines behind the travois traded off regularly, and I think they were stronger than me to begin with.

When I felt spasms running down my spine, I thought about Nailor and added my pain to the ledger. His was one score I would settle.

As we neared the top of the shaft, I saw bright light. The rescue team had set up arc lamps and a medical center. Medics met us. They loaded Freeman on a transport and flew away.

I saw the body bags as I stepped into the open. They lay in several rows in the dimness, just outside the bubble of light cast by the arc lamps. Marines do not stack their dead in haphazard piles. We show respect for our fallen and lay them out in rows. In the poor light, the black plastic bags looked like open graves.

Revenge, I thought. *The only cure for this disease is revenge.*

If I resigned, what I did with my time would be nobody's business, but generals have privileges that civilians do not. I needed my Corps and my rank to get Nailor.

An officer escorted me into a transport, and said, "Admiral Hauser is on the horn."

I sat in front of the console and stared into the screen.

Hauser stared back. He studied me, then, in a soft voice, he said, "You need rest, General. I know you won't listen to me, but you're killing yourself."

"Where are they attacking us?" I asked Hauser.

"Maybe we should . . ."

I remembered what Nailor told me, and asked, "What happened in Washington, D.C.?"

He took a breath as he composed his answer. "MacAvoy has a war on his hands." Hauser went quiet, purposely giving me a chance to respond. I didn't. He hadn't asked me a question. What did he expect me to say?

"How well do you know Washington?" he asked.

"I know it."

"They've taken everything from the Potomac to Stanton Park."

That was less than half the city, mostly the southwestern corner. They'd have the Capitol and the Mall, but who cared. I replayed Nailor's words in my mind. He'd thought he'd have the whole city by the time I climbed out of the mines.

"What about MacAvoy?" I asked.

Hauser smiled. He said, "They underestimated him. They thought they were fighting a by-the-book officer, but they got MacAvoy instead. I'm not sure what you know about his tactics . . . they're barbaric and really, really effective.

"He's come up with an answer for shielded armor. He waits until they walk by tall buildings, then he fires artillery at them."

"Shells don't get through shielded armor," I said.

Hauser smiled. "Not at the Unifieds, at the buildings. He brings the buildings down on top of them . . . buries them alive.

"They wanted a general who would try to match wits, but they got MacAvoy instead. They might have captured the entire city by now had they been fighting anybody else."

I asked, "How did they land in D.C. without our spotting them?" and Hauser's smile faded. Okay, yes, it wasn't meant as a question; it was an accusation. His blockade had failed.

Hauser told me about the stealth destroyer. He listed the targets . . . Bolling Field to cripple us, the Pentagon to cover their tracks, and the Archive Building. The destruction of the Archive was a death blow to the Enlisted Man's Empire. The Archive stored the data for cloning. Clones are sterile. Now that we no longer had the ability to build new clones, the Unifieds wouldn't need to beat us in war; they could simply outwait us.

PART IV

THE ASSASSIN

CHAPTER FIFTY-TWO

Location: Mazatlán, New Olympian Territories
Date: August 4, 2519

I found Brandon Pugh in a park in a wealthy residential area not far from shore. Mark Story, the local police chief, had told me where to find him. He also warned me that Pugh was a dangerous criminal, a gangster I'd be foolish to trust.

I set Story straight. I said, "I can trust him. I can trust him because he's already crossed me twice, and the next time he steps on my toes, I'll bury him."

Story smiled, and asked, "Would you kill him?"

I was almost out the door when I turned, and said, "Killing people who disagree with me is how I make my living."

Pugh would probably have preferred for me to stay away from Story, but I no longer cared what he wanted.

It was nighttime. In the weeks since I had first arrived, this part of Mazatlán had morphed into a regular town. Lights shone from the windows of houses in which families now lived. Streetlamps lit sidewalks and streets. There weren't many cars, but families and young people walked the neighborhoods.

Ritz, who drove out with me, said, "I've never seen the Martians so content."

That just about summed it up.

The night was warm and dry, a perfect night for swimming or drinking yourself drunk on the beach. In another life, I might have lit a fire on the beach and downed a few beers. That wouldn't get me drunk, but, depending on the company I kept, I might enjoy myself.

I had expected to find Pugh surrounded by thugs. Gangsters of his sort are always on guard. Having sent Freeman into the mountains to kill Ryan Petrie, he had a lot to fear . . . more than he knew.

He was far from alone when Ritz and I rolled up in our jeep. He had his entire organization around him. That included tough guys and bookkeepers, slick operators and thieves. There were women, too, but they looked like wives, not prostitutes.

Kasara saw me, came to hug me, saw the change in my face, and backed away. Her uncle read me as well. He asked, "Who have you come to kill?"

Both Ritz and I had M27s in our hands. I suppose we did look like we had come to kill someone.

As Kasara backed away from me, the park went silent. Kids had been playing, screaming, laughing as we arrived. Now they went silent. After a year trapped in Mars Spaceport, these children had developed a sense about how to behave when the situation turned serious.

Maybe it wasn't only our guns that alarmed them. I had showered and changed into a crisp, neatly pressed service uniform. I had shaved and washed my hair. I didn't look like I had just come from a battlefield. One of the nice things about wearing armor into battle is that you seldom get bruised.

My eyes, though, they gave me away. Maybe a man's eyes are the windows to his soul or possibly they're just the stool pigeons that give away his thoughts and intensions. Kasara looked into my eyes and knew that something was missing. Pugh looked into my eyes and saw something new and dangerous.

"I'm not here to kill anybody," I said.

"Wayson, what happened?" asked Kasara. She hovered a few feet away from me, watching me closely, possibly waiting to see if I would explode. She kept her eyes fastened on mine.

A voice shouted through my inner chaos, begging me to say that nothing had changed. I had tender feelings for Kasara, but I didn't love her, so I ignored that voice.

She had once been beautiful, but what she'd suffered on Mars had taken that away. The glow of the fire accentuated the sunken hollows of her cheeks, and I couldn't see the color of her eyes.

A few seconds passed as we regarded each other in a

standoff. I don't know if Kasara was afraid of me or afraid of rejection, but she kept her distance. Pugh was afraid. All the kingpin's horses and all the kingpin's men couldn't protect him from the Marines with the guns.

Pugh and his men had brought their families to the park for a party of some sort. The women sat around a table covered with food served on paper plates. I saw the trappings of games—a finish line for races, plastic swords, and long straps of cloth that might have been used as blindfolds in a game of Blind Man's Battle.

Neither ignoring Kasara nor specifically paying attention to her, I said, "We found Ray Freeman. The doctors aren't sure if he'll last the night."

"Freeman, I didn't know that man could be hurt," said Pugh.

"Apparently, he can," I said.

Most of the people remained silent and sober. A few feet behind Pugh, a man sat alone at a table. He had a cast on his arm. Hearing about Freeman, he smiled. By the fading bruises on his face and the way he clenched his teeth, I knew that his jaw had been broken, and I had a good idea about who had broken it. He was a big man. Until he'd run into Freeman, he'd probably been Pugh's fiercest enforcer.

Standing in front of his family and his employees, Pugh didn't allow himself to show fear. He sat silent, trying to form questions that would not make him sound overly concerned.

I asked, "Want to take a drive with us?"

Pugh looked at his minions, then back at me. Perhaps he hoped that his friends would forbid us from taking him. Nobody moved. He said, "I'm not sure that's a good idea."

"Sure it is," I said. "We can have the conversation right here if you want. I don't mind, but you seem like a man who values his privacy."

Pugh nodded. Two of his men started to object, but he told them he would be back shortly. I'd read the Bible a time or two. I wondered if Christ told his apostles the same thing before walking off with the Romans.

Kasara darted between us. She said, "I'm coming along."

Pugh put up a hand, and said, "Kassie . . ."

I interrupted, and said, "We have room for a fourth."

So there it stood. Kasara and her uncle climbed into the jeep. She sat behind me on the passenger side of the jeep. Pugh sat behind Ritz.

"Where are we going, sir?" asked Ritz.

"East," I said.

"East," he repeated. "East to anyplace in particular?"

"East to where the town is dark, and we have the street to ourselves."

We were on the west side of town, not far from shore, in an area with families and streetlights. The engineers had not yet reclaimed the east side of town.

After a few miles, we left the lights and sounds of Mazatlán behind us as we entered an ancient neighborhood with unlit streets and run-down hundred-year-old homes. Most of the buildings had faded away, many had collapsed. The chain-link fences that surrounded each property seemed good as new.

No one spoke until I said, "Pull over here."

Ritz drifted over to the side of the road and stopped. There we sat, everybody watching me, waiting for me to set the tone. I said, "Help me make sense of all of this."

A strong wind blew through the neighborhood, rattling fences, whistling through broken windows and fallen doors. The partial moon did little to brighten the sky. Stars winked between patches of cloud.

Pugh said, "I told you, Freeman went to kill Petrie as favor to me."

"Yeah, I got that," I said. "The Unifieds sent a lot of firepower out to stop that from happening. I went through that village; they had tanks and guns. The Unifieds sent four gunships and a lot of men. Why did they care so much about Petrie?"

Silence. I saw Kasara's face in the filtered moonlight and the glow from the dashboard. She looked worried. She looked from me to her uncle and back again.

Pugh said, "Maybe they weren't protecting Petrie. Maybe they were after Freeman."

"No doubt," I said. "How did they know Freeman was on his way?"

He shrugged his shoulders, and said, "I have no idea."

I said, "Well, Petrie is dead, and so are a lot of his men. Can you tell me why the Unified Authority would have loaned Petrie tanks and jeeps?"

Kasara said, "Wayson, you're not being fair. How would he know that?" I heard scolding in her voice.

Pugh, though, he understood. He said, "Are you sure they were his? Why would a gangster living in a camp in the mountains want tanks? People in my line of business don't overdo their firepower, it scares away our customers."

Fair point, I thought. "Then why were they there?"

"If I had to guess," said Pugh, "I'd say they didn't belong to him. I'd say they still belonged to the Unies. I'd say the real owners of those tanks might have placed them in Petrie's camp for safekeeping."

"But if Petrie is a play . . . was a minor player, why would the Unifieds trust him to guard their equipment?" I was guessing, trying to make sense out of a puzzle with missing pieces.

"He was a big deal on Olympus Kri. He was the only one who kept his organization running on Mars."

I thought about that. Could Petrie have been some kind of U.A. strongman before the alien invasions? Not likely. If he'd had friends on the Linear Committee, they would have slipped him off Mars.

"So you told Freeman about Petrie and asked him to make a hit. Is that right?"

"You sent a man to kill Ryan Petrie?" asked Kasara.

"Kassie, we're fighting for our lives here. You don't see it, but there's a war going on, and the first ones to go will be the ones who play nice," said Pugh.

"Oh, in that case you should be real safe," Kasara said, sounding sarcastic and angry.

"Kassie . . ."

I cut him off. I asked, "What else did you tell Freeman?"

Pugh started to say something, then stopped and rethought the comment. He seemed to riffle through a list in his head, sometimes even nodding to himself as he did. After some inner dialogue, he said, "I've told you everything . . ."

He was a bright man, not especially honest, and always looking for an angle, but bright. Watching him now, I got the feeling he would rather die than give me whatever information he was hiding. Men like him always wanted some form of hidden insurance. Shoot them during a card game, and you would inevitably find aces up their sleeves.

Pugh was hiding something. It might not have been particularly incriminating; it didn't need to be incriminating for him to hold it close to his vest. Hell, he had already confessed to selling me out. What could be more incriminating than that?

I toyed with the idea of drawing my gun and threatening him. It wouldn't have worked. I could have threatened Kasara instead. No. No, I really couldn't have done that. Even now, I felt tenderness toward her.

She sat silently, watching me and her uncle. If she'd known anything, she would have told me.

Do you love her? I asked myself. Maybe I would come back to find out after I finished with Nailor.

"I showed him where the Unifieds landed . . . the ones who tried to kill you. I showed him their diving equipment. That was when he agreed to take care of Petrie; before that, he didn't seem very interested."

I said, "Brandon, you've been holding out on me. Diving equipment?"

The party had ended by the time we returned to the settled side of the city. The park sat dark and mostly empty. I noticed two men sitting in a clearing, concealed by trees and bushes. Sentries, Pugh's men, sent to watch for his return and probably unarmed.

Pugh made no effort to signal them as we went by. I suppose he didn't need to. They knew he was in our jeep. How many EME jeeps would be on the streets of Mazatlán at that time of night?

We passed the park and entered a wealthy neighborhood, driving past large homes that did not quite qualify as mansions along a street that snaked its way down the face of a hill that overlooked the ocean. Pugh had moved into a large home with a million-dollar view that might well have needed a million dollars' worth of repairs.

The house wasn't empty. People had gathered just inside the house, dozens of them. As we pulled to the front, the door swung open, and Pugh's henchmen filed out.

They saw him and us and made no move. We had guns and he wasn't bleeding; they had no reason to attack and plenty of reason not to. I've seen men who can beat a gunman with a knife. Maybe some of Pugh's boys could, but that always depended on the gunman's readiness and the guy with the knife's proximity.

Pugh wanted us happy. He wanted allies. In a loud voice that all his men could hear, he announced, "Harris, I'm taking you out back." He'd said that to us, but he'd meant it for his men. He was telling them that everything was fine and copacetic and that they should back off.

So Pugh and I and Ritz headed down the steep slope toward the back of the house. The only person who followed us was Kasara. She clearly knew her way around the place. I wondered if she lived here as well.

The porch at the back of the house was as old as mankind and so rickety I thought I could topple it with a sneeze. Because the house was built on the side of a steep hill, the stilts supporting that porch were twenty feet tall.

Ritz stared up into the wobbly matrix of planks and beams and whistled. He asked, "Is the whole house built on toothpicks?"

It wasn't the porch that Pugh wanted to show us. He answered Ritz by saying, "The foundation is cement."

Ritz said, "So what, the porch is like a burglar alarm? If any bad people try to break into your house, the porch falls down on top of them?"

Pugh looked at me, and asked, "Is he always this funny?"

"Not when he gets angry," I said.

The old thug didn't have an answer for that. Apparently tongue-tied, he opened the door and led us into the space under the house.

There, sitting on the crumbling concrete slab, were three sets of SCUBA gear. I took one look at them and saw exactly what Freeman must have seen, and a cold chill ran down my spine. Standard Marine combat armor is watertight and good to go for a swim of twenty or thirty feet. Of course, the engineers who designed our gear meant for us to use it in outer space, where bodies burst open because of the lack of atmospheric pressure. The SCUBA gear Pugh had hidden under his house was designed to protect clones against external pressure, to keep a man's guts and lungs from collapsing under the considerable weight of deep, deep water.

The clones who had tried to kill me hadn't just come from the ocean, they'd come from deep beneath the sea.

CHAPTER FIFTY-THREE

Location: Flying from Mazatlán to Washington, D.C.
Date: August 5, 2519

Hauser and I sat across the table from each other on his shuttle. Perry MacAvoy joined us via a confabulator. Looking at him through the window, it looked like he was actually in the cabin.

"They've gotten smarter," said MacAvoy. "They used to start wasting their batteries the moment the shooting started. Now they're carrying spare batteries, and they don't switch their shields on without encouragement."

"What kind of encouragement?" asked Hauser.

"Snipers and mortars, mostly," said MacAvoy. "When we pick off a couple of guys in a platoon, the rest of them turn on the juice."

I asked, "How is your situation?"

MacAvoy and I were members of an exclusive club to which Hauser would never be admitted. We were ground pounders, foot soldiers, men who took their chances on the battlefield. Hauser fought his battles from the comfort of his bridge, drinking coffee, dressed in his service uniform, making his ship perform the same sorts of maneuvers we performed on our feet.

"They took back some of the city, but they aren't getting any more," said MacAvoy. "We can keep them bottled up as long as they don't get reinforcements. They're down to thirty or forty thousand men; sooner or later, they are going to run out of stiffs."

"Maybe not," I said. "They may have just as many men as we do."

"Bullshit," said MacAvoy.

"It doesn't matter if they do," said Hauser, sounding formal and more than a little prissy. "We've got our entire fleet blockading the planet. They might have been able to slip a spy ship or two past us . . ."

"And a destroyer," said MacAvoy. "They slipped that bitch right under your nose."

"Yes, thank you for reminding me," said Hauser. "I had almost forgotten about that.

"We have our ships parked tight around the planet right now."

"That would hold them if they didn't already have their boots on the ground," I said. Then I dropped the punch line; I said, "They're hiding in Cousteau underwater cities. Admiral, the reason you didn't spot them flying into the city is because they came in underwater from the Chesapeake Bay."

When I explained about the SCUBA gear that Pugh had shown me, Hauser said, "That doesn't prove anything . . . nothing at all." Then I brought up something Hauser should have noticed on his own. I said, "Gunships and transports keep materializing above the ocean, either you're running a shitty blockade, or those birds are already down here, down deep, someplace where our satellites don't see them."

MacAvoy said, "Speck. How the hell are we gonna hit 'em down there?"

That was going to be a problem. Four hundred years had passed since the nations of the world merged under the watchful umbrella of the Unified Authority. There'd been no reason to maintain a Wet Navy for over four hundred years. All of our boats now floated in space. Submarines ceased to exist. Once mankind turned its attention to colonizing space, guarding oceans no longer mattered.

Back in 2110, as more and more nations signed pacts with the Unified Authority, the French government created the Cousteau Oceanic Exploration Program, an initiative that involved the creation of several underwater cities. The initiative died after a few short years, and no one knew what became of the underwater cities.

Somebody once told me that one of the cities, which the French had named Mariana, was built in a deep trench somewhere in the Pacific. From what I had heard, Mariana could only hold a few thousand people, but it might have been one of the smaller sites.

This was all theoretical. The French had supposedly shut the Cousteau program down in 2115. The cities they built must have survived, though. All of the attacks—the Pentagon, Sheridan Penitentiary, and Washington, D.C., had taken place near coastlines. We always spotted their gunships and troop carriers coming in over the ocean and assumed that meant they had been dropped there from outer space. Bad assumption.

Hauser and I spent the rest of the flight discussing undersea cities and how to destroy them. We hadn't come up with any workable solutions by the time we reached Washington, D.C.

As the shuttle touched down, Hauser asked me a question that I didn't want to answer. He asked, "How much of this is personal, Harris? How much of this is you and your need for revenge?"

Amazingly, I hadn't even mentioned Franklin Nailor at this point.

We had gunships and fighters flying over Washington, D.C. We had troops and convoys evacuating the city. Not all of the civilians we evacuated came willingly, but most did. We sent troops to patrol neighborhoods and armed those who stayed behind with orders to shoot looters on sight.

MacAvoy's soldiers enjoyed shooting looters. They considered looter shooting a cross between MP duty and target practice.

We touched down in a secure area on the northeastern corner of the city, and I immediately recognized the trappings of a war zone. Soldiers patrolled the perimeter of the landing field. Looking around the field, I saw tanks and sentry drones and guard towers.

Standing beside me as we prepared to step off the shuttle, Hauser whispered, "This all seems a little draconian, don't you think?"

I said, "This is how you fight battles when you're not floating in space."

He caught my drift, and said, "Oh."

Hauser seemed nervous. He was a talker under normal circumstances. On this day, he couldn't stop talking. He made stupid little puns and hemmed and hawed.

We had come to take a tour of the battlefield. A fighter escort circled overhead. MacAvoy had a gunship prepped and waiting just a few dozen yards away. He met us as we stepped off the shuttle and saluted. He asked, "Are you sure you don't want some time to rest before we head out?"

Hauser said, "Now is as good a time as any."

I said, "I don't know about you soldiers, but we Marines don't rest until the battle's over, General."

He said, "I always heard it the other way around. I always heard that you Marines didn't battle until your rest is over."

I called him "Cannon fodder." He called me "Leatherneck."

Thomas Hauser rolled his eyes and boarded the gunship ahead of us. We followed like dogs on a leash.

Never let it be said that armored gunships are fast, aerodynamic, or shielded. They are slow, ponderous, bloated birds covered with weapons and heavy armor. They don't have shields because you can't fire rockets and bullets from within a shield, and the whole point of gunships is to deliver missiles and rockets and chain-gun fire. Gunships aren't really helicopters; they're more like flying tanks.

The overhead rotors ran merry-go-round laps around the gunship as we strapped ourselves into our seats. The whirl of the rotors rocked the bird and everyone inside her. The churn was loud, too. Every turn of the blades echoed in my ears.

"Any news on Travis Watson?" I yelled to MacAvoy, as the rotors spun faster, and their noise increased from a throb in my temples to an actual headache.

"We found his limo," said MacAvoy. "It had several bullet holes, but there wasn't any blood. We found it abandoned in an alley beside an apartment building."

"Did you search the building?" asked Hauser.

"I hope he's someplace else," said MacAvoy. "That was the first building the Unifieds attacked. My men sort of demolished it during the fighting."

"Sounds like the Unifieds are looking for Watson as well," Hauser observed.

"Maybe not anymore," said MacAvoy. He looked at me and smiled. "Watson isn't really the commander in chief with Harris around." He turned in my direction, and added, "With any luck, they'll go after you instead."

Hauser nodded, and said, "Good thought."

Seeing that Hauser was already nervous about touring the battlefield, I said, "Yeah, maybe we should let them know I'm on this gunship."

"There's no rush," said Hauser. He didn't like flying in a clumsy bird inside the atmosphere. He looked nervous and fidgeted. "If telling the Unifieds we're on this ride brings them out of the sewers, I'm all for it," said MacAvoy. "Hell, if it brings their asses out, I'll attach a streamer that says 'Vote for Harris.'"

The engines became louder as we lifted off. I could tell that Admiral Hauser was nervous by the way he jolted in his seat every time the gunship dropped or hiccuped. Trying to be heard over the engine, MacAvoy yelled, "The front is about six miles ahead of us. We've got them pinned down tight. That's the good news."

The side doors of the gunship hung open. Gunners sat beside the chain guns, ready to fire at anything that moved. The noise of the rotors thudded in my ears, making it hard to hear and harder to think. Below us, the city seemed to unfurl like a scroll, like a three-dimensional map with realistically rendered holographic buildings. The streets were empty.

Three fighters flashed past us. I didn't know they'd been behind us or see them go by. They were hundreds of yards ahead of us by the time the thunder of their engines shook our ride. The gunship shivered in their wake, and I felt my stomach lurch into my chest.

Looking through an open door, I stared at geometric shapes that made up the skyline, skyscrapers and towers forming its lower edge, cutting into the sky like the ridges of a serrated blade. August in Washington and the sky was such a light blue that I almost dismissed it as white.

Somebody fired a rocket at us. They could only hit us with rockets, not missiles, because gunships transmitted radio waves and other distractions that baffled the computers on missiles. The problem with rockets was that they were no more intelligent than bullets. Missiles lock on to targets, often tracking their motion or their heat. Rockets simply fly in the direction that you point them; missiles make course corrections. But while missiles are more accurate, their brains make them vulnerable.

Thunk-a-thunk-a-thunk-a-thunk. The gunner to my right responded with his chain gun, firing rounds that could pierce a tank or a truck as if they were made of paper. When I was in boot camp, one of my drill sergeants fired a chain gun at a nearby hill, then he sent my platoon with shovels to dig out the slugs. That little task took all night. We had to dig more than twelve feet down before we finally found them.

That was the same kind of gun that Nailor and his soldiers had used to massacre the men I left guarding the ridge while I looked for Freeman. A bullet that can split armor and bury itself deep in the earth can cut a man in half. I reminded myself of that as I thought about the score I would soon settle.

"Did he get them?" asked Admiral Hauser.

MacAvoy shook his head. "They fire their rockets, then switch on their shielded armor. It takes more than armor-piercing bullets to kill those bastards. You either have to bury them or catch them with their shields down.

"So far we're having more luck burying them."

Off in the distance, I saw Sunny's building, sticking out of the ground like an old-fashioned bayonet. It was tall and silver-gray, its tinted windows a perfect mirror of the sky. I pointed, and asked, "Have the residents been evacuated from that building?"

"Yes. We've evacuated everything west of 16th Street," said MacAvoy.

That must have been a massive effort; it included a third of the city and a lot of high-priced real estate. You can't just relocate rich people and politicians; you need to transport them someplace nice and send soldiers to patrol their neighborhoods for looters while they're gone.

The sight of Sunny's building, pointing like an accusing finger, unnerved me. I wanted to ignore it, tried to put it out of my mind, tried to put her out of my mind. I gave in. "Did you keep records of the people you moved and where you stashed them?" I asked.

"Sure, we did. And we treated them properly, too. No shitty relocation camps for these natural-borns. We placed them in hotels and houses outside of town."

"And you kept records of who went where?" I asked.

"Sure," said MacAvoy.

So I asked what I needed to ask, protocol be damned. I asked, "Is there a way I can check on someone you relocated?"

MacAvoy didn't seem to hear me. He pressed the pointer finger of his right hand to his earpiece and stared out the open door to his left.

Seeing Sunny's building, I felt the weight of my betrayal. She and I had never fought. We rode bikes together and went for long drives.

Bullshit, I told myself. The truth was that the only place Sunny and I fit together was in bed. We came from different worlds. I reminded myself that she and I had never belonged together. She didn't like my friends and refused to introduce me to the people in her life. She always wanted to be alone with me . . . "wanted me to herself," she would say. It got boring quickly. There were times that we made love because we'd run out of things to do.

Another rocket struck the gunship; this one hit low on the cockpit, causing the bird to buck. Apparently, Unified Authority Marines were no more capable of transporting heavy artillery underwater than we were. They seemed to have a good supply of handheld rockets, but I saw no tanks or jackals or missile batteries on the ground, not that I was looking. When the second rocket hit the gunship, I still had my eyes on the apartment building.

One of the gunners swung his chain gun, tracking the smoke trail from the rocket. He fired. The low *thunk-a-thunk-a* blended with the thud of the rotors, neither burying it nor being buried beneath it.

I wondered how soldiers could stand having a Military Occupational Specialty that kept them flying around in an airborne target, the grinding of the engines numbing their ears. The crew wore headsets, probably noise-canceling headsets. Maybe that was their secret. My MOS was infantry, all Marines specialized in infantry first, then we added other skills afterward.

I tapped MacAvoy on the shoulder. When he turned to look at me, I pointed toward the apartment building, and shouted, "There, that building. Is that behind enemy lines?"

He shook his head, and answered, "No. It's on our side of the line." He pointed out the door and two blocks ahead to a wide diagonal street. "There. That's Massachusetts Avenue. That's the line. Everything between Massachusetts and the river is theirs."

"I need to know about someone who lives in that building," I said, repeating the question that MacAvoy had ignored earlier. I pointed to Sunny's building, and asked, "Is there some way to check?"

MacAvoy listened to me, thought about it, and yelled, "Yes." He didn't like my asking for favors, and that was exactly what I was doing, asking for a personal favor, but I didn't care. I didn't love Sunny, but I felt like maybe I owed her something. We'd shared moments, and I betrayed her. Betrayal is something we took seriously in the Marines.

Yelling to be heard above the rotors, I said, "The name is Sunny Ferris . . . Sunny spelled S-U-N-N-Y. That's with a 'U' as in 'uniform.' Ferris . . . F-E-R-R-I-S."

MacAvoy stared at me, his face implacable. Had I made him angry with my request? Had I shown weakness? Check that, I knew that I had. He stared at me, muttered something, but didn't react.

Feeling like I had just made a fool of myself, I didn't ask if he'd heard me. I sat there, worrying about Sunny, but it wasn't Sunny I imagined as I studied the building on the edge of the war zone: It was Ava Gardner, Ava, who might have been my one true love or might have been the furthest thing from it.

The last time I'd seen Ava, she was lying on a bed, in an apartment, in a luxury condominium, on a planet called Providence Kri. We were evacuating the planet, but she begged me to leave her behind. She had given up. She no longer cared if she lived or died.

No, once again I was lying to myself. She cared. By that time, she'd seen so much death that life no longer mattered to her. She wanted to die. I kissed her one last time and said she could stay and die if she liked. She thanked me as I left. A few days later, the aliens incinerated the planet.

What if Sunny was still in that apartment building? What if she had missed the evacuation? Stupid as it sounded, even to me, I thought maybe I could make things right with Ava by rescuing Sunny.

At the moment, though, the gunship continued flying in the wrong direction. We cut through a splendid late-summer sky, hovering below lazy clouds and above a battered stretch of city.

Another trio of fighters screamed past us in silence. When the thunder of their engines finally caught up, it drowned out the noise of the rotors. I felt the vibrations of their wake, but it no longer bothered me.

"Harris, she's not in our records," said MacAvoy.

"What does that mean?" I asked.

"It doesn't mean anything," said MacAvoy. "She could have been on vacation somewhere when we evacuated the area or she may have stayed in the building. Sometimes people refused to leave.

"At any rate, she's not in our records. We didn't move her."

I looked back at Sunny's building. I needed to go there. I needed . . .

MacAvoy interrupted my thoughts. He shouted, "There, Harris, ahead at ten o'clock."

A column of maybe as many as fifty U.A. Marines moved through an alley between a couple of three-story buildings. They saw us coming. As they moved through the shadows, they switched on their shields. In the daylight and shadows, I noticed the change in color more than the glow of the shields. Their dark green armor turned brown under the orange glow of the shields.

Our pilot fired two rockets at the Unifieds as they raced between the buildings and out to the street. It was a world in reverse, this war with the Unifieds. Normally, soldiers ran for cover in battle; these bastards had to run away from it.

One of the buildings came down on the last third of the platoon burying ten or fifteen men. The bastards would have fired back at us, but the only weapons they could carry once their shields went up were the fléchette cannons attached to their sleeves. They might have been carrying rockets, but they would have dumped them in the alley before switching on their shields.

"Damn fine shooting," MacAvoy said as he patted the pilot on his shoulder.

The Unifieds didn't bother firing fléchettes at us; we were a couple hundred yards up and a quarter of a mile away. Their fléchette cannons didn't hit shit after a few hundred feet, but men in shielded armor can afford to fight up close and personal.

I'd been trained for shoulder-fired rockets; they're big, five or six times the size of an RPG and several times more powerful, and they weigh nearly thirty pounds. The bastards had fired two at us today, and we hadn't been in the air for thirty minutes. How could they have smuggled so many rockets into town?

"You got any idea how many of those rockets they have?" I asked MacAvoy.

Hauser, looking nervous now that the rockets were in play, sat quietly watching us. War takes on a different meaning when you find yourself in the center of it.

My question clearly irritated MacAvoy. He asked, "How the speck would I know that?"

"They've fired two at us so far," I said.

MacAvoy said, "Yeah, we call that 'smooth sailing' around here. Normally we'd have seen six or seven by now. They have hundreds of 'em."

"Hundreds?" I asked.

He thought about it, and said, "Thousands."

"Do they seem to be running out?" I asked.

MacAvoy shook his head, and said, "Maybe. They've only shot two at us so far; maybe things are looking up."

Hauser, listening to us, exhaled sharply, making a dismissive-sounding, fruffing noise. He rolled his eyes, then went back to staring out at the ground.

I thought about the situation. Those rockets were heavy, they weren't waterproof, and they were clumsy to carry. You couldn't swim with them, not even if you had the SCUBA rigs the bastards who tried to kill me were wearing.

The Unifieds killed Don Cutter, attacked the prison, and tried to blow up the Pentagon all at the exact same moment, a coordinated strike. A lot of planning goes into that kind of staged assault. The brains behind these assaults wouldn't make meticulous plans for one attack only to launch the next haphazardly. That wouldn't make sense.

Say the Unifieds started smuggling rockets and armor into the city weeks or months ago, a luxury apartment building like Sunny's would make an excellent munitions dump. It was big, protected by a civilian presence, and it had a transient population. People moved in, bringing their possessions in moving trucks that no one inspected. Stuff a dozen large apartments with rockets, and you'd have enough inventory to fight a fourth world war.

With MacAvoy flattening buildings in their part of town, hiding their armory in a neutral zone would make sense. I thought about Sunny's building. Her neighbors were lawyers and senators and wealthy people, people with influence. Hell, MacAvoy had just complained that he couldn't just relocate them; he'd had to place them in nicer billets.

No one in their right mind would search a building with such influential residents; you'd end your career.

CHAPTER FIFTY-FOUR

We toured the front line from four hundred feet up, flying over empty streets and an abandoned waterfront. A few days ago, this area had been as elegant as any riverfront property on Earth. The pilot took us inland, flying over the Capitol; the Mall, with its museums and monuments; and rows of empty government office buildings.

No one had done any shooting around the Mall, not on our side or theirs. Talk about an abandoned city, Capitol Hill looked like it had been cleared using a neutron bomb.

I asked MacAvoy, "Remember that building I asked about when we were flying in?"

He said, "Yeah, the one you kept staring at. You have some scrub stashed in there or something? Was that the girl you asked about?"

When I didn't answer, MacAvoy realized he had lit off a nerve and went silent.

"Can you drop me there?" I asked.

"Harris, if you're pining over some gal, I'll send you a battalion."

Hauser, who hadn't said more than a word or two the entire hour, chose this moment to speak up. He waved a hand, and said, "Don't bother, General. Haven't you heard about Harris? He can't get his heart started in the morning without people shooting at him."

"I heard you got shot a few weeks ago," said MacAvoy. "Isn't that why you went missing? You got gutshot?"

He was right, and I hadn't fully recovered yet. I had a habit of pushing myself too far too quickly. Hauser was right as well; my M.O. included visiting front lines.

"Don't worry about that. That was last week," said Hauser. "This week, he's storming underground caverns . . ."

"It was a mine shaft," I said.

". . . running one-man missions behind enemy lines . . ."

"Unless I am mistaken, the general just told us it was on our side of the fence."

". . . and you just mentioned the Cousteau undersea cities; are you planning on swimming down to the underwater cities as well?"

Visiting a Cousteau city was exactly what I planned to do though I wasn't about to admit it. I wouldn't actually swim down—no one could—but I planned to pay the Unifieds a visit.

And then some of the pieces of the puzzle collided together in my head. I had been abducted by the Unifieds on Mars. They captured me and my entire battalion. That much was known. We also knew that they tried to reprogram me. The scientists who designed the Liberators didn't give us all of the neural switches they placed in the later models, so the Unifieds settled on brainwashing me instead. They managed to reprogram the rest of my men, though. They all converted to the other side.

And they changed sides at the worst possible time, right as the Unifieds launched an attack on Mars Spaceport. I suppose that was how the Unifieds had planned it.

After we won the battle, we searched the spaceport and Mars Air Force Base, looking for the labs in which the reprogramming had been done. We found nothing. It was as if the entire episode had been a dream.

It hadn't been, though. When I returned to Earth, I had the ability to commit suicide, something that had originally been programmed out of me. Something else, I had a new phobia—a fear of the ocean. The very thought of traveling down to the Cousteau project had me terrified, with a deep-seated, paralyzing fear. When I looked into the dark blue water, I imagined giant squid and alien fish with sharp teeth and lantern scales. I imagined the fish at the bottom of the deepest trenches. I imagined the creatures that might live around an underwater city.

What if my indoctrination didn't take place on Mars? I asked myself. Just because they'd captured us on Mars didn't mean we'd stayed there. That would explain why we never found the lab. Maybe my newfound fear of swimming didn't have anything to do with reprogramming; maybe it was an accidental by-product of being trapped at the bottom of the sea.

I saw no reason to discuss my "suicide fetish." That was what the late Admiral Cutter had called it, a "suicide fetish." He might well have mentioned it to Hauser.

Ignoring Hauser, I asked, "Can you get me to the building?"

MacAvoy shrugged his shoulders, and said, "No problem. We can get you there. Maybe we can rustle up a box of chocolates and a bottle of wine. Could come in handy."

I chose to ignore that comment as well.

Hauser said, "At least call in if you need help."

I said, "That'd work great if I had a phone."

Hauser wasn't carrying anything, and neither was MacAvoy. You don't generally carry telephones or personal communications equipment when you survey the battlefield. Usually, the communications console in your bird is enough.

I said, "Look, General, give me an hour. If you don't hear from me, send in your troops."

Head four blocks east from Sunny's front door and you'd find yourself standing in a Unified Authority barracks building. Four specking blocks. I know this because MacAvoy pointed it out as we flew by. At least his men wouldn't have far to travel if they came to get me.

As we neared Sunny's building, I handed out assignments. I told Tom Hauser to find a map showing the Cousteau underwater cities. I wanted precise locations and a means for reaching them.

He said, "I hope you don't mean submarines. The Navy hasn't had a submarine fleet for three hundred years."

"The Unifieds are coming and going," I pointed out.

"Mais oui," he said.

"May we? May we what?" I asked.

"*Mais oui*—it's a French term. It means that the Unifieds have probably recovered the boats the French used to build those cities and we're out of luck."

"You speak French?" asked MacAvoy.

"I speak some French," Hauser corrected. He added, "Just like you speak some English." At least, it looked as if that was what he'd said. I couldn't be sure; he spoke softly enough that the sound of the engine drowned out his voice.

MacAvoy didn't notice him mumbling or didn't care. He asked, "Nobody speaks French anymore. Why do you want to learn a language that nobody speaks?"

Hauser answered with a knowing grin. I knew what he was thinking, though. He was thinking that languages were a hobby of intellectuals, something that Neanderthals like MacAvoy could never understand. He probably lumped me in with MacAvoy, the bastard.

Sounding colder and more commanding, I said, "Figure something out and figure it out fast; we need to know how they reach those cities and how we can reach them."

"So you do plan on going down?" asked Hauser.

"I didn't say that."

"Do you plan on going down yourself or sending men?"

"I'm not sure. Are you headed up to the *Churchill* after this?"

He nodded.

I said, "Find out what you can. Once I'm done down here, I'll take a transport up so we can strategize."

I turned to MacAvoy and gave him his orders. I said, "Ray Freeman was running a recon op on a city in the mountains in the New Olympian Territories when the trouble started. I'm not sure what he stirred up, but it brought the Unifieds out of hiding."

"Are you ordering me to open a second front?" asked MacAvoy.

I could generally spot it when officers were afraid or unhappy about the orders I gave. Their voices betrayed them. If the idea of starting a second war bothered Pernell MacAvoy, he did a masterful job of camouflaging it.

We were nearly to Sunny's now. There had been very little fighting in this part of town and very little damage. The buildings around Sunny's condominium had survived the fighting and evacuation unbroken. Most of them stood ankle high beside the behemoth in which she lived.

"That depends what kind of reception the locals give you," I said. The Unifieds upped the ante the last two times I visited."

MacAvoy smiled, and said, "Maybe they'll raise it again."

He liked to fight, that clone.

Not wanting to telegraph my plans to the enemy, I had the gunship touch down three blocks east of the apartment building. She dropped to a few feet off the ground, and I sprang out.

I hadn't bothered forming a plan. I had entered a demilitarized zone; the Unifieds would shoot any of ours they caught strolling this close to their border, and we would gladly shoot theirs.

As I watched the gunship's ponderous ascent into the skyline, I realized the fallacy of the stalemate. They would shoot any of our soldiers they spotted and we would shoot any of theirs, but how would we recognize theirs? They were only sending natural-born troops into our territory. How could we identify them? Natural-borns came in all shapes and sizes.

We were clones; in uniform or out, they could recognize us. Even me. I was a different make—taller and meaner, but I had the same face, the same hair, the same complexion. I gave in to impulses far too quickly. Had I thought about it, I would at least have changed out of uniform. Dropping into demilitarized territory wearing my Charlie service uniform . . . why not paint a target on my back and enter with a marching band?

The street was empty. When MacAvoy said his men had evacuated the area, he wasn't joking. From what I could see, they'd done a good job of it. I cleaved to the shadows and awnings as I traversed that first block. At six-foot-three and wearing Marine khakis, I made an easy target. Had there been people around, I could have tried to blend in with the herd. In this no-man's-land, there was no camouflage to be found.

I reached the street, looked both ways, and dashed across. There were cars parked on both sides of the road, mostly expensive ones. Sunny came from a wealthy family and was a lawyer, albeit a fairly young lawyer. Judging by the stories she told me, young lawyers served their time in ignominy, doing legwork for lazy partners, bottom-feeding on lousy cases that no experienced lawyer would take.

The next block was one of those downtown shopping malls, an open-air arcade along which all of the buildings had matching façades. I passed an expensive-looking dress shop, maybe one that Sunny frequented.

The two three-story buildings ahead of me were identical twins, with black granite exteriors and tinted-glass windows. The slate-tiled courtyard that separated the twins was lined with benches and picnic tables. The stores were closed and dark and silent: a gourmet coffee shop, a high-priced sandwich shop, a jewelry store, a shoe store for men.

I paused at the next corner to make sure no one would see me, checked both ways in search of guards and loiterers, then trotted across the street.

Sunny's apartment building filled an entire block, tall and sparkling with silver sides and acres of glass. It jutted out of the ground straight and narrow, a giant sword stabbing out of the earth and into the sky.

I approached the front doors of the building, and they slid

open automatically. I hadn't expected that though I didn't know why.

Entering the lobby, I spotted two men. They were natural-born and wearing civilian clothing. They might have been Unified Authority Marines or they might have been residents. They could have been both. But if MacAvoy was right, and this building had been evacuated, there was little chance that anyone I saw would be friendly.

Unifieds, sympathizers, or civilians, they were startled by my sudden appearance. They stared at me. One, an older man with patches of white in his hair, looked confused to see me. The other, a boy in his twenties, reached into his jacket for what could have been a gun, a phone, a wallet, or a key.

I didn't have a gun, or I would have pulled it. Instead, I sprinted across the lobby and caught the boy as he brought out his hand. He had a pistol. It was not an S9. In fact, I didn't recognize the make. I caught his hand as he brought it out of his coat, and forced the gun free.

The old one tried to slip behind me as the young one took a swing at me with his free hand. Using his right arm like a lever, I pivoted, playing my weight and momentum to force my attacker forward, then drove him face-first into the old guy. They crashed into each other with an *oof* and a *clunk*, and I grabbed the young guy by the hair and slammed his forehead into the bridge of the old guy's nose, following up with a knee to the small of the young guy's back, incapacitating him, then I backhanded him across the nape of his neck as he went down.

The old guy might have wanted to jump to action when I first started wrestling his partner, but seeing his pal collapse, he panicked, and I finished him with a slash across the throat.

I hid the stiffs behind the security desk, made sure they'd stay dead, then fleeced them of anything useful. I found a gun on the old guy as well. They both had elevator keys. I checked their wallets. They had credit cards and civilian IDs.

I took the young guy's jacket. He was shorter than me, and the sleeves of the jacket barely reached my wrists. The jacket concealed my khaki uniform, though, and that was enough. I took their keys and their guns.

Somewhere along the line, my combat reflex had begun,

and suddenly Sunny became less important than reconnoitering the premises. EME intelligence had no method for identifying Unified Authority Marines. They could move through our territory unrecognized. We were a clone minority in a natural-born world.

I adjusted the jacket as best I could, then walked to the security door and found it open . . . completely open. Somebody had removed the door from its frame. That somebody might have been one of MacAvoy's soldiers, by the way. They would have removed security doors and any other obstacles that slowed down the evacuation.

I walked through.

I could have taken the stairs, but I chose the elevator on the off chance that someone might see me. Residents ride elevators, criminals take stairs. I didn't want to attract any unwanted attention, so I rode the elevator up to the third floor and had a look around. The lights were off, the hall was silent. I stepped out and walked the floor from end to end without seeing people. I thought about forcing the doors of a couple of condos but decided against it.

So far, the building was as advertised, abandoned. Yes, I had run into a couple of gun-toting assholes in the lobby, but they might have come to explore, just as I had. I didn't really believe they were random assholes, not for a moment. This was a combat zone, and looters generally prefer to travel in locales where they are less likely to be caught. Until I found confirmation one way or another, I would assume they were Unifieds.

I decided to take the stairs for the next few floors, preferring to enter and exit halls without the fanfare of flashing lights and sliding doors. I climbed to the fourth floor and found it empty, just like the one after that, and the one after that. When I reached the seventh floor, I found the lights on and doors open.

Having grown up in an orphanage and spent my adult life in barracks on bases, I'm never quite comfortable in luxury buildings or empty halls because the sounds that I associate with life tend to disappear in the air. My footsteps make no noise on the plush carpet. The walls squelch voices, the doors don't creak. I approached the nearest open door and listened to silence. No one spoke, so I flitted down the hall, peering into doorways like a ghost haunting a castle.

The first apartment I passed seemed empty enough. The lights were off, leaving the room lit by whatever lingering daylight slipped in through an enormous window that faced east. It was late in the afternoon by that time, so the sun had already migrated to the west.

I stole into the apartment like a shadow and moved around the living room, looking for anything suspicious. I found nothing.

I had no idea what incriminating evidence I had hoped to find . . . a pallet of rocket launchers, a closet filled with armor, a Da Vinci–esque mural of Tobias Andropov and the Unified Authority Linear Committee eating their last supper.

I searched the bedrooms. The bed in the master bedroom was neatly made, its cover tight. Not so much as a wrinkle showed. The sinks in the master bathroom were dry.

Maybe they really were doing the same thing as me, I thought, referring to the men I had killed in the lobby. Maybe they had come to search the building. Maybe they were scouts.

I checked the closets, the extra bedrooms, the kitchen. Nothing of interest. There was food in the pantry and milk in the fridge.

Sunny lived on the thirty-eighth floor. Less than a month had passed since I'd been shot; I didn't feel like jogging thirty-one more flights, so I took the elevator instead.

The door opened, and I heard voices. There were men in the hall. They could have been civilians, of course, but I thought that the same thing that had attracted Sunny to the thirty-eighth floor might also interest officers from an invading army—the view. From her window, Sunny could look past George Washington University and catch little cerulean glimpses of the iron blue Potomac beyond. Sunny's apartment faced west. Upper-floor apartments that faced east might well offer a strategic glimpse into neighboring boroughs like Cheverly and Landover.

In an era of satellites and stealth generators, hijacking an apartment building with a panoramic view might not seem like much, maybe only a petty victory; then again, I still wondered if they might have stashed something inside this building.

I stepped off the lift, saw two men chatting in the hall to my right, and turned left. I kept my arms loose, my hands out and to my sides. They hadn't seen my face, and my height marked me as natural-born. The jacket might even have looked familiar to them. If those guys were Unified Authority general-issue, they might have known the man to whom this jacket had belonged.

In the quick glimpse I caught of them, I saw men in their thirties. Both had short hair. They paid no attention to me as I slipped away. Did that make them civilians?

Officially, I was running this unofficial op to search for Sunny. *Once you know that Sunny is out of the building and safe, what are you going to do?* I asked myself. I would explore. There were ten more floors above this one. I could search an apartment or two on this floor, then return to the elevator and ride it to a higher floor. I had no idea what I was looking for, but I wouldn't consider my recon complete until I had visited the top ten floors.

I looked up the hall and saw Sunny's door.

The door was closed. I didn't have a key to her apartment—she'd never offered me one—but I had a foot with a boot on it. *That might make too much noise,* I told myself. Civilian or not, the two guys down the hall would come to investigate if they heard me kicking in a door.

They weren't civilians, though. I wasn't fooling anybody; they were U.A. For some reason, I wanted to make myself believe I was in neutral territory when I knew damn well I wasn't. The two men I'd killed in the lobby weren't residents. They'd had guns. Had I not caught them off guard, they would have made the first move, and I might have ended the day hidden behind the help desk instead of them.

I reached into my pocket and pulled out one of the little pistols I had taken from the stiffs. I steeled myself to kick in the door and deal with the fallout, but I tried the knob first, and the door swung aside.

I felt the stirrings of a combat reflex as I entered Sunny's apartment.

The lights were off. The room was silent. I saw familiar trappings, chairs on which I had sat, a sofa on which I had once spent an uncomfortable night, a dining-room table at which I had eaten. Looking through the window at the back, I saw the familiar view. At night, that part of the city lit up like a field of stars.

I had killed two men downstairs without giving much thought to it. I had explored multiple floors of a building on the edge of occupied territory. Now I stood on familiar turf, an apartment in which I had spent many nights, and my heart had begun beating like an African drum. I still had steady hands, but only because I had slipped into a combat reflex.

My body, and on some unconscious level my mind, had prepared for war. My Liberator DNA didn't come with pre-cognition that warned me about danger, but veterans of the battlefield learn to recognize premonitions from jitters. Soldiers either develop that talent, or they become statistics.

Most of my battlefield premonitions had been along the lines of the duck-and-jump variety. This was different. I couldn't put my finger on what my emotions were telling me, but a moment later, a man dressed in combat armor stepped out of Sunny's bedroom. In the moment before I killed him, I noticed something in his hands, a metallic cylinder about the size of a shoe box, maybe fifteen inches tall and six inches in diameter.

I'd experienced the gas that Unifieds carried in cylinders before. A whiff of that and my brain would reboot, almost as if I'd had an epileptic seizure. That was the first step to reprogramming, the only part of the reprogramming process that worked as effectively on me as on any other clone.

I should have shot the bastard. Hell, I still had that stealth pistol in my hand, but I was primed to fight and flat-out forgot about it. Instead, I charged at him, leaping over Sunny's cream-colored leather sofa, and crashing into the bastard while he still had that cylinder in his hands. Had he shot me with his fléchette cannon or activated his shields, he would have won the fight before I got to him.

He looked up from the metal cylinder, and saw me hurdling the sofa. Then I landed on top of him, wedging my right forearm under his chin, hoping to crush his throat. He struggled to buck me off, but he didn't activate his shields. Fighting for air, pushing against my face with his left hand, he raised his right arm. I was so focused on his shields that I'd forgotten about the fléchette cannon and barely managed to bat the arm away before he fired.

With my left arm pinning his right, my right arm across his throat, and his armored glove in my face, I didn't have the situation under control. Trying to keep his eyes from connecting with the optic-controlled menu in his visor, I butted my head against his, knocking his helmet askew but hurting my head far more than his. All the while, the bastard kept digging his armor-plated knees into my thighs.

He rolled and turned his head, trying to right his visor so he could control its functions. Not especially strong, but protected from my knees and fists, the bastard had me beat even though he didn't know it. He brought his right knee up, hoping to connect with my groin. He missed, but only because I swung to the right and rebalanced my weight higher up his body, rendering the arm I had pinned across his throat useless. I scrabbled for a purchase, hoping for a handhold I could grab to lock the bastard in place. He jerked his right arm back and forth, prying it out of my grip for just a moment, then he aimed that specking cannon at my knee. I swatted his arm away, but that gave him enough wiggle room to throw me to the floor.

I rolled away, sprang to my feet, and dashed to the front door while he causally sat and adjusted his helmet. I had dropped the pistol and the other one was buried in my pocket. As he stood, an orange-gold glow materialized around him, meaning that I no longer had the option of shooting the bastard.

Sunny wouldn't thank me for what I did next, but I had no choice.

During our wrestling match, I'd liberated a grenade from the bastard's belt. Running for the door, I pulled the pin from the grenade and dropped it.

The son of a bitch shot at me. The fléchette dug tiny holes in the wall ahead of me as I leaped behind the sofa and crouched to stay low. The guy was now toying with me. He was sealed from harm in his shielded armor and thought I had no place to run. About that, he was wrong. I counted to three, then sprang for the door, which I threw open and pulled closed behind me as I tumbled into the hall.

Even if he'd shut off his armor and found the grenade that I'd left on the floor behind the couch, what would the bastard be able to do with it? If he lowered his shield in time, he could open the door and jump out like I had . . . and I would shoot him as he entered the hall.

His armor would protect him from the shrapnel, but I had something else in mind.

I had sprinted forty feet down the hall by the time the grenade exploded, launching Sunny's front door so hard that it stabbed through the wall on the opposite side of the hallway. Fire alarms screamed along the hall.

I stared into the room and saw what I'd expected to find. That Marine's shielded armor might have protected him from shrapnel, but it wouldn't stop the percussion from sweeping his armor-clad ass out through the window. *Happy landings,* I thought.

"Did you see what happened?"

I looked away from the bloodless carnage of Sunny's living room. The two men I'd seen standing near the elevator had come to survey the damage.

I shook my head, and said, "Man . . . it looks like a grenade went off in there."

"A grenade," one of them repeated. "More like a bomb."

A strong wind blew in through the shattered glass wall. Sunny's leather furniture had been blown to shreds and splinters. The sofa had entirely disappeared, probably washed out the window with the U.A. Marine. Her entire dining-room set appeared to have suffered the same fate. Her desk and entertainment center, on the other hand, now existed only as unrecognizable piles of debris.

I checked the floor for the canister that bastard had been holding. Gone. Maybe he took it with him.

"Did you see anyone come in or out?" asked one of the looky-loos.

I shook my head.

Other people came to see what had happened, all dressed like civilians, all the right age to qualify as Marines.

With my brown hair and brown eyes and clone facial features, I did not want to wait around any longer than necessary. I backed away from the crowd as more men arrived. Keeping my head down and hoping not to be noticed, I entered a stairwell.

"Hey! Wait," someone shouted in my direction. He quieted down quickly when I shot him between the eyes. I opened the door to the stairs, leaped the entire first flight, pushed off against the wall, and leaped the next one.

Sunny lived on the thirty-eighth floor, that left seventy-two more flights of stairs until I reached the bottom. I had not fully recovered from my experiences in the New Olympian Territories, and at this pace my knees would turn to jelly long before I reached the street.

I made my way down two or three floors before I heard the door open and the footfalls of the herd of men pounding after me. Had I had the presence of mind to steal a second grenade during my wrestling match, I would have dropped it on the stairs and escaped on the next floor. When a grenade goes off in the tight confines of a stairwell, few people survive.

I held my little gun out and ready. Two floors down, then four, then ten; my legs hurt, and my heart ran cycles it wasn't meant to hit. My guts knotting like a rope, I ducked into the next doorway, not even bothering to see what floor I was on.

I stepped into an empty hall and closed the door behind me. Maybe the men who were chasing me would continue past this floor, but I doubted it. I checked the closest apartment and found the door locked. I could have kicked it in . . . maybe, and maybe I could have hung a sign in front of it that said HE'S IN HERE.

The next door was locked, and so was the one after that.

As I tried the next door, I heard the door to the stairwell open and ran as best I could toward the elevator. My strength mostly gone, I found an open door down the next hall and stepped into it.

If Sunny's apartment was on the thirty-eighth floor, this one might have been somewhere in the high twenties. It looked out east into an extended cityscape and the flatlands beyond. With the pistol still in my right hand, I placed my left hand on to the armrest of a leather chair as I doubled over and forced air deep into my lungs.

I wasn't sick in the *here comes the puke* sense, but my heart was pumping and my lungs burned. My head hurt, but I wasn't dizzy.

If the Unifieds had followed me onto this floor, they could have stood right outside my door without my hearing them. The thick carpeting in the halls would absorb the sound of their footsteps. The doors and walls were designed for privacy.

I went to the bathroom and sipped water from the tap. I went to the bedroom, hoping for a change of clothes. All I found were dresses and lingerie.

I returned to the window for another look. Day had ended in the east, and night would soon settle on that horizon. A few streetlights had flickered to life. I didn't know how long I would need to hold out. MacAvoy would have sent men to collect me by now. He'd probably come at the head of his column.

One thing about Pernell MacAvoy—he didn't waste time worrying about the subtler things in life. Most commanders try to win battles using the least amount of force that will still guarantee them victory. Not MacAvoy. Be it battle or skirmish, he came to crush the opposition, and he brought as many men as he could muster, logistics be damned. When his men came to find me, they would march right up to this building. I hadn't found apartments filled with rockets, but I had killed four U.A. Marines so far, and the night was still young.

The door to the apartment opened. Either the Unifieds had found themselves a passkey or they had a device that scrambled computerized locks. I heard the soft whir of the bolt sliding and turned in time to see the door open. By this time, my combat reflex had waned, and I chose to hide instead of shoot.

I dropped to the floor and belly-crawled into the master bedroom and, beyond that, into the master bathroom, ending up on the tile floor wedged between the toilet and the shower. I aimed the little pistol at the bathroom door, held my breath, and willed my heart to beat slowly.

They didn't give the room much of a search, might not have even stepped in the door. They didn't so much as peer through the bathroom door.

I waited another minute before squeezing out from behind the toilet. The difference between live Marines and dead heroes is often the extra minute the live ones wait before crawling out of their hiding places. That's probably what separates live hares from dead ones as well.

The Unifieds really hadn't spent much time searching the apartment. I came out from behind the porcelain and chrome, the little pistol still ready, and saw that the apartment was indeed empty. I mentally chided the U.A.M.C. for the laziness of its recruits, then I saw what they must have seen, the reason they gave up so quickly. Out on the street, tanks had rolled into the neighborhood. Gunships hovered in the air, flitting between the buildings like prehistoric hummingbirds. Jeeps and Jackals led the procession, followed by a full battalion of men.

The Unifieds must have spotted the battalion's approach and interpreted it as an invasion. Maybe they were right. As I watched the force roll in, I realized that MacAvoy might have used rescuing me as an excuse for carving new boundaries. If he didn't run into resistance in this demilitarized area, he might just keep rolling west, but he was going to encounter resistance. Of that much, I would make sure.

CHAPTER FIFTY-FIVE

The three men standing in the hall were dressed like civilians and armed. I shot them. I opened the door, shot the first man I saw, then the two men gabbing with him. *This is a war zone, assholes, stay alert or die,* I silently told the dead men.

The men had been standing outside an open door, so I went to the door for a peek. Inside the apartment, a man held a large hammer. I shot him.

These men hadn't come looking for me. They had other business in mind. A line of crates ran parallel to the glass wall on the far side of the apartment. I knew the contents of the crates without opening them—DL-148 shoulder-fired rockets.

I had come to this building looking for Sunny, and now I

was doing scouting. Here were rockets, and powerful rockets at that. Around the corps, our grenadiers told jokes about "burying enemies at 148 Dreary Lane." The address "148 Dreary Lane" referenced the name of the rockets, "DL-148s."

I looked at the line of boxes and the dead man lying near the window with the rocket launcher in his hand and the Army parading up the block, and realized that I had stumbled into something a lot more dangerous than a few rogue officers vacationing in my ex-girlfriend's abandoned apartment building. Of all the gin joints in all the towns in all the world, these bastards had selected this one.

Specking coincidences, they shoot you in the ass every time, I thought.

This building had approximately one thousand apartments, five hundred of which faced east toward MacAvoy's advancing army. *They couldn't possibly have men with rockets hiding behind every door, could they?* I wondered.

I'd heard stories about bullets bouncing off skyscraper windows. Somewhere along the line, somebody had told me these windows were nearly unbreakable and that they were stronger in the center than along the edges. I picked up the dead guy's hammer and swung it like a baseball bat, rolling my wrist at just the right moment and connecting with the window along the side. The glass shattered like a poor man's dreams.

The spot I hit exploded into a million microscopic pieces. A moment later, the rest of the window slipped free from its mold and dropped in one jagged scale.

I borrowed a page from Ray Freeman's playbook and fired a rocket at an empty stretch of road. I aimed in the general direction of the approaching soldiers to make sure they saw it but several hundred yards ahead of them. My rocket flew through the window, crossed open air leaving a very traceable smoke trail, and left a fiery crater in the street.

MacAvoy's troops couldn't have missed it.

I was feeling pretty good about myself as I watched one of the EME gunships fly toward the smoke. I remembered the way MacAvoy's pilot had responded earlier that afternoon, stood rooted in place just long enough to see the bird turn so that one of her chain guns faced in my direction, and I bolted for the hall.

I was already out of the room when the gunship opened

fire. Let me tell you, the fifty-cal armor-piercing bullets that gunships shoot aren't slowed by skyscraper glass or aluminum-frame walls. Those bullets entered one side of the building, drilled through walls and halls, and exited the building on the opposite side.

I had hoped to warn MacAvoy. Instead, I had initiated a firestorm. It wouldn't matter any longer if the Unifieds had a thousand men standing at a thousand windows firing a thousand rockets; they would not win this one. Never in a million years.

A single well-placed missile would bring down this entire building, and so would the right shell from a tank. The fighters circling outside had bombs that could reduce the entire neighborhood to rubble. I'd seen it happen. Early in my career, I had served under an officer who referred to this as his "urban renewal plan."

I sprinted toward the stairs, not bothering to look back at the damage that gunship had inflicted in the hall.

Someone had propped the door to the stairwell wide open, so I slid in like a baseball player stealing home. I sprang to my feet, and started down the first set of stairs. Dozens of men ran ahead of me. Judging by the clatter, hundreds more were at my back.

I found myself panicking along with the Unified Authority Marines. In another minute or two, the Army of the Enlisted Man's Empire would bring down this building and everyone in it. Anyone unlucky enough to trip in this stairwell, be he in shielded armor or wearing civilian clothing, would find himself buried under a thousand thousand tons of rubble, so we all had the same need—we needed to escape. Then again, the bastards were Unified Authority Marines. I pulled out my little pistol and shot the guy in front of me in the back of the neck. The way he fell, it probably looked to everyone else like he tripped, and his dead form tackled four people in front of him. I leaped over his corpse and kept running.

Then MacAvoy shut off the lights. I didn't know if his men turned off a circuit breaker in the building or cut through the cables to the entire neighborhood; all I knew was that the stairs went from dim to dark, then to dusk as the emergency lights produced what little glow they had to offer.

When I reached the landing for the twenty-third floor, I shot the guy to my left in the gut. He fell, and people trampled him; I lost track of what happened after that. If it weren't for the combat reflex saturating me with adrenaline and testosterone, I wouldn't have lasted these five more floors. Now though, with my endurance boosted and mind alert, I had all the strength I needed to continue. Without looking back, I aimed my gun over my shoulder me and fired three shots. Somebody shrieked.

None of the people in the stairwell carried rockets. Only a few wore armor. As I crossed a landing and approached a ledge overlooking the next flight of stairs, I pushed the man to my right over the top of the rail. It didn't take much strength, just a quick shove, and he cartwheeled over the railing.

Killing him might have been a mistake. He fell onto the next landing, crashing down on five or six people, who formed a human snowball that clogged the next flight of stairs. As I reached the sixteenth floor, a tangle of heads, backs, and limbs formed a dam at the top of the stairs. While other escapees stood staring, mindless and confused, I climbed over the rail and swung myself so that I dropped onto the next set of stairs. Dozens of Unifieds saw what I had done and tried to follow. When I did it, I'd been alone. With so many men clamoring on such a short stretch of rail, they climbed on top of each other, kicking and punching and trying to knock everyone else out of the way. A few of them might have followed me down to the next landing, but I saw a steady stream of men falling past the stairs and dropping sixteen floors.

When I lowered myself, I landed on the heads and shoulders of the men ahead of me, inadvertently causing a human avalanche that conveyed me down to the next landing. Men fell on top of me, behind me, in front of me. I shot some and clambered over others.

Somewhere deep inside me, I realized that I had become a vampire feeding off the panic of these men, these enemies of my state, these sons of bitches who had returned to my world hoping to reclaim it for themselves. In the darkness of the stairwell, I saw their writhing bodies as silhouettes, as shadow-men; they were something less than human, and I felt no worse about killing them than I would about stepping on roaches or ants.

That was when I threw that little pistol away.

I had slipped into combat reflex overdrive, killing for the

fun and the adrenaline boost in my blood. That was happening more and more frequently. Killing enemies in battle came with the job; shooting men in the back as they ran for their lives held no honor.

About the same time that I had tossed away my pistol, the lights came back, and soldiers wearing the uniform of the Enlisted Man's Army and clear plastic breathing masks entered the stairwell. They had guns and they had orders—anyone who surrendered was a prisoner of war, anyone who resisted would be shot.

As I stood, a captain approached me and asked, "Does your shirt match your pants?"

I looked at my pants—khakis with blue piping. All the while that I had spent hiding my blouse, it never occurred to me that my pants would give me away. I opened the jacket, and the captain said, "General Harris, would you come with me, sir? General MacAvoy would like a word with you."

CHAPTER FIFTY-SIX

The real battle for the capital began that evening. Everything else had been a prelude, just a feint that enabled the Unifieds to establish a beachhead from which they could infiltrate our strongholds.

I had exposed them.

With that jacket off and my blouse on display, MacAvoy's soldiers recognized me. They gave me an Army helmet and a flak jacket and led me outside. Warm darkness now covered Washington, D.C. In that darkness, a gunship flew low to the ground, taking advantage of a wide avenue to fly lower than the rooftops. The men in that bird were hunting, daring any Unifieds to fire their rockets, while fighters circled overhead, and tanks rumbled down the boulevard.

The building across the street lay in ruins, its walls unrecognizable, a mere corner still standing while flames danced on its bric-a-brac slopes. I looked along the street and saw glowing light shining from street gutters.

I pointed and told the captain escorting me, "There! Under the street."

He didn't even give it a glance before saying, "Yeah, yeah, they're under the street; there's not much we can do about it. We don't want to blow up the streets if we can help it, sir. General MacAvoy wants to keep the collateral damage to a minimum."

He seemed so specking nonchalant about my spotting; that was what bothered me more than anything else. I started to say something and stopped myself.

A platoon of men in shielded armor appeared around a distant corner. They looked like phosphorus creatures, like something that lived deep in the oceans, with phosphorous light glowing from its skin. I supposed these men had lived deep in the ocean before they invaded.

The gunship swooped in, firing chain guns. A standoff. The gunship's chain guns couldn't penetrate their shields; they couldn't harm the gunship with their fléchettes.

I heard a fizzing noise and looked in time to see the explosion. Someone had fired a rocket from a building two blocks away. The gunship did a half flip in the air. Clearly injured, it pivoted and returned fire. A missile hit the window from which the rocket had been fired, and the entire front of the building caved in and poured into the street in a flash of fire and light and white smoke.

A few feet from where I stood, one of our soldiers pulled a grenade and tossed it at the Marines in the shielded armor. The guy had a good arm; he threw that pill an entire city block. The grenade hit the sidewalk, and bounced into the enemy platoon, where it exploded. Out here in the open, the pop of the grenade didn't seem nearly as visceral.

"Better get in the jeep, sir," said the captain. "It's getting hot around here."

It could get a lot hotter, I thought, remembering Thomas Hauser's inability to stop that stealth destroyer. I asked myself what other surprises the U.A. Navy might have up its sleeve. I knew the answer. The Unifieds had one of our fighter carriers in their fleet as well—the *de Gaulle*, piloted by a crew of reprogrammed clones. *For all you know, they might have more,* I reminded myself.

I stepped into the passenger's side of the jeep. Up in the sky, a fighter pilot must have seen something of interest. He took his jet hypersonic, vanishing so quickly that I didn't even see the flame from his engines, and all that remained of his bird was a loud boom.

That jet wasn't only the vehicle that left the scene in a hurry. The corporal driving our jeep gave the captain and me a moment to buckle ourselves in, then he sped off, tires screeching.

"What are they going to do about those glowboys?" I asked the captain.

"Ignore them," he said with a smirk.

"Ignore them?" I asked.

"Ignore them and keep out of their way," he said, adding a shrug to signal that he had stated the obvious. Seeing that his answer hadn't satisfied me, he said, "General MacAvoy's orders are to capture them if they're still around when their shields run out of juice and to bury them if they're stupid enough to stand near a building."

It sounded so specking simple. In my experience, the U.A. Marines were the terrors of the battlefield. Yes, their weapons were short-range, but they could kill us, and we couldn't touch them.

Seeing that I still didn't understand, he said, "We contain them with our tanks, sir. Their fléchettes don't penetrate tank armor, and they can't fire rockets when their shields are on.

"Look, sir, they're only dangerous when they're fighting troops, they don't have any answer for heavy armor."

Armor. I laughed. I was a Marine, and as a Marine, my primary military occupational specialty was infantry. I seldom dealt with mechanized cavalry and heavy armor.

MacAvoy was beating the Unifieds better than I ever could. I wasted time searching for elegant solutions; he happily relied on brute force. They weren't used to his methods.

General MacAvoy had moved his headquarters to a two-story portable in the shadow of the now-ruined Pentagon.

The captain led me into the building, a long Quonset-shaped

structure made out of a metal-and-plastic composite that insulated its occupants against heat, cold, and indirect hits. The missiles that destroyed the Pentagon would smash this structure to splinters, but MacAvoy didn't bother with details like that.

He had a perfectly good office, but that wasn't where we met. As we entered the building, I spotted him standing a few feet from the door, berating two colonels and a major.

"Oh, I'm sorry, ladies. Were you having your nails done this evening?" he asked with faux concern.

"No, sir," said one of the colonels, sounding unsure about whether or not he should answer the question.

"Then why the speck aren't you out there with your men? I hope to hell you don't think those worthless birds over your boobs make you special! Those are eagles, damn it, not chickens. If I wanted cowards for colonels, I'd drop the eagles and decorate you with chicken feathers instead."

He saw me standing near the door, stared at me for just a moment, then turned back to the officers, and shouted, "Why in speck's name are you sons of bitches still breathing my air? Get out of my building!"

They saluted.

He returned the salute.

They rushed out of the building. As soon as they were gone, MacAvoy said, "Those are some of my better officers. I think I'll put them down for medals and promotions when this one is over."

He stood there for a moment, lost in thought. MacAvoy stood five-ten, of course, a man nearing retirement with mostly white hair. He was thick and solid, a brick of a man with an incisive internal compass that never questioned whether north was north or south was south.

"Did Grayson tell you that we mobilized V Corps?"

I hadn't even noticed the captain's name, but he had to be Grayson. I asked, "You're sending an entire corps into the Territories?"

As we spoke, I removed my flak jacket. It was not tight, heavy, or constricting, but I wouldn't describe it as a comfortable fit. I folded the jacket over once and placed it on an empty desk. MacAvoy's Corps of Engineers had provided him with a building and furniture, but he had not yet selected the personnel to man it.

Most high-ranking officers surround themselves with posses of ass-lickers. Not MacAvoy. The way he beat down his officers, I wasn't sure anybody wanted to kiss his ass. Entourage officers avoided benefactors like Perry MacAvoy. He liked visiting the front and watching the action up close; they preferred admirals and generals who specialized in summits and diplomacy. Tom Hauser, for instance, had a congregation shadowing his every move.

"Did you find your girlfriend?" asked MacAvoy.

My girlfriend, I repeated to myself. The question left me confused. At that moment, Kasara and Sunny occupied no real estate in my head. *My girlfriend?* I thought of Kasara first, then realized he meant Sunny. I had gone to that building searching for Sunny. I had been to her apartment . . . had destroyed it with a grenade. Hell, MacAvoy and the Unifieds had left the entire building in tatters.

"The only people I saw were Unified Authority Marines," I said.

"A lot of people left town before we started evacuating," he said. "I'll tell my men to keep an eye out for her, but she's probably off in Chicago or Seattle watching us on TV."

I thanked him.

"Hell, who knows what we'll turn up looking for your gal," he said, "You sent us searching for Travis, and we discovered an invasion. You asked me to meet you at your girlfriend's apartment, now the whole damn city is in flames. Damn good thing we're activating V Corps; we'll probably run into the whole specking U.A. Army in the Territories."

He led me up to the empty second floor of his headquarters. The bottom floor had furniture. The top floor had no desks, no partitions, no chairs, just light fixtures, which he had set on dim. There were large windows at either end of the building; one faced southwest toward the remains of the Pentagon, the other northeast to the Potomac and the lights of downtown.

In a hollow voice, he said, "They took back most of my view. I used to control the riverfront; now I don't even have Capitol Hill."

I walked to the window. The world outside was dark and

dotted with tiny lights. Looking to my right, I saw the 14th Street Bridge, an unadorned stretch of road that spanned the river without suspension towers or cables. From this second-floor spot, I saw monuments and government buildings across the river, but they were so distant they looked like miniatures instead of the real buildings.

An unsteady darkness covered Washington, D.C. Off on the horizon, artillery flashed. No stars showed in the sky. Dual layers of clouds and smoke obscured them.

MacAvoy came and stood beside me. We both stared out the window, trying to read the flashes of light as if they held some sort of code. After a moment, he asked, "Did you ever play football?"

"I never did," I said. I wrestled and boxed. Whenever my teachers gave me a choice, I always selected combat training instead of phys. ed.

"It's an interesting sport, football," he said. "You have two kinds of defenses in football—man-to-man and zone. We're running a zone operation out here. If the Unifieds want the capital, they have to fight us for it. If they want a foothold in the New Olympian Territories, they can fight us there. There's no place they can go without having to fight us; that's a zone defense.

"Harris, Hauser says you want to fight man-to-man. He thinks you're making this your own personal war."

"Does he?" I asked.

"He doesn't know who it's about, and he doesn't know what it's about, but he says you're after somebody."

"Did Hauser play football?" I asked, unable to imagine him wearing pads and breaking tackles.

MacAvoy laughed, and said, "He strikes me as more of the chess-club type."

"But he thinks I'm adopting a man-to-man defense?" I asked.

"He thinks you are headhunting."

Headhunting? Two particularly bright flashes lit up the horizon. It was like watching a lightning storm.

"We'll lose some tanks and some gunships, but the fight is already won," said MacAvoy. "They thought they would run into the Marines, not the Army."

"Oh, shit, MacAvoy, let's not make this a battle between

soldiers and Marines," I said, though I wouldn't have minded a stupid argument.

"Depends on the mission," said MacAvoy. "I think they expected to run into you when they invaded. They expected to face a Marine using Marine tactics. They weren't counting on artillery and gunships.

"They didn't get the fight they had prepared for, and it's going to cost them."

Before leaving the Territories, I had already known that I would need Admiral Hauser's help. He was a by-the-regulations-type officer, meaning I would need to sell him on the idea of my private retribution. That would require meeting him on his terms, on his ship, where he held all the ace cards. I had requested a one-on-one with him before I arrived in Washington, D.C. I could have told Hauser my plans before climbing on the gunship, but I thought he might be more generous if I met him on his ship.

My ride, the military transport that would carry me to the *Churchill*, landed a few yards away. We watched the bulky, nearly wingless bird through the window. Her booster rockets flared as it touched down on heavy skids. That bulky warhorse of a ship would take me to space and from there to whatever boneyard Franklin Nailor had chosen for a hiding place.

MacAvoy watched me instead of the transport. Once she landed, he said, "You're going to get your fight, Harris. I hope it's the fight that you're looking for."

CHAPTER FIFTY-SEVEN

It was already late in the evening, and, of course, no light shone from the remains of the Pentagon. Those ruins were the opposite of light; they were a black hole, a vortex attempting to ingest the flatlands around them. Streetlamps still shone around the vast parking lot, casting tiny islands of light in a black sea.

As I approached the rear of the transport, two men met me. Both were clones, but I recognized them both.

We traded salutes.

"Lieutenant Nobles," I said, "if you're my pilot, this ride could be dangerous."

Nobles said, "It can't be worse than the time you had me dodging three battleships in an outer-space graveyard."

"I don't know; you're taking me to meet with an admiral."

"Am I meeting with the admiral as well?" asked Nobles.

"Nope."

He smiled, and said, "Sounds like a safe flight to me, sir." We traded salutes, and he left for the cockpit.

The second man was General Hunter Ritz. He asked, "You always fly with that boy, don't you."

I said, "More often than not."

Ritz looked more regulation than usual. His uniform was pressed, the gigs on his blouse formed ruler-straight rows, and his shoes reflected the dim light that trailed out of the transport.

I said, "You know, you look a lot like an officer I used to know named Ritz, but he never dressed as natty as you."

Ritz said, "The way I hear it, I may be running the show any day now, Harris."

I chose to play innocent. I said, "I'm not sure what you mean, General."

He said, "Admiral Hauser told me you wanted locations for underwater cities."

We started up the ramp, and Ritz hit the button to close the doors behind us. The motor that moved those heavy iron doors made a loud, grinding noise.

"Sounds like a tall tale," I said.

"Is he down there, sir? Is that where Nailor is hiding? Are you going after him?" asked Ritz. He was the only person who could have known what I had in mind. I'd told him about Nailor on Mars, and the name came up again when I finally made it out of that specking mine. He'd been with me, too, when Pugh showed me the SCUBA gear. Ritz had put it all together. I hoped he didn't share his theory with Tom Hauser.

Caught with my hand in the cookie jar, I saw no point to playing innocent any longer. I said, "Something like that."

"Admiral Hauser doesn't know about Nailor, but he knows you're after someone."

He'd told MacAvoy, too. *Who needs an entourage when I have a public affairs officer like Hauser telling everyone my plans?* I asked myself. My irritation must have shown.

Ritz said, "I did some digging around, and I've got good news and bad news for you, Harris. The good news is that Navy Intelligence knows which Cousteau city Nailor is hiding in. The bad news is that Hauser knows I was dicking around with his spooks."

I kept my expression even as my insides went black.

"I hope you boys are strapped in," Nobles yelled from the cockpit. "We're going wheels up."

Normally, I flew in the cockpit with Nobles. This time, feeling like I had just been kicked in the balls, I remained in the kettle with Ritz. I sat on the bench and looked around the shadowy cabin. I admitted something to myself as I sat there, I admitted that I didn't want to go to break into a Cousteau city. I had hoped that I would find Nailor in Washington, D.C., maybe even in Sunny's building.

"One of the undersea cities?" I asked. Suddenly, I saw the reality of going down to those cities. I had to face the reality that I would go to the bottom of the ocean, to the dark heart of the universe I most feared.

Ritz nodded. "Hauser's boys tracked him down. He knows that I asked his boys for information about Nailor, and he's got a pretty good idea why you want to kill him."

"Now that's bad news," I said.

"What are you going to tell Hauser?" asked Ritz.

"I'll make a deal with him," I said. "I'll offer him intelligence in exchange for Nailor's head."

"How are you going to get down there? Hauser told me he doesn't have any submarines."

"Yeah, I thought about that," I said. "I have a pretty good idea where I can find one."

"You know, Harris, maybe we can hit the cities with a bomb. It would be just like hitting a ship, right? You can't survive in space; you can't survive underwater. Destroy the city, and everyone inside it dies.

"I don't see why you need to go down after him."

From a logical standpoint, he was right, of course. I could

not think of a single good reason for me to go, but I had some very compelling bad ones. I wanted revenge. I wanted to see the man die, to make sure he died, to know how he had died, and to know that I had done it myself.

As a Marine, I had thousands of enemies and no enemies at all. We were at war with the Unified Authority, making every U.A. sailor, soldier, and Marine my foe. But if the war ended tomorrow, I would never give those sailors, soldiers, and Marines a second thought. They weren't really my enemies, just citizens of an enemy state.

That wasn't the case with Nailor.

I started to make up excuses about gathering intelligence, but they were hollow, and Ritz would have seen through them. He knew the same truth I did.

Rather then apologize or make more excuses, I saluted Ritz myself and went to the cockpit to visit with Christian Nobles. He seemed glad enough to see me, and he didn't ask any questions that made me choose between duty and revenge.

He asked, "Do you ever think about retiring?"

"What's the matter?" I asked. "Are you feeling old?"

He said, "Not old, just tired. Sometimes I think I'd like to start another life."

CHAPTER FIFTY-EIGHT

Location: The EME *Churchill*, orbiting Earth
Date: August 7, 2519

"Kill the head, and the body dies, too," I said.

Hauser listened and smiled. He said, "Isn't that backward? I always thought the saying went, 'Kill the body, and the head will die.'"

We sat in his office on the *Churchill*. This space had

belonged to the late Don Cutter before Hauser inherited it. This was the room in which Cutter had died. I remembered the way Cutter had organized this room; I'd spent a good deal of time in here. Hauser had changed some things around. He'd brought in a newer desk, a different chair, and placed new bookshelves along the wall behind the desk. Nothing else seemed to have changed.

I remembered hearing that the man who killed Cutter had shot him while he sat at his desk. I scanned the distance from the hatch to the desk—twelve feet, maybe, fairly close range—and hit with a shotgun. Perhaps the changes in interior decoration had more to do with necessity than taste. Cutter's desk and everything behind it must have been shredded and covered with blood.

I said, "It works both ways. When was the last time you saw a body walking around without a head?"

"What about MacAvoy?" asked Hauser.

"He has a head."

"Yes, I suppose it's just his brain that's missing."

"You might want to give him a little credit," I said. "He's doing a hell of a job defending Washington, D.C. The Unifieds don't know what to do with him."

"Maybe so," said Hauser, reluctantly conceding the point. He didn't like MacAvoy, but he didn't have a good reason for disliking him. I wondered if Hauser ever questioned himself about being a snob.

He said, "This guy, Nailor, he was the one who shot you on Mars. Ritz says you ran into him in the Territories."

"He killed a lot of my men there," I said.

"Yes. Yes, that's what Ritz said as well. Look, Harris, you can't turn this into your own personal war. That's not a good course, not for you or the Enlisted Man's Empire.

"I hear you're a reading man, Harris. Have you ever read *Moby-Dick*?"

I'd read the novel, but I didn't feel like giving Hauser the satisfaction. I didn't answer the question.

He said, "Your job, General, is to win the war, not kill your own personal white whale."

I left my seat and walked over to the desk. I stood over Hauser, not intentionally menacing him, but I communicated a certain amount of threat simply by standing so close. I said, "If you think I'm getting in the way, I'm happy to resign my commission, Admiral. I can do this on my own."

"No, that's not what I mean," he said, then he thought about my offer, and asked, "Would you really resign your commission over a vendetta?"

"Hell, I've been ready to give up my commission since day one. I didn't want to be a sergeant when they made me a sergeant. I didn't want to be an officer when they bumped me to lieutenant. I hate this officer shit. I wasn't designed for it.

"Killing Nailor, that's another story. I'd cut off my hands and my nuts for a shot at that bastard."

Hauser gave me a malicious smile as he asked, "Your hands and your nuts? You wouldn't be much of a Marine . . . Oh well, lose one set, and I suppose the other's worthless."

"You think I'm joking?" I asked.

Calm, even though I had raised my voice, Hauser said, "No. I know you're serious. You're also narcissistic and vindictive. I know, he shot you on Mars, then he buried you in the Territories. He's going to die if we sink those cities, General. I question the wisdom of committing so much effort to killing a single individual."

"It depends on the individual," I said.

"The Enlisted Man's Empire needs you, Harris, and you're talking about retirement and personal vendettas. I find that pretty sad. Maybe all those clones have overestimated you."

I said, "Once I settle things with Nailor, I'll get back to work."

"Do you think so?" asked Hauser.

"Look, Admiral, I need to get him out of my system. Once I kill the bastard, I'll have my head on straight."

"Do you think so?" Hauser repeated in the exact same tone of voice.

"What do you think?" I asked.

"About Franklin Nailor? He isn't worth this much effort. If that was Tobias Andropov down there, well, to capture the former head of the Linear Committee I'd be willing to do whatever it took. For Nailor? I wouldn't hijack a submarine and dive to the bottom of the sea for a high-profile thug like him."

"Andropov's never shot me," I muttered.

"Harris, this fight has become personal to you. It's clouding your judgment. What do you really know about Nailor?"

I said, "I've read his file. He's not a military man. He worked for the U.A.I.A."

That was the Unified Authority Intelligence Agency. He was a spook, not a soldier.

"Do you know what he did at the agency?" asked Hauser.

I didn't. All of his records had been deleted.

Hauser said, "He might have been a janitor for all we know."

"What do you want to bet he did interrogations?" I asked.

"Maybe so. That would make him a bastard, but it also leaves him low in the chain of command," Hauser pointed out. "I'm not ready to commit my fleet to settle your vendetta. You may not have noticed, General Harris, but we have a full-blown war on our hands, one I'm not convinced we're winning.

"They marched right up to Sheridan and took back their war criminals. They killed our highest-ranking officer. They took over the Pentagon, and when we tried to stop them, they blew it up."

Hauser and I glared at each other, neither of us willing to give the other what he wanted. I wanted an assassination; he wanted me to turn the other cheek.

"You know, I always heard that there were only three underwater cities; turns out there are eleven of them." Hauser fiddled with a couple of buttons on his desktop, bringing up a three-dimensional globe with red dots marking the eleven locations. He said, "Now that we know where they're hiding and how they're communicating, we've been able to intercept their messages. That's how we know that Nailor is here, he's in this city," Hauser said as he pointed to a city near the middle of the Atlantic Ocean. "The water around that city is several miles deep. Do you have a submarine that can take you down that far?"

"No," I admitted. "I know where I can get one."

"Really?" asked Hauser.

I nodded. "They have everything I need right here," I said, giving the globe a controlled spin and pointing to another dot on the map, one in the Pacific Ocean, about an inch off the shores of the New Olympian Territories.

Hauser said, "Unless I am mistaken, that is another

underwater city, which means that it is also on the bottom of the ocean. How do you plan to get to it?"

I said, "Ah, now, that's the beautiful thing. We don't need to go down to that city. They'll send their submarines up to us."

"Why would they do that?" asked Hauser.

I said, "Because we're going to drop some bombs on their doorstep. They're either going to need to surface or go down with their ship." Trying to lighten the mood, I said, "Think of it as *drowntown*, instead of *downtown*.

He didn't laugh, didn't even smile. He said, "So you plan on dropping bombs to force them to the surface. What's going to prevent them from sending a distress signal? What's stopping them from warning all the other cities?

"Right now we have an advantage. We know where they are, and they don't know we know it. We have the element of surprise on our side."

When I pressed my finger to the red dot, the name of the city appeared. I looked at it, recognized it as gibberish, and tried to ignore it. I said, "This city is unique. This is the one Cousteau city that won't warn the others. This one is at war with everybody else."

Hauser looked at the dot, then looked at the name and sounded it out. A dubious expression on his face, he said, "What's so special about Quetzalcoatl?"

"Is that how you pronounce it?" I asked. He spoke French. Maybe "Quetzalcoatl" was a French word.

"General Harris, you were about to explain to me why the people in that city won't warn the other cities when we attack."

I said, "Because the people in Ketsaalcoddle . . . in that city are no longer affiliated with the Unified Authority. The people in that city are reprogrammed clones."

The man who had assassinated Admiral Cutter stood five feet ten inches tall. He had brown hair and brown eyes, but he wasn't a clone. He looked like a clone at first glance, and he blended in with the crowd on the *Churchill*, but he had been a natural-born, as was Lenny Herman, the man who blew himself up in the Pentagon.

The men who attacked Sheridan were natural-borns as well. We didn't have any blood samples because the guards had not so much as nicked a single one of them, but we had the security feed. The men who entered the penitentiary were Unified Authority Marines in glowing orange uniforms. Ritz called them "glowboys." A lot of officers did.

The Marines that went after Freeman in the New Olympian Territories had been U.A. Marines as well.

In every attack, the assailants were natural-borns, but there was one exception—the men who came after me. They were clones; we had the corpses to prove it.

While confessing his many sins, Brandon Pugh told me that the clones who had come to kill me were looking for an alliance. Nailor and his friends had formed an alliance with Ryan Petrie and his mountain tribe, so Pugh and his gang looked for friends in the sea. They turned to clones, clones who wanted to fight both us and the Unified Authority.

The Unifieds had converted our clones, but, apparently they hadn't been able to keep them in the fold. Travis Watson wasn't the only natural-born working at the Pentagon, maybe not even the most important; Howard Tasman worked in the big black cube as well. MacAvoy's intelligence group said that he had probably escaped with Watson. I hoped he did. I wanted to ask him how converted clones could have turned on the Unified Authority.

I explained what little I knew to Hauser. I pointed out that the attacks on the Pentagon, Sheridan Penitentiary, and Cutter were all carried out by natural-borns. I finished by saying, "The clones who attacked me entered the hotel five minutes after the other attacks. They were five minutes late."

"Maybe they ran into traffic," Hauser joked.

"I think they knew that the other attacks were coming. I think they waited to make sure the Unified Authority was committed, and only then did they make their move."

"But you don't know anything," said Hauser.

"I know that all of the other attacks were carried out by natural-borns," I said, then added, "and that the Unifieds typically dump their dirty jobs on clones. If their clone-recruiting efforts were going so well, why didn't they send clones to attack Sheridan? Ketzu . . . Ketzaqual . . . this city is the closest Cousteau city to the penitentiary, so why not send clones?"

"It's a theory. It sounds good, but it's still a theory," Hauser said. His words were skeptical, but I could tell by his expression and the tone of his voice that he wanted me to make the sell.

"Fair enough," I said, "It's a theory, and let's put it to the test. If I'm right, we capture an underwater city, a fleet of submarines, and we might just find a way to rehabilitate several thousand reprogrammed clones. If I'm wrong, what do we lose?"

Hauser said, "We lose the element of surprise."

I said, "Now weigh that against what we get if I'm right about this. We get submarines. If we can take Kezukotal in one piece, we might recover some significant intelligence. Hell, we might learn enough to win the war."

Hauser said, "I'll make a deal with you, Harris. You want to go down for an assassination; that seems like an unnecessary risk to me. Add an intelligence angle to your operation, and I'm in."

CHAPTER FIFTY-NINE

Location: Pacific Ocean, one thousand miles off the coast of Mexico
Date: August 12, 2519

An immaculate morning—ice blue sky, cobalt sea, clouds so thin they looked like fading steam. We flew in low, three feet above the water and six hundred miles from shore.

The Navy sent fighters and bombers, and the Marines supplied fifteen transports and nine amphibious personnel carriers, two-story hovering saucers that rode upon cushions of air. APCs worked well on deserts and oceans, but mountains and valleys caused them problems. They were too wide for city streets.

MacAvoy contributed an armada of gunships. The gunships would chase any submarines that tried to escape. Even at their slowest speeds, Tom Hauser's fighters couldn't shadow a submarine without falling from the sky.

Far overhead, unseen and outside the atmosphere, one fighter carrier, two destroyers, and three battleships oversaw the operation. If the Unifieds tried to intervene, Hauser's capital ships would respond.

I rode to the show on one of the personnel carriers along with a battalion of Marines. The floating platform was big and clean, spotless as the day it first floated out of the factory. It hovered above the water, steady as a football stadium and just about as big. Eight hundred combat-armor-wearing Marines sat on padded benches on the bottom deck, waiting for orders.

Ritz and I stood in an office near the bridge. We stood beside a large, three-dimensional tactical display that showed the surface of the water and one hundred feet below it. For now, all it showed was a whole lot of blue and an invisible sky.

This was a Navy operation, run by Admiral Hauser. The Navy provided the bombers and the torpedoes. If the reprogrammed clones came up shooting, my Marines and I would calm them down. If the converts simply surrendered, we would board their ships and bring them home.

Hauser elected to fight this battle in open space from the bridge of the *Churchill*, thousands of miles above the action. I knew I was judging him harshly, writing him off as another scared sailor hiding inside his ship, but, really, he didn't have much of a choice. His massive, heavy, and not particularly aerodynamic fighter carrier was not equipped to fly in the atmosphere, where Earth's gravity would tug at it and wind currents would push it around.

Hauser said, "It's not too late to change your mind, General. They won't know we're here until we drop the first torpedo. Are you sure this is how you want to proceed?"

I studied his face on the screen. He wore a determined expression. A slight smile played on his lips, probably from the excitement of the coming battle. The Unifieds had been hitting and hiding for so long, now that we knew the location of their mouseholes, euphoria had set in.

I said, "Let me know when your bomber arrives."

A Navy bomber dropped out of the sky. An ugly, angular creation made out of a metal-ceramic composite, the AC-221

Hummingbird had a multifaceted face that looked like a poorly cut diamond. Her rusty black color stood out in the sky. She was an atmosphere-traveling jet with nonatmospheric flight capacity, a jack of all trades.

She positioned herself three hundred yards above the sea.

Hauser said, "Okay, she's dropping the Observer."

The Observer was a true antique, an underwater communications buoy that transmitted low-frequency electromagnetic waves, signals that could penetrate the thermocline—the thin layer of water that separates warmer surface waters from the colder depths.

In warm waters like these, the thermocline started about one hundred feet down. The Observer piloted itself through the layer to waters with less dramatic temperature shifts in which it could map and read the ocean floor without distortion. Standing on the APC, Ritz and I received its signals and charted the maps it sent back.

Hauser's engineers had rigged space-Navy torpedoes for this operation. Apparently they swam underwater every bit as well as they flew in the grand vacuum. For the purposes of this exercise, Hauser's engineers had armed most of the torpedoes with nuclear tips.

In the military vernacular, all flying machines were nicknamed "birds." The Navy's love of wildlife apparently extended undersea. Hauser looked away from the camera for a moment, and said, "Give me a status on those fish?"

He looked back at me, and said, "General, you might want to prepare your men."

The first wave of torpedoes dropped out of the Hummingbird like a flock of penguins diving into the sea. Two feet long and sleek, they stabbed into the water as neatly as needles slip through cloth, then they formed into a tidy cluster that reminded me of a school of fish. I watched their water ballet in 3-D holographic detail on my virtual display.

While most of the cluster of torpedoes floated twenty feet under the surface of the water, one lone tactical-tipped torpedo sank down, past the thermocline and past the observer. The torpedo's NERVA-based propulsion system ignited, and it dashed through the water as gracefully as a jet soars through the air.

The torpedo slowed to a mere fifty miles per hour as it neared the silty ocean floor.

"How deep is it down there?" I asked.

"Twenty thousand feet," said Hauser.

"That's pretty deep," I said.

"The French built Cousteau cities in trenches with geothermal vents," said Hauser. "I guess they wanted to save on heating bills. *C'est la guerre.*"

I didn't understand that last comment and didn't feel like asking what it meant. I got the feeling that we stroked Hauser's ego when we asked him what this or that meant. I also had the feeling that he didn't speak his dead languages as fluently as he wanted us believe.

The tactical display showed a holographic image of the ocean floor as the French had mapped it several hundred years ago. One of the screens on the side of that display showed the ocean floor as the Observer's sonar mapped it today. Both displays showed a nearly flat ocean floor. If there was a trench down there, it was a wide one.

One of the screens showed the world through the eyes of the lead torpedo, a simplistic style of tracking that searched for obstructions and ignored other features. The image on the screen was blacker than space. From the torpedo's perspective, the darkness of that ocean plain was as solid as granite. The torpedo relayed its feed to the Observer, which broadcast it for us to see.

As the torpedo cut through the dark water, it decelerated to twenty miles per hour, a nearly unmanageable pace for equipment designed to travel at two hundred times that speed.

That speed came into perspective when a tiny spot of light appeared on the torpedo's eye display. It looked no bigger than a pixel, then a dot, and slowly grew into a spot, at which point the torpedo nearly came to a stop.

Hauser said, "The Observer has run sonar, radar, and light tracking. There's no sign of movement. They're either asleep down there . . . or they're not down there at all."

"Wake them up," I said.

"Last chance to change your mind," Hauser said.

"Change my mind?" I asked. "Why would I change my mind?"

Ritz remained uncharacteristically mute as he watched the proceedings. He didn't offer any useless opinions or refer to the clones as "Repromen." He normally made jokes at times like this, his irreverence sometimes endearing and sometimes a source of irritation.

I asked him, "You see any problems?"

Ritz said, "No, sir." He'd called me, "sir." That made me nervous.

"Do you want to proceed, General?" asked Hauser.

"You okay?" I asked Ritz.

He hesitated, then said, "Yeah. Yes, sir."

I told Hauser, "We agreed upon this operation, Admiral. I believe it is time to execute."

On the tactical, the swarm of torpedoes hovering near the surface dropped below the line marking the thermocline and scattered. If the clones boarded submarines as we expected them to do, the torpedoes would shadow them from beneath.

The lone torpedo, the one that would target the city itself, drifted within several hundred yards of the large red oval representing the city. I said, "Gentlemen, I give you Quetzalcoatl."

I had spent several minutes learning how to pronounce the name correctly, and now knew it was the name of a Mesoamerican god as well. I hoped Hauser would refer to it as a Mayan god so I could call him on it. It had actually been a lesser known tribe called the Nahua that worshipped Quetzalcoatl, not the Mayans.

I knew nothing about the Nahua other than their worship of Quetzalcoatl, but that wasn't the point. Pretending like I knew something, so I could one-up Hauser . . . that was the point.

Hauser made no comment, however.

The torpedo exploded. Had it had a nuclear tip, it would have destroyed the underwater city. The tactical device produced a more controlled explosion calculated to rock the city without destroying it.

"Think we got their attention?" I asked Ritz.

He looked at me and said nothing. He stood slack-jawed and stiff, like a Marine at attention, but I saw sadness in his eyes. Until their reprogramming, those men had been our men.

The Observer had a communications array capable of broadcasting underwater using ELF (extremely low frequency) electromagnetic waves that could travel all the way to the ocean floor. Using those electromagnetic waves, Hauser sent a message to Quetzalcoatl. The message he sent was, "Surrender . . . Surrender . . . Surrender . . . Surrender . . . Surrender . . ."

Nobody involved in planning this operation believed that reprogrammed clones would have the capacity to surrender. It wasn't in their programming, original or hijacked.

Once the lead torpedo exploded, another torpedo circled in from a different angle, broadcasting a video feed that suggested that the people in Quetzalcoatl had both received our message and understood it.

The outside of the city was encased in an opaque dome that rose above the silt like a mushroom-shaped shadow. Looking on that screen, I had no concept of its size. If anything, the city was dwarfed by the sprawling plains that spread out around it.

We could have hit the dome with more torpedoes, but the clones responded as expected. They evacuated their hideout without putting up a fight.

The first Turtle launched almost immediately. Over the next hour, another thirty took to the sea.

Turtles were the Cousteau equivalent of fighter carriers. They were enormous mobile domes. The French had built them for transporting workers, equipment, and materials to construct the undersea cities. They were designed to carry everything from cranes to girders to desalinization equipment. I'd never actually seen a Turtle, not even a picture of one, but I'd read their design specifications, and they were enormous. If God ever flooded the world again, Noah wouldn't need to build an ark. He could borrow a Turtle and fit the whole damn zoo inside.

If my suspicions proved true, the Unifieds had used them for more than moving zoos and building supplies. The reason our radar had never detected U.A. gunships until they had nearly reached land was because their gunships and transports had traveled by Turtle, below the surface, below our radar, and out of the range of satellite surveillance.

Each Turtle was a floating disc, 120 feet in diameter, 10 feet tall around the edges, and 40 feet tall at the center of its convex shell, and capable of launching gunboats, transports, even Harriers, anything with a vertical liftoff. To launch its cargo, the Turtle would rise to the surface of the water, and its shell would open like a lid.

Traveling under the water with its shell closed, the Turtle didn't look like a mobile launchpad; it looked like a flying frying pan with a lid.

"Well, well," said Hauser, "a UFO."

"It isn't flying," I said.

"An Unidentified *Floating* Object."

I sent a message to the Marines piloting our APC. I told them to follow that first Turtle as she came to the surface. We didn't have enough personnel carriers to shadow every Turtle and sub that emerged from the city. We'd send gunships after some and fighters after others if need be, but I wanted to be there when we captured that first clone-controlled boat.

The giant submersibles had been created for peacetime purposes. They didn't have guns or torpedo tubes. The Unifieds might have added defenses, but it seemed unlikely. The Observer checked that first one for the seams that would indicate missiles hatches and torpedo tubes.

"Look's like she's unarmed," said Hauser, who sounded just about ready to break out champagne and cigars. The converts had launched their enormous, slow-moving, defenseless underwater platform, which we now chased with a nuclear-tipped torpedo, a gunship, and an amphibious personnel carrier. The clones on that boat couldn't hold their breath forever. When they surfaced, we would be waiting. If they tried to dive back to the bottom of the ocean, we could blow them out of the water with the torpedo. Sinking the Turtle was a viable option. We would sink one of the converts' boats to indicate our resolve to the others.

The French may not have armed their Turtles, but they wouldn't send them to the bottom of the sea swimming blind. That boat undoubtedly had sonar and radar arrays; even if they had been created for navigation purposes, they would detect the torpedo nipping at their heels. They had probably located our gunship and our APC as well, but the men piloting the Turtle seemed not to care.

Watching that floating puck, I realized that a boat that big couldn't have floated up the Chesapeake Bay unnoticed. Even if it made it across the bay, it couldn't have traveled the Potomac. It was too wide and too tall.

I looked at the tactical. By this time the converts had launched dozens of Turtles. The floating platforms traveled in every direction. On the display, they looked like a scattering school of jellyfish.

I said, "Admiral, this can't be all of it. There needs to be something else, something smaller than these boats."

Hauser had done his homework. He said, "You mean the Mantas. They'll be out soon. I bet they're using the Turtles as decoys. They'll send the enlisted men on the Turtles and load their officers on the Mantas."

I hadn't heard about Mantas, but seeing as the boats called "Turtles" were round, slow-moving tin cans, I had a pretty good idea about what a Manta might be.

We tailed the Turtle for two hours. It meandered at a painfully slow ten miles per hour, heading east toward the Territories while rising to within fifteen feet of the surface. When I went outside and peered over the edge of the APC, I could see it clearly though I couldn't tell if it looked more like an island or an enormous fish.

After two hours spent chasing the ponderous sub, I became bored, so I had a gunship put an end to the chase. The crew fired a couple of RPGs off her bow. The grenades exploded, and the Turtle stopped moving. It just hung there, the world's biggest dead fish in the world's largest vat of formaldehyde. All the while, the communications officer on the APC transmitted the message, "Surrender . . . Surrender . . . Surrender."

At that moment, everything seemed so promising. We had no idea what had become of the scientist Howard Tasman, but I thought he might still be alive. I thought we could capture the converts and store them someplace safe until Tasman returned, then he could figure out the riddle to unprogram these clones so that their loyalties returned to the Enlisted Man's Empire.

The Turtle remained where it had stopped. Other ships rise and descend at odd angles, but not this boat. She remained flat the entire time she slowly ascended from the abyss.

I returned to the bridge and asked the communications officer if the clones had responded. He shook his head.

I stood over him as the communications officer repeated the message, "Surrender . . . Surrender . . . Surrender."

The Turtle rose again, and the apex of her shell cleared the surface of the water and waves rolled over it. There she floated, like a reef, just under the waves, like a kraken or a whale or some mythical leviathan, the silver hump breaking the surface of the water during the troughs between waves. She hovered at that depth for several minutes, then she rose another few feet like a sandbar in a spectacularly low tide. Waves crashed into her mound and dissolved into foam. The wet skin of the boat sparkled under the sun.

Thinking that the clones meant to surrender, I had the communications officer broadcast a new message. He said, "Attention Unified Authority vessel, according to the Enlisted Man's Empire Articles of Surrender, we are hereby authorized to commandeer your ship."

We didn't have submarines, but we did have divers and watertight combat armor. Men in dark armor dived from the edges of the APC, plunging into the royal blue water. They looked no bigger than minnows as they approached the gigantic silver dish that was the Turtle, placing charges around the submersible to prevent her from submerging again. If the Turtle tried to dive, those charges would blow holes in her shell.

We lowered a ramp from the APC to the roof of the Turtle. A company of armed Marines stormed down the ramp. From a distance, they must have looked no more significant than ants crawling over an egg. As the divers performed their acts of sabotage and the Marines crowded onto the shell, the Turtle sat still and helpless.

I looked over at Hauser, and asked, "Is she sending distress signals?"

He shook his head, and said, "Silent as a lamb."

There was a tense moment. When the gunship signaled the crew of the Turtle to open hatches, the ship vibrated wildly—she practically convulsed. She shuddered for a moment, causing a few Marines to lose their footing, but she didn't sink or swim. She stayed where she had breached, a robotic island.

I asked, "Can we open her without breaking her apart?"

"Sure we can," said Hauser. "It may take a few minutes. If

your men have laser torches, tell them to cut the main hatch. My engineers tell me they can fix it."

"What's happening with the other Turtles?" I asked. Looking at the tactical display, I saw that many had surfaced.

"They seem to be giving up," said Hauser.

"It could be a trap," I said. Those boats almost certainly used nuclear reactors to power their engines. For all we knew, the clones could have rigged the reactors to explode.

I thought about Curtis Jackson, the highest ranking of the converted clones. I'd once considered him among my most promising officers. He'd been tough and resourceful, the kind of Marine who would sacrifice himself and a few volunteers in exchange for destroying an enemy company. Now I had to worry about his sacrificing himself to kill my men.

"Harris, check out the display! Here come the Mantas," said Hauser.

The tactical display had changed its focus so that it now showed an area that spanned hundreds of miles. The Turtles now showed as discs about the size of the head of a nail. The Mantas, which were one-tenth the size of the Turtles, looked like glowing fleas.

I watched them emerge from their underwater nest and scatter. From this angle, I wouldn't have attempted to count the little submarines, but I didn't need to. The tactical display tallied every torpedo, Turtle, and Manta. If a pod of whales swam by, it might have counted them as well.

Seeing the Mantas scatter, I asked, "Do we have enough torpedoes and gunships to catch all of them?"

Hauser laughed me to scorn, and said, "Harris, the fastest Manta is doing sixty-two knots. I could requisition an additional squad of gunboats from Fort Irwin, have them stop for chow in Los Angeles, and still nab those Mantas.

"Unless those clones have added self-broadcasting submarines to their fleet, General, we'll catch them."

His confidence was irritating but infectious. All I could say was, "Very well."

Still sounding melancholy, Ritz said, "General, the men on the Turtle have opened the hatch."

"We should go have a look," I said.

He didn't answer.

He looked so specking dour, and my anger flared. I shouted, "Damn it, man; what is the matter with you?"

He just stood there looking silent and brittle . . . Hunter Ritz looking "brittle" seemed about as plausible Mount Everest looking small. Ritz was a wild man, as irreverent an officer as any who had ever honored the Corps. He was the man who ran head-on at gunships and never sat still in briefings. No superior officer ever received proper respect from the bastard, and death didn't faze him; now, here he stood, in a freshly pressed uniform and calling me "General" and "sir."

In a quiet voice he said, "We're not going to bring them in alive, sir."

"We already have," I said.

He said, "I fought side by side with some of those men on Terraneau, and Earth, and Mars."

So that explained the freshly pressed uniform. He had dressed for a funeral.

I said, "Ritz, they've already come to the surface. That pretty well qualifies as an unconditional surrender."

He didn't respond.

I shook my head, and said, "Suit yourself." He remained on the bridge while I went to help capture the "Repromen." Ritz's term, not mine.

I jogged out to the boarding area, where most of my Marines still waited by the gangplank. As I approached, they snapped to attention and saluted. I returned their salutes as I brushed past them and hopped the foot-high gap between the end of the plank and the roof of the Turtle.

Dressed in my armor and bodysuit, I had no idea if the wind felt boiling hot or freezing cold. I couldn't smell the salt air or feel the sun on my shoulders. My armored boots slid as they clattered onto the Turtle's rounded shell, and I struggled for a moment to catch my balance.

The Marines who had gathered around the hatch watched me in silence. I think they feared me more than the converts inside the boat. Well, they didn't fear me so much as my rank. Generals are trouble. They're like Greek statues come to life, like gods with hearts made of marble who send men to their deaths. Generals and gods seldom notice men for their good deeds and readily punish them for their bad.

Standing on that curved, metallic shoal, preparing to enter the hatch, I noticed something inside me—I was scared. I was petrified. First, I noticed how fast my heart was pumping, then I realized that I wasn't scared of anything inside the Turtle. If anything, that hatch looked like an exit from my fears.

It was the water. The great aqua plain stretched to the horizon in every direction, flat and deep and beautiful, like a floor made of polished sapphire. The Turtle had long stopped vibrating; I might have collapsed if it so much as quivered. But it sat solid as a mountain beneath my feet.

This was fear, not just an anxious moment. It festered in my gut. Trying to hide it, I straightened my back, threw my chest out, and kept my chin level. I strode toward the hatch, asking the Marines around me, "What are you waiting for, an engraved invitation?"

My M27 out and ready, I felt my blood pressure drop and my heart slow as I entered the enclosed, shadowy depths . . . and saw the first dead body. Death and darkness welcomed me in.

Every last man on the boat had died. Some lay on the floor. The dead pilots sat at the controls.

They were all clones, and from the blood welling up in the ears of the men not wearing helmets, they all appeared to have died from a mass death reflex. I had no idea what the death reflex did inside their brains, but it was brutal.

I walked through the corridors that circled the cavernous cargo hold in the center. Dead Marines lay everywhere. Some held guns. Some lay empty-handed.

As I approached the bridge, I heard the automatic broadcast from our APC still droning on. It said, "Surrender . . . surrender . . . surrender."

The pilots, there were three, sat up nearly straight, strapped in their seats, their heads hanging as if in shame. *They must have surrendered,* I thought. They brought their boat to the surface. Maybe a conflict in their programming would not let them surrender. Or maybe they could surrender, but not to other clones.

One way or another, they had surrendered themselves to death.

CHAPTER SIXTY

Location: The EME *Churchill*, orbiting Earth
Date: August 12, 2519

"Just what exactly happened down there?" Hauser demanded. "General Harris, you assured me that we were going to capture clones."

Watching Hauser's anger fascinated me. He wouldn't allow himself to swear or pound the table and barely raised his voice, but he was castigating me nonetheless. Back in boot camp, angry drill sergeants screamed at me, threatened me, prognosticated that any girl I ever slept with would be syphilitic, and called my nonexistent mother a whore. Had they dressed me down this gently, I might have mistaken it for praise.

"You were going to capture them. You were supposed to bring them in alive. This wasn't a battle. This was . . . this was Masada."

Masada . . . Masada. I ran the name through my memory several times before I pieced it together—Romans versus Jews. The Jews had a fortress on top of a butte, inaccessible and impossible to attack. When the Romans finally broke through the walls, they found only dead Jews. The Jews picked suicide over capture.

I started to mention that dying from a mass death reflex hardly qualified as suicide, but Perry MacAvoy spoke up in my defense. Unwilling to leave Washington, D.C., he joined us via confabulator.

He said, "From what you told me, General Harris never said we'd capture anybody. He said we'd capture equipment and an underwater city. We got their city; we got their subs, and we didn't lose a single man. As far as I can tell, only God could have run this operation any smoother.

"What were you hoping for, Tommy? Were you hoping the sea would part, and the converts would march out on dry land?

"I wish the natural-born assholes the Unifieds have out here would die from a death reflex. I'd give my last working nut for a little divine intervention of that sort. Shit, we shoot these bastards, we stab these bastards, we blow their testicles to kingdom come, and the only thing we get outta their damn ears are brains and earwax."

We'd already heard the news from the capital. The Unified Authority showed no sign of weakening despite heavy losses. We had more equipment, tanks, gunships, fighters, etc., but they had dug in tight as ticks. They hit us from the buildings we wanted to keep whole with an endless supply of rockets and traveled below streets we could not afford to demolish.

Even worse, public sentiment had shifted in their direction. We were a military empire, conquerors of a home planet that didn't welcome our return. Now that the Unifieds had returned, the indigenous population's attitude toward us had gone from strong dislike to hate.

Hauser asked, "Do we even know what caused the reflex?"

I shook my head. "Howard Tasman might be able to explain it."

I wished I had some way to ask him. He was gone. Travis Watson was gone. Sunny was gone. I had failed them all.

MacAvoy took a stab at it. He guessed, "Maybe the Unifieds programmed them to die."

"Why would they do that?" asked Hauser.

"To stop us from programming them back the way they were."

"That wasn't a battle," Hauser said in a soft voice that resonated with regret. "That was an extermination."

"We didn't exterminate anyone," said MacAvoy. "Harris didn't even fire a specking shot."

I didn't respond. We'd fired off a couple of rockets to get their attention, nothing more.

His voice still softer and sadder, Hauser said, "I served a tour with Curtis Jackson. He served on *Bhutto*. That was my first command."

I had served with Jackson as well. He commanded the

regiment I took to Mars on an ill-fated operation. The Unifieds captured us. I was brainwashed; they were reprogrammed. Now they were dead. Hell, to us they'd been worse than dead since we left Mars. They'd been a ticking time bomb waiting to explode, but in the end, they'd imploded instead.

"I'll tell you what. If you're scared that there are clones holed up in Gendamwortha, let me put you at ease," said MacAvoy. "They're all natural-born down there. They are all enemy soldiers, and not a one of them is going to have a death reflex."

The name of the Cousteau city MacAvoy referred to was Gendenwitha, but he didn't worry about pronouncing it correctly.

Hauser ignored the general. Looking at me, he asked, "It's entirely possible Nailor has left Gendenwitha?"

Gendenwitha sat halfway between the United States and Europe. Apparently enamored of local mythologies, the French named Gendenwitha after an Iroquois woman who, according to legend, had been transformed into the morning star. I had looked it up.

The story of Gendenwitha reminded me of Ava, which made me think of Sunny. I felt a familiar wave of guilt. Did I feel guilty for cheating on Sunny or for abandoning Ava?

"Have you received any intel indicating he is somewhere else?" I asked.

"We haven't heard anything," said Hauser.

"Then he's still there," I said.

There were only two Cousteau cities in the Atlantic Ocean. Gendenwitha was fifteen hundred miles from Washington. Anansi, the next closest site, was four thousand miles away in an oceanic black hole called the Romanche Trench.

I really hoped Nailor was in Gendenwitha.

"What if it turns up empty?" asked Hauser. "What if the Unifieds have moved everyone they have to Washington, D.C.? What if they moved their troops to the Territories?"

"I've got plenty of prisoners. You're welcome to interrogate them till your nuts fall out," MacAvoy offered.

"You'll still get your intel," I said. Hauser and I had come to an agreement. He'd agreed to help me get to Gendenwitha if I did some simple reconnaissance while I was down there.

We were about to destroy all of the underwater cities in one big sweep. Admiral Hauser wanted to make sure we searched one of them for its secrets before we buried it at sea.

I said, "You're not after Nailor; he's my problem. I'll still deliver your package either way."

Hauser thought about this and smiled. He said, "Fair enough."

CHAPTER SIXTY-ONE

Location: Norfolk Naval Base, Virginia
Date: August 13, 2519

We had to strike the other underwater cities before the Unifieds figured out what happened to Quetzalcoatl. Hauser's engineers spent the night getting a Manta ready for the mission, and I spent the night doing preparations of my own.

I dyed my hair blond, placed blue dye in my eyes, and glued a beard to my chin. Would people still recognize that I was a clone?

Ironically, my disguise made me look like what most clones were programmed to see when they looked in a mirror, except I was taller. I came armed with a sniper rifle and a pistol and a knife. Hauser's engineers had also built a dirty bomb into the rear compartment of the Manta I was taking, just in case. If that little package went off, it would turn Gendenwitha into a highly radioactive bubble on the bottom of the sea.

The Manta sat on the water beside the dock, looking like a fighter jet designed by an engineer with a strange sense of humor. She had the same dart-shaped fuselage as a Tomcat, only it looked like her wings had been put on backward. They were broad at the front and tapered at the back. She was also a lot less sleek.

Most fighters only carried a lone pilot though a few carried a navigator as well. The Manta had tandem seats for a pilot and navigator along with tight accommodations for thirty-six passengers.

"You say you've tested this thing," I said to the flight instructor.

"Ten hours' worth," he replied.

The three of us stood around the bird . . . fish; the third being Ritz. Quiet and stolid, he seemed to be in mourning for the Marines who'd died when we captured this boat.

"Did you recharge the batteries?" I asked. Did this thing even have batteries? More likely she ran on nuclear power, meaning I would be sitting in a miniature nuclear reactor with a second nuclear device, the dirty bomb, just a few feet away. Nukes spooked me—nukes had always spooked me. In another minute, I would pilot this nuclear-powered accident down into the depths.

Nukes spooked me, but that was a fear I could work around. My fear of the deep was not. Seeing the ocean had temporarily paralyzed me when I boarded the Turtle, and that didn't involve diving under the surface. Now I was going down, down, down, and, frankly, my ability to perform might turn to mush. I suspected I could make it to Gendenwitha with most of my marbles, but I wouldn't be in the right frame of mind for a delicate and dangerous op. Fortunately, I didn't come empty-handed. When I explained my situation to a doctor in the base infirmary, he gave me something powerful to calm my nerves. Remembering the way I had frozen while I entered the Turtle, I hoped the pills rendered me unconscious.

We had to step on the wings to reach the hatch. I noticed that the bottoms of the wings were deep beneath the water. "Why are the wings so thick?" I asked.

"They're not wings. They're ballast tanks," said the instructor. "This isn't like flying, you won't need wings to stay afloat."

"What do they do?" I asked. I was nervous. Even stepping off the dock bothered me.

The water was a chalky, bluish green. The Manta was a steel-colored tube. The sky was gray. Everything looked dismal.

"Ballast tanks? You fill them with water to make the boat heavier; that's how you make her go down."

"How do I make the boat lighter again?" I asked.

"By flushing out the water."

"Won't I need that air?" I asked.

"You'll have plenty of air, General."

I was not entirely ignorant. Hoping to combat my nervousness, I had done some reading. One of the differences between the ships that went into space and the ones that went to the bottom of the sea was the kind of pressure they endured. In space, the pressure came from inside the ship, and the hull was designed to contain it. Undersea vessels had more to deal with; by the time I reached Gendenwitha, this Manta would have thousands of pounds of water pressing down on her every square inch.

I stepped on the wing, then on the spine, and into the hatch.

The interior of the Manta was reinforced with steel ribs.

"Admiral Hauser says you have misgivings about going underwater," said the instructor.

Yeah, he gossips like an old witch, I thought.

"Did he?" I asked. I hadn't told him about my phobias, but Don Cutter may have. Cutter knew about them because he was the officer in charge when I disappeared on Mars. He'd also temporarily relieved me of command and ordered me to undergo psychiatric evaluation.

Once he knew he'd be taking Cutter's seat, Hauser would have gone through his files. He would have read all about me and my psychological inventory; the son of a bitch probably knew things I didn't know.

"You're going to enter the city through a moon pool. Are you familiar with the term, General?" asked the flight instructor.

I nodded. I knew what a moon pool was, and the very thought of it played havoc with my phobias.

Moon pools were holes in the understructure of oceanic architecture. Instead of having enclosed docking bays like spaceports, the underwater cities had holes in their floors. The holes didn't allow water in because the cities had highly pressurized atmospheres that canceled out the pressure of the water.

The flight instructor said, "General, it takes a great deal of pressure to force the water out at depths like the ones you will be entering. It will take your body nearly a full day to adjust to that pressure and another day to readjust before you can return to the surface."

I remembered an old term I'd heard in school. I asked, "Are you sticking me in a hyperbaric chamber?"

He shook his head, and said, "The submarine will take care of that. Her atmosphere is computerized and self-adjusting. You've got a long, slow ride ahead of you, sir. There's really no way around it."

I reminded myself that this man was a flight instructor, not a deep-sea diver. Anything he knew about decompression and submarines was nearly as new to him as it was to me.

He spent a few minutes going over the controls, and that was really all the time we needed. The instructor didn't teach me how to "fly" the Manta; the boat piloted herself—type in the destination, and her computers handled the rest. She knew when to fill her ballast tanks and when to purge them. Her communications gear was no different than the gear in our spaceships except that signals couldn't travel millions of miles underwater. Any messages I sent or received would be short-range.

That was good. The shorter the range, the better as far as I was concerned. I didn't want the Unifieds asking me to identify myself as I drifted toward their base.

It's funny how phobias play with your mind. Death did not bother me; oceans did.

CHAPTER SIXTY-TWO

The flight instructor left, but Ritz remained behind. He said, "Harris, maybe I should come with you."

I said, "I appreciate the offer, General, but I'd rather go alone."

He said, "You're scared, aren't you? Are you scared of Nailor or the ocean?"

"Tough choice," I said. "I generally spend vacations on a beach, and Nailor, he's just a tiny speck. I could . . ."

"Nailor shot you and left you for dead. I don't know about

your vacations, but I heard about the way you acted when you boarded the Turtle. I heard you were scared of the water."

"Is that what you heard?" I asked, noting how precisely he had hit both nails on the head.

"Yes, sir. That's what I heard."

I decided to change the subject. "How about you?" I asked. "You've been acting like you're at a funeral. You're dressing like an officer bucking for promotion. I don't know if you noticed, Ritz, but you just called me 'sir.'"

"General, we lost most of the First of the First rescuing Freeman. Fifteen thousand clones died yesterday. Fifteen thousand. I told you we wouldn't bring them back alive, and we didn't. The only thing those boys did wrong was breathe. They didn't even know about the possibility of reprogramming when the Unified Authority caught them."

"It's not my . . ."

"No, General, it's not your fault. But they still died, and the killing isn't over. Maybe you'll survive this mission, maybe you won't. I get the feeling you don't care.

"So maybe we'll survive this war, and maybe we won't. We've become a disposable empire. We're throwing away good men to hold on to a planet that doesn't want us because we don't have anyplace else to go.

"That's what I saw when we were in the mountains. I saw good men dying in a fight they'd already lost."

Thank you for the cheerful good-bye, I thought. *He's all done,* I thought. When an officer goes into a funk like that, you can't leave him in command. I thought about bringing him with me, but moods like his were absolutely contagious, so I thanked him for his offer and told him to go ashore.

Then I took my medicine and hit the autopilot. The sooner I conked out, the happier I would be.

As I waited for the drugs to make the phobias go away, I told myself that the launch would be the worst part of the trip, floating helpless, staring out across the docks, worrying about what to expect. My fears played havoc with my brain, leading me to see dark shapes under the water that weren't really there. I imagined fins slicing across the surface and reminded myself that a shark would kill itself before it could harm this boat with her thick hull. Any shark that bit the Manta would end up with shattered teeth.

Logic and phobia exist on different planes. They are as alien as dinosaurs and angels and just as unlikely to interact.

The trip to the city would be long. I had over a thousand miles to travel before I reached Gendenwitha, and the Manta topped out somewhere around fifty miles per hour. Twenty hours, I hoped to sleep through it. Even if Nailor was down there, no one was guaranteeing that he would wait around until I arrived.

This is a mistake, I thought, and I wanted to call it off.

In the distance, dockworkers loaded crates onto transports. Two APCs sat on a large landing pad. They were a welcome sight. I wouldn't need to sail this fish all the way back to Norfolk when I returned from Gendenwitha. Hauser was sending those amphibious personnel carriers to retrieve me and the spy equipment he had loaned me.

I didn't know if Hauser planned to sail the Manta back to port or sink her, and I truly didn't care.

As if piloted by a ghost, the Manta's autopilot engaged, and she pulled away from the dock and headed out of the harbor. My heart pounding loud and fast, my lungs swelling as they tried to hoard every breath, my head aching, I forced myself to check the gauges. My heart sank when I saw a gauge indicating that the ballast tanks had started to fill with water.

At some point before the Manta started her long dive, I began talking to myself. The submarine had a plastiscreen up front, and that was the only viewing port on the boat. Once we left the harbor, she started her descent. Water and sky were the only things I could see, and soon the sky disappeared. This was a dark operation, so I didn't have radio communications.

"I specking hate this," I said. A moment later, I added, "The speck am I doing here?"

Since there was no one else to respond to the question, I answered myself. I said, "This was your idea, asshole. Please tell me you're not losing your nerve."

Then I thought, *Shit, I'm talking to myself.*

This would have been a good time to spot Gendenwitha. It didn't happen that way. The submarine spent the next forty minutes hovering ten feet below the surface while she finished filling her ballast tanks. During that time, I pulled my rifle out of its case and field stripped it.

Obeying some logical impulse that now escaped me, I had elected to take a sniper rifle with me on this op. With a base accuracy of fifteen hundred yards, this was a great weapon for snipers and hunters, and a shitty choice for indoor combat. From stock to muzzle, the rifle was forty-four inches long, too big for concealment.

"You know why you brought this," I chided myself out loud. I did know why, though I didn't want to admit it to myself. "You didn't come for recon. You came here to assassinate the bastard."

The bastard, of course, was Franklin Nailor, but I'd have happily killed Tobias Andropov or any other Unified Authority war criminals I happened to see while I was down there.

I was getting sleepy. I told myself it was the medicine that had me talking to myself. Maybe it was.

A plastic button on the pilot's yoke lit a pale red and a Klaxon purred a single, lengthy note. I stood in the doorway, holding that rifle, staring at the glowing button, knowing what it meant, and no longer caring. We were about to dive whether I was ready or not.

This boat didn't need me to reach her destination. I was a passenger; I had no more control over this rig than a flea has over a dog. Something beeped, something else buzzed. I didn't care. The Manta shuddered, and my brain drifted, drifted, drifted because of the medicine.

The stuff the doctor gave me never quite knocked me out. I fell in and out of sleep. When I felt the urge to use the bathroom, I walked to the head. When I was done, I curled up in the nearest seat. At some point, I went back into the cockpit and stared into the dark depths ahead. I recognized their endlessness, and thought, *Oh shit, I hate going down there.* That was the extent of it. No sweat. No fear. No combat reflex.

Twenty hours, thirty hours, I no longer cared how long the trip would take. I hadn't brought books, but I was in no shape to read them anyway. I should have been bored. Time passed slowly, but now that I had luded, time no longer mattered. Medicinal magic.

I sat at the plastiscreen, staring out into the darkness as I had so many times on spacecraft. Space is not dark in the way so many people imagine it. Space is clear. There are billions of stars in our galaxy; after some fashion, each one is or was a sun. You may find yourself in a five-hundred-million-mile stretch in which there is no sunlight, but there are suns and stars in every direction that you look. In the ocean, there are no stars at all.

The Manta didn't have headlights. She didn't need them. Her computers saw through darkness using sounds and magnetic detection. At some point, the Manta would make contact with Gendenwitha. What happened after that was anybody's guess.

Anybody monitoring their traffic control would probably have questions as my Manta sailed toward their moon pool. I would need to be alert. That didn't scare me, though. The drugs didn't slur my speech or leave me disoriented. Even after I started waking from the haze, the medicine left me feeling calm. My not being worried probably should have worried me, but I wasn't feeling any pain at that moment.

I remained in the pilot's chair, searching for sea monsters. No recognizable life-forms swam past, though I did see a galaxy of tiny phosphorous lights in the distance. They might have been plants or chemical bubbles or fish with lanterns on their heads.

At some point, my fears started to return, like blood reentering a limb that has fallen asleep. The phobias started as a tingle, a distant ache that remained in the background, making too much noise to ignore. With time, the panic came clawing back.

I fidgeted in my seat. I pulled out my pistol, an S9, and checked the clip. It held a depleted uranium wafer, good for hundreds of fragmentlike fléchettes. I would have stripped it for the distraction, but then I saw something in the distance and stopped.

Lights shone along Gendenwitha's outer dome, revealing an enormous convex surface that was too regular to have occurred in nature. Those lights didn't illuminate the entire structure, just scattered patches. From what I saw, Gendenwitha was larger than a school, larger than a shopping mall, larger than a military base. As the Manta approached, I willed myself to calm down, taking deep drags of the cold, recirculated air and holding them in my lungs.

I expected some traffic-control goon to appear on a monitor, but, apparently, undersea runways didn't operate like the ones in space. Seemingly of her own volition, the Manta dropped below the lights and passed under the dome.

As the Manta passed under the city, I twisted my neck so that I could stare up through the plastiscreen. The city stretched on for acres and acres, with shimmering circles that shone bright white like stars; I realized they must be the moon pools. The pools were round, perfectly round, and I discovered they were enormously wide as the Manta passed below one. Nothing was visible through most of the moon pools, but we coasted past one in which I saw the silhouettes of five Mantas parked side by side.

Because of its immense size, I couldn't see all the way across Gendenwitha, and any maps of the city had been destroyed when the Unifieds blasted the Archive building.

I realized that I was trying to judge the shape of a forest by its trees. I had reviewed an internal map of Gendenwitha before boarding the Manta, but that hardly prepared me for what I saw. I could not, for instance, tell what held the city in place. It might have stood on one enormous column like a giant mushroom. It might have had eight legs like a spider. For all I knew, the Manta might have entered a single enormous tunnel, and the rest of the city might have been built into the ground.

Portions of the ground beneath the city reflected the white and yellow light that shone from the moon pools in a gleam of silver. It was as if chrome-skinned hills lined the ocean floor. It took me a moment to figure the riddle out: The Unifieds had parked their Turtles down there.

The Manta traveled past several empty moon pools, then changed direction and rose toward one in which three other Mantas waited.

As we approached, rising toward the light, I stashed my rifle on the floor beside the pilot's chair. I strapped my knife to the inside of my right calf and flipped my pant leg over it. I was dressed like a U.A. sailor, wearing the dark slacks and button-up blouse of their service uniform.

My hands were damp. They left moisture prints on the arms of my chair. I breathed a sigh of relief as the Manta inched into place beside the other subs, and the cockpit emerged into the air. Water dribbled down the plastiscreen, but the area the submarine had entered was dry and brightly lit.

CHAPTER SIXTY-THREE

I took a deep breath, opened the hatch, and stepped out onto one of the wing-shaped ballast tanks. Emerging from the confines of the Manta, I began to shiver in the frigid air, air so cold that my breath seemed to turn to steam.

The Manta's autopilot function had brought her right up to the catwalk that led across the moon pool. I grabbed the handle, stepped onto the ladder, and pulled myself up, my palms nearly freezing to the cold, metal rails.

Looking around the room, I was struck by an overwhelming sense of déjà vu. No matter where I looked, I felt an oppressive sense of familiarity.

The moon pool was as big as a football field, only round. My Manta had churned the water as she broke the surface, sending wavelets that lapped at the well-like wall that surrounded the pool. I stood in the center of a narrow-but-sturdy catwalk that ran the entire diameter of pool.

Staring down at the glowing yellow lights that shone into the depths below unearthed some nebulous memory in my head that refused to sharpen into focus. Racks of bright lights hung from the ceiling. Would you call it a ceiling? This chamber was a dome; at what point did the walls become the ceiling?

A few men worked on the deck that surrounded the moon pool. They wore jackets and gloves. I would have liked to have killed them for their gloves. I didn't count that impulse as inhumane. In a few short hours, Hauser's bombers would drop torpedoes on all eleven underwater cities. Killing those men would not even rob them of an entire day.

I looked down into the water and felt my legs go weak. The fear I had felt stepping onto the Turtle had been nothing compared to what I now experienced. It had been a taste, a precursor. I couldn't shake the nagging feeling that I had been here before, that something terrible had happened in this place.

Walking quickly, I crossed the catwalk, my hands in my pockets, my right hand wrapped around my pistol.

"Hey, where's your jacket?" one of the men asked, as I stepped onto the deck. "D'you forget it on the Manta?"

"Worse," I said. "I forgot it from the start."

The man shook his head and returned to work.

Anxious to get away from the cold, I headed toward the exit, somehow sure that the rest of the city would be warmer. As the hangar door slid open, a burst of warm air blew in. The heat felt good, but it reinforced my feelings of déjà vu.

The hall I had entered was narrow, maybe eight feet wide, and circular. It was brightly lit. I had expected the relatively narrow fit and the circular shape, but, for some reason, I had thought it would be dark. I had the strongest impression that I shouldn't turn left, as if something dangerous waited for me in that direction. It made no sense. I almost turned left just to prove to myself that there was nothing there to fear . . . almost.

I turned right, and true to my continuing sense of déjà vu, found myself standing in front of a large door that looked entirely too familiar. *This opens to the city,* I told myself.

It did, but the city was nothing like I had expected. I had expected someplace dark and nightmarish, like a man-made forest with girders instead of trees. The expanse that awaited me on the other side of the door looked like every other military base, only abandoned and housed under a gigantic dome.

The buildings looked like they had come off an assembly line. Some stood one or two stories tall, a few stood six, but all were the same color, made of the same material, and with identical windows and doors. The domed ceiling above the city seemed to stretch on forever. And it was bright; the glow coming from that dome was every bit as radiant as a noonday sun. When I turned away from it, spots flashed in my eyes.

I didn't know if this was how the French had originally

envisioned their underwater cities. They had built the shell, but I thought the Unifieds had filled it in.

A man on an electric cart drove past me, not giving me a second glance. Except for the wheels, his vehicle was silent.

The place was a ghost town.

This was not the first time I had visited a military base that had been largely vacated for war. I recognized the signs the moment I saw them, the empty buildings, the motor pools filled with vehicles, the roads on which few people drove, and the sense of anticipation in the air.

Trying to behave like a natural-born lieutenant, I walked with purpose, scowling at the few enlisted men I passed and not quite meeting the gazes of senior officers.

The way I saw it, I had two objectives and one destination. I needed to find whatever building served as the strategic command center. The data Hauser wanted would be on the computers inside that building. If Nailor was here, I'd find him in the command center as well. He'd billet someplace else, but that was where he'd spend his days.

Finding my way around their city came easily enough. I'd spent my entire life living on Unified Authority military bases. The Unifieds had planned Gendenwitha the same way they planned all the others.

The walk from the moon pool to the command center was nearly two miles. When I found a building with sedans parked beside it, I thought I might have located the right spot. I needed to verify this, of course, and the only way to do that would be to have a look around.

No one stopped me as I entered the building. They left the entrance unguarded. Why guard it? Who could break into an undersea city?

I entered the lobby, saw the gathering of majors and colonels waiting to enter the officer's mess, and knew I had found the strategic command building. Standing across the lobby, I could see round tables covered with white linen tablecloths. A waiter in a white jacket guided officers to their chairs.

As a lowly U.A. lieutenant, I knew better than to linger near such a dining hall, so I walked past, feigning no interest. The feelings of déjà vu had completely vanished by this time, even though I now stood in a building as familiar to me as my own home.

When a herd of officers walked in my direction, I stepped into the head and found that this head had the same fixtures as the heads on the *Churchill*. Like the admin. buildings at Benning and Anacostia-Bolling, this one had its mess hall and its officer country on the first floor, meaning that all the serious work would be done one floor up. I headed up the stairs and found the computer room easily enough. Peering through the windows in the doors, I saw, a large, quasi-refrigerated storehouse with rows of computers the size of coffins.

The room was vacant, with soundproof walls that eliminated outside noise, allowing nothing louder than the soft hum of electronics inside its doors. The only people who entered this area were the techs who maintained the equipment, officers sending coded messages, and spooks. Rooms like this were the domain of intelligence operations. The computers, the communications equipment, and even the environmental controls carried encryption.

I found a terminal with a holographic keyboard and a touch screen, neither of which meant anything to me. I'm a Marine; my computer expertise didn't extend beyond the optical controls in my combat visor and the keyboard on my stove. Had Hauser wanted me to snoop through data banks, he would have been disappointed—I wouldn't have known how to access them.

Hauser, however, had provided me with a modicum of spy gear—a device made out of some sort of stiff cloth that was the size and shape of a large bandage. My job was to wrap this device around the conduction cable that ran between the computers.

The terminal was a chest-high cabinet with a metal shell that probably weighed two hundred pounds. It sat wedged between two larger computers that I could not have moved without a forklift.

I thought this next moment might be the most dangerous part of the entire operation—stealing data without being caught. From where I stood, I could see the hall outside through the window panels in the door, and people in the hall could also see me. The walls were soundproof, so I wouldn't hear people walking by, maybe stopping to watch me work. I sighed and set to work, knowing that there was nothing I could do.

After one last check through that window, I wrapped my fingers around the edges of the terminal and pivoted it from side to side, slowly walking it out of its parking space so I could see the cables on the ground behind it. I turned it to the left, then the right, at first only able to pivot it an inch or two. Once I had wiggled it free from its neighbors, I pulled it an extra foot away and found a long, flat cable that ran from the terminal and disappeared into the floor. It might have conducted data; it might have conducted power, possibly both.

This was espionage, and I was a Marine. I didn't break into things, I broke them. My Military Occupational Specialty was infantry, not computer science. If Hauser didn't get what he wanted, it would be his own damn fault for sending a Marine to do the work of a spy.

I dropped low to the ground as if inspecting the bottom of the terminal. Then, on the ground, hidden from the view of any passersby, I pulled the stiff cloth swatch from my pocket, reached as far as I could to get behind the terminal, and wrapped Hauser's device around the cable. At this point, the success of my espionage objective was out of my hands.

My instructions were to watch the spying device. A red stripe would appear along its spine if I had placed it correctly. That stripe would turn green once it had gathered the data Hauser's intel team had programmed it to record.

So I remained on the floor on all fours beside the terminal, looking for all the world like a computer tech who had come to fix a malfunctioning machine, and that was where I was when Colonel Franklin Nailor stepped through the door. I hadn't known his rank. If I had been forced to guess, I would have thought he was a general because of the authority he wielded and his swagger.

Of all the gin joints in all the towns in all the world, I thought, but there was nothing coincidental about it. I was in the strategic command center of a military base, in the information-systems section, the domain of intelligence officers. Nailor's insignia indicated that his MOS was intelligence. I was in his backyard.

I'd only seen the man in person once, and that time I was lying on the floor helpless and bleeding. He'd looked larger-than-life on that occasion, him standing and me on my ass, my back filled with buckshot.

Nailor looked at me and through me. I was a tech and a lieutenant; in his world, that made me no more significant than a tadpole. He grunted a quick question, "Any problems with the sending gear?" I shook my head, and said, "No, sir." Not bothering to respond, Nailor gave me a cursory glance and walked past.

I noticed Nailor peering at me again, a puzzled look on his face. Hoping to appear in my element, I neither returned his stare nor turned away from him. I pretended I was busy checking cables.

The little twerp was short, shorter than the computer towers. He might have stood five-five on his toes. I must have already known he was short, but seeing it firsthand made more of an impression. He had blond hair, which he parted down the middle like a girl. Between his hair and his eyebrows, there was a round scar with jagged, furrowed edges. It looked like someone had stamped him right between the eyes with a pipe or the muzzle of a shotgun.

Strange as it sounds, the little bastard intimidated me. Maybe it was the arrogance that he radiated. His expression was a constant smirk. It was as if he sized up every man he had ever met and knew he could beat every one of them.

I tried to imagine killing Nailor, but I only saw images of defeat. I saw him laughing at me, treating me like a corpse, playing with me. That strange sense of déjà vu had returned when he walked in the room.

This was my chance to kill him. I had the pistol and the knife. Maybe he was tough enough to beat me in a fair fight, but I hadn't come to fight fair. He'd walked into the computer facility alone. I could kill him and . . . I couldn't kill him, not yet. Whatever data that spy piece was supposed to gather, it hadn't yet gathered it. If I killed Nailor now, someone might come looking for him.

This is your chance, I told myself, but killing Nailor would need to wait.

He glanced at me again and walked over to the terminal I was pretending to examine. He stuck his head behind it, and said, "That's an encryption bandit. What the speck are you doing?"

I hated the bastard. I wanted to run. I wanted to dash for the door, to hide. In my head, visions of him choking me flashed like the warning lights on an overloaded nuclear reactor before it explodes.

"You're nothing if not observant, Nailor," I said, forcing myself to sound calm and reasonable. I had my S9 pistol out where he could see it. I tried to force a smile. "There's a little red strip on the back of that . . ." He'd called it an "encryption bandit." Of course he'd known what to call that thing; the bastard was a spook. "You and I are going to chat until the strip turns green."

His eyes dropped down to the gun. I was scared. Hell, I was petrified, but I held the gun fairly steady, and I faked that killer glint in my eye. He scared me, but my S9 sure as speck had his sphincter puckering.

I said, "You know, Franklin, you look a lot smaller when you aren't hiding behind a shotgun."

He looked me right in the eye, and recognition finally showed. He sneered, and said, "Harris. You're the one hiding behind the pistol."

Damn, he was calm. His demeanor, his absolute lack of concern, he intimidated me more than any man I had ever met . . . even more than Freeman . . . Freeman, who could have lifted this little turd with one hand and snapped his neck with the other.

"Do you recognize the place, Harris?" he asked.

"Should I?" I asked, feeling my resolve melt around my feet. *Shoot him!* I thought. *Shoot him!*

He laughed, a scorning, derisive sound that came drenched with déjà vu.

"This isn't the first time you've been in a Cousteau city," he said.

"You're full of shit," I said, though in my heart, I knew it was true. The feelings of déjà vu were too strong, too constant, too . . . crippling.

"We brought you here from Mars," he said.

"Here?" I asked.

"Not this city, one like it. We have a lot of cities."

"From Mars . . . the brainwashing," I said. "You were in on that?"

"Harris, I've seen you cry like a baby. I've seen you so scared you filled your pants. I know when you're scared. You're scared right now."

"Maybe," I said. "Good thing I've got the gun."

The little bastard had gotten under my skin. He stood there with that confident smirk on his face, as he said, "If you're so tough, why don't you put it down?"

"Put down the gun?"

"That's right, tough guy, put down the gun, and we can fight man-to-man, a fair fight."

I didn't respond. I just stood there, silent and watchful, the muzzle of my S9 pointed at his face. *Are you scared?* I wondered, not really sure if I was mentally checking on his state or mine. He showed no signs of fear, but there was a curious twitch in his eye. Out of the corner of my vision, I noticed the subtlest of movements. It wasn't a person, just a shadow. I noticed the way the contours of the shadows shifted, but it meant nothing until I heard the swish of the pneumatic door.

I wasn't caught off guard and the big fellow charging through the door did not have the element of surprise, but he forced me to show my back to Nailor for a crucial split second. I turned, fired three fléchettes into the bull-necked bastard's face, and felt Nailor's foot crash into my lower thigh before I could turn back to address him.

That was a smart move on his part. He didn't have a clean shot at my groin or my neck or even my head, but by kicking in the back of knee, he caused my leg to buckle, and he followed up with a swift elbow across my head that sent me to the floor.

The sense of déjà vu overwhelmed me, only now it felt more like prophecy than memory . . . me lying flat on my ass, feeling dazed and confused, him standing over me, once again bigger than life. I had the gun, but his elbow had smashed me behind the ear, and my reflexes had slowed. He kicked the gun out of my hand before I had the sense to aim it, then he kicked me across the jaw, and lights popped in my head.

I felt a moment of paralysis. It probably was fear, but after everything I'd been through, it might have been fatigue as well. Even with a slow-starting combat reflex, I was tired, weak, indecisive . . . beat.

Nailor laughed and kicked me, the point of his shoe digging into my ribs. The little bastard drew back his right leg to kick me again. I spun on my ass and kicked his left foot out from under him. As he fell, I shot my foot between his legs and stamped with my heel. I don't know if I hit his unit. If I did, I crushed it. I hit the joint where the thighs connect with the pelvis, and something broke.

Nailor let out a noise between a roar and a squeal. He sat up on his elbows and tried to pull himself away. Our eyes locked. I saw fear in his. He would have seen nothing in mine. There was nothing behind my eyes at that moment, not hate, not fear, and nothing remotely related to compassion. I would just as happily have beaten him to death or snapped his neck, but the S9 was closer, so I picked it up and shot him twice, once in the neck and once in the face. The fléchettes passed through him and lodged themselves in the floor.

A long, thin stream of blood squirted from the wound in his throat. His mouth hung open as if he wanted to hurl one final insult. He might have been gasping for air when my second shot hit him in the left eye and bored through his brain.

When a kill is close and intimate, I often read the final truths in the dying man's expression. What I saw in Franklin Nailor's face was surprise. Right up to the moment that I squeezed the trigger, he hadn't expected me to shoot. Even after he attacked me, he must have thought I would be too scared to defend myself.

Blood dripped out of his head and throat. Using his blouse and trousers for handles, I dragged him and his bull-necked friend to a waste compartment. The big guy was a clumsy lift, and I felt weak as I hoisted his bulky corpse to the top of the compartment and tipped him in. He nearly filled the compartment.

I lifted Nailor and crammed him in headfirst. His neck snapped as I folded his back and legs down over his head to fit him in, then I tore off Nailor's trousers and blouse, and used them to sop up the blood from the floor. The cloth was silky and stiff, made to resist moisture, not to absorb it. The blood smeared. I turned the trousers inside out and they sponged up most of the mess. Taking a quick glance through the window, no one would notice the stains on the floor. I left so little blood, anyone sent to investigate might think that some tech had cut his hand.

I opened the trash bin and loaded the bloody rags on top of their dead owner. Nailor was naked and lying ass-end up, humiliated in death in ways that he could never have been in life. So many things passed through my head as I saw him there, a crushed insect, the menace now evaporated out of him. No witticism left my lips. Seeing him there, the enemy who had left me buried in a mountain, now folded and exposed, I felt no relief, just a sense of emptiness.

And, of course, now that my ribs were bruised and my homicidal deed was done, the strip on the encryption bandit was green. Had it been green a few minutes earlier, I might have been ready when Nailor walked into the room. Silent and morose, I removed the encryption bandit and pushed the terminal back into its slot.

It struck me as odd. Nothing was broken. The computers stood straight and tall as ever, forming a perfect wall. You had to look for the bloodstains on the floor to find them, and the bodies were stashed in a closed compartment, buried under a layer of paper and coffee cups; yet, there was still this unmistakable air suggesting that something had happened.

I slipped out of the building and retraced my path. These were the desperate moments, the time when things go wrong. So much could happen. The grunts at the moon pool might look inside my Manta and spot my rifle, some tech might wander into the information-systems area and pull out the trash, the encryption bandit could have triggered a silent alarm, or someone could see me and realize I was a clone.

I had entered Gendenwitha as a spy and an assassin, roles that do not come naturally to Marines. We shoot, we storm, we protect. We don't steal, and we don't carry out vendettas . . . at least we're not supposed to.

I turned down one empty street, then down the next, always listening for the sound of alarms. This was a city under the sea, locking it down wouldn't take much. Only a skeleton crew now manned this post, but there were enough men to kill me if they trapped me. Strangely, I cared about getting away. I, who had given up on life, now wanted to survive.

I reached the domed wall that separated the city from the moon pool. Before entering, I turned back and looked at the city. In another hour or two, Hauser's bombers would release torpedoes into these waters. The dome around this city would shatter, burying the world behind me in depths so black that only glowing fish could survive them.

It shall be a habitation of dragons and a court of owls, I thought. A Biblical passage remembered by a synthetic man who had a life but no soul. Maybe death goes better for those without souls. When I died, I would sleep untroubled by my sins. At the moment of his death, Franklin Nailor might have tried to wish his soul away.

I had hoped that killing Nailor would come with some sense of closure. It didn't. As I entered the gloomy underworld environ that surrounded the moon pool, my knees went weak. My heart pounded, and my breathing sped so fast that I barely absorbed any oxygen from my lungs.

Panic. Marines cannot afford to give in to panic.

The corridor wound around the wall of the moon pool and wended on, a wraith of a path and barely lit. In my mind's eye, it led to a torture chamber in which men lay on racks, and bodies lay stacked like cordwood on the floor. *He said you were brainwashed here or someplace like it,* I reminded myself. Maybe that image was a relic from an erased memory.

I walked past the door to the moon pool, slipping by quickly, not even sparing a backward glance. *Marines exorcise their demons,* I told myself. *Carry them with you into battle, and you endanger the men who depend on you.*

I walked to the end of the hall and discovered a maze of smaller hallways that led . . . I was pushing my luck. Sooner or later they would discover Nailor. *What will I accomplish by finding the place where I was tortured?* I asked myself. *Will that make the demons go away?*

By this time I had entered the maze, and I found that I knew the way through it. I didn't find labs or torture chambers on the other side. I found a brig. I found a row of holding cells for criminals.

Memories as jagged as shattered glass danced in my head. The images cut at my brain, a pain that felt every bit as real as a knife in the gut. Mostly I saw myself locked in a cell, lying on a cot, paralyzed and terrified, watching some sort of drama that would determine . . . was it my ego or my id that refused to release more information? All I could remember was a choice, one fate meant pain and the other meant death. Both came with humiliation.

Nailor had been there. I heard him shouting my name. I heard him taunting me. *You killed him too quickly,* I told myself.

Coming this far hadn't exorcised my demons, it had empowered them. The door at the other end of the hall led to the labs, the torture chambers, the place where the brainwashing had occurred.

I stared at the door, took a long deep breath, and turned around. Maybe I could have freed myself by continuing on. Or maybe the demons would have whittled my psyche down to sawdust and sticks.

CHAPTER SIXTY-FOUR

Hauser and his navy waited for my signal. They wouldn't wait forever. Unless I gave them a compelling reason to stay their hand, they would destroy Gendenwitha. Bombers now circled all eleven Cousteau cities, ready to wipe out these centuries-old marvels of engineering with a single swipe.

It looked to me as if Hauser's attack would destroy nearly

empty anthills from which the armies' ants were gone. The Unifieds had cleared nearly all of their men out of Gendenwitha though they hadn't abandoned the old city. I suspected the other cities sat empty as well. What other territories had those bastards infiltrated?

I entered the moon-pool area. It was cold; my breath immediately turned to steam. The workers were still there.

One of them looked at me. He asked, "Still can't find your jacket?"

He was a nice guy, a friendly guy. I wanted to let him live.

I shook my head, and asked, "Can you believe it?"

"Hey? What happened to your face? Did you fall down?"

Maybe Nailor had hit me, or, possibly, I hit my face when I fell. I said, "I tripped on some stairs."

The son of a bitch was a natural-born who had joined the Unified Authority, and that made him the enemy, but I really did not feel like killing him. I had nothing against him, and he would die soon enough without my pulling the trigger. *Let the son of a bitch go as long as he can,* I told myself.

He said, "You're the only guy I ever seen come here without a jacket and gloves."

I smiled, and said, "It's warm enough in the Manta."

He stood up straight and his eyes narrowed. The friendliness left his voice. "Where exactly are you taking her?" he asked.

I made one final attempt to grant him a reprieve. I said, "I'm taking her to Washington."

"Washington?" he asked. "You got orders for that, pal?"

He sounded more sarcastic than suspicious. It didn't matter. I shot him. I shot the two men working beside him as well. I shot them and left them where they lay, on the cold, metal floor. By this time it no longer mattered if anybody found them. I had made it to my boat. I had escaped.

I pulled myself up onto the catwalk and let myself into my Manta. Once I had sealed her and pressed the right buttons, she slid under the surface. Still struggling to control my fear of water, I took in the sights as my submarine glided beneath the city. I studied the great disc of her floor, a giant circle spotted with moon pools with rows of white and yellow lights.

I realized that the vista was a thing of beauty and symmetry. For each light on one side of the great disc, there would be a similar light on the opposite side. Perfect symmetry. I thought about the crystal formations in snowflakes. *Are they as perfect as this?* I asked myself. My thoughts turned to civilizations long gone.

Once the Manta passed from under Gendenwitha, no person would see those lights again. It was an undersea galaxy, and soon it would be extinguished. I wished my fears would go with it. As the Manta emerged from under the city, I felt the ocean close in around me. The pounds per square inch that the Manta was fighting were nothing compared to the PSI in my head.

Killing Nailor had gotten me nowhere.

So what did you get out of it? I asked myself. I wanted to say I would sleep more easily. That bastard had tortured me and played with my brain. He'd nearly killed Freeman. The world had been made a safer place by Franklin Nailor's death. At least mine had.

I searched through my things and pulled out the little vial of pills that would see me to the surface. I took the pills and hoped they'd do their work quickly.

As the Manta slid into the empty abyss, my thoughts turned to Hell. I thought about canyons of sulfur filled with buttes and volcanic geysers. I thought about demons with horns and cloven feet that tortured victims beyond the boundaries of insanity. *A terrible fate,* I thought, but it didn't frighten me as much as the hell at the bottom of the ocean.

So this was where I learned my fear of deep water. They had brought me here and taught me to fear Franklin Nailor and giant squid and sharks. I searched for whales and squid and other unearthly creatures, spotted tiny flowing lights in the distance, but nothing that looked alive.

I was already starting to get drowsy when I loaded the encryption bandit into a little beacon buoy, a bullet-shaped container about the size of my forearm. *You'll see the sun before I do,* I thought. The brass cylinder didn't know sun from darkness, but I did. I'd seen too much darkness. How long ago had I been trapped in that mine? Now I was three miles under the Atlantic.

"Darkness." The word ran through me, and I thought about

Nailor, folded upside down, dead and naked. I was glad I had killed him. In my heart of hearts, I wished I could murder him a second time the way some people believed that the demons of Hell killed and reassembled their victims. *Maybe he has a twin,* I told myself. My thoughts had become dreamlike.

I placed the beacon buoy into a tube and launched it.

The buoy didn't need to decompress. It would rise like a rocket to the surface, where Hunter Ritz waited on an APC to collect it. Ritz would personally deliver the encryption bandit to Hauser.

What secrets would it reveal?

The Manta rose quickly. I would be trapped in her for fifteen hours, but that didn't mean I had to spend those hours on the ocean floor. I needed to be clear of Gendenwitha when the bombers dropped their nuclear-tipped torpedoes. I was far away . . . far, far away. I sat in the pilot's chair and nearly slept.

EPILOGUE

Location: Norfolk Naval Base, Virginia
Date: August 14, 2519

Hunter Ritz was not alone on the amphibious personnel carrier, but he sat apart from the other men. He'd brought an entire battalion.

According to the last report he had heard, the Navy had demolished the underwater cities, which meant that Harris had killed Nailor and broken into the Unified Authority's computers. The news was good out of Washington, D.C., as well; MacAvoy's troops had the Unifieds on the run.

All good news, but Ritz's instincts told him that the war was far from over.

While his men assembled on the deck, Ritz waited in a ready room just off the bridge, looking out at Norfolk as the APC hovered into the harbor. It was the middle of August, but a gray day nonetheless. A slab of gray clouds filled the sky, minimizing the noonday sun to morning light levels. Green and gray water filled the harbor. Dreary.

Ritz had already pulled the encryption bandit out of the buoy and placed it in an armored case for safekeeping. The case was a foot long and two inches wide, too small to weigh as much as it did. He wondered if it was radioactivity-proof as well as bulletproof and suspected it was.

The docks were made of concrete, with thick wooden posts and rubberized ledges that acted like bumpers. The APC didn't fly high enough to jump the docks. It flew beyond them and up a ramp meant for launching harbor boats and other small crafts into the water.

Ritz looked down at his men, standing alert, their guns ready. He took pride in these men. He had been a private and a corporal, and a sergeant. Now he was a general, a ridiculous rank that he considered a joke. He had the temperament of a corporal, and that was the only advancement that he had ever wanted.

The APC breezed up the ramp and hovered to the launchpad, where it settled to its skids.

Nothing had changed at Norfolk. It was as if the war had occurred in another universe. Sailors busied themselves on nearby ships. Dockworkers hauled cargo. The place was a colony of clone-sized ants, everyone working, everyone assigned his specific duty.

Ritz's duty was to deliver the case. Standing at the window, he saw the transport that would fly him to the *Churchill* sitting on the other side of the launchpad just one hundred yards away.

He saluted the captain of the APC and trotted down the stairs. *Maybe it really will end,* he thought to himself. What if the data Harris stole held something big? What if it gave away the Unifieds' plans? What if it named their spies and bases?

The end is in sight, he thought, and he smiled. He didn't believe it, but he wanted to.

Ritz crossed the deck. He had hundreds of armed men around him, loyal Marines, armed and ready to fight.

Kevin Rhodes, the director of data encryption at the EME Intelligence Agency, stood at the bottom of the gangway. Rhodes was a natural-born, a tall, slender man who dressed like a politician—gray suit, red necktie.

He flashed his government ID at the Marines guarding the gangway, and they let him past. Rhodes was supposed to be there. The Navy clones would need his help deciphering the data on Harris's encryption bandit.

Ritz strode down the gangway and joined him. They shook hands. *That's how civilians salute,* Ritz told himself.

He didn't like spies, and that included Rhodes, though he could see that the man tried to be pleasant. Marines lived in a straightforward world of black-and-white, allies and enemies. Spies lived in the shadows, where the black was never complete and the white was gray along the edges. You might never know who to kill in their world, or who to trust.

Rhodes pointed at the case, and asked, "Is that the encryption bandit?"

Ritz nodded.

"I can't wait to see what you found. I mean, this could win the war for us. It's going to take some time to decipher everything, but it's bound to be a gold mine—battle plans, inventories listing men and materials . . . a gold mine."

They walked across the launchpad, heading toward the transport. It sat at the edge, its rear hatch open, the ramp waiting for Ritz and Rhodes.

"Have you heard anything from Travis Watson?" asked Ritz.

"They still haven't found him?" asked Rhodes.

"It's like he left the planet."

Rhodes shook his head. "That's funny; I thought the Army might have found him and hid him away."

Ritz shook his head.

"How about Tasman? Were they able to find him?"

"Same story," said Ritz. "We haven't found hide nor hair of Watson, or Tasman, or Emily Hughes—Watson's fiancée. Some of MacAvoy's soldiers found the car Watson used to escape."

"Well, if the Unifieds know anything, we'll find it in here," Rhodes said, pointing at the case.

Ritz carried the case with a newfound respect. He liked Watson; locating the man and bringing him home safe had become something of an obsession with him.

They walked up the ramp and entered the kettle of the transport. Rhodes said, "We haven't found Watson or Tasman, but we have located one person of interest. We found Harris's girlfriend."

"Is she alive?" asked Ritz.

"Alive and well," said Rhodes.

This was good news. He was supposed to meet Harris when his submarine emerged. Harris would be happy that his girl was safe.

"I brought her with me," said Rhodes.

"She's here?" asked Ritz, surprised that she'd been allowed on base.

"She's right behind you."

Ritz turned around in time to see her step out of the head. She was as tall as a clone—maybe a fraction of an inch taller. She smiled at him, a gentle, happy smile. Her entire face seemed to light up with that smile.

"Rhodes, this is a classified . . ."

"General, I feel like I know you. Wayson's always talking about you," she said, and she reached out her hand to shake his. She had brown hair and blue, blue eyes. *Darker than sky blue,* he thought to himself. *How the speck could Harris ever cheat on her?* he wondered. His final thought.

Though he knew she should not be on the transport, Ritz shook her hand, felt the pinprick through the soft pad of the palm just below his thumb and the quick electric shock that came with it. He tried to pull his hand back, but that was an involuntary reaction. The shock disabled him. She had aimed the tiny pin perfectly. The poison entered a vein that led into his wrist and from there into his circulatory system. Before he recovered from the shock, the poison had entered his heart and started the trek to his brain.

Ritz fell to his knees as if preparing to tie a shoelace. Sunny held on to his hand, keeping the needle in place far longer than needed. The poison would enter his brain in less than a minute, but she held on to his hand, looking into his eyes, smiling.

"So you are Hunter Ritz," she said. Her smile remained warm, but her eyes hardened. The blue that Ritz had assessed as "darker than the sky" became harder than cobalt.

She released his hand as he tumbled backward, onto the metal floor. "It would have been better if we could have reprogrammed you," she said. "With all this security, I couldn't smuggle a canister in."

She knelt beside him and stroked his cheek with her finger. "You really know your security procedures, Ritz," she said. "You run a tight operation."

Sunny wondered if Ritz could hear her or if the poison had paralyzed his awareness along with his body. He wasn't dead yet, but he would be in another moment.

His eyes remained open, but she had killed men with this poison before; she knew that their eyes stayed open after they died. Ritz's mouth fell open as he struggled for air.

A line of drool trailed out of the corner of his mouth. Sunny brushed it away with a finger as gently as a mother cleaning an infant child. She wiped her finger dry on his collar. Then, to see what it would feel like to force the air out of a dying man's lungs, she pressed down on his chest until she heard the air rattling in his throat.

"I better go, dear. They're expecting this transport to go wheels up, and I'm the only person on board who knows how to fly it." She paused. "Do you know how to fly one?" Then, seeing that his eyes had turned to glass, she corrected herself. "Did you know how to fly one?"

She stepped over Ritz's body, taking the case from his limp arms.

Sunny left for the cockpit without saying another word. General Hunter Ritz died without speaking. They both left the naval base in silence.

AUTHOR'S NOTE

I am going to keep my author's note shorter than usual because this book is considerably longer than any of my previous Wayson Harris novels. The good folks at Ace have indulged my oversized manuscript, but they might balk if I wade in with two thousand words in notes and explanations. That said, I still have one piece of business to which I must attend.

So, here we go.

I want to begin with a true confession. I happened to reread Robert Heinlein's *Starship Troopers* while writing this book. The truth is that everyone writing military science fiction has benefited from the work of Robert Heinlein, though some less directly than I. This book includes a phrase that I filched from *Troopers*: "Wet Navy." Heinlein used this term to distinguish between today's navies, which travel the seas, and the navies of the future, which will probably fly in space.

I saw the term and was awed by its elegance and simplicity, and so I borrowed it—but I want to give credit where credit is due. Thank you, Mr. Heinlein. Thank you for so many things.

Don't miss exciting military science fiction featuring Lieutenant Wayson Harris from

STEVEN L. KENT

Earth, A.D. 2508

Humans have spread across the six arms of the Milky Way Galaxy. The Unified Authority controls Earth's colonies with an iron fist and a powerful military—a military made up almost entirely of clones . . .

THE CLONE REPUBLIC

ROGUE CLONE

THE CLONE ALLIANCE

THE CLONE ELITE

THE CLONE BETRAYAL